A COLD SEASON

'An itchy tension-cranker of parental paranoia' *SFX*

'The underlying dread escalates to scenes of real terror. Atmospheric throughout and disturbing to the end' Ramsey Campbell, author of *The Kind Folk*

'This is a very spooky story. You'll love it if you're into tales of the occult, or a fan of film classic *The Wicker Man* . . . disturbing, in a devilish *Midsomer Murders* kind of way' Judy Finnigan, *The Daily Express*

'A scary read that will chill you to the bone . . . Beware if fact and fiction suddenly start to blur' *crimesquad.com*

'A terrifically chilling tale. A sterling debut which bodes unspeakably well for its author and beyond' *scotspec.blogspot.com*

'An assured and finely-crafted piece of work, probably the best horror debut since Joe Hill's 2007 novel, *Heart-Shaped Box* . . . you need to read *A Cold Season*. Just make sure you know where the light switches are' *readerdad.co.uk*

'Alison Littlewood's *A Cold Season* has taken the horror world by storm' *thisishorror.co.uk*

'*A Cold Season* is an intelligent, sensitive book. Its chills are delivered with precision . . . Littlewood excels at driving home a feeling of discomfort' *spooky-reads.com*

'A career defining masterpiece that exuded chills and almost . . . *hurt*, in a frightening way. Hands down one of this year's greatest novels' Matt Molgaard, *Horror Novel Reviews*

Alison Littlewood is the author of *A Cold Season*, published by Jo Fletcher Books. The novel was selected for the Richard and Judy Book Club, where it was described as 'perfect reading for a dark winter's night.' Her second novel, *Path of Needles*, is a dark blend of fairy tales and crime fiction. Alison's short stories have been picked for the *Best Horror of the Year* and *Mammoth Book of Best New Horror* anthologies, as well as *The Best British Fantasy 2013* and *The Mammoth Book of Best British Crime 10*. Alison lives in West Yorkshire, England, with her partner Fergus.

THE UNQUIET HOUSE

ALISON LITTLEWOOD

Jo Fletcher
BOOKS

First published in Great Britain in 2014 by

Jo Fletcher Books
an imprint of Quercus
55 Baker Street
7ᵗʰ Floor, South Block
London
W1U 8EW

A CIP catalogue record for this book is available from the British Library

ISBN 978 1 78087 646 7 (PB)
ISBN 978 1 78087 647 4 (EBOOK)

10 9 8 7 6 5 4 3 2 1

Typeset by IDSUK (DataConnection) Ltd.
Printed and bound in Great Britain by
Clays Ltd, St Ives plc

To Fergus
For showing me the unquiet houses

PART ONE

2013 – The Arrival

CHAPTER ONE

It was five months after the death of her parents that Emma Dean first saw the house, so in an odd way it had become attached to them in her mind, though as far as she knew they'd never seen it. It was someone else's passing that had brought her here, one that hadn't touched her so deeply, and it was strange to think that it had affected the direction of her life just as much.

Mire House. It wasn't a prepossessing name; it wasn't a prepossessing start. She couldn't find it, for one thing. It was supposed to be a little beyond the road that ran through a village called West Fulford – she hadn't seen a North, South or East Fulford on any map – so she'd followed it through the village and past a country park and over a little bridge, and then she'd turned off into a narrow lane which led nowhere in particular. It wound between farm buildings and broken-down barns and out again until she reached a junction unmarked by any sign. There she turned around and retraced her route. This time she took it slowly, pulling tight over to the hawthorn hedge so that she could look to left and right without finding herself stuck in the middle of the road if anything rushed around the next bend. There was nothing, only a dip with muddy verges and the damp dirty shine of puddles in the road.

It was if it had never existed, and that, at this moment, seemed a more cogent explanation than that she was lost. She had never seen the house; she had never met Clarence Mitchell, the distant relation whose death at the age of eighty-two had made it hers. She didn't know why he'd left it to her; he had a grandson, after all. She had considered finding the boy and asking *why*, curious to know what had happened within the family to make this happen to her, but the thought only summoned the image of her own father's face: his eyes watery, his skin sallow and a little loose, no longer the strong man who'd once hefted her on his shoulders and made her laugh.

Now the house was hers. *Hers.* And she couldn't even find it.

She let the car roll onwards into the bottom of the lane and glanced to the side. There was nothing but a field that rose away from her, tufted and rough and silvered by the breeze, and then she saw a small interruption to its curve and she squinted. What she was looking at was a chimney. There was a building set into the lower ground on the other side of the hill.

She accelerated towards the end of the lane, driving with purpose now. She was the *owner*. She had property. She should try to look as if she knew what on earth she was going to do with it. She turned right and went onward, spotting the turning at the very last moment, and she pulled into a lane even narrower than the last.

The house was set in a dip in the land where the humid air seemed to hang in place. It had been so near all along, and yet now she was looking at it, it looked like it was sitting in its own world, tucked away from everything and everyone. Emma loved it at once. It was hewn from blocks of stone which were deep grey in the damp air. It was tall and grand, and looked much older than she'd imagined; the style was of an earlier era than its age implied. The door was nestled into a porch and footed by three wide steps. There was little decoration, though the upper windows each had a small gable topped with a simple stone globe. Another globe was set over the porch and Emma thought there was writing carved into it, something she couldn't read from where she was sitting in the car. She stared up at the house, and all she could think was: *He didn't even live here.*

Mire House was beautiful, and imposing, and alone. She had a sudden image of herself coming down to breakfast in a silken gown, trying not to splash it with milk as she poured it onto her cornflakes, and she let out a brief giggle, a sound too high and too loud for the quiet interior of her car. It hung there, echoing in her own ears. *No. She was an owner now.* An adult.

Alone was the word her mind was trying to add, but she pushed it away. *Independent* was the word she substituted, already knowing it wasn't the right one, not quite.

Her parents would surely have loved this place. Had they even known about it? It had been described as a second home in the will and she had thought it must have been meant for holidays, but judging from the blankness of the windows and the air of quiet, it hadn't been used for anything in a long time.

She didn't get out of the car. She wanted to gaze at the house a little longer. Behind it were only the low-rising hills which were sliced by the narrow lines of drystone walls. It looked cut off from anywhere and anything, but as she looked around, she realised it wasn't quite alone, that there was another building close by after all. It was only a short distance away down the lane but it was masked by a stand of trees. She could make out part of a wall and, lower down, the lines of a fence. She returned her gaze to Mire House – *her* house. It had octagonal gateposts clutched by stems of ivy and it only occurred to her now that she could have driven through them. She wasn't a guest.

Instead, she stepped out of the car and walked through the gateposts. The drive was a mixture of gravel, scabbed earth and weeds, but she could still imagine ladies dressed in finery being driven up to the door and servants rushing towards them with umbrellas as they exclaimed in lady-like fashion about the dampness of the day.

The day *was* damp. She sniffed at the air and as she did so a squadron of midges descended. She batted at them and they divided around her before settling again. They moved with her as she walked towards the door and her hairline started to itch. The scent in the air was sour and metallic, with the more musky under-note of rot. There was a river close by, wasn't there? Perhaps the smell was coming from there. Yes, definitely the river. It couldn't possibly be the house.

She tilted her head back and looked up at the windows, seeing only the heavy grey sky reflected in them. The house was hers. *Hers.* She smiled. It was odd that she already felt so proprietorial as she pulled the keys from her pocket. As she went to open the door, she wondered that she could feel so close to belonging to a place she had never seen and had no intention of doing anything with other than selling, as quickly and effortlessly as she could.

CHAPTER TWO

Emma could see at once that the house had not been used as a holiday home, or anything else. It didn't look as if anyone had been there in a long time. Cobwebs laden with dust darkened the corners. The staircase wrapped around the square hall, which was floored with black and white tiles half-covered with grime. She found herself tiptoeing, her steps sounding like an intrusion. She peered into the first room on her left. It was a bright, spacious drawing room with large windows looking onto the front and side of the house, but it was dulled by the drab walls and heavily patterned carpet. It had a cornice like the frills on a wedding cake and a yellowed-looking chandelier. Hairline cracks spidered across the ceiling. There was a smell in here too: musty and unaired.

Emma walked to the side window, noting the cracks in the frames, the blackened wood beneath. The view was of thorny twigs jutting from a flowerbed, the colourless remnants of dead leaves, with a narrow strip of unkempt lawn beyond, and through the trees she'd seen earlier, more of the neighbouring property; it looked broader than she'd first assumed, and taller. It might even have a tower.

She stood there for a moment, sensing the weight and breadth of the house above her. It had six bedrooms. *Six.* A ridiculous number. She smiled, thinking of how her dad would have fussed around it, noting all the things that needed doing, and then she remembered and her smile faded. She still hadn't decided what to do with her parents' place. She was living in a small rented flat in Leeds. While her mother's illness had dragged on and on she'd imagined that after it took its course, her dad would live there alone and that she would visit more often. It hadn't worked out that way. The heart attack had taken him within weeks of her mother passing and now their house too lay empty. She hadn't been able to bring herself to sell it. The very idea of cutting those ties had brought on bad dreams in which she simply disappeared, leaving no one to even remember her name. They were dreams from which she'd woken in a cold sweat. Now there was Mire House.

She looked around the room once more. Oddly, she knew the exact shade she would paint it if she were to live here: a soft sage green, traditional yet fresh. It would fit; it would belong.

Emma looked across the front lawn and the wall and into the road beyond, the bright metal of her car incongruous outside it all, like a visitor from a different era. The window was clouded with dirt and the carpet was greasy, but even so, she knew that if she were to stay here, this room, on the first floor in the centre of the building, would be hers. It was painted a shade of blue that was a little too dark, but it had a pretty little fireplace that was edged with flowered tiles and it felt like a place in which she could stay. Of course she *wasn't* staying, but it was nice to imagine waking here to the distant sound of bird-song through the glass, the soft hum of farm traffic somewhere along the road.

She turned to leave and blinked. Her first thought was that that she was seeing things, that the door in front of her had doubled somehow, but then she saw that one of them was a little narrower than the other. She hadn't noticed the second door, which was set into the same wall as the entrance. She didn't remember seeing it from the landing on the other side and for a fleeting moment she thought of the stories she'd read when she was young, tales of impossible doors leading to strange and magical lands. She shook her head in amusement. The landing had narrowed in that place, hadn't it? She stepped forward and opened the door. It swung outwards, revealing only a cupboard. One side was lined with shelves and the other held a single high clothes rail. Something was hanging from it. She leaned in and made out the shape of a man's three-piece suit, the shoulders of the jacket misshapen against the curve of the hanger. There was a sour, unwashed smell. She thought of Clarence Mitchell. Was it his, saved for some special occasion, perhaps? She had a sudden image of a funeral – the suit was black, after all – and she grimaced.

He didn't even live here, she reminded herself, and she closed the door and went to explore the rest of the rooms.

It wasn't until she entered the master bedroom – the largest one, next to the blue room she was already thinking of as hers – that she saw through the tops of the trees that marked the edge of the garden. When she did, she realised her neighbours were not as she'd expected. She had assumed there would be a house, a farmhouse perhaps, like the one she could now glimpse a little further along the lane, but instead she saw a stone structure with a neat grey-tiled spire. The property next door was not a farm or any such thing: it was a church, and she realised she could see into the graveyard too, the crooked stones ranked across the rising hillside.

She could never have imagined owning anywhere like this. The house was too big for her. It had too many rooms. She would disappear within it. If she was to speak her voice would echo from the empty walls, too loud and too flat, and she knew she wouldn't like to hear it. But then, she hadn't spoken. There was no one to speak to. It crossed her mind that perhaps it was only that the house echoed her own emptiness, her *aloneness*, and she shook the thought away.

And yet, the house was beautiful. It was run down and drab and unkempt and unclean, but even so, something in it called to her. She could easily imagine this place filled with life, with parties, the distant laughter of children. Another brief image: herself smiling, calling down the stairs to her own children as they kicked off muddy boots in the hallway, a man behind them, his face a blur. She smiled at herself. She wasn't even seeing anyone, not just now. But still, it was a shame – *wrong*, even – that somewhere so lovely should be locked up and abandoned. And one day perhaps that *could* be her. For a second she pressed a hand to her belly, smoothing down her top. This place would need a fortune spending on it, a fortune she didn't have. *Unless she sold her parents' house.* The thought slotted neatly into her mind as if it was something she'd been planning for years, as if it was natural. But it *wasn't* natural. It wasn't anything she'd been able to do. She wasn't ready.

Emma let out a breath she hadn't realised she'd been holding and a mist rose in front of her face. The heating probably hadn't been on for a long time; it might not even work. It had been ridiculous to think of staying here, even for a moment. People her age didn't have houses like this. It was too much. Her flat was what she needed: somewhere she could never really be alone, in the heart of a city. In a city things were never as silent as this; a silence so deep it would only leave her at the mercy of her own imaginings.

She gathered herself to leave and as she did, she heard the long slow creak of a door. She turned to see that it had swung wide open. The place was draughty, too, then: *perfect*. She half smiled as she headed outside. It was as if the house itself was showing her out.

The grass was so soft and giving that Emma sank into it as she walked. It was thick with moss and moisture seeped around her feet with each step. When she looked back she found she had left a trail of perfect footprints, each one still bearing the pattern of the soles of her shoes.

Midges and mire, she thought as she approached the boundary. This side ended with a wall and when she looked over it she saw a narrow path. It was choked with nettles and there was a hedgerow with dead stunted trees. Insects hung thickly in the air, soundless and weightless, as if this were their source. The scent of stale water was stronger here. So perhaps there was a marsh somewhere close by. She wondered if that was how the house had come by its name.

The trees at the opposite end of the garden were still clinging to their leaves, though most had already turned. Branches clacked as they swayed in the breeze. When she walked under them she could see the church, nestled so deeply into the earth it seemed almost sunken, speared into it by the weight of its spire. The grounds sloped upward from the boundary wall and she glanced at the hillside covered in gravestones. She pushed away the memories that rose at the sight of them; another grave-yard, pulling up in a slow heavy car, the cloying scent of flowers—

She took a deep breath. What did it matter if it was so nearby? It wasn't as if she was going to stay here. She turned her back on the place and made her way to the car, wiping her feet on the verge before getting in. It was no good, the damp earth ingrained in her shoes was already smearing the mat. She started the engine and looked back at the house. It was still beautiful. It still answered something within her, as if it was responding to some question she'd never thought to ask. It was also too big, too expensive, too irrational. She shook her head, trying not to look back once more as she drove away, but she couldn't help herself. The house was quiet and its windows were dark.

CHAPTER THREE

The city was stirring. Emma could hear the murmur of tyres on the road outside, the louder choking of a bus passing at the top of the street. She opened her eyes. Her room was a smooth white box. She'd been woken late by Jackie and Liam, the Irish couple upstairs. Their voices through the ceiling had been fast and raised, like something mechanical gaining speed and slipping into high gear. Their argument had gone on and on.

She pushed herself up, slotting her legs into the narrow gap between the bed and the wall. The flat was in a narrow red-brick terraced house which had never been meant to be subdivided. Her kitchen had once been a corridor and she shared a landing with Jackie and Liam. She had chosen it because it was close to work and because it had been new – the oven had still been coated in plastic film. The flat had no history, none of the accumulated grime of other people's lives.

But the past was always there, waiting to make its presence felt. Emma glanced at the table where she'd placed the letter. It had been sent after Clarence Mitchell's death by his solicitor. She tried to remember if her father had ever told her one single thing about the man. She thought there might have been something, the hint of some estrangement, but when she tried to recall the details they slipped away from her.

It struck her now that the letter smelled a little like Mire House, like stale, uncirculated air. It was a single sheet of paper, thin and brittle, folded once. He hadn't used her first name or even 'Dear'. *Miss Dean* was how he'd addressed her, terse and formal, as if she were some spinster in a Jane Austen novel:

Miss Dean,

I dare say, if you're reading this, that everything has gone according to plan. I thought long and hard about what to do, had plenty of opportunity. Some people never see it coming, and all that.

I don't really know you. I suppose that gets that out of the way. But I know my grandson, and I don't believe he would get the most out of the old place. Don't feel bad. It just isn't him, not really, and you – well, you're a mystery. But at least you have a chance to make something of it, a chance that I don't see in Charles' future. He's not meant for it, that's all: I can't express it better than that.

I suppose that's all that needs to be said. You'll find her a fine old bird, that's for certain. I wish you joy of her. Ah, but we can't know what the future holds, can we? Not for other people. We simply do our best. I never imagined my own future like this, but then we never do, do we? Time is short, and when we begin to see its end, doubly so.

Enjoy her.

Mr Clarence W. Mitchell.

Emma had stared at it, perplexed. It purported to be an explanation and yet it explained nothing; it only raised more questions. *I wish you joy of her?* She wasn't sure she liked how that sounded. She scanned it again, though she really needed to shower, dress, get to work. She still couldn't penetrate its meaning.

It occurred to her now to wonder if the mysterious Charles had come to her father's funeral. Weddings, funerals, christenings – the triumvirate that reunited families. She couldn't remember him – but then, she didn't remember much, only black suits and veils and brief glimpses of friends and neighbours with pale faces and dark clothes, sitting in pews, their hands resting on unfamiliar hymn books worn out from the press of hundreds of hands before them. She shook her head. There was no way of remembering and she didn't want to; a new day was beginning, something to fill with routine tasks and cups of tea and minor pleasantries, and then it would be behind her and she would forget all over again.

She put down the letter and went to the window, pulling back the curtains so hard that the plastic rings rattled against the rail. The fabric was a tasteful grey, the wall white, the view outside drab red brick. In her mind, though, was another window, wide and generous, its curtains dull and fraying from years of use, the view one of silent trees and the merest glimpse of gravestones; a place that was much more quiet and more permanent than this.

CHAPTER FOUR

It wouldn't take long, the woman had said, and it felt good to have finally done it. Emma had passed over the keys to her parents' house and she'd signed a form. The estate agent would take care of everything. It was all right, it was going to happen; the woman had reassured her of that in tones so breezy they would admit of nothing else.

She had started to pack. She hadn't mentioned it to anyone at work, didn't really need to. She could reach the office from the house in a little over an hour. They wouldn't even notice she'd gone until she updated her records for the payroll.

It didn't take long before the flat looked as empty and sterile as when she'd moved in. She could hear shouting in the street outside and the rattle of shutters from the corner shop. The television was on low, a soft burble, and as she listened, a tirade began in the flat above: Jackie's voice, berating or blaming, going on and on.

She found herself longing for quiet rooms, for grand spaces, for *air*. And then she remembered what Mire House was actually like: the musty smell, the emptiness, nothing around it except the graveyard, nothing for her at all. And the *cold*.

She shook her head. *Go now*, she thought. *Go now, before it's too late.*

If she stopped to think or to ask anyone's advice it would all become too much. She already knew what her workmates would say: *You'd have to be mad. I wouldn't take that on. A lass like you . . .?* They'd have her live somewhere she was *expected* to live, to be the person they expected her to be. Now she'd had a glimpse of something different.

Mire House wasn't a choice, not really, not any more. It didn't make sense but she felt as if she was already living within its walls, inhabiting those spacious rooms. In a little place inside of her, a place that was a little like love, she was *there*, not as a property owner or a developer, but a *custodian*. Even in so brief a time it felt that in some way she and Mire House were already connected.

CHAPTER FIVE

The boxes stacked around the walls didn't even begin to make the room look full. It was hard to believe it had taken so long to bring them inside. Emma knew that once her furniture arrived from the flat it too would be dwarfed. It didn't matter. She could choose new things later, once she knew what kind of furniture the house *wanted*. She'd already brought paintbrushes, rollers, cleaning things, white emulsion and sage green paint.

Before she began, she went to see her room. As soon as she walked in she knew that she'd made the right choice. She stood there for a moment, just listening to the sound of birdsong outside the window, and then she remembered what was in the cupboard and she frowned. The suit was still hanging inside, in *her* wardrobe. She stepped towards it but hesitated, remembering who had owned the house and what Clarence Mitchell had done for her. The suit was his, wasn't it? Perhaps she was being ungrateful, clearing it away. Still, she couldn't keep it forever, clinging to the memory of someone she hadn't even known. The house would be the memory, not those things. Perhaps if he'd seen what she was going to do with the place he would have been glad.

She pushed open the door, remembering the hunched shoulders, the dark fabric, the way the trousers had rubbed shiny where the dead man's knees would have fitted. It wasn't there. The rail was empty; there was nothing but an old pipe sitting on the shelf behind it, half full of whitened tobacco.

She looked down, then smiled at herself. The suit had simply fallen off the hanger and was lying on the dingy carpet, the sleeves folded across the body as if trying to cover itself. That was why she could see the shelf behind it; the pipe must have been there all the time. She reached for it and at once had an image of wrinkled hands closing over the thing, stroking its smooth barrel. The pipe was as polished as a prized antique, smooth as silk. It had been well-used. She could still detect the scent of sweet tobacco, the harsher tang of burning.

She picked up the suit, the fabric grimy under her fingertips, and as she did a knock rang out. It must be the furniture: perfect timing. She headed for the stairs. This meant she was really staying. It would be her first night in her new home, the beginning of something new at last.

The young man at the door wasn't in uniform, clutching a delivery note or a tracking device. He was tall and good-looking and his hair was dark blond and slightly curled and a little too long over his ears. At first he didn't say anything and then he held out his hand to shake. She looked at it.

'You must be Emma,' he said.

She frowned, realising it was too late to cover her surprise, then she put out her hand, already wondering: *sales ploy?* No doubt he'd go from first-name terms to some rehearsed patter designed to have her sign up for something she didn't need – but no, he looked almost shy now, sheepish even.

'I hope you don't mind me coming round. I know it might seem a bit – well, *off* – but . . .' His voice tailed away.

'I'm sorry, but have we met?'

'Oh – lord, yes, we have – well, not for a long time, though; I don't expect you to recognise me. I'm Charlie.'

Emma frowned. She was quite sure she'd never seen him before in her life.

'Charles. Clarence Mitchell's grandson.'

Her mouth fell open. She had no words; there was only a rush of shock and guilt.

'Pleased to meet you,' he added, and he grinned at her expression.

Emma shook her head. He seemed to be enjoying her surprise, though not in any malicious way; he was amused, that was all – and who wouldn't be? She hadn't yet spent a single night in her house – in his grandfather's house – and here he was, on her doorstep. Her cheeks flushed. Why had he come? He had every right to be angry. He would want the place back. She swallowed hard, her throat suddenly blocked. He might contest the will; he might even win.

He shook his head, still smiling at her. 'I'm really sorry. I didn't mean to disturb you, or make you think— Well, you know. I don't want anything. I just – after the funeral and all, I started wondering about family. It makes you think, doesn't it? I'd barely remembered I'd got another relative – another strand, so to speak. I was meaning to come down anyway to see some friends, so . . . well, I thought I'd call in. I can go, if you're busy.'

'Lord, no,' said Emma, 'it's me who should apologise. You took me by surprise, that's all. Come in, please. I was about to dig out the kettle anyway. I'm in the drawing room – through there.' She gestured, then let her hand fall. What was she doing? He must have been here plenty of times. Many more than her.

If he was offended, he didn't show it. He thanked her, leading the way into the house, and Emma saw only his straight back and broad shoulders as she followed after him.

The first thing she saw on entering the room was the old black suit, lying crumpled on top of a bin bag, where she'd thrown it on the floor. Charlie was looking at it too, his eyes a little out of focus, as if he was remembering. She bent and picked up the suit, brushing it down, as if it wasn't obvious she'd been in the process of throwing it away.

When she met his eyes, he looked quizzical. 'Sorry,' she said. 'I imagine this must have been your grandfather's.'

He shrugged. 'Not likely. More Savile Row, the old man. That looks like a charity shop reject.' His head tilted as he took in the shiny material, the patina of age. 'I'd chuck it, if I were you.'

She started to nod, then took in his words. *If I were you.* She threw the suit aside without looking and the bin bag rustled under it, coughing out dust.

He pulled a face. 'I know this might seem a bit odd, me calling in like this – but really, I've no claim over the place. I wanted to say that up front. Grandfather always did as he wanted and – Well, I didn't expect anything. I didn't come here because I wanted to check the place out – I hope you believe that.' His eyes were clear, his expression earnest.

Emma took a deep breath. 'Well, I had no right to expect anything at all – at least you knew him, had something to do with him. I'm afraid I'd rather lost track of that side of the family. And I was still—' She paused, then finished, 'I was sorting things out. It took me by surprise.'

He stepped forward and his hand twitched towards her, then he let it fall. 'I heard about your parents,' he said. 'I'm really sorry. I would have come for the funeral, but Grandfather was ill and my dad was so busy – he was ill for a long time, you know, not like—'

Emma couldn't help it; her eyes filled with tears and she stepped away from him. She had thought about her family, of course she had, but no one had spoken to her about them in months. It had fallen into the past for everyone but her, and she had buried it deep. Now it was here, a living, breathing thing.

'God, look at me – I only wanted to call in and say hi, get acquainted maybe. Look what I've done. Sorry.'

She blinked back the tears but she felt the blood gathering in her cheeks and her face growing hot. She shook her head. 'It's not your fault. It took me by surprise.' She couldn't look at him.

'For the second time today, eh?' His tone was light and she tried to smile, and then both of them jumped when someone banged on the door.

'Oh, God – the furniture.'

Now he did put out a hand, lightly touched her shoulder. 'Why don't you stay here? I'll see to it.' And he was gone.

She heard the sound of the door opening and voices buzzing in the hall, a chirpy, *'Be right back!'*, and Emma stood there staring at the boxes and the paint and wondering how on earth she had come to be here. The way she'd reacted, when he spoke of family – she hadn't known it could still hit her like that. It made her realise how numb she had been. *I didn't know*, she thought. *I didn't know I could still feel this way.*

In the end Charlie had them put the sofa in the middle of the carpet like a piece from a dolls' house and told them to carry the bed upstairs. She followed them up and opened her mouth to direct them, but Charlie went straight to it, the room she had chosen for herself, waiting only for her nod of confirmation before he held open the door for them. The delivery men were ready to leave and she signed their form and tipped them. Then Charlie reappeared with two steaming mugs in his hand, passed one to her and put his own down on the floor. He perched on the edge of the sofa and she saw again how inadequate it looked. Whatever must he think?

He looked around. 'God, this room is amazing.' His eyes shone with enthusiasm. 'Look at that cornicing. It's so – how old is this place, anyway? It'll be really dramatic in here when you're done, I'll bet.'

'I know,' she said. 'It was built in the thirties, I think, but it looks much older.' *Grander*, she thought. It was a time when people did that – made their homes look mock-Tudor or mock-Victorian or mock-Georgian, as if they were trying to escape into the past; making everything look like something else.

He picked up his coffee and Emma breathed in the scent of her own as the steam dampened her cheeks. She glanced at the tins of paint in the corner. At least it looked as if she was doing something, as if someone cared about the place at last. He followed her gaze. 'Ah, that's perfect,' he said. 'That's for in here, isn't it, that green? Tell me it is.'

She smiled her answer as she listened to him talk, drinking her coffee, letting it warm her as she thought of that odd flash of feeling when they'd spoken of her parents. She didn't know if she was trying to remember or trying to forget but in some way, in the last few minutes, it felt like it was all right for her to do both.

CHAPTER SIX

It didn't occur to Emma until later that the house had come as a surprise to Charlie too. They were still sitting in the drawing room, Emma on the sofa, him now cross-legged on the floor, as if he didn't want to impose on her by getting too close.

She blurted out the question, 'Had you ever seen this place before?'

'Never been here, sadly. My dad was going to bring us once, but it fell through. Grandfather paid for us to go to the States that year instead – not sure why. He was never that generous.' He paused. 'Well, not often. He was a driven man, you know. He was self-made and he believed others should be the same. But looking at this place, I can see why he didn't want us to come. It's a bit of a mess, isn't it.' He gave a rueful smile, then added, 'Actually, I don't think he'd been here in a long time. My dad had no idea why the old man hung onto it – he said Grandfather did some of his growing up around here and he liked this part of Yorkshire, but then it was like he changed his mind: he bought it, then just abandoned it, let it rot – I'm not sure why he didn't just sell up, but I didn't see much of him over the last few years. We used to see him every other weekend, but he could be difficult, you know, and then we moved further away, and – well, not so much after that. I do wonder if that's why – I mean—'

'Why he left the place to me,' Emma finished for him.

'Well, yes. Not meaning anything by it. But I did see him towards the end and there didn't seem to be any hard feelings.' He frowned. 'He wrote me a letter.'

Emma started. 'Me too.'

'I don't think anyone's written a proper letter to me in years.' He smiled. 'It was a bit of an odd one, actually. He said that sometimes things are for the best, and there were reasons that weren't for me to know. It was all very strange. But then he said I wasn't to think badly of him and – I don't, you know. I really hadn't expected anything, like I said. I didn't think he had a lot to do with your side of the family, but it's okay – it was his place. He did all right, Grandfather Clarence, and it was his choice, after all.'

Emma stared down at her coffee. It was going cold. She glanced at the window and saw the sky was turning a deeper grey. It would be dark soon and Charlie would leave and the house would be silent again. Now that he was here, filling the room with the sound of his voice, she found herself wanting to delay that moment.

'Do you want something to eat?' she asked. 'I brought a few things with me. Nothing spectacular, but—'

He smiled, revealing a dimple in his right cheek. 'Love to,' he said. 'If I'm honest, I'm starving. Actually, since you're being so hospitable, I can sing for my supper if you like.' He gestured towards the paint tins in the corner. 'Make myself useful.' He snapped out a mock salute. 'Will work for pizza.'

Emma pushed herself up. 'You've got yourself a deal.'

Later, while they ate, Charlie told her about the old man.

'He wasn't what you'd call a traditional grandfather,' he said. 'There were no trips to the seaside or packets of toffee hidden in his pockets. He didn't spend his time pottering about the garden. He'd dress in his best suits every day. He walked with a cane with a silver top, and he always looked at me as if he knew every thought going through my scrawny little head. That's how I think of him anyway, as if I was still ten and he was tall and strange and a little bit frightening.

'If you'd known him, you'd understand why I didn't expect anything from him. He was – *independent*, I suppose that's the word for it. When my dad was still with us, he always said if the old man set his mind on anything, he'd damned well get it, and watch out if you got in his way. And he had what he called his *standards*. He was of a different generation, I guess. I don't think I was ever smart enough or educated enough or distinguished enough for him – especially now, when I'm between jobs. I was something of a disappointment, I suppose.'

She would have liked to say, *No, of course you weren't*, but how could she? Judging by the meagre impression she had gained from old man's letter, the picture Charlie painted was pretty true to life.

You're a mystery. That was the best he could say about her, and perhaps that was for the best in itself. If he'd known her, she might have been a disappointment too, and he might have decided against leaving her the house. But of course, her gain was Charlie's loss. She swallowed down her reply as she remembered he'd said, *When my dad was still with us.*

'So your dad—'

'He died five years ago.'

'I'm sorry. I didn't know.'

'No reason why you should. I only really thought about your branch of the family after Grandfather died, and I suppose I only wanted to look you up because there's no one left, if I'm honest. I'm kind of *it*, and – well, family's family, even if we are only distant relatives.' He paused. 'The weird thing was, I didn't know Clarence had thought about your side of the family either. I think I heard someone mention your dad once – Junior, they called him, and I think it was him they meant—'

'He was called Arthur, after *his* father, my granddad, and yes, sometimes people did call him that, even when he was older.'

'I thought so. Anyway, when the subject came up – Clarence's *face* – well, it was like he didn't think much of him, or didn't approve or something. Sorry, but it's true, though I never – shit, hang on—'

He shuffled about and as he reached into his pocket Emma became aware of a low buzzing. It grew louder when he withdrew a mobile phone. 'Rick, hiya. I'm on my way soon. Just— why, what's up?'

He went quiet and a different kind of buzzing replaced the first, that of someone speaking. 'Shit. All right, mate, sit tight. I can come tomorrow. Yeah, don't worry. Don't even think about it. Take care, all right?' And he rang off, staring at the phone as if it might throw light on the brief burst of conversation.

'Is everything okay?'

'Yeah, it will be. My mate Rick – the one I came down to see – he had to cancel. Something about his girlfriend being ill. Never mind. I can— I'll sort it.'

'Sort it?'

'It's nothing. I'll head back home tonight, that's all. It's not that late. I was going to sleep on his floor, you see. Bit of a lad's break while Karen goes off with the girls to Huddersfield, but she's at home with flu or something, so . . .' His voice tailed off and he bit into his pizza, chewing quickly, as if he was suddenly in a hurry to leave.

'Shame.' Emma fell quiet. She felt all the weight of the house above her, the long corridors, the silent and dark rooms, waiting for nothing and no one. There were six bedrooms. *Six.*

She took a deep breath. How did she even know he was for real? Charlie – a potential heir to the property – had showed up on the very day she'd chosen to move in. And now this, a friend who'd let him down on that very same day. Wasn't that something of a coincidence? She shook the thought away. She had believed him when he'd said he had no thought of inheriting the house. And something else had stayed with her – the thing he'd said about being the only one left. It had made her think of her own parents, a whole line dwindling into nothing but her, her *alone*, and she found herself saying, 'You can stay here.'

His head swivelled around. 'Seriously? But you don't even know me.'

'I do now. It's fine, honestly. There's plenty of room.' And then she remembered. 'Oh, but no spare bed – no bedding, anything like that.'

He straightened. 'Neither has Rick. I've a sleeping bag in the boot and it's pretty comfy. At least if I'm tired enough.' He grinned. 'I could manage with that no problem, if it's really all right. It's a long way to get back and it'd be good to get some sleep before I head off. Thanks. I mean, really – thanks.'

'No problem. Pick a room.'

'Could be tricky.'

She smiled.

'One condition though,' Charlie said. When she looked over she realised how the light was fading; neither of them had switched on the lights and he was becoming an outline, only his eyes still gleaming. 'If you're being good enough to help me out, I could do some more on the house. I'd like to. Least I can do.'

Emma nodded, wondering why her heartbeat had quickened. 'Fine,' she said, and she smiled, though she could no longer make out the expression on his face.

Charlie followed her upstairs, carrying the large rucksack he'd fetched from his car. They paused on the landing, surrounded by doors, and he didn't wait to be asked – he pushed open the one next to her own, the one that let onto the master bedroom. Then he stopped and backed out again. 'God no,' he said, 'I'd rattle around in that one. And it's freezing.'

She stared at him in dismay. He was right, it *was* cold. She was no longer sure how he would fare, sleeping on the floor, but he'd never fit on the sofa either. He gestured towards the smaller bedrooms at the back of the house – the ones furthest from hers. 'I'll grab one of those, if that's all right. I'll be no bother, I promise.'

'You're no bother.'

'Thanks.' He smiled. 'It's kind of nice being here actually. It's been good catching up with family.'

She nodded. He was right, it was.

But he was looking all around, up at the ceiling. 'The heating doesn't seem to work – it'll be like ice in winter. Still, I'm sure you'll fix it up.'

She thought of trying to heat the whole place with those little fireplaces and the very idea made her shiver. There was a definite draught here; it must be colder outside than she'd thought.

He turned away, saying, 'Well, I'll get myself sorted. Thanks again, Emma. Good night.'

She replied automatically, and walked into her room. It was properly dark now and the tall window was a blackened slab save where the reflection of her own face shone, a pale oval in the bottom pane. She went over and looked out. The moon was bright and she could see further than she'd expected. Their two cars were parked close together in the driveway. The lawn was pocked with ink-dark blots that looked a little like footprints. The road was a strip of brighter grey, just visible over the top of the wall. She could see the shapes of the trees that bounded the house and beyond, the dark spaces of the fields. She turned to peer out to the other side, towards the churchyard, but a sound startled her and she turned. There was only the outline of her bed; then she saw the door of the cupboard where she'd found the old man's suit. It was open.

I'd chuck it, if I were you.

Now it sounded as if there were mice in there, a soft shuffling against the walls. She could suddenly feel her heart beating, some fluttering, trapped thing. She took a deep breath. She was being silly. She wasn't scared, not really; only startled. All the same, what rose to her mind was the image of an old man, his figure bent, creeping about, patting at the shelves in turn, thinking, *Where is it?*

Grow up, she thought, and strode across the room and looked inside. The cupboard was empty; the suit was gone and so were the memories it carried. The noise was probably just the building settling, one of those sounds that meant nothing at all. She closed her eyes. She had a sudden vivid memory of her mother's face, smiling at her. Emma had been crying over a fairy tale, the fate of some princess who didn't win the handsome prince, didn't live happily ever after. What was it she had said? *It's all right, Emma. You're just being fanciful.*

She found herself smiling. Yes, she *was* being fanciful. She closed the cupboard door and went to find some pyjamas. At least she was being rational now. A good thing too: tomorrow Charlie would be gone and she would be here alone. It was best that she should get used to it.

CHAPTER SEVEN

Emma didn't know when the house had changed. She had been sleeping, but when she awoke she had a sense that she had been listening to it all along, or if not listening, sensing it with her body, finding its rhythm, attuning herself to its ways.

She pushed the covers away, feeling too hot under them, but outside, the air was bitter. There was a sharp barrier between the two and once she'd crossed it, it was too late; the chill delved inside, embracing her skin, furrowing along her body, finding her spine, her legs, her feet. The room was dark, everything grainy and silver. The ceiling looked a long way off and the corners were dark, as if a child had sketched the room in stark black lines. She sat up and realised that the cupboard door was hanging open once more. *How ridiculous*, she thought. *Monsters in the cupboard, like in a story.* And then she saw the man standing quietly next to it.

He was half-dressed. He had hunched shoulders and a stocky body and slightly bowed legs, and she opened her mouth but the only sound she could make was a dry gasp. He didn't move but she knew that he was watching her. She couldn't see his eyes but she could just make out his rumpled vest and then she knew: the suit was his – he had come looking for it but he wouldn't find it because she had thrown it away. Now he'd come to see where it was and instead, he had found her.

Her hands flexed. She could feel the tainted material on her skin, that shiny-musty fabric. She could see again the way she'd thrown it down in disgust, just as if it wasn't wanted, wasn't *needed* any longer.

You're being fanciful, Emma.

She took a deep breath. She was in a strange house and there was nothing there, only an unfamiliar room full of shadows. But he *was* there. He didn't move but continued to stand there, and she could feel his gaze on her, though she still couldn't see his eyes. She could sense the hostility in his look. She became conscious of the cold on her own face, a bone-deep cold. She was alone, and for a moment that was the worst thing of all. She didn't know why she had come here, but then she remembered Charlie, sleeping at the other end of the house. He would banish this thing. He'd grin at her and laugh, his very presence denying the possibility of its existence.

Panic took her and she pushed herself to her feet and ran, hoping – *hoping* – that the man wouldn't stretch out his arm and grasp her shoulder as she passed. Then she was in the corridor and heading for Charlie's room. The worn carpet was no protection from the hard boards beneath and her steps rang out loudly. She banged on the door, and the moment she did, she felt ridiculous. If she was so scared, why didn't she just go in? There were no locks on the doors, nothing to stop her. And if she *wasn't*, why was she at his door?

He opened it, his face full of concern. She reached for his arm and started to cry. She wanted to be held and yet a part of her didn't want to touch him, this stranger in a strange house – in *her* house. Then he opened the door wider and put a hand on her arm and brought her out of the corridor, drawing her inside.

Charlie didn't switch on the light but a slanting glow lit the room anyway and she realised his room didn't have any curtains. There was nothing to shut out the moon which shone down, silvering the ancient carpet and the mound of his makeshift bed. She hugged herself. What must he think of her?

But he didn't touch her. He took a step back and waited. She no longer knew what she was going to say. She was no longer sure she'd seen anything at all.

'What is it?' he asked at last. 'A bad dream?'

'No. I woke up. I thought – I thought I saw someone in my room.'

He turned towards the door. 'There's someone in the house? Now? All right, I'll go and check. Have you heard him moving about – do you think he's still in your room? Should we call someone?'

Instinctively she grabbed his arm. She felt cool skin, the roughness of his hair, and she realised he was wearing only T-shirt and shorts. *He must be freezing.* 'No, don't – I don't think— that wasn't it, Charlie. No one's broken in. At least, I don't *think* they have. I— it's hard to explain, but it didn't feel like that.'

He frowned. 'What do you mean? Did you dream it, Emma, or should I go looking?'

She paused. 'No, I didn't dream it.' Her voice faltered. 'He was real. I *saw* someone. I felt him looking back at me. I had to go straight past him to get out of the room. I was scared he'd touch me when I went past.'

'And did he? Did he try to grab you?'

She shook her head. It hadn't been like that, not someone who *could* grab and hold on. But someone *trying* to touch her would have been bad enough. She just wasn't sure if she'd have felt it as a physical thing, a real thing. Now she didn't know which would be worse, her feeling it or not feeling it. She reached out for him again. This time it felt more intimate, chosen rather than a reflex. She closed her fingers over his arm. 'I'm sorry,' she said. 'It wasn't a dream – or I don't think it was – but it wasn't real either. I knew he wasn't real even while he was looking straight at me. Don't ask me how I knew that. I just *knew*. He wasn't *there*, not like we are, but he was still real.'

He looked at her and she replayed her words in her head, realising how stupid it sounded.

But Charlie didn't tell her she was being fanciful. He didn't tell her there was nothing there and he didn't try to reason with her or name her fear. He simply twisted around so that he was standing at her side and he put his arm around her. After a while he squeezed her shoulders and he said, 'I'll go and take a look.'

She couldn't see his expression as he walked out of the room. His footsteps receded, steady and sure, and there came the faint creak of a door opening and then silence. Emma listened to the sound of her own breathing. She tried to remember if she'd heard *him* breathing, the man in her room; she didn't think so. She wasn't sure what it would mean if she had. She still didn't think he had been a real person.

After a time she heard footsteps again but they didn't come back to this room. Instead they faded into another, and then came louder on the landing and then rhythmic on the stairs. After a time the same rhythm sounded, getting louder this time, and before the thought had fully formed in her mind that it might not be Charlie, it might be *him*, the door swung wide and she saw the outline of Charlie's hair. He walked in and smiled reassuringly. 'There's no one there,' he said. 'I had a good look around – I even looked under the bed and in the cupboard, and in the other rooms and downstairs. Unless someone kept slipping into a different room while my back was turned, we're on our own.'

She took a deep breath. 'No, I— I didn't think there would be. Sorry, Charlie.'

He frowned as the words sank in, and he tensed. Now he would say it: *There's nothing there, Emma. You're just being fanciful.* She could already hear the note of contempt that would be in his voice when he said it.

But he didn't say that. Instead, she heard a low chuckle. 'Well, you know what this means.'

I'm crazy, she thought. *That's what it means.*

'This house is even more interesting than you thought. It looks as if you've got a real live ghost.'

She turned the word over in her mind. *Ghost.* Had she really thought of it that way? She had only known that the person in her room had come from somewhere *else*, that it *belonged* somewhere else. She hadn't thought of it as a ghost – she hadn't thought to name it – but now she couldn't get the word out of her mind. It didn't fit with the way she thought of herself. She wasn't the sort of person who saw ghosts, or even believed in them. She pushed the idea away, something to think about later, and she forced herself to nod at Charlie. She really didn't want to go back to her room, not now, but she couldn't stay here.

'Thank you, Charlie,' she started. She found she wanted to say something else, to explain the whole thing away perhaps, but tiredness had overtaken her. She didn't want to think about it, not now. Later maybe, when she couldn't sleep or when she was alone. Charlie showed her out and she stood in the hallway, looking at the door to her room.

She knew her room was empty even before she flicked on the light and it flooded across the dingy floor and into the dusty corners. The cupboard door was open, though she couldn't see inside. The sense of presence which had been so strong when she'd awakened was gone.

She went to the door, reaching out to push it closed once more, and froze. The suit was back again. It was hanging on its yellowing padded hanger, not pulled awry but straight and neat, the trousers sharply creased around the white shine of the bulked-out knees, the jacket hanging squarely over the top. At once she thought of grabbing the thing and taking it downstairs and throwing it out of the door, but she stopped herself even before the movement began. She didn't want to feel that fabric on her fingers. Would the owner of the thing still be looking for it? Perhaps she'd feel his hand on her shoulder after all.

But maybe he'd already found it – she *had* thrown it out, hadn't she? She'd put it in the bin outside or left it in the drawing room, she wasn't sure which. It hadn't been something she'd wanted in the house. He must have come looking for it, and he'd found it and placed it in here. If she was to move it again, she might make everything worse. It might even call him back.

Then a thought struck her and she flushed with heat. Charlie had come in here, hadn't he? He'd been checking the place, being helpful. And he knew about the suit. *More Savile Row, the old man.*

He'd been downstairs too, while she hid in his room. Had he found the suit down there and brought it back up with him? The whole thing might have been some kind of joke. Heat spread through her. She'd thought he was helping, that he was being kind, and all the time he'd just been pulling some kind of trick. She frowned. Had she really seen a stranger in her room or had that been only another kind of trick? The kind that meant standing and watching her, in the dark – watching her sleep, maybe?

She shook her head. The suit was still there, in front of her eyes. Tomorrow she would take it outside and banish it forever; it would be gone and so would Charlie and she would get on with all the things she'd planned to do. For now, though, she had no intention of touching it. Let it stay there. She backed away and closed the door, making sure it snicked into place. It wouldn't open on her again; she didn't even have to think about it until morning.

She turned, still not liking to have her back to that door, just as if she were a child again, afraid of the monster in the wardrobe, and she got back into bed. The sheets had grown cold and she pulled them up to her shoulders, watching the door as she nestled her head into her pillow. Charlie had comforted her. He had been kind to her, had gone to see what was wrong, looking around the house in the dark and the cold. It couldn't have been him. She had seen a *ghost*, for God's sake. If she accepted that, it wasn't too much of a step to suppose it could have found its suit and put it back. And that was enough to worry about, without inventing trickery of another kind: without souring the kindness of the one person in her life who appeared to be intent on helping her.

CHAPTER EIGHT

When Emma woke, the events of the night before were so close to the surface of her mind that she opened her eyes and stared directly at the same spot where the man had been standing. She knew exactly where it was, that space between the doorways. She remembered the suit too, but for now, she didn't want to look at it. Instead she went into the bathroom and splashed ice-cold water onto her face.

To look into the cupboard and see that worn black suit would be to acknowledge that it had all been real. Had she really gone running to Charlie in the middle of the night? He must think she was mad. She probably *had* been mad. And yet she could still picture the man looking back at her, the malice pouring off him like a musty smell.

At least the house felt like her own again. Sunlight spilled around and beneath the curtains, filling the rooms with diffuse light. Despite her interrupted sleep, she felt refreshed. Today she would clean and paint and later, when she was ready, she'd come back up here with a bin bag and knock that suit off the shelf and into it, yellowing coat-hanger and all. She'd put it out with the rubbish, shove it down deep into the bin, and never think about it again.

For now, she headed downstairs. She could hear a noise coming from the drawing room. When she went in she saw Charlie, his arms stretched above his head, reaching into the corner with a roller covered in paint. He had almost finished. The soft green glowed in the morning sun. He turned and she saw that his face was spattered with it, that colour; it was in his hair and over his clothes. He grinned at her, but Emma felt nothing but dismay. It was *her* room. This was what she had been planning to do first, the thing that would make the house truly her own. Now he had taken it from her; there was nothing left for her to do.

'Morning,' he said, his voice bright, as if he hadn't noticed her expression. 'Nearly there. Doesn't it look good?'

She swallowed, fighting the lump in her throat. It did look good. He must have been working for hours. She was being childish; she should be grateful. 'It does. Thanks, Charlie. This must have taken you ages.'

'Ah, well – that'll teach me to pick a room without any curtains. I woke up at dawn, so not much choice.' As if to underline the point his jaws stretched in a sudden yawn and when he tried to cover it with his arm it looked as if he'd dipped that in the paint too.

Emma's cheeks flushed. His eyes were red as if he'd been rubbing them, and his hair was flattened at the back and spiked haphazardly at the front. He'd probably barely slept, what with her running to him in the middle of the night and then being awoken with the sun. 'I'll make us some coffee,' she said, 'and see what I can find for breakfast.'

'No need: I made egg butties – might be a bit cold now, but should still taste okay. I left you one. And I found a coffee grinder in one of the boxes – I hope you don't mind.'

'Of course not. It's good of you.' She glanced at the window, wondering just how late it was. She'd slept the day away.

'I had a look at the hot water too. There's an immersion – should be piping in an hour or so, I reckon.'

'You have been busy.'

'Least I can do.'

'Hardly. You didn't have to do anything. I know you must have things of your own to be doing.'

'Well – but we're relatives, and all that. Even if it is only distant.' The last words came out in a rush. 'And anyway, I couldn't head off without seeing if you were okay. Last night – whatever it was you saw – well, I would have been worried about you, that's all.'

Emma opened her mouth to say there was no need, then looked away. What *had* she seen? It felt further from reality than ever. And yet he'd said *what you saw*, not *what you* think *you saw*.

'Grandfather used to see ghosts.'

She met his eye, startled.

'Seriously. He never talked to me about it, though. He told Dad, who told me. Of course no one believed him and after a while he just stopped talking about it, apparently. I got all excited about it when I heard – I even tried to ask him about it, but he just gave me this look, like it was a serious matter, you know, and certainly not for the likes of me. Not something to laugh about.'

Emma shook her head. 'He saw something *here*?'

'Hell – I didn't mean that.' He frowned. 'Actually, I don't know where he saw it. I never really got the whole story, and I never thought to ask where he was. I suppose it might've been about the time he bought this place, but it's not all that likely – he didn't stay here very long.'

'Do you have a photograph of him?'

He looked surprised. 'Why?'

'Well, I— Never mind. I'm not sure. It was just a stupid idea.' She hadn't even seen his face, the man last night. And anyway, she'd got the impression of someone who wasn't quite that old; he was stooped, yes, but not a man in his eighties as Clarence Mitchell had been.

She pushed the thought away and looked around the room once more. It did look better – it looked *right*. If she half-closed her eyes she could picture it with furniture in place, and how she'd sit and read a book, light falling across the page. She could almost see it: a dark winged armchair with a high back, grand enough for its position in the room, and a tall, elegant standard lamp, and her sitting there quite straight – and she found she couldn't breathe. There *was* someone sitting there. The armchair was faded, the arms rubbed almost bare, and the windows were clouded because he was smoking; she saw the wreaths of smoke quite clearly, obscuring his face, leaving nothing but the dark smudges of his eyes.

She blinked and he was gone, but she was quite sure that it had been the same man, the one she'd seen last night. The only difference was that he was wearing his suit. He had found his pipe too. Of course she was imagining things, but she found herself trying to remember what she'd done with that; she could remember picking up the suit, ready to throw it away, but not the pipe. She thought, though, that the last time she'd looked in the cupboard, the pipe had been gone.

She blinked. There was only the window, full of soft brightness.

'Are you okay?'

It must have been a trick of the light, that was all. She was seeing things, summoning them out of shadows and bad dreams. She was tired and she was hungry; that didn't mean she'd seen a ghost. Perhaps she'd just been spooked by the big old empty house last night – and yet the house didn't feel frightening to her. It felt like home. It felt like *hers*.

'Emma?'

She started. She had almost forgotten Charlie. She turned and smiled and he looked reassured. He grabbed hold of the roller again. 'I'll get this finished, then I'll head off.'

Then she would be alone. Perhaps that would be better; when she knew the house was truly empty she wouldn't be listening for odd sounds from dark corners. She wouldn't imagine she'd seen someone where there was nothing. Still, she couldn't help feeling vaguely disappointed. As she left the room, she breathed in deep; the paint fumes filled her lungs, almost – but not quite – masking the richer, spicier scent of pipe tobacco beneath.

CHAPTER NINE

'Well good luck, almost-second-cousin, or great-grand-niece-in-law-by-marriage or whatever it is that we are.'

Emma smiled. 'It was good to see you,' she said, and she found that she meant it. He held out his arms and she hugged him back, feeling the warm strength of his body under his sweater. She suddenly wanted to apologise again for waking him in the middle of the night, but it didn't feel necessary – his smile was clean and open, and she didn't want to remind him of her behaviour.

He picked up his bag and she watched while he slung it into the boot. The air was cool but the sun was shining, making everything bright and clear. 'Take care of the old place.' He glanced up at the windows and said approvingly, 'I know you will.' He got in and rolled the window down and waved out of it before reversing away down the drive.

Emma watched the car pulling out of sight, not sure how she was supposed to feel. She wasn't afraid, that wasn't it, but she was alone. It was odd that she had become accustomed to his presence so quickly. Now, though, the place was hers. There'd be no more coming downstairs to find things had moved without her moving them – *no more suits reappearing in a wardrobe.*

She frowned, remembering she still had to clear that thing away. It would be the first thing she did when she went back inside. For now, though, it was a bright clear Sunday. She looked over at the church. It was strange that no one had rung the bells or come for morning service. It was as quiet and still as it had been before. She pulled the front door to, then found herself checking around before walking down the drive. But there was no one about; she probably didn't even need to lock the door around here anyway.

The church was a sagging single-storey building, settling into the green earth like a tired old man. A faint mist rose from it, looking almost like a sigh. Its windows were intricately webbed and she could see the traces of colours, mostly faded and greyed on the outside, but one of them was glowing as if a candle was burning somewhere inside. The path to the door was made of old worn slabs. The wooden door was silvered and cracked with age.

The slope rising behind the building was covered in gravestones that leaned and tilted towards one other like homecoming drunks. Everything was damp with dew and she could hear dripping from the trees. It looked the ideal of a country church, except that it was closed on a Sunday morning. She could imagine it back in the day, a hotbed of gossip, the chance to meet and mingle with neighbours seldom seen in the midst of harvest or planting or whatever else people around here used to do. She could imagine how it had dwindled over the years, with people no longer forced to attend, either through belief or obligation, or simply moving away. She had no religion herself, had never felt any desire to reach for the church, not even when arranging her parents' funeral, but it was a little melancholic now, seeing such a building fall out of use.

When she tried the iron ring set into the door it swung open. She had an image of herself walking in on the middle of a service and rows of people turning to look at her – but there was only a shadowy vestibule with short stone benches on either side. There was a noticeboard, though, and she leaned in, propping the door open with one foot so she had light enough to read by.

There were requests for help cleaning, for cake-baking in support of a coffee morning, a thank-you to a group who'd been round to clear the gutters. In the middle was a notice: *Next Service*, it said, and there was something about the vicar being ill, and in large black letters, next Sunday's date.

No service today, then. Emma leaned in further and tried the inner door. It would be good to look around when nobody was there; she wasn't planning on going next Sunday. It was locked, however, and she stepped out again into the bright air, closing the outer door quietly behind her – odd how churches engendered quiet in people, even when they were empty. She turned towards the path and that was when she saw the bench.

It sat next to a path that led around the front of the church and up through the graveyard. It looked old but solid, made of stone that had darkened where the morning damp lingered. Large clear letters were carved deeply into the backrest. She went closer, and read: *O taste and see that the Lord is good. Psalm 34:8*

The corner of her mouth twitched. *Taste and see.* She had a sudden image of the local children, their tongues sticking out, trying to lick the letters. She looked along the path and saw that there was another bench like this one, a short way along. It was set into a space between the gravestones and grass was growing thickly around its base. Like everything else here, it appeared to be sinking into the earth. It looked quiet, peaceful, a good place to sit and look up at the trees and let time pass. She walked to it and read: *Rejoice in the Lord always: and again I say, rejoice. Philippians 4:4*

There was another, further down the path, this one facing the back of the church.

Behold, I am the Lord, the God of all flesh. Jeremiah 32:27

She had expected inscriptions in memory of husbands and wives, the beloved so-and-so, but this was sweet, a nice thing to do. As she walked, she remembered having to sing hymns as a child in school. 'All Things Bright and Beautiful', or her then-favourite, 'Lord of the Dance': something about dancing with the devil, an odd one for children perhaps, but she had liked the tune.

The next was, *Nothing shall by any means hurt you. Luke 10:19*

She smiled. It was an odd collection of verses and she wondered how on earth they had been chosen. It looked as if they'd been set here at different times. She had reached the end of them, though: the path ended with a last irregular stone and then there was nothing but the graves spreading away, with trodden-down grass marking the walkways between them.

Then she saw there was one more after all.

A rougher path led between the headstones to the boundary fence, beyond which she could see the grey mass of Mire House. The last bench was close to the edge, positioned underneath an overhanging yew tree so that it was almost lost in shadow.

She stepped onto the grass and her feet sank into the soft ground at once; she would be leaving a trail of footprints as she edged between the memorials of people long gone. She wanted to see the view from the bench. Looking behind her, she would be able to see everything, the whole graveyard and the church nestled among it all, peaceful, sleeping.

When she stood in front of the bench and read the words, she frowned. She bent, sweeping the lettering clear of dead needles that had fallen from the tree, but the letters were cut clear and tall as the rest and their meaning did not change: *My God, my God, why hast Thou forsaken me? Matthew 27:46*

She hugged herself, suddenly feeling colder. There was a twinge inside her – a feeling like loss – and she swallowed it down. She forced herself instead to focus on *why?* – who would have carved such a thing? Why had they chosen it? It was from the Bible – it must be, the chapter and verse were written there – but it was a hard sentiment to use in such a way.

If not for those words, this would be a lovely place to sit. The bench faced her own house; from this position she could see straight through the gaps in the trees at the edge of the garden. But to sit here, knowing those words were at her back, somehow wouldn't be the same. She wished she could reach back through time and understand. Perhaps it was only meant in some educational way; they were the words meant to have been spoken by Christ on the cross, weren't they? In a moment of despair, of loss that must be borne before everything changed. Perhaps it was meant as a reminder of that sacrifice, or maybe – and the thought made her lip twitch – it had been a mistake, they had instructed the stonemason using the wrong verse number and he had etched it into the thing anyway. But she had no way of knowing why it was there; it was just a shame it was so bleak.

She couldn't push from her mind the image of a lone figure sitting hunched on the seat, despairing and desolate – but still, it was a beautiful place and she was lucky to be living next to it. There was surely no need to ever feel desolate in a place as lovely and comforting as this.

CHAPTER TEN

When Emma opened the door to the cupboard she could smell the stale scent of tobacco, stronger than ever. She covered her hand with the bin bag before using it to lift the hanger, feeling the weight of the suit. She had half-expected it to be gone again when she came back, but no, it was still there. She found herself wondering once more if Charlie had been playing some trick – or even if he'd made a mistake; perhaps he'd thought she'd wanted to keep it after all, and had hung it in here earlier in the day. But neither explanation felt likely. She wrinkled her nose as the scent of unwashed skin reached her. She stuffed the clothing down into the bag and twisted the top around, trying to shut that smell inside, but it was no good; it was in the air now too.

She headed downstairs and rather than just leaving the bag in a corner, she went out through the kitchen and thrust it straight into the wheelie-bin, pressing it down between the other sour-smelling rubbish.

Then she gathered her cleaning things from the kitchen and went back upstairs. Her footsteps sounded loud now that she was alone, echoing through the house and into all the empty spaces.

She would clear out the cupboard properly, clean it and make it hers. She'd hang a second rail below the first on which to place her clothes. It wouldn't take long. First she rummaged through some boxes, extricated her radio and tuned it to a morning show. The music was bright and cheerful and a little too loud – she'd need it that way, to hear it in the cupboard – and she went inside and began to replace the musty smell with that of bleach. She scrubbed dark spots from the shelves, revealing faded white paint. It started to look better at once. And then she stopped. She could hear another sound beneath the strains of the music: steady thuds, like the echo of footsteps. She listened. The tune segued into the DJ's patter. In the spaces between the words there was nothing; only the house, breathing around her.

When she went back to work she could see her own breath, rising in a white mist, although she didn't feel cold. Then there came a soft thud. After a moment came a second, so faint she wasn't sure she'd heard it, and a loud skitter that made her heart leap. Something scraped against the wall just outside and the cupboard door slammed closed behind her.

Emma whirled, clutching the cloth tightly against her chest, her eyes staring, and she didn't breathe. The beating of her heart was almost painful. Inside the cupboard it was almost pitch-dark, with only a faint glow coming from around the doorframe. Every fibre of her being was intent on listening. She took a breath that caught in her throat, chilling her lungs. She put out a hand and touched the door but she didn't try to open it. She only waited as the music tailed off then a voice rang out, loudly, making her jump once more. It was only the DJ, only the radio. There was nothing else, no other sound, though it *felt* as if she should be able to hear something else. She turned and saw only a dark space behind her. She forced a deep breath. Something must have fallen in the room outside, or one of the boxes had overbalanced, that was all. She didn't need to be afraid. Mire House was her *home*.

Footsteps, she thought. *It had sounded like footsteps, at least until that awful clatter.*

She put her hand to the door handle and pushed. It didn't move.

Emma frowned. She tried again, harder, and felt the mechanism give, but it wouldn't press. She pushed outwards instead, and the door rattled in its frame, but it did not open.

She took a deep breath. *Don't be ridiculous. Don't be* fanciful.

She must be trying to open it the wrong way. It was an old house and things didn't necessarily work the way she was used to. She tried to move the handle again, upwards this time, then down, and then any way at all. It still didn't move and she strained harder, gripping it with both hands, then banging into the door with her shoulder. She stopped, found herself opening her mouth to call out, then closed it again. Someone had come into the house and come up the stairs and heard her in here and they were here now, holding the handle from the other side. It must be Charlie, playing another joke. She'd left the front door unlocked, and the back. That had been stupid. Why on earth had she done that? Especially after what she thought she'd seen in the night.

She let go of the handle and stepped back. Her hand was shaking. She bent and looked at the strip of light under the door, then, quietly, she knelt and pushed her face as close to the floor as she could.

She thought she could see something partially blocking the light, but she couldn't get low enough to see it properly. She stood again, knocking her head against the shelf and bit her lip. She didn't want to cry out – she wasn't sure who might hear her. She grabbed the handle again, quickly, as if to take someone by surprise, and jerked on it, but it still didn't move.

She stepped back, breathing hard. Who the hell would do this? Some joke this was, sneaking up on someone in their own house – a woman, on her own – and scaring her.

'Who's there?' Her voice was sharp, although she'd meant for it to be louder. 'Who is it?'

As she listened the music changed to some seventies thing: Marc Bolan singing T. Rex's 'Metal Guru'.

She banged on the door, hard, the blows wrenching her shoulder, but she didn't care, and when the door didn't open she did it again, harder. Then tears came, fucking *tears*, but she blinked them back. *Charlie*, she thought. She didn't know why, only that his name was there: someone she could go to for help, or someone who would play tricks, put a dirty old suit back in her room as if to say, there: that's the real owner, come home again. She didn't know which Charlie he was.

She grabbed the handle and wrenched hard on it, bruising her palm, and this time it came free. She gasped in spite of herself and pushed, and something outside rattled against the base of the door. The door gave a little further and then it stopped. She hammered on it this time, hard, *blam-blam-blam!*

There was no sound from the other side, only the radio going on and on, though the tone of the music seemed to have changed.

'Let me out.' Emma's voice didn't waver: good. She didn't want to betray her fear, didn't want to give them the satisfaction. Who was it, anyway? What the hell gave them the right? She gave the door a kick for good measure and again it rattled but it did not open.

'*Shit.*'

Emma could feel her hand resting against the wood. It was still shaking. Her knees felt shaky too; she wanted to sit down. She looked behind her, into the dark, as if she would find some answer there, but it did not come. She looked back at the door. It no longer felt as if anyone was there. It didn't feel as if anyone was going to help. The house was empty and it was hers, only hers. And her parents couldn't come to her, full of concern at the noise she'd made. There was no one here she knew, no neighbour or friend to look in on her. She couldn't shout through the ceiling to bring Jackie and Liam. There was only the church with its quiet graveyard and no one there – and anyway, even if she could shout loud enough, she'd put on the radio – the *radio*, for God's sake – just as if she'd wanted to drown out her own calls for help.

She remembered the dreams she'd had before she'd come to Mire House, the ones in which she simply disappeared, with no one to miss her or look for her, and she curled her hands into fists. There must be someone she could contact. She reached for her back pocket and found it empty. Where had she put her mobile phone? She peered around but it was still dark, so she ran her hands across each shelf, finding only cold dampness where she'd already cleaned and dry dust where she hadn't. Then something cool and smooth brushed against her wrist.

She grabbed for it, whatever it was, but she didn't recognise the shape. It didn't feel right: it was almost silken against her skin but it was too slender and she couldn't think what it was. Then she leaned closer and *smelled* it, and now she knew. She swept her arm across the shelf and it clattered into the corner, sending up a stronger waft of that rich, dried scent, the tobacco scent, and she cried out, a despairing wail that made her suddenly think of the bench in the churchyard.

My God, she thought, *my God . . .*

No. Emma, pull yourself together.

She breathed in deeply, leaned towards the door and said, 'Tell me who's there.' She forced herself to speak steadily. 'This isn't funny. Open the door, now.'

Nothing happened; no one replied. She rattled the handle, then frowned and lowered herself to her knees again. She pressed her face into the musty-smelling carpet, trying to see under the door, and then she *did* see, in her mind's eye: the boxes she'd stacked against the wall, the paint roller leaning against the skirting, the new clothes rail. She squeezed her eyes closed. She knew exactly what had happened.

There was no one there, had never been anyone there. She'd heard the sound of the radio and that was all because she had done this to herself. It was just her and her own stupidity, and now she was stuck and she had to *think*.

She sat with her back to the door, running her hand across her face. She'd propped the rail against the wall and now it had fallen across the door. It must have jammed behind the boxes. She tried to replay the sounds she'd heard: the scrape and slide of something against the plaster, the duller thud as it came to rest.

And the door handle? She tried to picture the rail somehow catching under it and preventing it from turning, but she couldn't. She remembered that feeling, the way she'd *sensed* somebody standing there, gripping it from the other side, and she tossed her head, trying to dislodge the thought. Now she really was being fanciful. No one was there; this was a problem of her own making, only that, and she was the one who would have to get out of it.

She'd simply have to push harder, hard enough to move the door and the rail and the pile of boxes that was keeping them in place.

She knew it was useless before she even tried.

She'd been so enthusiastic when she'd carried everything up the stairs. The books had been the worst. The boxes had grown heavier in her arms as the day wore on, until she'd been stopping to rest each one on the stairs partway up. Now they were stacked outside, all in a pile, and they were *heavy* . . .

No. It *had* to be possible. They couldn't be *that* heavy, could they?

She reached above her head and held the handle down and pushed backwards with her whole body, trying to brace her legs against the floor. Her feet slid over the worn carpet, but whatever was on the outside of the door *didn't* slide, didn't even move. She screwed up her face, but stopped herself. She wasn't going to cry. It wouldn't help. She knew that from before; she'd allowed herself to cry at the funeral and then made herself stop and she knew she couldn't allow herself to start again, because then she *wouldn't* stop, there'd only be the pit and blackness and despair . . .

My God, my God . . .

The DJ was talking again, some burble that no longer sounded like language. It didn't make sense any more, nothing did. There was only this narrow room and no way out of it, no way back. She hid her face in her arms, as she had when she was a little girl afraid of the dark.

She shook her head, trying to shake loose the negative thoughts, and pushed against the door once more, as hard as she could, but it was no use. She'd given it all she had and it still hadn't moved an inch. She curled her hand into a fist and hit the wood, hard, a resounding blow. What the hell was she going to do? No one was going to come – no one even knew she was here. Even Charlie had gone. She was due at work tomorrow; she had to get out of here before then – she had to *sleep* before then, in her own bed, or she'd be useless. They'd be angry with her.

She took a couple of steps back, then paced forward; moved back, then forward. She thought suddenly that maybe she wouldn't make it into work at all. She might still be stuck in here, not even able to call them. No: surely that wouldn't happen? At least, if it did, she would be missed. They'd come looking for her, wouldn't they?

At the address she'd given them when she took the job: the address in Leeds.

She made a choking sound, but fought it back. It was bad enough she'd got herself stuck in here; she wasn't going to sound pathetic too. That would mean she'd given up. It would mean she'd failed.

She had to find something to use as a lever, something to force her way out. She looked around, though she could see nothing. She reached out, touched a cloth she'd left on the shelf, a useless lumpen thing. And there was the bottle of bleach, and a bowl of dirty water. There was nothing else . . .

That wasn't true: there *was* something else. She couldn't see where the pipe had fallen but she knew it was there. She lowered herself to the floor yet again, and had to force herself to put out her hand, to run it over that grimy carpet. When she touched the wood, smoothed by someone else's hand, she caught her breath.

She bent and tried to slip the stem of the pipe under the door. She wasn't really sure how it would help, but anyway the mouthpiece – *the thing he'd held between his lips, slid under his tongue* – jammed against the floor. She cupped the bowl in her palm, feeling the old grain close against her skin. The stem wouldn't fit into the narrow gap. She forced it anyway, and after a moment, she felt the pipe give. It twisted in her hand, almost as if it were a living thing, and then it cracked. She pulled her hand away. The pipe had splintered; it was useless. *Useless.* The shards were sharp. She flung it back into the corner and it banged against the wall and she heard something spatter dryly across the carpet. Then she smelled it, deep and rich in her throat. She had a sudden image of the man she'd seen, looking for his pipe as well as his suit, throwing open the door and finding her instead.

But no one did open the door. No one came.

She realised she was thirsty and she thought at once of that bowl of greying water on the shelf, the scum floating in it, the bubbles of bleach. She imagined being stuck in here so long she was desperate enough to sip the caustic liquid and she bit back a laugh.

My God.

Her head was beginning to ache. She put a hand to her forehead and realised it was throbbing in time to the music. The DJ was playing something older still now, softer and somehow mocking, and she thought, *I'll turn that damned thing down*, and she screwed up her face as Buddy Holly began to sing 'It Doesn't Matter Anymore'. She sat there, focusing on nothing, thinking of nothing, resolutely forcing herself not to cry.

It was the tone of the music that roused her, a subtle change she hadn't even noticed at first. She wasn't sure what had been playing before but now the tone was crackly and distant, as if she was listening to an old scratched record, not the constant prattle of the radio DJ and a stream of modern pop songs. She didn't recognise this. It was Big Band music, a jaunty, endless tune. She wasn't sure there were any words, but then a wavering voice began to sing, the voice cut-glass, the sound fragile, almost as if at any moment it might break.

She let her head tilt back. The light under the door, low as it was, was fading. The music didn't fade, though; it swelled around her, and it was *right*, somehow, for the way the house felt. It was *old*. She imagined those notes moving through the empty corridors, reaching the drawing room downstairs where people had once danced, taking each other in their arms and spinning, spinning, across the floor.

She opened her eyes onto the tight black space within the cupboard and closed them again. She was hungry; dull pains in her stomach were echoing the ones in her head. No one had come: of course, no one had come. Emma was alone: that was the way it was, the way it would stay, for ever and ever, amen.

Her throat hurt. She thought of the bowl. *Thirsty*.

No: someone must come. Someone would surely come.

After a while she curled up on the floor. It was cold there, and hard. She had no idea what time it was. She closed her eyes and tried to sleep. It wouldn't hurt any more if she could only sleep.

Emma lifted her head and listened to the sound of footsteps outside the door. Someone was walking about the room. The music was still playing, but the sound was distant, as if it were coming from a long way away. It could be the middle of the night, but she had no way of telling. It went around and around and the footsteps moved with it. Now she imagined two people, and in her mind they were dancing. She opened her mouth to speak, but somehow she didn't make a sound; she didn't want to – she didn't want to see who was out there, didn't want them to see her.

The sound cut off suddenly, music and footsteps and all, and there was only her own rasping breath. Her throat was dry. The feeling was coming back into her limbs, pins and needles where her arm had been trapped beneath her, soreness in her hip from lying on the floor, pain in her hand where she'd banged it against the door. Her head was the worst, the ache dull and *heavy*; she couldn't think. Silence was thick in the air and all around her, pressing in close.

There had never been any sound, never been anyone there. She must have been dreaming.

After a moment she lowered her head again and she slept.

Eventually, the light came back. In the distance she could hear a dull *beep-beep-beep* and she realised that her mobile phone was ringing somewhere.

Dad, she thought, and shook her head. No, not him. Not now, not ever again.

She pulled herself up, her limbs stiff and cold. There was more light coming under the door. Her head felt a little clearer. It was simple, wasn't it? Door, rail, boxes: all she had to do was move them. Had she really spent the night in here?

She'd turn the handle and the door would open, just like that. She turned it, paused, and pushed. The door didn't move. She thought of the dirty cloth, the bowl with its dirty water. She needed the loo. Soon she would need it badly. At least if she had to go to the toilet in the silly little bowl she wouldn't be so tempted to raise it to her lips; to close her eyes and drink.

The sound was small at first, and yet familiar to her now. It felt, on some level, as if she'd been hearing it on and off for hours, though when she tried to think, she couldn't identify when it had started. It was footsteps: footsteps on the stairs.

She half-sat, staring into the darkness. It didn't matter, wouldn't help: it was the old man, that was all, looking for his suit or his pipe. He'd never really find them because he wasn't really there. He wouldn't be there again tomorrow or the next day; it didn't matter how many times she heard him or saw him.

She shook her head. The footsteps were coming up the stairs: slow this time, very slow.

'Emma?'

She frowned. The voice was quiet, so low she wasn't sure she'd heard it. How did the ghost know her name? Did it know *her*, really – had it been watching her all along? Then recognition came, and with it a flood of warmth.

'Charlie!' Her voice was dry, little more than a croak. She stood, ignoring the stiffness in her limbs, and hammered against the door. Her hand hurt but she didn't care. The door shook under her blows. She could hear his voice again, more words, though she couldn't make them out. It entered her mind that it was the radio, only the radio, but then there were scraping noises and the banging of things being thrown aside and the door opened.

She froze, her hand still raised. Charlie was there, his face creased in puzzlement, and there was so much *light*; it was day again and she could step forward and just walk out of there, but she didn't move. She could barely see his face for the brightness. It was Charlie who stepped forward, putting his arm around her, saying something to her, but she still couldn't make it out. It was his warmth that she clung to, and she realised that she was crying after all; the tears had crept out of her while she was too stunned to stop them and her face was wet.

CHAPTER ELEVEN

It wasn't until Charlie wrapped the duvet around her that Emma started to shiver. It was as if the cold had been buried deep inside and now it was leaving. She sat on the sofa in the drawing room surrounded by that perfect green paint and he put a mug of hot tea into her hands. She could get up and walk around if she wanted. She had been to the toilet and drunk about a gallon of water. She could have a shower, let the heat bring her back to warmth and life and reality.

She thought she'd explained what happened but she couldn't really remember. Her head felt fuzzy. *Someone came*, she thought, and a smile spread across her face: she couldn't help it.

Charlie didn't smile back. He still looked worried.

Maybe he isn't really here, she thought. *He's gone and you're still lying upstairs, only now you're dead.* She shuddered.

'Are you all right, seriously? I thought – I didn't know what to think. Were you really in there all night?'

She nodded and took a sip of tea. It was too milky but she didn't care. Then she thought of something. 'How – I mean, why are you—?'

'Why am I here?' He spread his arms, let them fall again. 'Emma, I really have no idea. I didn't intend to be; I'm not sure what made me come back. Yesterday – I got a call from my mate, just as I was heading off, and he said his girlfriend was feeling better so I dropped in after all. I don't think they're getting along so well – she'd gone off to her mum's – so we had a boys' night in, drank some beer, watched a film, and I stayed over. I was passing close to here on the way back, so – I don't know, I just suddenly thought I'd pop in, I suppose. I expected you'd be at work, to be honest, but – well, this house, it gets under your skin, you know? I thought I'd take another look at it before I left. And then I knocked, and you didn't answer but the car was there, so—'

Emma was staring. 'Shit,' she said. '*Work*. Christ, Charlie, what time is it?'

'Just after ten – Emma, you can't possibly be thinking of going in. Tell them what happened – they'll understand, won't they?'

'I have to get dressed.' She fought her way clear of the covers, her hands shaking; tea dripped across the carpet.

'Emma, *stop*. You're in no fit state. Sit back down, I'll call them for you. Don't worry, I'll say I'm a friend and I'll tell you're sick – you *are* sick, for God's sake.'

She sank back down. He was right, she felt dizzy. Her stomach was empty and it hurt. She needed warmth and – and *safety*, at least for a time. She supposed she should sleep, but the thought of settling into another confined space, wrapping herself tight in the bedclothes and closing her eyes, narrowing down the world – no, she didn't want that, even though she knew she needed it.

She watched him while he took her phone and found the work number she'd programmed into it. He drifted away, murmuring. She caught occasional words, but she could hear his tone and he sounded businesslike, to the point. It didn't take long.

'All done,' he said. 'I told them you might need a couple of days; they said it's fine.'

'A couple of days? Charlie, I don't—'

'Well, you have them if you need them.'

She paused, then said, 'All right. Thank you. I really don't know where I'd be if you hadn't turned up.'

'I do.' He glanced towards the stairs and gave a rueful smile. 'It's not worth thinking about. Look, just relax. I'll stick around for a bit, make sure you're okay.'

She took a deep breath. 'You don't have to – if you need to go, it's fine. Something like that couldn't happen twice, after all – anyway, I'll make sure it doesn't.'

'I know.' He spoke more softly. 'But I *want* to, Emma. I don't like to think about what might have happened if— but then, I suppose someone from work would have come looking for you.'

'Maybe. They don't even know I've moved, not yet. They will, of course.'

'You're staying here, then? Even after—'

'Of course. It was just an accident. It could have happened anywhere.' But it *hadn't* happened anywhere. It had been here, in the house she loved. She frowned, thinking of the people who had drifted from her life, the ones who couldn't come to help her any longer. She smiled back at Charlie. 'Of course, it would be nice if you wanted to stay around a little longer. It'd be a pleasure to have you.'

CHAPTER TWELVE

Emma stared at the place where she had seen the man standing, watching her in the night. She was no longer sure she'd seen anything but a shadow, but still, on some level, the thought of him was with her all of the time. She realised she had been skirting it like a bad memory, walking around that piece of floor as if there was something wrong with it, or as if the air had gone bad, *something*. There was no one there and yet look how carefully she had been avoiding that *no one* with her gaze. She hadn't opened the cupboard door yet either. She was being fanciful and she didn't care.

Everything else was coming together, though, forming around her: dust and shadows were being replaced by smooth gleaming paint; the vision she'd had of the place was beginning to emerge. Everything she did looked as if it had meant to be that way, as if it *belonged*, and as she thought of the word it felt full of promise, drifting through her mind, bringing comfort as, somewhere, Charlie began to sing.

She went to the window and looked out across the lawn and into the lane beyond. She had barely left the house since she'd moved in. She'd decided to take some time off work after all. She was so close to the rest of the world and yet she felt enclosed here, safe. Peaceful. Then she looked down and saw the man standing in her garden.

She froze. His back was turned but she knew it was him, the same man she'd seen in the night. He had found his suit. The greasy shine of the fabric was even more obvious in the daylight, as were the places it had worn thin. It looked a little too small, and he had one hand in his jacket pocket, stretching the fabric even more thinly across his back. In the other hand he held a thick black stick. As she watched, he raised it a couple of inches before banging it down again into the ground. He looked as if he was watching for someone coming down the lane, someone he didn't like.

For a moment she thought of Charlie, playing a practical joke maybe, then she heard his voice, so close she felt his warm breath on her ear: 'Who's that?'

She jumped. 'You see him?'

'Of course I see him. What's he doing on your lawn? Is he a neighbour or something?'

'I don't think so.' Somehow she didn't think that was it. The man was from here, *of* here. She could sense it.

'I'll go and ask him.'

By the time she'd taken in the words and whirled around, Charlie had already gone. His footsteps were on the stairs and she went after him, half feeling as if she was chasing nothing but a dream, the ghost of a sound; that it was Charlie, after all, who wasn't real.

By the time she caught up with him he was standing on the gravel by the door. He too had his back turned. She stepped outside, the air cool but pressing in damply, like clammy hands. The man with the stick had gone.

'He must have been passing by,' Charlie said without turning. 'I missed him.' He made to walk towards the lane, but Emma reached out and caught his arm. She didn't want him treading across that soft grass. She thought she could see a faint trace of her own footprints from the day she'd moved in, but there was nothing else, no other footprints, not even an imprint to show where he'd punched his stick into the ground.

She looked up. The signs of the failing day were already written in the sky; the top of the clouds were smeared with grey even as their undersides were turning to gold. It was cooler now and she remembered the night before, the way the chill had sunk into her. She shuddered, and she felt Charlie's hand on her shoulder. That too felt cold.

'You know, you don't need to leave,' she said.

He didn't answer, and the words hung in the air between them.

'There's no rush, is there?' She cleared her throat. 'You could always stay here a little longer.'

Later, she opened a bottle of wine. They drank it sitting on the floor in the drawing room. Everything was quiet. She leaned back and Mire House enveloped her. She felt warm, even though the temperature was falling again, and she smiled at Charlie.

The wine was such a deep red it was almost black, and it was rich, dulling her thoughts. She liked the way Charlie looked, his muscles loose, everything so effortless. He hadn't mentioned the man they'd seen in the garden again; perhaps he was right, it had been a passer-by, and she *had* only been dreaming the other night.

'A penny for them,' Charlie said.

She shook her head and pushed the hair out of her eyes. 'I like this,' she replied.

'It is nice. But – well, I can't stay forever, Emma.'

'I know that. But for now – you're okay here, aren't you?'

He took a sip of his drink, his lips marking the top of the glass.

'I know the room isn't— Maybe we could sort out a better place for you to sleep.' He didn't answer, just kept looking at her with a steady gaze, and she looked away. 'I mean—'

'Why did we never meet before, Emma? Since we were kids, I mean.' He frowned. 'I suppose if my dad and yours didn't get along . . .'

Emma stared down into her glass, peering at the murky fluid. The moment – the warmth – had gone and instead there was an empty space, waiting. It was always waiting; it was just that sometimes she managed to forget it was there.

'I didn't mean to remind you of anything.'

'No, it's all right.' She couldn't look up from the glass. Her eyes were stinging, as if tears were going to come. Thinking about it made everything worse.

She still didn't look up as he sat at her side and put his arm around her. She closed her eyes. It felt good; *too* good. It would be easy to sink into him, to rest her head against his chest, as if he could take it all away, fix everything, *rescue* her, for God's sake.

No. She wasn't there to be rescued. Soon he'd be gone and she would get on with her life. She couldn't start to rely on him – not on *anyone* – or one day she'd turn around and they wouldn't be there any longer. People did that: they died or they left and she would be alone again. She needed to learn to be comfortable with it. Still, even as she thought it, she felt hollow inside.

He rested his head on hers and she found herself leaning against him. Her flesh was tightening, as if in anticipation. Then he shifted away and the moment passed, like so many other moments had, each small possibility fading away into nothing.

Then they turned and leaned in towards each other, and their lips met. Even as they kissed she thought, it was only *now*, but it felt good, *right* even, and they drew in closer, his arms around her after all, his hand grasping at her shoulder. She felt the coldness of his skin through her clothes and she opened her eyes and saw that his were open too and he was looking right back at her.

CHAPTER THIRTEEN

Emma lay awake, thinking of Charlie sleeping at the other side of the wall. He had taken the bedroom next to hers. He couldn't have stayed in the other room, the one where he'd woken at daybreak. Now he was only a short distance away.

She pulled the covers tighter and bit her lip. Soon he would leave: he would pretend to be sleeping one morning when she left for work and when she got back he would be gone. He probably wouldn't even leave a note. He'd go back to wherever he'd come from and she would never see him again.

His arms around her had been so warm, his touch on her shoulder so cold. He hadn't acted embarrassed when they pulled away from their kiss and cool air filled the space between them. She told herself it was all right. Everybody needed someone, didn't they? And they were connected – they were all that remained of family lines that had been joined at some time in the distant past, before they were even born. She reminded herself that they were not so closely bound as to make it wrong. She didn't have to be alone, not all of the time. She felt her lips pulling into a smile as she remembered their kiss.

When they'd turned in she'd stepped towards him, stretching onto tiptoe and kissing his cheek, just brushing the corner of his lips. She'd poured glasses of iron-smelling water for them to take up. The stairs were hard under her feet, the sound of their steps loud against the silence. She imagined having his arm around her while she slept – warm, solid, *there* – and she pushed the idea away.

He had taken the room next to hers. She wondered now if that meant anything. But Charlie had needed a place where he could sleep without being woken by the sunrise. He'd looked into the other rooms before he'd made his choice.

And then she'd entered her own room and closed the door. She'd looked towards the place she'd been avoiding – the one opposite the foot of her bed – and she'd taken a deep breath and gone towards it, stepping deliberately into the space. There was nothing, no sudden chill, no sense of anyone watching, no breath. Nothing there at all.

But when she'd seen him last, the old man had been outside. She walked to the window. The lawn was a silvered patch of moonlight, the shadows of trees reaching their spindly arms across it. There was no figure standing among them. Now that her back was turned to the room, though, she could feel the shadows gathering behind her; it felt as if the air were coalescing into some more solid shape, taking on form, hands and limbs and eyes; eyes that looked at her from dark hollows.

She turned and the room was empty. Of course it was empty: she was alone. There was no one in the house but her and Charlie. And then a thought struck her and her mouth twitched. He had taken *the room next to hers*. Charlie had the master bedroom after all. Of course it didn't mean anything. Sometimes things were simply what they were. For now she had a comfortable bed, warm covers and a whole night in which to sleep before she rose and saw him again.

CHAPTER FOURTEEN

Emma raised her head from the pillow. She didn't know if she was dreaming or waking or half-asleep but she could hear a sound. It meandered through the air, almost like words, almost taking form before drifting again. It felt like something from the distant past that had never left; the house had stood through the years and now she felt the things within it had lingered too, not just solid things but memories.

She shifted, trying to find a cool place on her pillow. The air on her cheek was cold but everything else felt hot. She knew that she was dreaming when she got out of bed and found herself in the corridor, standing in her bare feet, and she did not shiver.

Then the words rang out, clear and harsh: *You little . . .* and nothing more, the sentence cut off, curtailed as if with violence. Then there was a loud clatter, as if someone had crashed through a door or hammered against a window. She pictured fragile glass jumping in its frame.

The landing was illuminated by moonlight that flooded in through uncovered windows and open doors, spilling through the banisters and down into the dark well beneath. Somehow Emma was not afraid. She went to the edge and looked over into the hall below just as a shape moved out of vision. She had the impression it had been heading towards the front door.

Emma froze. Dreaming or not, now she did feel cold. There was another presence in the hallway below; she could sense hostility. She could almost hear them breathe. And then the words came again, so clearly they might have been spoken next to her ear:

Get out.

CHAPTER FIFTEEN

Emma left the house early, stepping out into a thin, mean autumn morning. The sky was a pale glow of unsteady light; it looked like it might fail completely rather than grow. The car started with a dry wheeze that deepened when she pressed on the accelerator. She didn't take off the handbrake, not yet. She pictured the journey, the country roads all the same, with endless hedges edging drab, empty fields beneath the grey shroud of the sky. Then she would reach the motorway, join the tide of dull humanity being drawn towards the city. It was all impossibly far away.

She remembered the kiss, Charlie's mouth against hers, the way it had sparked feelings within her she thought she'd forgotten, like something awakening. *Life*, she thought. And she smiled and she switched off the engine. She surely had a little more time. Work wasn't as important to her as it once had been. She had a life here now.

She sat there, her eyes half-focused, letting the world blur around her. Everything looked distant, even Mire House: a reality that lay on the other side of some transparent but indissoluble veil. When she focused again she saw Charlie. He was standing at the bottom of the steps, by the side of her window. His gaze looked unclear and his hair was dishevelled.

She got out and opened her mouth, but he spoke first. 'Changed your mind? Good. There's something you should have a look at.'

He opened the door for her and ushered her inside as if she were a guest. For a moment she thought she heard something behind him, a brief high sound; then it faded and Charlie turned.

'Look at this,' he said. 'This is what I think you should see.'

The hall was empty save for some shoes lying at the foot of the stairs and a few rags discarded in the corner. Charlie's face was full of suppressed excitement. 'Do you see it?'

She didn't see. He pointed down at the floor and she looked again. The whole space was criss-crossed with muddy footprints.

'*Look.*' He took an exaggerated step across the floor, carefully placing his heel, then laying down his foot. She saw what he meant. The muddy print next to his foot was small, too small. She went closer.

'Do you see it now?' His voice was lower, almost calm.

She looked across the tiles and saw how many prints there were: some were a little larger and some smaller, but they all belonged to children. She had a sudden image of them running around the hall and she shook her head. It didn't mean anything; the marks could have been there for years; she simply hadn't noticed them—

'They weren't there before,' Charlie said, as if reading her thoughts. 'I know they weren't, because the first time I saw them – when I came down earlier this morning – I cleaned them all away. Now they've come back.'

Emma remembered the sound she thought she'd heard when Charlie led her into the house: a child's stifled giggle. Now she thought she could detect the lingering trace of tobacco in the air.

She'd seen a man standing at the foot of her bed in the middle of the night. She'd seen his suit hanging in her wardrobe after she'd thrown it out.

And Charlie had been there each time.

She looked up at him now, trying to read his expression. He gave a smile. 'It looks as if you really do have ghosts. It probably just means you're special.'

She shrugged his words away. There had to be some explanation; there had been no laughter. She had only heard the house settle and taken it for something else. She forced herself to smile as Charlie's words dissipated in the air between them.

Emma had started to paint the dining room at the back of the house while Charlie tried to fix some of the panelling upstairs. She could hear the *bang, bang* of his hammer, the pauses while he pieced things together. This room was tall and a little narrow. She didn't quite like it. She could smell damp even through the sharp tang of paint, and she thought mould was blossoming through it already, shadows that would eventually darken and stain the walls.

Here at the back of the house she could almost sense the mire the place was named for. It had a faintly musky scent that made her want to find its source. She could imagine the moisture spreading through the walls, bringing decay with its touch, reaching across the ceiling and through the door, into the hallway. It had brought the cold with it too; as she worked, the mist of her breath hung in front of her face.

Then she heard the tolling of a bell.

She shuddered: it was as if the sound had come from somewhere within – but it sounded again, full and resonant, and she laid down her paintbrush. *Fanciful*, she thought as she went to take a look.

As soon as she stepped onto the gravel a clammy breeze brought with it the sound of bells and she turned towards the church. It didn't sound like a call to service – it didn't sound *organised*, though she had never heard the bells before and didn't know how they should sound.

The heavy ring set into the church door clanged under her fingers as she twisted it and the door opened, letting out a dry stone smell. This time the inner door was unlocked and it opened onto streams of misty light, thick with dust, and rows of pews stretching into the distance. A man was standing in the aisle, facing her. She looked for his black suit but no, this man was taller, his bearing straight and his hair just touched with grey, and he was thin, very thin. She realised the bells were quiet now, that everything was.

The man carried an air of vague anxiety, but when he came towards her his smile was genuine. 'Hello,' he said.

'I— hello. I didn't mean to interrupt. I heard the bells and thought I'd call in.'

'You're not interrupting, love. New, are you? We welcome new faces here.'

Emma found herself blushing. 'Well, I don't usually – I mean . . .'

'Not an attender, eh? Well, that's all right too. I don't come much myself, truth be told.'

'I just moved into the house next door.'

'Painting, was you?'

Emma had forgotten the state of her clothes; her top was spattered with paint. 'I'm sorry. I didn't think to change.' She glanced around the church, the windows brilliantly coloured, the roof a mass of exposed beams, the bosses obscured by the poor light.

He grinned, instantly looking almost boyish. 'Well, I won't tell if you don't. Name's Frank Watts. I come in to potter about – do a few repairs, give the old girls a workout.'

Emma frowned, then he gestured upwards to where the bells must be hung and she understood.

'You getting on all right, are you? Big old house, that.'

'It was my— a distant relative's. I inherited it.'

'Ah. Sorry. Or, good for you, not sure which.' He winked.

'I just moved in, so I'm new here. My name's Emma. I—'

'Yes, love?'

'Well, I was kind of curious. About its background, I suppose. I'd never been here before, so it's nice to talk to someone who knows the area. I don't suppose you know anything about the house?'

His eyes clouded. 'Well, not that much. There's stories, I suppose you'd say. I live nearby, but I don't have a lot to do wi' it, you know.' His eyes went distant and he paused. 'It was empty before you, for a good long while. Someone called Mitchell bought it, but he just left it to go to ruin. And a ways before that it was the Owens, but – well, they kept theirselves to theirselves.

That's about it, love.' There was something in his eyes; he looked guarded.

'Do you know what happened to them?'

He shot her a sharp look. 'Well – they were getting on, you know. She passed a good few years ago – I'm not sure really. Then he went – well, a while back. An' I never really knew the Mitchell feller. He din't stop here long, never seemed a part o' the place.'

Emma frowned. 'In the house?' she asked. 'Did Mr Owens die in the house?'

He put out a hand as if to quiet her. 'Steady on, love. Nowt like that. No, he din't go in the house. Not that far off, though.' He paused, grimaced. 'He were out walking – yes, I believe that were it. Near the river, I think.' He brightened. 'So not in the house, no, love. Don't you worry about that. It's a nice place, I'll warrant. Big place, though. You married?'

She shook her head. 'A relative's staying here for a bit. Then it'll just be me.' She regretted telling him of their relationship at once. *Barely related at all*, she thought. It surely wasn't worth mentioning to anyone else.

'Aye, well, love, I'd best crack on. Nice to meet you, like.'

Emma smiled back, nodding. 'You too.' She'd already forgotten his name. They said their goodbyes and she walked away, her footsteps loud on the stone floor. Then she stopped and turned. The man – *Frank*, that was it – twisted away as if he didn't want her to know he'd been staring.

'I had a walk around the graveyard the other day,' she said. 'Nice place. I did wonder, though – who came up with those inscriptions, Frank? The ones on the benches?'

'Oh – all sorts, love, over the years. Someone'll come along and sponsor one, and they get to choose, you know. It ends up a bit of a hotch-potch, but it's all the Good Word, you know. If you'd like to come along one Sunday—'

'But who chose the one along the back fence? It's a bit – well, full-on, isn't it?'

He didn't reply.

'Do you know it? It says *My God, my God*—'

'I know what it says, love.'

His voice was quiet and didn't invite further questions, but Emma pressed on, 'So do you know who picked it? They must have been – I don't know—'

'I know who it was,' he said. 'It was a long time ago, love, and she was deep in grief, so I dare say that was the reason. And it is part of the Word, after all. So I don't reckon anyone'd want to take it down, though there's probably quite a few would've liked it not to have been there in t' fust place.' He drew a sigh and sank onto a pew, as if suddenly tired. 'She'd lost a child, love. I'm not sure what her name was – it's a long time ago. But it's funny you should ask, for all that.'

'Why's that, Frank?'

He met her eyes. 'Because you're living in her place, love.' He paused. 'The woman who had them words put on that bench – the same person built your house.'

CHAPTER SIXTEEN

The ground about the bench was seeping water, welling around Emma's shoes wherever she stepped. It was on a slope, but the ground was drenched with run-off from the hills beyond. She could see Mire House from where she stood, its stone darkened with damp, sitting on the hillside, and she thought for a moment of a squat toad – but no, the house was beautiful. It had always been beautiful. It was strange to think that the woman who had it built had also sat here, her despair so strong she'd had it carved into the stone.

She looked at the inscription now – *Why hast Thou forsaken me?* – and she touched a finger to the lettering's smooth edges.

After a moment she sat down on the bench. It was damp beneath her and she felt cold at once, a bone-deep cold. She thought of the footprints she'd seen in the house, that brief high giggle. Had she really heard it? In this bleak place it was easy to believe that she had. Was it the woman's lost child she'd heard? But then, who was the man she'd seen – her husband?

Emma closed her eyes, feeling little more than a lost child herself. Her dad's face rose before her and she realised that she had never felt lost when he was there. When she was little her mum would put her to bed but whenever she felt afraid it was her dad who told her stories, and the princesses would live happily ever after and the wicked witches and stepmothers and nasty sisters and the monsters would all be dead. And she found herself remembering the one thing that did scare her, the thing she'd asked him once: 'Why did they have to die, Daddy?'

'Hush. It was because they were bad.'

But she knew they *weren't* all bad. Cinderella's real mother had died too, hadn't she? That was how the story began. For a moment, she had listened to the sound of his breathing. 'Daddy, will you die?'

He had smiled at first, but then he'd surprised her by laughing. 'Not for a long, long time, love.' He was halfway out of the door before he added the usual words: 'Sleep tight, little Em.'

But she hadn't slept tight. She hadn't been able to stop thinking about what he'd said, or rather, what he *hadn't*. He hadn't said *never*. He hadn't said *no*.

Now here she was, sitting on a bench in a place her parents had never seen.

She blinked and looked about her. Ranks of gravestones, greened or blackened with moss and rain and time, were spread all around her. And she wondered: if she could wake in the night to see a man standing at the foot of her bed, hear the giggle of some long-ago child, feel the sadness of a woman sitting on a bench – why not her parents? Why had she not seen her *own* ghosts?

The yew tree whispered above her head. Somewhere there was the sharp cry of a bird, but there was nothing else: no answer came.

Then she remembered another sound, one she'd heard what seemed a long time ago and yet was no time at all: *Get out*.

She shook the thought away. She didn't even know when those words had first been spoken, or why. What she'd heard was only an echo – was probably never even meant for her. She stood and looked down at the words carved on the bench. It was another echo, nothing more, nothing that need touch her. She glanced back towards Mire House. It was waiting and it wasn't empty: Charlie was there with his grin and his laughing voice. She should be there with him.

She tried not to focus on the stones as she walked back through the graveyard, the words written on their faces all that remained of the lives and loves long fallen into the forgetful past.

CHAPTER SEVENTEEN

The mould looked darker now, like clouds harbouring bad dreams. Emma painted over it, her movements aggressive. She would banish it, make the room bright and clean and new. She frowned. Upstairs, Charlie had replaced the flimsy curtains in the master bedroom with the thicker ones he'd taken from the drawing room. He seemed quite at home in there, although it hadn't yet been painted, and she set her own brush down with a twinge of annoyance. He had said, *I could paint it for you. Dark red would look good in here, don't you think?*

She didn't know why she was so annoyed. She had simply found that she didn't want to accept his choice – and yet somehow she couldn't imagine the room any other colour. That only made it worse.

She was being ungenerous. If Charlie hadn't come back here ... She had a sudden image of herself trapped in that awful cupboard, nothing to eat, only dirty grey water to drink. She shuddered and looked up at the ceiling. It struck her that she hadn't heard the sound of Charlie's hammer for some time.

She left her own work and headed up the stairs, taking each tread slowly, calling his name as she entered the master bedroom.

The room was empty. Charlie must have moved on some-where else. She crossed to the window and ran her hand over the sill.

The trees were losing their leaves and everything looked a little more bare than yesterday. She could see the yew tree more clearly now though, and through the slats of the fence, the paler outline of the bench. She started. Someone was seated there, perfectly motionless, just sitting with head bowed, a dark shape against the foliage. It looked like a woman. She stared, trying to make out her features, and she realised she was wearing a veil. She closed her eyes. *My God*, she thought, *my God* . . . and she looked again and the woman was gone; there were only twisting branches that gave the impression of a human figure.

She was being fanciful, that was all.

A sound rang out from the hallway, strident and loud and *real*. Emma rushed onto the landing. She could hear tapping from below, irregular and disordered, like rapid footsteps. She went to the top of the stairs and looked down. Something shifted in the corner of her eye, as if she'd been just a little too slow to see it, and then someone laughed.

'Charlie?'

No answer came back. She didn't know where he was. She listened for the sound of his footsteps but heard nothing. Instead, coming from downstairs but softer – on carpet – was a soft shuffling. At once an image sprung into her mind of the old man, squat and unkempt, dragging his feet as he emerged from the drawing room, the hems of his trousers pulling along the floor.

She leaned over the balustrade. There was only the hallway, quiet as a held breath. She stretched out further, trying to see the door that led into the drawing room. It looked as if it was shifting in some draft, but as she watched it swung wide. She jerked back. She couldn't see but it *felt* as if someone was down there. Their anger was souring the air.

When the voice came, it was louder than she'd expected, more *present*.

'Get *out*.'

And then she saw him, quite clearly, striding across the space below her. There was a bald patch on top of his head; the shoulders of his jacket were grimy. He vanished and the front door slammed.

'Charlie?'

She looked around, but she couldn't see him anywhere. There was only the silence. She drew in a deep breath. *An echo*, she thought; *it was only an echo*. Anyway, there was no reason to believe the man meant her harm. What did she think, that people came back from the dead – people who'd had their own families, children, wives, people they loved – with the sole intention of frightening the living? She closed her eyes and thought of her mother and father. Of course it didn't have to be like that.

But then, her parents *hadn't* come back. There was only this man with his rough words and gruff voice. *Get out.* She shook herself. Charlie would know what to do. He wouldn't be afraid.

But the man had come to *her*; he had stood at the end of her bed.

He had locked her in the cupboard and left her to die.

No. It *wasn't* that way, it couldn't be. And at least it was some kind of link, a connection to a world she couldn't glimpse or even imagine; the place her parents had gone and she could not follow. Except that now, she could follow *something*. She pushed herself away from the balustrade and turned towards the stairs. It was only when she reached the top that she heard the footsteps behind her; only when she set her foot on the first step that she felt the hand, firm and warm, in the middle of her back.

PART TWO

1973 – The Second-Best Suit

CHAPTER ONE

Frank didn't know how Sam Holroyd knew that Mire House was haunted, but Sam wasn't saying and he couldn't just ask. Sam didn't brook being asked to explain himself. He'd said it was haunted and so it was and that was why they were all afraid, dutifully opening their eyes wide. There were four of them. Sam, at twelve, was a full year older than Frank, and there was Sam's brother, Jeff, who was eight and Frank's little brother, Mossy. Mossy's real name was Michael, but he'd been rechristened Mossy for his short, thick hair. *A rolling stone gathers no moss*, their dad always said and Frank always wished it was true. He liked to be outside, going about the farm. If anyone was a rolling stone it was him, and yet still Mossy clung, most of all when he was least wanted.

'There was a mad old bag who built it,' Sam said. 'People have seen 'er. If she grabs a hold of you, you're dead. Anyone'll tell you.'

Frank frowned. No one ever *had* told him, and it was *them* who lived nearest; their farm was just up the lane and his dad had never mentioned anything at all. Still, it wasn't the sort of thing his dad talked about. Which of the sheep had caught on pregnant and which hadn't, that was more the kind of thing his dad discussed when they sat down for tea at the big old table, things that made his mum flick a tea-towel at him and tell him to eat his stew. Not ghosts or anything interesting.

Sam led the way down the lane, stomping especially hard as if to show he wasn't afraid. His boots were caked in mud like Frank's own, though they looked newer. Sam's dad had the farm on the other side of the hill and it was bigger than theirs, a fact Sam never minded pointing out. Sam thought he was better than Frank as well as richer. His trousers were flared and he kept boasting how he was growing his hair to look like Marc Bolan's; though Frank knew Sam's mum would never let him, he never said anything.

They rounded the corner and broke into a run past the church – Frank was never sure why they did that, he hadn't asked about that either – and skidded to a halt behind the garden wall of Mire House. Frank didn't know why anyone would want to live in a place called Mire House, but it was grand enough: grey as the rain and twice as bleak, as his dad always put it. Now it wasn't raining and white clouds were gathered behind it as if they'd arranged themselves as a backdrop. Frank wished he was anywhere else, walking in the fields maybe, alone with his thoughts, hearing only the wind whistling through the old church bells. If he left now, though, Sam would wait for him in the schoolyard on Monday, making *buk-buk-buk* noises and waggling his elbows.

Sam twisted around. His dark hair hung across his face and his eyes gleamed through it. 'It's your turn,' he said, and then those magical words: 'I dare you.'

Frank shrugged, trying to look unconcerned. 'What d'you mean, my turn?'

'It were me went in t' bull pen.'

'You put one leg in.'

'Aye, well, it were more'n you.'

Frank let out a spurt of air. He bobbed up and looked at the house and saw more of those pale clouds, reflected in the front windows. It looked as if they were hiding secrets. It didn't matter to him, really, if there was an old lady there, did it? It was far more likely that the old man who owned the place would get hold of him. He wasn't made of smoke; he would have real hands, real knuckles. He might even have a belt or a cane.

'You have to go and look in t' window.'

'Do not.'

Sam looked down on Frank through hair that wasn't curly enough to be Marc Bolan's. Suddenly Frank wasn't even sure he liked his friend Sam at all. Sometimes he was mean. He'd found a bird's nest once, a tight round thing that was lined with down and had four small blue eggs in it. It had been in the hedge at the top of the long field and he'd pulled it free and held it out and laughed. 'You have to crush them,' he'd said, holding one out with his index finger and thumb, demonstrating. 'Like this.' And he'd squeezed hard, just with that single finger, and he'd gone red in the face, which had made Frank want to smile. He didn't smile though. He'd only watched, because that was what he was supposed to do, and at first he didn't think anything was going to happen but then the egg shattered and a spurt of blood came out, and something else, not like the usual kind of egg at all; something that was damp and lumpy and gooey, and it fell to the grass and Sam had made a high-pitched noise in his throat and they'd run.

Frank was never sure what had happened to the nest. He supposed Sam must have thrown it down onto the grass, but when he went back he didn't find it, though he did see the thing that had come out of the egg, the feathers clotted tight to its fragile bones, its eyes closed and scaly-looking, never having opened. Its claws looked far too large and they were the exact same colour as Frank's hands. Its body had burst open and tiny black insects were crawling in and out of it. He had wondered if he was supposed to feel sick, but instead he felt tired and resigned and a little sad. He had kicked the dead thing under the hedge before walking away.

Now he knew he had to go and look in at the window of Mire House. It wasn't even the thought of what Sam would do on Monday; it was because the idea was now out there, and it would stay out there until it was something he'd done and it was in the past.

He didn't look at Sam again – he wouldn't give him the satisfaction – but he felt Mossy's hand on his back, two sharp pats, as he pushed himself up. He felt a momentary guilt that he'd ever wanted to get rid of his little brother.

He crept alongside the wall until he reached the gatepost. The fancy hexagonal pillar was strangely narrow and looked expensive; he was used to the big rugged slabs at the farm. Beyond it, weeds were pushing up through the driveway. Everything was still; there was not even the bark of a dog or the slinking shadow of a cat. It didn't look as if anyone lived here. No wonder Sam said it was haunted. It wasn't somewhere Frank ever came, even though they lived so close by. His dad always said, *Stay away from that there feller*, and he was happy to do so. It was more fun playing at the farm anyway, or sneaking away to the river, though he was strictly forbidden to go there too.

Suddenly he wondered if the place really *was* haunted. Perhaps it would be worse, after all, if the hand that landed on your shoulder was made of mist.

He leaned in, looking around the garden. There wasn't much cover. He took a deep breath just as he heard Sam's whisper behind him: '*Chicken . . .*'

He remembered the best way to do something you didn't want to do: something his dad had told him once. The words came to him now: *Do it like you mean it. Look as if you belong.*

He couldn't remember why his dad had said that, or what he'd been tasked with – standing at the front of school assembly and doing a reading perhaps, or walking through the top field when the heifers were out – but he knew it was good advice. He stood up, as straight as he could, then he began to walk, quite steadily, up the drive. He hadn't realised the gravel would be so loud under his feet. He kept going, hearing a gasp behind him – he knew that was Mossy – and he went to the nearest window. It was higher than he'd thought; he'd need to stand on tiptoe and pull himself up. That wasn't good. It wasn't what people did when they were somewhere they belonged, doing something they had every right to do.

He leaned against the stone and looked back down the drive, seeing a flash of movement: Sam, ducking behind the gatepost. He was watching, making sure Frank did what he was supposed to do. His heartbeat quickened. He didn't want to move but knew he couldn't stay where he was, trapped between the wall and Sam's gaze. It *was* like being in assembly, with everyone looking at him and waiting for him to do something. He let out a sigh. There was no other sound, nothing he could detect inside the house, no car in the lane; only the brief wailing call of a curlew coming from across the fields. He wished he was up there now, with only the wind in the grass for company.

He couldn't crouch here any longer. He pulled his boots from where they'd sunk into a narrow strip of empty flowerbed, reached up and caught hold of the sill. The old paint was flaking; he could feel bits sticking to his skin. Then he looked in at the window.

He didn't know what he expected to see. The room was dark and old-looking but grand too, with ceilings much higher than at the farm, where his dad had to stoop to pass under the doorways. The furniture barely filled it: a table, an old dresser, two high-backed chairs. One of them was facing the window and there was someone sitting in it.

Frank stared. The man was stocky with hunched shoulders and he wore black clothes. One hand held a pipe and smoke rose from it, forming a pale cloud in front of his face. It was the only thing that caught any light. Frank wondered why he didn't light the lamp that stood behind the chair or sit closer to the window, but they were only passing thoughts; mostly he was frozen. He could see the man's eyes, nothing but dark pits. He was facing the window but Frank had the feeling he wasn't really seeing anything because his gaze was fixed on something far away – or on nothing at all. But he knew the exact moment when the man's eyes focused and he looked at Frank.

Neither of them moved. Then the man whipped the pipe from his mouth and stood up. As he strode towards the door he threw the pipe onto a table and Frank saw ash spilling across the surface. He got a clear look at the man's greying shirt and his waistcoat, knowing all the time that he should be running, but he still hadn't moved. He let himself drop to the ground and rubbed the flakes of paint from his hands. They wouldn't come off and he felt a moment of panic. He heard the rattle of a door handle and he ran, scattering gravel, as behind him the front door opened.

He heard a voice, deep and gruff and angry: 'Bloody little buggers.'

Frank let out a gasp and then he was laughing, the sound whipping from him and rising into the air. Mossy stood in the gateway, wide-eyed and staring, and that was funny too; he laughed louder and grabbed his brother's arm as he passed, spinning him around and dragging him away. All he could see of Sam and Jeff were their backs, the flashes of the soles of their boots as they ran away up the lane. They were a good way ahead, *too* far ahead.

He glanced back; the lane was empty. The man was standing in the middle of the driveway, his hands clenched, his face scrunched up in fury. He had beetle-brows and his legs were bowed and his waistcoat was taut across his belly, as if it was a size too small.

Mossy pulled on his hand and he started to run again, already thinking of all the things he was going to say to Sam for the way he'd run away and left them.

CHAPTER TWO

If she grabs a hold of you, you're dead.

Frank couldn't stop thinking of those words. He hadn't been scared when Sam had told him about the ghost, not really, though he wasn't quite sure why. He'd been scared of the old man, that was for certain. If he got caught trespassing he'd get a good hiding, and his dad would probably say he'd asked for it. But it was more than that. The memory of the old man's eyes, suddenly shifting focus and fixing on his, had stayed with him. He rolled over on his bed. He should never have gone into the garden. It felt as if he'd set something in motion. He'd never really thought about the house before, even though it was so close; not even when he'd cut down the path at its side to get to the river. It was like a blank spot in his mind, something he'd never really considered. Now that he had, things had changed somehow, the thought was *there*, all at once beckoning and taunting him. He hadn't liked the place, he knew that now. He hadn't even liked stepping over the boundary between the grounds and the lane, falling under its shadow. It hadn't felt like a good place; the person who lived there hadn't looked like a good man. He wondered now whether its resident had cast a pall over the house or if it was the other way around.

He kept trying to remember when he'd had the thought about whether it would be better if a hand seized your shoulder to find it was see-through; to know that he could pull away and find it was nothing solid after all. *If she grabs a hold of you, you're dead.*

But ghosts couldn't grab, could they? Their hand would slip straight through. And what if a thing like that happened in daylight? Ghosts were supposed to come out at night, but having looked in at the window of Mire House, he wasn't so sure that was true. Maybe it could happen in the daytime, when it might be hard to see a ghost. If a misty hand had touched him when he'd been running down the drive, how would he even know?

Maybe that was why he couldn't stop thinking about the place – because somehow something had already touched him. It was all Sam Holroyd's fault. If he hadn't dared him . . .

Frank shook his head. He was being stupid, wasn't he? He'd only looked in at a window. He hadn't done anything wrong, not really. For all the old man knew he might have called around there to see him on purpose. He had an image of himself walking up to its great front door and knocking, inviting the fierce old man round for tea, and he let out a giggle.

He stifled it when he heard a quiet knock on his door. Then it was pushed slowly open, before he even had the chance to call out. Mossy was standing in the gap. Frank scowled. He was about to say something – *get out*, probably – and then he saw the expression on his brother's face. He looked tired and a little sheepish. He was already wearing his pyjamas. Frank didn't like Mossy being in his room, but he couldn't bring himself to send him away. His brother climbed onto the bed and sat next to him. He hadn't said a word.

'What do you want?' Frank's voice was soft. This time, when Mossy looked up, Frank realised he'd been crying. 'What's up?'

Mossy shrugged. Then he whispered, 'Were you scared?'

Frank looked at him. He hadn't liked the way the house had lodged in his own thoughts; he didn't like the idea that Mossy had been thinking about it too.

'*I* was scared,' his brother said.

Frank sighed. He wasn't going to admit to being scared. Mossy didn't usually admit it either and it was better that way: he'd have to learn. If he admitted to being scared of things in front of the others, it'd be even worse. 'It was nothing,' he said. 'Just an old man.'

Mossy turned his head and looked at him. 'Not him,' he said. 'I wasn't scared of the old man.'

Frank felt his arms go cold all at once, each little hair prickling as it spread over his skin. He didn't like the look in his brother's eyes. He didn't want to think about what it might mean. He glanced towards the window. Their house was set back a way from the road, in a wide yard all of its own. There were outbuildings around it; from here, all he would see were the barn and the lane and the fields. If he pushed aside the net curtains and opened the window and leaned out, he would be able to see the church steeple. He would need to lean further to see the house, but he knew it was there, on the other side of the churchyard – the *graveyard* – and the old man was inside it, smoking his pipe perhaps, staring into space with those blank eyes.

He took a deep breath. He wasn't sure what he was going to say. Then Mossy pushed himself to the edge of the bed. 'Night night,' he said, and Frank automatically replied as his little brother walked out of the room.

I wasn't scared of the old man.

Frank wrapped the covers tightly around his shoulders and leaned back against the pillow. When he closed his eyes, though, it wasn't the old man he thought of; it was Sam Holroyd, the so-called friend who'd run off and left them. Sam Holroyd, who'd dared him to step across that border in the first place.

His lip twisted. The place was still there. It wasn't going away. Perhaps next time it was Sam who needed to go up to the door: maybe he even needed to go inside.

CHAPTER THREE

It was early on Saturday morning and a light ground mist still hung over the grass. Everyone was there except Mossy, who had chosen to stay and help Dad put new chicken-wire around the hen coop. It wasn't something he'd normally do and he hadn't really told him why, but Frank thought it was something to do with what he'd said the night before: *I wasn't scared of the old man.*

Now they were at the big house again but it was clear that no one was going inside because the old man was standing in the garden. He was motionless, staring out at the road. The only thing that moved was the curl of smoke from his pipe.

Frank still hadn't asked what it was his little brother *had* been scared of and he wasn't sure he wanted to know.

They crouched in the lane, Frank and Sam and Jeff, occasionally bobbing up to see what they could see. Sometimes, the old man did move; he raised the hand in which he held a thick wooden stick and punched it down again into the ground.

Frank looked at Sam. 'It's your turn,' he said in a low voice. 'As soon as he goes in you can go and knock on the door. You 'ave to count to ten before you run.' He didn't say Sam should go inside, though he knew that was exactly what he should do; the only thing that could make up for Mossy's fear. He thought Sam would argue anyway, but what he didn't expect was: 'I've already done it. It's your turn again.'

'You have *not*. We was all the'er last time, and you was first away.' Frank leaned over and spat. It was something he'd just started to do; he'd copied it off his dad.

'An' then I went back agin later. Din't I, Jee?'

Jeff's eyes had started to shine. He looked at his brother as if he'd just come up with a brilliant idea.

'You're lyin'.'

'Not.'

'Are.'

'Wanna make summat of it?' Sam leaned towards him, his chest puffed out. Frank suddenly knew it was hopeless. Sam would do anything, say anything, rather than go and knock on the old man's door.

Anyway, no one was going to knock. The man still stood there, his head twitching now and then towards the lane. He kept banging the stick so hard into the ground Frank knew it would retain its print for days to come. *His backside would too*, he thought, *if he got caught*.

He sighed. It was two against one. 'You won't mind going past him then,' he said, 'if you're so brave.' He pointed down the lane, towards the path that led to the river. One side of it flanked the old man's wall. His mother would tan his hide if she knew he'd even thought of it – she got tight-lipped if anyone even mentioned the place – and he shifted uncomfortably. It wasn't as if the river was much fun for playing out. They couldn't even reach the water, not really. There was a little bridge over the worst of the miry ground, a concrete slab with a thin metal pipe for a handrail, but it didn't lead anywhere very much. It looked as if it would be fun to play on but it wasn't. They could sit on the edge and dangle their feet, but what lay below looked like nothing but grass, long and lush. It wasn't grass, though. It was mire.

'All right.' Sam's voice was low. Frank looked at him and saw the older boy was only pausing, making him wait. Then he straightened and smiled. 'We'll all go. If, you know, *you're* so brave.'

Frank thought of the way Mossy had come into his room, his quiet knock, his downcast eyes: the way he'd gone to his big brother when he was afraid. And he *had* been afraid, he and Mossy both, but he hadn't allowed it to show. He couldn't. He was the eldest. 'All right,' he said. 'You first.'

Sam led the way down the lane. Frank was behind him and he couldn't see his expression but the back of his neck looked pink and he didn't think it was caused by the coolness of the morning. Maybe he was wondering if the others were still behind him, following at his heels. He tried to walk more quietly just to spite him. Then he looked into the garden and saw the old man's head turning slowly to watch their progress. He could hear the sound of his stick punching the earth. He was still wearing his scruffy black suit. It bagged at the knees. Even from here, he could see it had an unpleasant shine.

Sam started to whistle. It wasn't a good whistle. Frank knew it was supposed to sound as if he didn't care, like he wasn't scared, and for a moment it almost worked.

The old man made a dirty noise – a deep, rasping hawking sound – and he spat. Spittle flew from his lips, a wet gobbet that landed on the ground in front of his feet. Frank saw this quite clearly because he had reached the gateway; there was no longer any wall between them. He felt exposed, as if he'd stepped out of the bath and someone had seen him; the cold was close against his skin, his belly contracting. He became aware of his own breathing, too light and shallow.

Ahead of him, Sam started swinging his arms, high and fast, trying too hard to look casual. They had reached the path. It was narrow and overgrown with rosebay willow herb and nettles that brushed against their legs. They started to sting even through his brown corduroys, but he didn't really feel it. Then Sam stopped and Frank had to stop too, to avoid bumping into him. Behind him, Jeff's footsteps ceased.

'Nice day!' Sam yelled the words, shattering the quiet. Frank stared at him, horrified. The older boy had half-turned to look back at the old man. He raised an arm and gave a cheery wave, then pursed up his lips and blew a long, loud raspberry. In the next moment he started to run.

Frank was frozen. He heard the plants whipping at Sam's legs but he was really listening to the silence underneath that, until Jeff forced his way past him and he realised he would be left alone. He had expected the old man to chase after them but he was still standing there, an isolated figure in the middle of a wide lawn, and then he caught movement from the corner of his eye and he realised he wasn't alone after all; there was someone standing behind him, wearing dark clothes. It was a thin woman with wide skirts and something covering her face. He shifted his focus to where she stood only to find he was mistaken after all; there was nothing but the shadow of clouds, moving across the grass.

He shook his head. He had been so *sure*. He could still almost see her, reaching out to grasp the old man's shoulder. Now he didn't look angry any longer. His lips were pressed into a bloodless line, his forehead furrowed with creases, but his eyes were sad. Frank felt an overwhelming urge to shout at him to run with them, to run away; then the shrieks of laughter from up ahead roused him and he forced himself to move.

He didn't stop running until he reached the bridge and found them, Sam almost doubled across the handrail, laughing fit to bust. He slapped his thigh; he'd copied that from *his* old man. 'Your face,' he said. 'Your *face*!'

Jeff was standing in the middle of the bridge, laughing too; now he laughed even louder. When he slapped his thigh in just the same way Sam had, Frank had to fight back the urge to scream.

'See?' Sam gasped. 'He's just a silly old sod. Dunno what you was scared of.'

'Silly old sod,' Jeff repeated. 'Silly old sod.'

Frank stood there, not knowing what to say or what to do, until the two of them subsided and the sun climbed higher and Sam turned and led the way across the mire and towards the river.

There was no bridge over the actual river. It was not inviting or even approachable; it didn't make a noise, chattering over pebbles like the rivers in stories did. It was something they could sense, but they rarely *saw* it because of the reeds that spread around it. Frank had tried to paddle in it once and he knew that what looked like long grass was always mire. He'd sunk into it and the water had overrun his boots and run down to his toes, and later he'd found it had a bad smell, that water. It was odd that he couldn't detect it from here on the bank. He'd had to use the reed-grass to pull himself out again, clutching sharp handfuls to help him gain purchase. The river had no clear definition. It seeped into the land on either side; there was no distinct point at which land was land and river, river.

Now the only sound was the slapping as they batted midges away from their faces and arms. No one spoke but he knew they must be thinking of going back. Mossy would be waiting for his big brother by now and he felt a stab of mean triumph that he'd got rid of him at last.

Sam was standing with his back to Frank, staring out over the river, and he pulled back his arm as if to throw something into the water. Frank knew without looking for a splash that there was nothing in his hand; there were no stones to throw. There was nothing to do here, nothing with which to make a den, nothing to shoot at even if they'd thought to bring the catapults they'd made from sticks and elastic bands, no trees to climb. They were bored already and too hot and being eaten alive, and the only reason they hadn't gone home was the old man that Sam had insulted.

He looked back the way they'd come. Beyond the bridge he could see the top of the house, and further off was the tip of the church spire. All of it was still there, waiting. Maybe the old man was there and maybe he wasn't: *And the woman. Maybe she's waiting too.*

He shook his head. The woman had never been real in the first place. But a part of him still wondered if that was why the old man had been so horrible? *Bloody little buggers*, he'd called them when Frank peeked in at his window. Maybe he couldn't help it. Maybe he'd been touched by the ghost after all, been claimed by it in some way, and now he was stuck there all alone with no one but ghosts for company. He shivered. Still, it was no use staying here, waiting for nothing. They could be stuck here for ever. 'I'm off,' he said.

Sam looked up and shrugged as if he wasn't bothered.

'See you later.' He started to pick his way across the wet earth, his boots making an unpleasant squelching noise. Then he heard other noises behind him, the sound of the others following. Sam, who was older than him by a year, was taking his lead. He smothered a grin and kept going, his back a little straighter than before.

The old man's garden was empty. There was only a bare expanse of uneven lawn, darkened with damp and pocked with holes punched by a thick black walking stick.

'You should go inside,' said a voice at his ear. 'It's your turn to do summat.'

Frank twisted away as if Sam had struck him. The boy was like the midges, he wouldn't let go. It didn't matter how much you batted at them. He wasn't going inside, he was going home to eat his dinner and get pestered by Mossy.

Mossy. He thought for a moment of the way he'd been last night, subdued and small. Yes, that was it; he'd seemed smaller than he usually did, and quiet and somehow warm, but not in a nice way. It was like he'd been last summer when the scarlet fever was about to take hold.

I wasn't scared of the old man.

No, his brother hadn't been scared of the old man, and nor had Sam when he'd blown that raspberry as they'd walked up this same path. And what had he done to them, after all? Nothing, just shouted at them. What was he going to do about it if they went inside? Frank could say he thought he'd seen his brother going in there and he'd gone to find him. He'd get told off, that was all. He might get marched around to his parents' by the scruff of his neck.

He remembered the woman he thought he'd seen, standing behind him. There were worse things than sticks. But ghosts didn't exist.

'Well?' asked Sam.

His tone made up Frank's mind for him. If he went into the house he could tell Mossy all about it and his little brother would know that he didn't have to be afraid any longer.

'Come on then,' he said. 'We'll go in together.' He turned to face Sam. He saw that the older boy was trying to hide the fear in his eyes and that was good; it made him feel a little taller. And Sam would have to go in after all. It served him right for starting this whole thing. 'You're the eldest,' he said. 'It's about time you acted like it.'

Of course the door would be locked. The old man hated them and he had seen them playing around his house and there was no way he'd leave the door open. That was what Frank told himself as he crept alongside the garden wall. Sam was behind him and Jeff in the middle. They hadn't talked about what order they'd be in and he wasn't sure how, once again, he'd ended up in front.

The man would come out and get him, or the woman would. He thought of her materialising out of nowhere, right behind him where he couldn't see, and he swallowed.

He turned and Sam glared at him. Frank sighed. There was no point in putting this off; he might as well just go. He glanced up the lane towards home. He was hungry. He wasn't sure how far into dinnertime it was but judging by the sun, which was riding high, he was going to be late.

He felt a hard nudge in his back. 'Gerron wi' it then.'

He crept out from behind the gatepost. When he'd gone a short way up the drive he stepped onto the grass and into the shadow of the house. The ground felt unpleasantly unstable under his feet, damp and soft and liable to shift at any moment. From here he couldn't see into the upper windows – they reflected back only the sky – but lower down, he thought he could see the top of the chair the old man had been sitting in. He couldn't tell if he was sitting in it now. He could imagine his expression, though, if he could see Frank. He might be readying his stick at this very moment. But he thought of Mossy, clinging, whining Mossy, and he went on.

It was only when he was part-way across the lawn that he thought to look down and saw the trail of perfect footprints they were leaving in the grass. Even if the man wasn't watching him, he'd *know*. He might come after them.

He tiptoed across the remaining stretch of grass and across the top of the drive towards the porch. The noise of the gravel couldn't be helped; it was just something else he had to do. The door looked taller than ever as he walked up to it, and unwelcoming. He turned and Sam was there, but he didn't look so bold any longer. He gave Frank a thumbs-up that made him think of school and children, *little* children, and he wrinkled his nose and turned and reached for the handle. When he turned it there was a loud metallic noise and he felt the catch release.

The hallway was bare and unlit. He heard the sound at once, but for a moment he didn't recognise it as music. It didn't have the tinny quality of his radio; this sounded worse. It had a scratchy, fizzy tone that made him think of the old films his mother liked. It didn't just sound as if it was coming from a long way away; it sounded as if it was coming from out of the past. It drifted down the stairs, through the spindles and along the balustrade and across the black and white tiled floor. He could hear footsteps but they weren't dashing towards him; they were coming from inside the house, light little steps that made him think of dancing.

Warm breath huffed against his ear and he jumped. It was Sam, laughing silently. 'Old git,' he said. 'Gerron wi' it then.'

Frank didn't bother to glare. He wasn't sure he cared what Sam thought of him any longer. He turned his attention to the hall. There was a coat rack in one corner with an overcoat hanging from it, a pile of boots and shoes beneath that. They all looked like men's shoes and Frank remembered something he thought he'd heard once: that the old man's wife had died.

Sam pushed past him and let out another smothered giggle. 'God, look,' he said. 'We're goin' ter be in trouble.' He pointed down at the smeared footprints they'd left behind. Frank looked around at the floor. It hadn't been particularly clean to begin with, but now it was worse. Jeff hop-skipped across it, shaking the mud from his boots.

'Stop it,' Frank hissed.

'What for?' Sam pointed upwards. 'You deaf or summat?' He turned to the nearest door and disappeared into the room.

For a moment Sam vanished; then his face appeared in the doorway. 'What's up? Come on then.'

Frank's bowels clenched, as if he suddenly needed to go.

Jeff walked ahead of him and through the doorway. Now it felt more than ever as if they'd crossed some threshold Frank couldn't see and didn't want to. He glanced up the stairs, hearing the soft footsteps and the music, then he went after his friends.

It was the same room he'd looked into the day before. Now he could see it better, but the first thing that struck him was the smell; it was stale and cloying and he could almost hear his mum tut-tutting over it. She'd never let a room get in this state. The carpet was thin and gritty and the air didn't feel clean in his lungs. It felt as if his skin was being coated with something greasy. He rubbed his fingers as if he could feel it, but of course they were clean, he hadn't touched anything. He looked at Sam as the older boy reached out and touched the side of the chair the old man had been sitting in. Frank caught his breath in an audible gasp.

Sam's gaze shot towards him. 'Godsake. Nearly give me an 'eart attack.' He whipped his hand back to his side and Frank could breathe again. Then Jeff pointed at the side table, two sharp jabs, and Sam went to it and picked up the pipe, just like that, and pretended to smoke it. He poked his nose in the air. 'Call me sir,' he said, 'and summon the servants.'

Jeff laughed, a loud, high-pitched noise.

Frank looked around the room. He saw another chair just like the first but pushed back against the wall, and a big old dresser that must have taken four men to move. There was a table that might once have been grand but was old now, the top scratched and the legs chipped, and dining chairs and a fireplace and a set of fire irons on a stand. Everything was set back against the walls as if someone was about to play some sort of party game. The air was wrong and *they* were wrong, and he realised those things didn't matter, not really, because something else was very wrong indeed.

'We've got to go,' he hissed and they froze. He could tell from their faces they'd noticed it too: the music had stopped. He couldn't hear the old man's footsteps. He wasn't sure when he'd last heard them, or even if those same footsteps had become a little louder before they'd ceased, as if each one was on the tread of a stair.

'Run for it,' he said, and he pelted for the door.

The old man was standing at the bottom of the stairs, motionless, as if he were listening. Sam and Jeff burst from the room behind him and into Frank's back, sending him staggering. He stumbled towards the entrance and his foot slipped on the mud in the hall and he landed, hard, on his knees. He stretched out his arms to catch himself and saw only the flash of Sam and Jeff's legs as they passed, the sound of their feet deadening as they cleared the threshold.

Frank ignored the pain in his knees and pushed himself up, and the old man grabbed his elbow and dragged him the rest of the way to his feet. He shook him and Frank's head rocked on his shoulders. The man wasn't gentle, wasn't playing. Then he pulled him closer and Frank stumbled again but towards him this time; it was the old man's body that kept him from falling. He could *smell* him, the same musty smell as the house but stronger and sharper, tinged with sweat and anger. He turned to stare up at him and caught the man's sour breath full in his face.

'Whe'er's t' other one?' the man said, gripping Frank's arm tighter. 'Whe'er is he?'

Frank stared. He could see the old man's stubble jutting from his chin, and some of it was dark and some of it was white. His nose was pocked with open pores and short black hairs were growing out of it. His waistcoat – such a smart thing to wear, so odd to have on in the house – was as dirty as everything else. 'Whe'er's 'e gone?'

Frank shook his head. 'Sorry,' he said. His voice came out all breathy and jerky as if he was still being shaken. ''E's nor 'ere. 'E's at 'ome.'

The old man's eyes were full of anger and hatred. The back of Frank's neck prickled. The old man wouldn't stop staring and he had the distinct impression he was looking straight through him.

'The *other* one,' he said again. 'I saw 'im. Where'd he go?'

Frank knew that his eyes were wide open and fixed and he knew he shouldn't stare like that, but somehow he couldn't help it because he had realised something about the old man and it made his belly feel hot and loose and his legs turn to rubber. *He was afraid.* The old man was afraid.

He shifted his grip and got hold of Frank by both sides of the collar and pulled him up close. His breath was strong in his face and Frank could see the rheumy rims of his eyes and the veins threading through his skin.

'Now see 'ere,' the man said. His voice was throaty and each word was accompanied by a gust of that bitter smell. It made Frank want to wrinkle his nose but he didn't dare. It was odd, though; the man didn't sound angry any longer, just tired, really *tired*, as if he didn't want to be saying these things but felt he had to. 'See 'ere. Just you see he keeps away. I don't want 'im 'ere. You tell 'im. Tell 'em all.' He nodded towards the door. 'Your little friends – stop sodding about. Keep 'em away and it'll be fine wi' me and fine wi' you. See?'

Frank didn't see but he nodded himself and he felt his top loosen as the man relaxed his grip. It had ridden up, exposing his ribs.

The old man pointed towards the door, though his eyes still looked unfocused. 'Get out.' He gave Frank a push that sent him slithering backwards. 'I said *get out*.'

Frank didn't move, then he heard a distant shout, almost a shriek – *Jeff*, he thought – and he started to run. He expected a meaty fist to land on his collar and snatch him back, but it did not come; his fingers brushed the side of the door as he passed and then he was on the stone steps and the day was too bright but the air was blessedly clean and he welcomed it in, running freely now across the lawn and into the lane. When he reached the road he doubled over, gasping in more of that clean air. He could still smell the old man's breath – he could almost taste it on his tongue. He rubbed his fingers against his trousers, brushing away the feel of those dirty clothes, seeing as he did how filthy his own clothes were – but this was *new* dirt – and he saw the back of his hand was grazed from where he'd brushed against the door and the knees of his corduroys were scuffed from falling in the hall, and red had smeared through where the skin had broken underneath. Suddenly he wanted to cry. He looked up the lane and saw no one; they had run away again, run off and left him, and then a shape emerged from the hedge and he realised they were waiting after all, Sam and Jeff, and he sniffed back the tears.

He looked around once more, and saw another dark shape, this one standing in the doorway of the fine old house, watching him as he tried to walk in a dignified way up the lane, doing his best to hide the way his legs were shaking.

CHAPTER FOUR

There had been someone else there. Frank couldn't banish the thought as he stared down at the thing Sam held in the palm of his hand. It was making him feel sick, not just the sight of the thing or the knowledge that Sam had stolen it but the *smell*. It was the same stench the old man had breathed into his face: the foulness of his breath and the trace of whatever sad meal he'd last eaten. Sam was holding the old man's pipe.

He took another breath and closed his eyes. When he did that, the smell wasn't so bad: it was burnt, but also rich and spicy. He opened his eyes and found he'd actually begun to reach out as if he was going to touch that slender smooth stem that had been in the old man's mouth. He snatched his hand away and Sam laughed, though it wasn't his usual laugh. Mossy laughed too. They'd found Mossy waiting for them. He'd been told to fetch Frank in for his dinner – they were waiting to eat – but he hadn't dared go past their own gate. Now his eyes were fixed on the pipe and he didn't blink.

'Get rid of it,' Frank said. 'You shouldn't 'ave tekken it.'

'I din't mean to. If 'e 'adn't come down t' stairs . . .' Sam said this as if coming downstairs was the old man's fault, as if they hadn't been trespassing. Frank swallowed and looked back down the lane. He kept expecting to see the old man marching after them, brandishing his stick, but there was only the lane, banked by tall hedges thick with wiry hawthorn, grown about with dog roses and underpinned by stinging nettles. Sam sighed and tightened his grip on the pipe – *Don't touch it*, thought Frank – and drew back his arm as if to throw the thing away.

He gasped and reached out and grabbed hold of Sam and everything stopped. Their eyes met. After a moment, Sam lowered his arm.

''Ere, then. 'Ave it.' He thrust it towards Frank and Frank slowly shook his head. 'Tha'll take it or I'll wang it.'

Frank knew that was true but somehow he still couldn't reach out and take hold of the pipe. It was as if it carried something of the old man with it, as if he would be tainted by his touch, but from the corner of his eye he could see Mossy looking at him, wondering what he would do. He reached out and took the pipe. It was slippery-smooth under his fingers – odd that it should feel so *clean* – and he shoved the stem into the waistband of his trousers and pulled his top down so that his mum and dad wouldn't see.

'What're you goin' ter do wi' it?'

Frank ignored Sam's words. Mossy was pulling on his arm and part of him wanted to tell him to stop but he didn't. He just nodded and took his brother's hand and started to walk away. He felt better as soon as he entered the farmyard.

'What you goin' ter do wi' it?' Sam's voice called after him, louder this time, but Frank didn't take any notice. Mossy's hand twisted in his but he gripped it tighter and kept them both walking towards the house where his mother was standing on the step, her pinny on and her face red and her eyebrows drawn down like thunder.

CHAPTER FIVE

The pipe lay where Frank had hidden it, on his shelf at the back of a pile of books, with a stack of bubblegum cards on top of them. It would have been easier to slip it under his old teddy bear, but he couldn't bear the thought of the bear ending up smelling like the old man, and anyway, it wasn't as if he had any use for the books. Downstairs, he could hear his mother clattering pots onto the table for everyone else to have their dinner. He wasn't allowed any; he'd been told to go to his room and not come out and the first thing he'd done after he'd slammed the door shut was hide the pipe. Now he worried that he could smell it in his room, that his mother would. He screwed up his face and rolled over onto his back and the bedsprings creaked under him. It wasn't *fair*. He'd only been late and now he was being punished as if the old man had actually caught him. His arm hurt where he'd gripped him and that wasn't fair either. He rubbed it, staring up at the ceiling.

There were voices downstairs too. They did not sound happy.

He closed his eyes and wondered what the old man was doing now. Perhaps he'd be sitting in his chair again, staring into space, his hand reaching for his pipe; he'd be frowning when he realised it had gone. Frank felt anger nestle sourly in his stomach.

He needed food to settle it, but thanks to Sam there wouldn't be any. He could smell it, his mother's chops and gravy, and saliva flooded his mouth. He gathered it on his tongue, wondering if he could spit it clear of the bed, then he swallowed it down. He could just imagine the old man marching up the lane towards the farm, each step stomping so hard it left a perfect imprint in the road. He shook his head. Surely it was more likely he'd think he'd mislaid his pipe, put it down in one room instead of another. His mum did that all the time, losing her knitting or her book, huffing and puffing while she looked for them. She never thought to blame him or Mossy or burglars, so why should the man? There was no reason, after all, for children to steal a pipe. He thought of Sam again, no doubt tucking in to a big plateful of food, and he pulled a face. The least he could have done was to keep the pipe himself, not pass the cursed thing – yes, *cursed* – on to him.

He slipped off the bed and went to the shelf and picked it up. It was so smooth it made him think of the old man's hands, strong and rough, holding it. The smell really didn't seem so unpleasant now. It was still an old man smell but somehow it made Frank think of his granddad, who had died a few years ago when he was really small. It was funny: he hadn't thought of him in a long time. He looked again at the pipe. If he was old, would he treasure something like this? He almost thought he would. It didn't look cursed. He felt another spike of anger towards Sam. Why couldn't he have taken something the old man wouldn't have missed? It wasn't just unfair, it was stupid.

He turned and went to the window, pulling the net curtains back and pushing it open. He could see the spire of the church and it looked bright and peaceful in the early afternoon sunshine. The air was at once sweet and warm and he longed to be enveloped in it, not thinking about anything else. And then it struck him that his parents would be at dinner for an hour yet.

He could put the pipe back.

The old man wouldn't be angry any more. Mossy needn't be frightened. Sam would see he had more sense than him, and his parents would never know.

Once he'd had the thought, he didn't stop to consider. He slipped the pipe back into his waistband, pulling a face at the coldness of the wood against his skin. He pushed aside his Airfix models from the broad windowsill – he'd abandoned the Spitfire when Sam had told him he'd stuck the wings on backwards – and he pulled up his chair. He stepped onto it, the seat sagging beneath his weight, and clambered onto the sill. It was awkward and it dug into his sore knees. He peered out to the side. He knew that the drainpipe was there because his mum had read him a story once about someone doing this very thing and she had caught the look in his eye and glared at him. *You mustn't*, she'd said. *Such things is only for stories. Anyone else and the drainpipe'll come right off t' wall and tek you wi' it.*

He didn't think the drainpipe would *tek him wi' it*, though. It was a big old chunky thing, topped with decorative ironwork. It was fixed to the wall with solid-looking brackets. He'd examined it before and he thought it would do, although he'd never actually tried it. He saw now that half the trick would be shifting from where he sat and getting a grip on it. He managed to get both legs onto the sill and he reached out and wrapped both palms around it, then felt himself slipping before he'd even thought to let go.

For a moment his stomach fell away. He could picture it perfectly, dropping all the way to the ground and landing with a thud on the paving beneath. It would crack his skull. There would be blood. He wasn't sure how he would hide that from his mum. It was only as he realised there might not be any need, that he might never have to face her again, that his grip tightened and he swung around and his toe caught in one of the brackets. His cheek jarred against the metal and it hurt and he closed his eyes. It was a few seconds before he realised he was motionless, just hanging there, and that his arms were getting tired.

After that it was easier. He let himself down hand over hand, thinking about the bruises he would have after this. He decided he would show them to Mossy. He could already imagine how wide his little brother's eyes would go when he told him the tale, and then there were flagstones under his feet and it was so unexpected, the solid ground under him, that he staggered and had to steady himself against the wall of the house.

He straightened his clothes and got moving, trying to walk quietly across the rough surface of the yard.

Mire House stood with its back to the sun and its face in shadow. Frank had intended to walk straight inside without giving himself the chance to pause or let his nerves prickle but he stopped at the gate anyway. There seemed to be something different about the house. It took him a moment to realise what it was, and then he had it: it was waiting.

Although the day was warm, the air was harsh in his throat. It was impossible to know where in the house the old man was. Frank pictured himself walking up to the door and knocking and handing over the pipe. Perhaps that would be the best thing – but there was no way of knowing how the man would react; he might be marched home after all, or worse. And he could imagine his mother's face if he appeared, being dragged by the ear, when all the time she thought he was upstairs. He frowned. If she'd relented by now she might have filled a plate and carried it up to him, only to find the room empty. But it couldn't be helped. The only way was to keep doing what they'd started – sneaking about and trespassing. It was funny how one thing led to another. That was something his dad always said when the horse threw a shoe just as the blacksmith put his prices up, or when the rain came down just before harvest and the tractor went on the blink. *There's always something.* He looked up at the house, wondering what was going to go wrong this time.

The pipe was digging into his skin. He wanted to move it but he didn't want to touch it again, not before he had to. Better, if he got caught, that the old man didn't see it; better he didn't have anything that could show Frank was nothing but a thief.

He pursed up his lips. He *wasn't* a thief. He'd pinched some of Mossy's toys before, but that didn't count; it wasn't anything Mossy hadn't done back. He took a deep breath. As before, there was no point in waiting. Waiting meant his mum and dad finishing their meal and going to find him. Waiting would make everything worse. He stepped out onto the driveway just as sunlight speared from behind the building, making him squint. Now the house was a dark shape. He told himself he hadn't been able to see anything anyway and started to walk.

The door handle was cool under his fingers, almost cold, and when he tried to turn it he had the awful thought that it was locked, but no: it turned and the catch clicked and he froze, listening. There was no sound until he stepped into the hall and then he heard the rhythmic scraping of a spoon against a pan. If the old man's dinner was ready, he might come out at any moment. Frank hurried, trying to walk quietly, and saw with dismay that he had left new muddy footprints across the tiles. He looked up just as a door at the back of the house creaked. He had to hide. He looked towards the man's sitting room. That was where the pipe belonged – but what if he got trapped in there? That only left the stairs.

He knew it was a bad idea even as he started up them. The treads were made of dark wood and they let out tired, airy squeaks as he went up. He kept to the edges, knowing from all the times he'd crept up on Mossy that was the best way to stop stairs from creaking. He found himself at a corner, edging around it with his hands spread against panelling that felt sticky under his fingers. He saw there was a passageway all around the top of the stairs and there were a lot of doors. He snatched the pipe from his waistband and stared at it as if it could tell him where to go. He walked to one of the doors and pushed it open.

The bedroom was bright after the hallway. It was painted blue and yellow curtains with little white flowers swayed at the open window. There was a narrow fireplace that didn't look as if it had been lit in a long time. It wasn't until he'd stepped inside that he caught the stale scent hanging in the air. It smelled as if someone had slept too long and without brushing their teeth, a smell that the open window had failed to freshen, and he knew at once he'd made a mistake: this was the old man's room. If he came upstairs, this is where he'd head. The candlewick bedspread was rumpled and grey-looking, obviously used; he should have seen it at once.

There was little else but a dresser with a record player sitting on the top and a few other items squeezed in next to it: a chipped crystal vase, empty; a picture in a frame; a button with a cluster of threads attached; a comb, and an ashtray. That was where he would leave the pipe. He padded across the carpet and put it down, gently, so that it scarcely made a sound, and then a noise came from the landing and he realised it was too late; he was trapped after all. His heart thumped in his chest. He glanced at the window but it was too small to climb out and anyway, it was far too high, and he didn't even know if there was a drainpipe. And then he noticed, close to the door by which he'd entered, another door, narrower than the first. He had no time to consider where it might lead before he rushed towards it and pulled it open and closed it again behind him.

It was dark inside. He knew without being able to see that he was in a small space. He could sense the walls, close and pressing inwards, and it was stuffy and too warm. The soft bulk of clothes pressed against his side.

He heard footsteps moving about the bedroom. A narrow crack of light penetrated the door frame and he thought about pressing his eye to that gap, trying to see through, but he daren't move. He'd only knock into something or make a noise, and what happened then might be terrible.

More footsteps came, just two or three this time, and a harsh scratching, so loud that Frank jumped. Then, starting faintly and building in volume, there was music. Frank realised it was the same that he had heard before. The steps multiplied, quick and light, as if the man was tiptoeing around. Suddenly he had the image of not just one person out there but two, dancing together while Frank cowered in the dark.

It stopped and the footsteps became louder again. They were heading straight towards him. Frank caught his breath and edged backward, and the handle on the other side of the door rattled before falling still. Frank's throat was dry. He licked his lips and found they were parched too. He was cold all over. It was as if the dark was touching him with its indifferent hands. He felt a long way from home and he thought of Mossy and then his mum and dad and he realised with a lurch in his stomach that they didn't even know where he was.

He closed his eyes. It didn't make any difference. He could hear a voice under the strange crackly music that went on and on; it was his mother's voice. He couldn't remember when she'd said the words, probably because she had repeated them so many times: *Don't talk to strangers. Stop, look and listen before you cross the road.* And most of all, every time they went anywhere: *Never wander off without saying where you're going.* And then she'd rub his head, so hard that sometimes his hair pulled and it hurt, and he'd duck away and squirm. He would do anything now to feel her hand in his hair. He silently swore that if he could be somewhere else and have her with him he wouldn't pull away again; he wouldn't even complain.

He imagined someone reaching out from behind him in the dark and resting their hand on his shoulder. He pulled himself in smaller, wrapping his arms around his body. He closed his eyes and waited but it didn't help. He expected the door to be yanked open any second and for the yelling to begin, but it didn't happen. He bent and looked at the line of light under the door. It wasn't quite regular and he didn't know if that was because someone was standing on the other side of it. He sniffed. If it was the old man, wouldn't he be able to smell him?

There was a soft creak, as if someone standing outside had shifted their weight. Frank swallowed, battling the dry lump in his throat, and he stepped backward, his arm outstretched. It seemed he might just keep moving until he emerged in some fantasy land, just like in a book. But his fingers brushed something hard and there was fabric, coarse and hairy, and he thought of some kind of animal but standing upright, something that could somehow *see* him, and then he was sure he could hear it breathing. He could *feel* it, the heat radiating from its body. He still couldn't see but he knew that someone was there. He staggered away, stumbling into a hard edge. And then he sensed something else, tendrils of it reaching towards him on the air, something he could almost smell: *fear*. Someone else's fear.

He stumbled forwards again, towards the door. He brushed against something and it rattled and he decided he didn't care. It was too late anyway: the old man must have heard him. He must know he was trapped in the dark and he was only waiting now to teach him a lesson, and all Frank wanted was for it to be over.

He felt his cheeks and they were wet and he realised he was crying and he felt a sudden raging thirst. He had to get *out*. He flailed, bashing his hand against the door handle, then grabbed it and twisted and at first it turned but then it jammed and turned back, *against* his hand. He tried again but it wouldn't budge. It was as if someone was holding it from the other side. He tried it with both hands but it wasn't any use and then he heard a shuffling sound behind him, something limp and soft dragging itself across the floor.

He banged against the wood and called out: '*Please—*'

The door opened and light flooded in. The man stood there staring down at him with disgust in his eyes, and something else; it looked a little like surprise.

The tears on Frank's cheeks felt cold. Whatever he'd felt before, the thirst, the *fear*, had gone. He looked behind him and saw only a small cupboard lined with shelves and a rail full of ratty jumpers and greying shirts, and something lying on the floor: a heap of fabric, a brown tweedy suit that he must have knocked from its hanger. That must have been the sound he'd heard. The thing looked crumpled but clean, almost new.

The old man was still staring at him. His cheeks looked sunken and horribly unshaven. His ears were large, the lobes rounded as if they were on upside down. He looked angry, but not as if he were going to lash out. As if in denial of this impression, he reached for Frank's shoulder, and he pulled away with a little cry.

'Tha's still 'ere,' he said.

Frank had no idea what he meant. He did not reply.

'What're you doing in 'ere?'

Frank couldn't find any words. The man twitched, as if he was going to touch him, and Frank did the only thing he could think of: he pointed towards the dresser. 'I brought your pipe,' he said. 'My friend took it. He din't mean to. We was messin' about, and now I've brung it back.'

'So you're not 'im.'

Frank shook his head. 'It wan't me as swiped it.' He crossed the room and picked up the pipe and held it out. This time the man took it. He held it in his hands as if it were some rare and precious thing, and then he slipped it into the pocket of his jacket. He was wearing his black suit again, the one Frank's mother would say was 'nowt but holes and air'.

'I dun't mean that.' The man blinked, and his eyelids looked heavy. Now he didn't look angry; he looked tired. 'One of yer mates ran up 'ere, couple o' weeks back. Left footprints all ower, he did. An' I shut 'im in that cupboard, just like you, on'y – when I opened t' door – 'e'd gone.'

Frank pressed his lips together and looked back into the cupboard. It was just a cupboard. There was nowhere to go, nowhere to hide that wouldn't be spotted in moments. ''E must a' run out again,' he said, 'when you wan't looking.'

'There weren't no time when I wan't lookin', lad. I were 'ere all t' time, standing right outside this 'ere door.' He kicked at it.

'I din't mean owt,' Frank said. 'I din't mean to come in. I on'y wanted to gi' you that.' He shrugged. 'Sorry, an' that.' He looked down at the floor.

'So you're not 'im.'

Frank shrugged. He didn't really know what he meant and he didn't want to think about who the 'him' might have been. He certainly didn't want to think about anyone vanishing in a closed cupboard; that made him think of the woman he thought he'd seen, the one with the dark clothes and the pale face. It struck him once more that was what was wrong with the old man: she'd touched him and his thoughts had gone awry. He'd started seeing things. He was so busy standing about waiting for children to come along and bother him, bashing his big stick into the ground, that he was imagining he'd seen them even when they weren't there.

''E looked like you,' the man said. 'Not *just* like you. Bit younger. Funny teeth.'

'Well 'e's nowt to do wi' me. An' I've allus come 'ere with me mates. We've never been by us sen.'

The man didn't appear to have heard. He was staring down at his feet. Frank saw he was wearing brown ribbed socks that had worn into holes and his big toe with its jagged yellowing nail was jutting from it. Strangely, he wasn't disgusted: he felt only pity. 'What d'you live 'ere for?' he said, 'out 'ere, all on yer tod? It's a big 'ouse. Lots o' rooms.' He stopped himself, biting his lip. It wasn't any of his business. His dad would give him a clip round his ear if he'd heard. Maybe the old man would.

But he didn't look angry. He met Frank's eyes. It was the first time he'd seemed to really *see* him. 'I dunno,' the man said, and his voice was quiet, barely a whisper. Frank found himself leaning closer so that he could hear; he felt sure, somehow, that there was more.

'I'll show yer,' he said, and stepped back, not towards the doorway but into the room. He went to the window and Frank knew that he could run, now, if he wanted to, but somehow he found he *didn't* want to. 'You 'ave to lean,' he said, 'down the'er.'

The man stepped away from the window and Frank took his place. He could see right across the garden and into the lane. He could just see the roof of the porch beneath and that some of the slates were cracked, and that was all.

'The'er.' The man squeezed in next to him and pointed.

Frank saw. At the apex of the porch was a globe made out of stone. He thought there were letters on it, but they were darkened with moss and difficult to make out.

'Read it,' the man said.

Frank leaned out further. 'E . . . L . . . I,' he said, and there was more, but it disappeared around the curve. There were more letters to the left of them, others beneath where they spiralled around, but they didn't make any sense.

'Eli,' the man said. 'Elizabeth.' He drew a long sigh, and Frank caught a whiff of stale breath.

'Is that what it says?'

There was another sour spurt of air, perhaps the nearest thing the man could get to a laugh. 'I don't know,' he said. He gave a wry smile. 'I never did know, not really, but I *thought* it did. *We* thought it did.' He smiled again, and this time there was sorrow in it too. 'It didn't mek much sense. We knew those letters weren't put there for 'er, but when my Lizzie saw it carved there, she said it were meant t' be: it was *s'pposed* to be our 'ouse. Course, we got it for a song – bought it from one o' Lizzie's sisters, married into it, she did, then decided she wanted nowt to do wi' t' place. I thought at fust it was charity, but she were just flighty: Antonia weren't never one for charity. On'y then my Lizzie died, see. All a long time ago now, I 'spose, though it dun't seem like it t' me. Prob'ly before you was even a nipper.' He gazed out of the window again, though he didn't seem to be seeing anything at all. 'We was going to live 'ere till we got old. We was going t' have children. Lizzie was allus the one who knew what t' do. She were going to come in and paint the walls green and fill it wi' laughter.

'You can't tell the ways, can you? Not really – you can't plan owt. Well, you can, but it's God's own sweet will as wins in the end. Her name means "my God is abundance", did you know that?' He let out a spurt of air. 'Cancer got 'er. Bowels.'

Frank blinked. He knew the man had said a funny word, but somehow it wasn't funny at all. He swallowed.

The man drew a long sigh. 'So tha's why,' he said. 'Tha's why I've got a big 'ouse, lad. It weren't meant for me – not just for me, anyroad.' He stared out of the window and Frank waited. He shifted his feet. He wasn't sure what he was meant to say.

'I should turn it off,' the man said, and he went to the worn-looking record player and picked up the stylus and swung it off the disc. 'It were our song, that. Dun't s'pose you'd like it.'

Frank realised the record had just been going around and around, making a soft hissing; he wasn't sure when the music had stopped.

'I listened to Elvis and Cliff and Buddy, all those,' he said, 'but it was the old 'uns I liked best, the ones I danced to wi' Lizzie, back in the day. When we wus courtin' and fust wed. The big bands: "Someday Sweetheart" and "Don't Sit Under the Apple Tree": songs where the words took a long time to begin and you could just listen to the music, let it carry you off.'

'I should go,' Frank said.

'Aye, well, I 'spose you should.' He tapped his pocket where he'd put the pipe.

Frank didn't move. Now he could go home, it didn't seem so pressing any longer. There was something else he wanted to say, but he wasn't sure how. Then it just spilled out: 'I think there's a ghost in your 'ouse,' he said.

The man raised his eyes, slowly and steadily, and he looked at Frank. 'I know,' he said.

Frank nodded again, and then walked towards the door. He could feel the old man's gaze on his back.

'Tha'll come back then,' he said.

Frank stopped and turned. 'Mebbe.' He opened the door and when the man didn't say anything else he walked down the stairs. He could hear steps above him but they stopped and he looked back to see him standing on the landing, watching him go. The man raised a hand at him and he raised a hand back before he walked across the black and white tiles, towards the outside and home.

It wasn't until he was halfway up the lane that the thought struck him. He stopped dead. It wasn't about ghosts or the man or his dead wife or anything about Mire House at all: it was about the way he'd climbed out of his window and shinned down the drainpipe. It hadn't been easy. It was bad enough going downwards: there was no way on earth he was going to be able to climb back up again. His mother was going to know exactly what he had done.

CHAPTER SIX

Frank didn't know why he'd expected to see the old man in church. He was never in church, even though he always looked as if he'd dressed for it. He twisted around on the unforgiving pew, searching for that dark suit, but of course it wasn't there. The old man wasn't *neighbourly*, as his mother would have put it.

Today Frank wasn't sitting next to Mossy as he usually did. This was because he was in disgrace. As if to underline the fact, his mother reached out and grasped his knee, preventing him from twisting in his seat. He fell quiet as the vicar stepped forward. He was a tall and bloodless man, everything about him pale and washed out, including the tufts of hair that clung above his ears. Everything about the church felt dry: the flags, the smell of old stone in the back of the throat, the vicar's voice as he began to intone, something about Job and endurance.

Frank pulled a face just as the vicar's eyes fell on him. He quickly looked down at the kneeling cushion tucked under the pew in front. Matthew James, a boy he knew from school, had tucked his legs under him and his muddy boots had smeared across the embroidery. Frank frowned. He wasn't sure which was worse, a thought that no one could see or damaging church property.

His mother dug him in the ribs as the vicar stopped droning on and everyone shuffled to their feet to sing 'All Things Bright and Beautiful'. He glanced at her. It wasn't fair, he had stood as quickly as everyone else. She wouldn't look at him. He knew she was doing it on purpose. She'd barely looked at him since he'd arrived at the door from his last visit to Mire House. He'd tried to sneak in – quietly, he'd thought – past the dining room, but he'd glanced in to see them all looking straight at him. He still remembered the way Mossy's mouth had fallen open, the mush of his mother's treacle pudding all chewed up inside.

She nudged him in the ribs again and they started to sing.

After the service everyone gathered outside, the men talking about the weather, the women about the trials of bringing up children. The vicar stood in the doorway, looking at them as if he wasn't sure what to do any more. The children didn't stand about; some took out their latest playthings to show their friends, while others ran up and down the lane or around the graves. Frank didn't join in. If he looked like he was enjoying himself, his mum would be down on him in seconds. She'd send him off home on his own. Instead he walked away from the others, along a quieter path that led between the graves. Tufts of grass licked at the base of each grey stone and lichen obscured the letters. He glanced at a few: *Dear Husband. Cherished Son. Beloved Wife.* He could see Mire House through the veil of trees that stood between them. If the old man still had a wife, he might be nicer. He might come to church and chat with the rest of them and no one would think to peek in at his windows because he'd be just like everybody else. From here he could see the porch jutting from the front of the house, the globe appearing flattened to a disc. He remembered the look on the man's face when he'd told Frank about the letters written there, the name of his wife waiting for them at their new home. Now she must have a stone just like these, her name carved into it once more, not in life but in death. It was only then that he realised he knew the name of the dead wife but not of the living man who lived so close by.

He shook his head. He didn't know why he was even thinking of such things. He'd never cared what the old man was called before; he had only made sure to avoid him. It wasn't like him. Normally he'd be thinking about his Sunday dinner. He turned and scanned the graves. They were all around him now, as if they'd gathered in to block his way home. Down the hillside he could still see his mum in her Sunday frock, together with his friends' mothers, their mouths all wagging but not a sound to be heard. She was a long way off. He turned back towards the house, wondering if he'd be able to spot the old man at a window, watching them but with nobody to talk to, and he noticed he wasn't alone in the churchyard after all: there was a woman there too, dressed all in black, just like the old man. She had her back turned and was looking towards the house.

She was tall, the woman, and slender, and a veil was covering her hair, but he thought that it was long and dark, though he didn't know why as he couldn't really see it. She stood beneath one of the yew trees that surrounded the church. They were ancient things; they had been there for years and years, according to his mother, and they were heavy with thick old branches holding out their poisonous berries like offerings. He looked back at the woman. She wasn't there any longer. Frank blinked.

There was a dark furrow in the tree's trunk, a broken branch hanging loose. Together, the shape they made looked a little like a woman; it had only been an illusion. He had fired his imagination with Sam's silly stories and now he was seeing things, just as he had before.

He forced himself to walk towards the tree. There was no reason to be afraid. It was just like monsters under the bed; he knew they weren't real, but if he thought about them too hard he would end up lying awake, mistaking his breathing for theirs. There was a bench under the tree. There was writing on the back of it.

My God, my God, why hast Thou forsaken me? Matthew 27:46

He pulled a face and backed away. That wasn't a nice thing to write. Perhaps the vicar had chosen it, maybe while he was dreaming up another sermon about endurance. It didn't feel that way, though. It seemed like the words had been there for a long time.

It was cold under the tree. Its shadow was sapping the warmth from the air. He looked at its fruit. His mum had told him about yew trees. Older than the church, and deadly; she said he must never ever eat any, not that he could see why he would. That was the reason for the church wall, she'd said, to keep people's cattle from straying and eating the waxy needles. It was odd, but until then he'd thought the walls must be to keep the badness out, not to keep it in. Now there was Mire House. Was that something they'd wanted to keep out too?

His mother's voice, raised and harsh, sounded like a curlew on the air. Frank whirled around and gave her a wave, seeing Mossy standing next to her, small and neat and good in his best clothes. He hurried across the tussocky grass, realising too late that he'd stepped off the path. It was people's graves he was walking on, the low mounds that must be hiding their bones. He grimaced and moved aside, edging by the back of the head-stones, but it was no use; he couldn't seem to keep clear of them. He tried not to see any of the names written upon them as he started to run.

The cake was not his mother's finest. It was chocolate cake, but it looked beaten; the top sagged and the edges looked dense, as if someone had sat on it. He'd thought he could smell baking that morning but hadn't dared ask what she was doing. There was usually afters, but he hadn't expected his favourite. She knew he loved chocolate cake. On his birthday she'd decorate one with hard little silver balls she bought from the grocer. There were no silver balls on this cake – if there had been, they'd all roll inwards and gather in its sunken middle.

Everyone was sitting at the table, Dad and Mum and Mossy, and the cake stood between them. His mother was wearing her pinny and the silver cake slice she got for her wedding was raised in her hand. Mossy grinned and licked his lips and made slurping sounds, and it was then that Frank realised he wasn't going to be allowed to have any.

She cut a big slice, extra wide, perhaps to compensate for its thinness. Frank could smell it, could see the thin layer of buttercream knifed through its middle. His mouth watered; he couldn't help it. His mum had got out the good plates, the ones with the gold rims and little roses around the edge, the ones he and Mossy weren't allowed to wash up on their own. She held one out for a moment before giving it to Mossy. He didn't start in; he knew better than that.

She cut another slice and passed it to his dad, who grunted and sat forward in his seat. It wasn't until then that she looked at him, her eyes sharp. 'There's cake for good boys,' she said.

Dad looked up. He *had* started in, had a fork halfway to his mouth. 'Now, Aggie,' he said. 'Let the—'

'There's cake for *good* boys,' she said again, this time with emphasis, and Dad shut up. He knew when he could argue and when he couldn't and this was one of those times he couldn't. 'Not for them as mess about. Not for them as plays silly buggers.'

Mossy, who had picked up his fork, looked at Frank, his eyes wide open. The sound of him catching his breath would almost have been funny under another circumstance, but not this one. Mum never swore. She told Dad off when he cursed, and if he did it on a Sunday, she'd slap his arm.

'Not for them as – as climbs down walls, and does stupid things, and risks breaking their necks,' she said, and this time her voice sounded funny and that was worse because she didn't sound angry any longer. She sounded as if she was going to cry. She cut another slice of cake, balancing it with her thumb, and plopped it onto another plate. She picked it up and slammed it down in front of her own chair. She never slammed the good plates.

No one looked at each other. It was as if nobody knew what they were supposed to do. They had all stopped eating. Only Mum picked up her fork, cut a small piece quite delicately and deliberately, and held it in front of her mouth.

'Mmm,' she said, and that was it: her voice had broken some kind of spell. Suddenly Mossy kicked the table leg. He couldn't seem to sit still. His cheeks were puffed out and air spurted between them. Dad made a choking sound in the back of his throat, then burst out laughing. She clanked her fork down without taking a bite and pushed herself up and started to pile pots on top of each other.

'Aggie – don't,' Dad said. He leaned back in his seat, tears pouring down his cheeks. Frank stared. ''E's learned 'is lesson. Give t' lad a piece.'

'I most certainly will not,' she said, and she turned and bustled towards the kitchen, her arms laden with dinner things.

Dad winked at Frank. 'Tha's done it now, lad,' he said. 'Tha's done it now.'

Frank sat there in silence while Dad and Mossy laughed and ate their cake, completely stumped as to what it was he had done.

CHAPTER SEVEN

It was well into the afternoon when Frank came downstairs. Mossy hadn't crowed over him because he'd had cake when Frank had had none, but then, he hadn't had the chance. He peered into the sitting room, which his dad just called *the room*. He must have pulled the curtains to stop the glare of sunlight on the telly because it looked dark in there. His mum always complained when he did that; she said it was like a blackout. Frank didn't know what that meant. Now his dad's snores drifted from the direction of the settee. He didn't know if Mossy was sleeping too or if he was just sitting there, all alone, in the dark.

Mum was in the kitchen and it was there that Frank went, pushing open the door very quietly to see her nodding at the table, her arms folded across her chest. The cake was on the side, underneath a wire cover to keep flies off.

He stood in front of her as she breathed deeply, dragging in the air and letting it go with a little *foof*. He could see the down on her cheek, the mole next to her lip, the eyebrows that were beginning to turn grey, catching up with the rest of her hair. She was older than his friend's mothers. He wasn't sure why, except that his dad sometimes joked about how she'd insisted she wasn't going to get married, that she was married to the farm already. It always seemed strange to Frank that it had been hers and not his dad's, that she used to do everything all by herself. Then she spluttered and looked up. Her eyes focused and she started to smile, then she frowned again, as if she'd remembered she was supposed to be cross with him.

'Mu-um.'

'Yes, our Frank?'

'I wondered—' He paused. 'I wondered if I could have a piece of cake, on'y it's not for me, it's for someone else.'

She raised her eyebrows in outrage. 'Now don't you dare tell me lies, Frank Watts. If you want cake, tell me you want cake. Don't go pretending it's for someone else or I'll crown you.'

He flinched. 'It's not for me, honest. It's for t' owd man.' He pointed, as if his mother could see down the lane and towards the mire from where she sat.

'Really,' he added, 'it's for 'im. It's just, he was talkin' to me t' other day. Said he lives there all on 'is tod, and there's no children, no nothing. She – his missus – died.'

His mother's brow straightened. 'How do you know that?'

'I teld yer. 'E teld us.'

'*Told*, Frank. He *told* you.'

'Tha's what I said.'

She pursed her lips. ''E's not friendly, yon.' She said it like a challenge. 'I've never known 'im 'ave a word to say to no one.'

Anyone, thought Frank, but he didn't say it out loud.

'I took 'im a pie once, long time ago. 'E din't want it.'

Frank sniffed. 'Aye, well. Prob'ly not. Can on'y ask though, can't I?'

'An you're not to call 'im t' *owd man*. 'E'll barely be in 'is seventies, if that.'

Frank shrugged: it sounded ancient to him, an impossible age. He didn't say anything, though, as his mum pushed herself to her feet. She did this as if she was supporting a great weight, and she sighed while she did it. She went over to the cake and lifted the cover and cut a slice. She put it onto a plate – one of the plain ones – and she sucked the chocolate from her thumb before holding it out. 'You're to tell *Mr Owens* I want me plate back,' she said, and she sat down again at the table, heavily, and with more sighs. Then she looked up as if in surprise. 'Still 'ere?'

As soon as Frank was outside, he wasn't quite sure what he'd done. But now he had the cake he had to keep on going. If he ate it himself, his mum would know. He walked down the lane, stepping carefully, feeling ridiculous. She should have covered it with something. Now it would be all dried up before he got there. Still, the old man probably wouldn't know any different. *Mr Owens*, he thought. *His name is Mr Owens*.

He went in at the gate. It didn't seem so bad falling under the shadow of the house now that he had a proper reason to be there. He marched up to the porch and knocked. The door was hard against his knuckles and he could imagine the dull sound being swallowed by the hollow rooms within. He didn't suppose the old man had many visitors. He banged again, louder, and he waited. It felt like a long time before he heard something inside.

The door was yanked open and Frank found himself tilting forwards, as if he was going to fall. Mr Owens looked down at Frank and the plate and then back at Frank, and his expression, for a moment, was empty.

'I brought you some cake, Mr Owens.' Frank put on his best voice, his Sunday voice. 'I thought you might like some. I – I asked me mum.'

The man stared at the cake, sniffing, as if he suspected it might actually be something else. 'Cake, eh,' he said.

Frank nodded vigorously. 'Cake,' he agreed.

'Tha'd best come in, then. Watch yer feet.'

He took the plate and Frank followed him into the hall, kicking off his boots at the door like a proper visitor. His feet felt cold at once, and slippery, and he realised the hall had recently been mopped; it glistened with pools of water.

They went into the big room and Mr Owens settled into his wing-back chair, blowing out his cheeks as if the effort had pained him. He held up the cake. 'Thank you,' he said, forming the words carefully, as if he too was putting on a Sunday voice. He looked around as if a fork would materialise, and said, 'Want some?'

Frank shook his head. 'No, thank you. It's fer you.'

Mr Owens nodded and tried to pick it up with his fingers. He licked buttercream from them and looked at Frank. 'P'raps I'll 'ave it later.'

'I'm to tek t' plate back. She said.'

He shrugged and started to eat, scooping rich chunks of cake into his mouth. Frank glanced around. He had thought the arrangement looked temporary before, as if the furniture had momentarily been pushed aside, but it was just the same now.

There was something he wanted to ask about, but he didn't know how to begin.

'Cat got yer tongue, lad?'

Frank took a deep breath. 'I thought I saw a lady. At chu'ch. An' in your garden. I thought I saw 'er twice.'

The man raised his eyebrows and went on scooping up cake. He was eating now as if he was hungry. He made a low grunting noise.

'I dun't think she were real.'

Mr Owens looked up sharply. His eyes were narrowed. He didn't answer.

'I wondered – I wondered, like, if it was—' Frank's words failed him. He shouldn't be here; he shouldn't have begun this subject. He was trespassing, any way he looked at it.

Mr Owens stopped chewing. Then he tossed his head and let out an odd rasping noise and Frank realised he was laughing. 'Tha thinks it's me missus.' He put the last of the cake in his mouth and swallowed. His Adam's apple bobbed, as if it was an effort. 'Tha's what tha thinks.'

'Aye.'

'It in't.'

'No. Sorry.'

'Tha should come an' look at summat.' Mr Owens picked up the crumb-filled plate but he didn't give it to Frank. He balanced it, instead, on the arm of his chair. 'Upstairs.'

Frank followed Mr Owens as he led the way back into the hall and up the stairs. He remembered the last time he'd walked up them and his face flushed, but Mr Owens didn't appear to be thinking about that. He led the way, his unwashed smell trailing behind him, and Frank wished he hadn't noticed it. It didn't seem polite to notice the smell of someone when he'd given them cake.

Owens led him to the same room Frank had been in before. He went to the dresser and pulled open the deep bottom drawer. It scraped as if the base was sagging and he took out a photograph album. Frank's curiosity overcame his reluctance and when Owens opened it, he leaned in.

The pictures looked old. They were held in with little corners so dry they popped off the page as Owens turned them. He stopped when he reached the image of a young man and a young woman. It couldn't possibly be Mr Owens, not only because he was younger and thinner, but because he was smiling. It was such a happy smile. The girl was shy-looking and had curling hair that Frank thought was golden but couldn't really tell because it was partially covered by a white veil, and anyway, there was no colour in the picture.

'Tha's her.' His voice held pride in it, and something else that was warmer, and it held sadness too. 'That who yer saw, was it?'

Frank shook his head.

'No. She's not like tha', is she? Bright, she was. Golden. She med me – she med me smile, and she med me laugh. She wor a good woman, our Lizzie.' His eyes misted, then seemed to darken. 'Tha' other – that in't 'er, lad. I dunno wha's up wi' 'er, but I wun't go near, not me. She seems – she dun't seem—'

'Nice,' Frank finished for him. 'She dun't seem nice.' He felt Mr Owen's hand on his shoulder; it made him jump.

'No, lad, you've 'it it there. She dun't seem nice.'

Frank thought of all the ways he could expand on what he'd said. *Dark*, he thought. *Mean*. But none of it was quite right.

He wasn't sure he could sum her up in words, the woman under the yew tree. It wasn't just the way she looked, but the *feeling* she gave him. He looked instead at the picture. The woman there *did* look nice. She was pretty. He put out a finger as if to touch her and drew it back. 'It's a shame,' he said. 'If yer goin' ter – *see* someone, y' know, who in't really there – that it should be '*er*, and not—'

'Aye, well, a lot o' things in't fair. I 'ave to look at that there bairn all t' time an' all, don't I. Just as if—' he drew in a long breath, 'as if I did summat wrong. We never had children, see, an' seeing that 'un, runnin round t' 'ouse – it's like looking at what we never 'ad, 'er and me. The ghost of some sort o' life we should 'ave lived.'

Frank found he couldn't look at him. He just stayed there, leaning over and staring down at the photograph. It sounded a little bit as if the old man was crying. Frank wasn't sure what he even thought about that, let alone what he would say. And then he let out a little cry and he *did* reach out, touching the surface of the photograph. He had seen the suit that the man in the picture was wearing. It was a three-piece, black, and with three buttons down the front. Frank turned and looked, not at Mr Owens' face, but at the buttons on his waistcoat. The buttons were straining at the holes, but other than that it was just the same.

'Aye, lad. Same suit.'

'But – but why?' Frank turned and looked at the cupboard set into the corner. He knew there was another suit in there. It had looked cleaner and newer than this one, and it certainly didn't smell as bad. 'Why don't yer wear that other one?'

Mr Owens tilted his head. 'Now, lad, it's not polite ter—'

'I know. Sorry. But why? That 'un looks knackered.'

Mr Owens gave a wry smile. Then he chuckled. 'This 'ere's me wedding suit, lad. It's the suit I wed 'er in and the suit I buried 'er in an' it's the suit I should ha' worn to our bairn's christening, if we'd been blessed. An' it'll be the suit they carry me off in when I'm done, an' all.'

'But—'

'Numore, lad, I teld yer. This 'ere's me best suit, even if it dun't look like it. Value in't just in't eye o' the beholder, tha knows. That's summat our Lizzie always said. Her sisters said she married down, right hoity-toity they was, but she always said you can't judge owt by its wrapping. Anyway, if I was fussed about all that I'd go about flashin' my watch-chain and spouting nonsense all ower, like t'other folk do. No: this 'ere's me best, an' if t'other folk can't see that it's their problem.'

He stared down at the floor. Frank didn't know where to look. He'd come here feeling all grown-up, doing a kindness for the old man, and now he'd put himself right back where he'd started, a naughty child who was in the doghouse.

'Now – ne'er you mind me, lad. I'm just grumpy, I 'spose. It's just, like I said – value in't in the eye o' the beholder.'

'Aye. Well, I'd best get on 'ome.'

'Course yer did. Yer mum'll be missin' yer.'

Frank pulled a face.

'Summat up?'

'Not really. She – I were in trouble. Just stuff.'

'Well, boys will be boys, I 'spose. Anyroad, it were right nice o' yer to come.'

Frank looked up.

'Tha can come again, if yer want.' Mr Owens held out his hand, and Frank stared at it. It took him a moment to realise he was supposed to shake. He put out his own hand and shook solemnly.

'Now, lad. I'd best get yer that plate, 'adn't I, before yer go.'

CHAPTER EIGHT

The schoolyard was grey under the grey sky, hemmed in by grey walls. Frank was grateful that Mossy wasn't around; he was still at little school. He was in no mood to have one of the 'young 'uns' trailing after him. During the week Sam preferred the company of the older boys and he was nowhere in sight. There was only a bunch of girls, busy skipping with a piece of elastic; one had a hula-hoop but she couldn't keep it around her waist. Frank didn't feel like going to find Sam. He wasn't sure he wanted company; something about Mire House – the *feel* of it, the stale air maybe – seemed to have clung to him. He still had a sense of its sadness, as if it had folded itself around him and wouldn't let go. He thought of the woman he thought he'd seen in the garden, the way he'd worried about her reaching out and touching him – *If she grabs a hold of you, you're dead* – and he shivered.

Frank sauntered around the corner, leaned against the side of the building and closed his eyes. *Grey*, he thought. As if in answer he felt the first warm drop of rain splatter his cheek. When he opened his eyes, Sam was standing in front of him after all. Frank glanced up into the sky. He was no longer sure it was raining; he wasn't sure where the moisture on his cheek had come from.

There was a smacking noise as Sam let the ball in his hands drop to the paving and caught it again. 'Ey up,' he said. 'You're t' keeper.'

Sam, telling him what to do. Sam acting like the leader, just because he was the eldest. Sam, running away up the lane at the first sign of any trouble, dumping his friends because he was chicken. *Buk-buk...*

'I'm not playing,' Frank said.

'Yes, you are.'

'Am not.'

Sam's eyes narrowed and suddenly Frank knew that he was thinking of it, too: the way he'd run away. The way that Frank had *seen* him run.

'You'll do as I say.'

Frank stared at him. He didn't pull a face and he didn't glare and it took a long time, but eventually it was Sam who looked away. Frank pushed himself off the wall. 'Come on then,' he said. He stripped off the jumper his mum had knitted and he didn't look at the others as he went, just dropped it on top of someone's blazer in the heap that marked the goalposts. In some corner of his mind he registered that there was no one from his year playing, it was all the bigger lads, and none of them looked very friendly. He wasn't sure why they'd asked him to join in.

He sniffed and looked towards the school entrance. Today the teachers on duty were Miss 'Hennie' Henshaw and Miss 'Skeleton' Scales and they were standing by the door but they weren't watching the pupils. They were having a right good natter, as his mum would have put it. Miss Scales' fingers were twitching as if she wanted a cigarette.

'Watch it,' Harry Alsop shouted as he came in close, but he didn't try to score; instead he collided with Sam, knocking him towards Frank so that he had to jump out of their way. Sam called out 'My turn,' and he took a half-hearted kick at the ball – he missed by a mile – and then he ran straight between the posts, into Frank, sending him staggering.

'*Sorree*,' he said, but his tone of voice didn't say he was sorry. It said something else altogether.

Frank straightened his T-shirt as he took his place again.

'Now you.' Sam nodded towards Thomas Furlow, who smirked and nodded and placed the ball on the floor, right in front of the goal. He backed away – it wasn't fair, it wasn't the rules – and booted it straight towards Frank. He tried to catch it, but it flew through his hands and thwacked into his chest.

'*Shot*,' someone else said admiringly, and Sam rushed in, curling his hand into a fist, and he rubbed it against Frank's hair. It pulled, the knucklebones hard against his scalp, and he felt his eyes begin to water. He blinked them furiously.

Sam started lining up the ball again. Frank didn't like the look on his face. He knew it was revenge. Sam had worked out that Frank thought he was a coward and he couldn't bear it. Now he was going to take it out on him. But Frank didn't have to put up with it. He walked off to the side and grabbed his jumper, shaking it out straight. He muttered, 'I'm off,' from the corner of his mouth and headed away, trying to act casual, knowing it wasn't quite working. He heard rapid footsteps on the tarmac and then Sam's hands were on his shoulders, pushing him into the wall.

'Yer'll do as yer told.' Sam's face was up close, his eyes narrowed.

'I'll not.' Frank's voice was quiet. 'I know what's up with yer.'

'You little—'

'I'm not playin'. I told yer.'

A whistle cut into the day. It wasn't a teacher's whistle, but they looked around and saw Harry shaking his head, then gesturing towards the entrance. Miss Henshaw and Miss Scales weren't talking any longer; they were peering at them through the throng of children.

'Later,' Sam said. 'You've 'ad it.'

He turned and sauntered away, whistling himself now, the tune to *We are the Champions*, a programme Frank had never liked and didn't watch.

CHAPTER NINE

Frank sat back on his bed, trying to read his *Hotspur* comic. He had read it already, more than once, but now nothing he looked at made any sense. He had seen Sam again on the bus home and he'd expected him to knock into him or say something mean, but he hadn't; he'd only given him a knowing look.

When he'd got home Mossy had started prattling on about some picture he'd painted and he'd just thrown down his bag and gone upstairs. Soon he'd get called down for tea. Dad would come in and after that they might go out again together to check the fencing or take some of the machinery apart and clean it and put it back together again. Sure enough, through the floorboards, he heard the rattle of the door. Still his mother's voice didn't come and after a while he went and opened the window and leaned out. It was cool out there, the air fresh against his cheek. He could see the church spire and beyond that, the house. Everything had changed since he first set foot on the driveway. Now he wished he'd never done it, even though Mr Owens hadn't turned out so bad. *Tha can come again, if yer want*, he'd said, but Frank wasn't really sure he did want to. Before all that, he'd had friends; not many, not around here, but enough. Now they weren't his friends any longer.

He drew a sigh. There was no point crying over spilt milk, as Mum would say. She'd tell him to *gerron wi' it*, not sit here moping. Maybe she was right.

He walked downstairs and he heard her voice even before he went into the kitchen. 'Thought you must 'ave 'omework?'

'Eh?'

' "Pardon", not "eh". 'Ave you done it, then? You might just catch 'em if so.'

'You what, Mum?'

'T' others. They're out lakin'.'

Frank frowned. 'Where's Mossy?'

'You can't expect 'im to stay in, just cos you are. He's out wi' Jeff. Sam said 'e'd keep an eye on them. A good lad, that.'

'Where'd they go?'

'Not far, unless they want a good hiding. Now, what are you—?'

But Frank didn't wait, he headed straight for the door and before she could stop him he started running across the yard.

The others weren't in the yard. They probably weren't even on the farm. Mire House was what he thought of first; it would be just like Sam to get Mossy into trouble, to get back at him. He ran into the lane, which was empty as the yard had been, and down past the church. He glanced in as he passed and the grave-yard looked empty too, the colours a little too rich, as if it was about to rain.

He slowed when he reached the house. He almost expected to see Mr Owens standing in the garden with his big stick, ready to ward the others off, but there was no trace of him. There wasn't even a light shining in a window, although the day was starting to fade, the sun turning a deeper gold. It didn't *feel* as if they were there.

There was somewhere else, though; the place they weren't supposed to go. He could see immediately how that would have appealed to Sam. He wouldn't have taken Mossy to his house – their mum was worse than his at keeping an eye on them. *You've 'ad it*, he'd said. No, the mire would be more suited to whatever Sam had in mind. Frank thought of Mossy's open smile, the way he trusted people, and anger rose within him. He hurried past Mire House and onto the path that led to the river. He didn't look back; he started to run.

He saw Jeff first. He was sitting on the bridge that crossed the worst of the mire, dangling his legs over the long grass. Sam wasn't there and he couldn't see Mossy, but then he noticed a dark shape standing beyond the bridge. He crossed it, ignoring Jeff. His legs felt at once cold and hot from running. His corduroys were covered with the gossamer of seed heads or cobwebs.

When he reached the broad bank of the river, there was nothing but the green and pale yellow of long grasses; and then he realised that Sam was there, standing off to one side. He was alone. His hands were on his hips and his lip was curled.

'Where's my brother?' Frank said. He knew it was no use acting scared. If he did, Sam wouldn't tell him anything. But he didn't tell him anything now. He grinned and looked over Frank's shoulder and Frank followed his gaze. Through the long grass where the water began there was a darker colour and he realised with a start that it was Mossy. As he watched, his brother raised one arm and waved. He didn't shout a greeting or anything else.

Sam let out a whistle – a *watch this* whistle – and Frank turned to see him throw something small and coppery – a coin – into the long grass, towards Mossy. 'We're playing a game,' he said.

'The buggeration you are.' Frank strode towards his brother. He immediately felt himself sinking. The ground only looked solid, he knew that. It was green, but it squelched like water. The river merged into the ground, no division between the elements. 'Mossy,' he shouted, 'get ower 'ere, *now*.'

He couldn't see his little brother any longer. He couldn't hear anything either. The river's progress was silent. Midges gathered about his face, as quiet as everything else. There was only his own breathing, and when he moved again, a sucking sound when he pulled his foot from the bog. 'Mossy!'

His voice came out too loud and too high, and this time, behind him, there came a giggle. It was Sam. Frank pushed the thought of him out of his mind; he didn't matter. He was thinking of Mossy's feet, sinking deeper and deeper into the wet ground. He was further in than Frank and he wasn't as tall or as strong.

He heard an answering cry a little way ahead of him. It was the sound made by someone who didn't want anyone to know they were frightened.

'I'm coming,' he called, and he took a large, exaggerated step. He was into the reeds. They were stiffer than the grass, more difficult to push aside. If he bent them under his feet they might stop him from sinking too far. They were slippery though, and treacherous; he grasped at the thin stems to steady himself and they dug into his palms but he didn't care. Mossy might not have the sense to step on clumps of reeds. He might not have the sense to hold on. If he went into the river – an image flashed before his eyes, but not of Mossy; oddly, it was the old man he saw. *You're not 'im.*

Frank shivered. The hairs were standing away from the skin on his arms. He caught sight of a flash of colour: Mossy's coat. 'Hang on,' he said, his voice lower now, just for the two of them to hear. 'I'm almost the'er, our Michael.'

There was silence, and he didn't know if it was because Mossy was reassured or because he was surprised at his brother calling him by his real name. Then the thought went out of his mind because he slipped, both feet this time, and in a second he was down, his hands plunging into muddy water.

He thrashed, grasping for the reeds, for anything solid, but nothing was; everything shifted or came away in his hands. Then he got his legs under him and he pushed himself up. He wasn't sure which way he'd been facing. It all looked the same. He took another step – the ground felt a little more solid this time – and he heard Mossy cry out, a sharp sound of panic. He turned and caught sight of someone through the reeds, but it wasn't him, not his brother; it was Sam, standing with his hands on his hips, smiling. It was odd, but for just a moment, it was someone else's face he saw: he shook his head and it was only Sam again, but surrounded by a dark shape, like mist. His stomach clenched. He remembered seeing the old man with the woman standing just behind him, touching him, and he remembered the thought he'd had: that maybe it was *her* that had made him go bad. He pushed the thought away. He had to find his brother. He shouted his name, but his cry sounded inarticulate, like some wild creature.

He waded into the mire, the uncertain, unreliable mire, and he screamed something: Mossy's name perhaps, though it might have been a wordless yell of fear, and then Mossy answered.

The sound carried to him clearly now. He couldn't think how he hadn't heard it before. His brother was wailing and splashing about, a frantic sound. Then he saw him, not in the river after all but among the reeds. He was covered in mud.

Frank kept going and reached out – for a moment he couldn't see anything – then he felt fabric and his hand closed over it. He kept hold and pulled as hard as he could. Mossy scrambled towards him, into his grip, and he yanked his brother all the way out of the mire. When they were standing on firmer ground he still didn't let go, he just stood there clutching his coat until hands started to slap at his own and he realised he was half strangling his brother.

'I couldn't find it,' Mossy said.

Frank's mouth fell open, and then he grinned and touched a hand to Mossy's hair. He left a muddy smear on his forehead and his smile faded. 'We're going ter be for it,' he said, and he shrugged. 'I 'spose it dun't matter. Come on, our Moss.'

He took his hand and stepped carefully back towards the bridge, ignoring Sam, tamping down the grass for Mossy. Now it felt firmer it was odd that he'd panicked like that. There was no way his little brother would have ended up in the river. Things like that just didn't happen. He hadn't meant to look at Sam again but he glanced around and saw he was still wearing that knowing grin as he tossed another coin in his hand.

Frank remembered what he'd seen – *thought* he'd seen – that woman, standing behind him. For a moment, she had even looked like a *part* of him. Then he focused on Sam's eyes and they looked blank and strange and dangerous. Frank wasn't sure it was the boy he knew, and then Sam shook his head and it passed. Frank still felt cold. He wished he was at home, safe in his own bed, his brother in the room next to his.

He hadn't expected Sam to speak but when he did, he sounded bewildered. 'What—?' and then he recovered himself and pointed at Mossy. 'He owes me some brass,' he said.

'He owes you nowt.' Frank glanced down at his brother. He was muddy and his eyes did not look trusting any longer and it was that more than anything that rekindled his anger. 'Tha'll not go near me brother again. I'm tellin' yer.'

A smile spread slowly across Sam's face. 'All right. I'll 'ave nowt to do wi' 'im. Soon as you pay us back.'

Frank let out an exasperated sound and dug around in his pocket. There was nothing there but a five-pence piece he was going to use to buy Black Jacks or a lucky bag, but it would have to do. He held it out. His hand didn't shake and he didn't look away from Sam's eyes.

Sam shook his head. 'It's not enough. And you know summat else, Frank Watts – I'm goin' to tell your mum. I'll tell 'er you threw Mossy in t' watter cos he went out wi'out yer an' you were mad. I'll tell 'er you were in trouble in t' playground. An' I'll tell 'er you went trespassin' in that 'ouse, an' all. She'll believe me – you know she will.' He paused. 'It wan't me that sneaked up to 'is window. It wan't me what went inside that 'ouse. Anyroad, she can go an' ask t' old man, if she wants proof. He'll tell 'er.'

Frank stared at him. No one said anything. Even Jeff was looking at Sam open-mouthed. No one ever told their mothers what they'd been up to; they just didn't.

'So 'ow about it? You goin' ter pay us back, or what?'

Frank stared, but then, slowly, he nodded. He had some money left from his spends the week before, and it was his birthday soon. Sam would have to wait – there was no way his mum would give him anything early – but what he got, he could have. 'I'll get you some brass,' he said.

Sam smiled. Frank knew the smile did not bode well.

'In yer dreams,' he said. 'It's not brass I want. There's summat I want yer to do for me.'

CHAPTER TEN

Frank found himself crouching by the drystone wall that ran along the front of Mire House. Everything seemed to come back to this place. Mossy was pinch-faced and silent beside him. Frank reached out a hand and grasped his shoulder.

Mossy looked at him, a question in his eyes, but it was Sam who answered it.

'Tha'll go in again,' he said. 'But this time you're not after a pipe or owt useless. I want summat good.'

Frank waited but he did not say more and he realised it didn't matter. It wasn't really the value of the item that mattered – just *summat good* – so much as the satisfaction in making Frank fetch it, like a dog with a stick.

'I'll wait 'ere and so will 'e.' He gestured at Mossy.

Frank had a sudden image of Sam taking his little brother and leading him back to the river. He shook his head and spoke, not to Sam, but to Mossy. 'You *will* stop 'ere,' he said. 'You dun't go nowhere. Not with 'im, not any more. Understand?'

Mossy nodded. Frank wasn't sure he meant it, but it would have to be enough. He looked at the house and sighed. It still didn't look like a nice house, but he'd taken the old man cake. He'd looked at pictures of his wife. He knew her name and what it meant and he had shaken his hand. But he also knew that Sam was right. The way his mum had been lately, always cross, glaring at him and stomping around – she'd believe Sam in a shot, even if Mossy stuck up for him. He didn't really have a choice, and it wasn't as if the old man had anything valuable anyway; the whole house was a wreck, everything old and worn out and broken.

Except 'er, he thought, remembering the look on the old man's face when he'd spoken of his wife. *And she's nowt but a memory*.

'Well gerron wi' it,' Sam said, and shuffled on his haunches. 'I'm not gerrin' any younger.'

It was so obviously something he'd copied from his dad that Frank let out a splutter. It earned him a clip round the ear. 'None o' your cheek,' Sam said, another phrase that sounded borrowed, but this time Frank didn't laugh.

He turned towards the house. The thought of actually doing it, of creeping inside somewhere he'd been invited to visit, taking something that didn't belong to him, made him feel sick. But if he didn't do it – he looked at Mossy. Sam would find some other way of getting at him, so he might as well get on with it. He'd grab something the man would never miss and run out again. He'd just have to hope he wasn't seen. He closed his eyes. He knew it didn't matter; even if the old man never knew, he could never visit him again. He wouldn't be able to look him in the eye.

He pushed himself up and ran, doubled over, towards the house.

The handle was familiar under his hand and he pushed on the door while he turned it to lessen the clang when it opened. The hallway was dark and it was only when he saw it that he realised how quickly the day was passing; the sun must have almost disappeared already.

Frank slipped inside. The house was waiting. Only the dust moved, drifting down from the stairwell, and Frank watched it and it struck him that maybe the old man had died. He might have gone upstairs, taken off that smelly old jacket that was a little too small, taken a last look at that stone globe with the name of his wife and laid down and given up. Maybe he was with that dark woman now. Maybe *she* was with *him*. He looked up the stairs. They seemed steeper than they had before.

And then he remembered something that the old man had said: *Value in't just in't eye o' the beholder, tha knows . . . If I was fussed about all that I'd go about flashin' my watch-chain.*

A watch-chain, that would do. If he took that, Sam wouldn't be able to accuse him of having failed. He bit his lip, imagining himself taking the one thing the man owned of any worth. But then, he didn't value it, not really. It was other things he treasured. Pictures. Memories. Those kind of things. *In't eye o' the beholder.*

He took a deep breath and started up, one hand on the rail. It felt dusty but he didn't take his hand away. If he fell, he'd be caught for sure. He looked down and saw the trail of muddy footprints he'd left behind. It struck him now that the old man might think the ghost had left them, the one who'd gone into the cupboard and disappeared. It seemed odd he'd never really thought about that before. He'd never seen a child, only the woman, and even then he'd barely thought the word *ghost*. He'd seen her, and so she simply *was*. It struck him how stupid it was that he'd just accepted that. He didn't know what she was or where she had come from and he didn't know what it was she wanted. Maybe she wanted *him*. Maybe she wanted him *here*.

He swallowed. His throat had gone dry. It flashed across his mind how doubly stupid he had been. If he'd thought about this he could have simply knocked on the door, pretended he'd come to visit and slipped something into his pocket when the old man wasn't looking. Now it was too late. The old man would be in his chair downstairs – he *hoped* – and if he came out now, Frank would be stuck. No, he had to keep going.

He reached the top of the stairs and glanced down at his feet. His boots were still muddy; there were tidemarks on his trouser legs. His mother would kill him, regardless of how this came out. He should have been in for tea ages ago.

He looked towards the bedroom and imagined stepping into that cupboard, that small stuffy space, and simply vanishing. He wrinkled his nose. Perhaps that would be best for everybody. He was nothing but a nasty thief now, wasn't he?

His eyes were itchy and he rubbed at them with his sleeve. Then he stepped inside the old man's bedroom. For a second he saw the old man sitting there on the bed, a shiny watch-chain held in his hands – actually *saw* him – and he blinked and the room was empty. He pulled the door to behind him. The photograph album was leaning against the side of the dresser; Owens hadn't bothered to put it away. He walked over and looked down at it. The man and his wife might have had children. Frank might have been friends with them, they could have laughed together, played together; the house would have been different then.

No. Somehow, he knew that the house hadn't been meant for playing, for laughter. It wouldn't forgive such a thing for entering its doors.

He saw now there was another picture, this one sitting on the dresser. The old man wasn't in it but it showed the same woman as in the album and it was faded and browned. The frame it was in looked like silver.

He couldn't take that.

The cupboard, that was where he kept most of his things, wasn't it? That's where the second-best suit was hanging. He might find the watch chain in there too. He walked towards it, his footsteps making no sound. *Quick.*

The shelves were stacked with old newspapers, brittle and yellow, damp-stained cardboard boxes, and clothes: old shirts, jumpers, things that looked like rags. The suit was hanging from a rail. Frank stepped inside. It was almost fascinating, like stepping into someone else's life. There were things in here Owens must have had for years. *Decades.* He noticed a small wooden box that looked as if it might hold something valuable and he opened the creaking lid and saw a jumble of rusted collar stiffeners. Nothing that was any use.

He bent and looked under the shelves. There was a larger box, with something yellowed like net curtains sticking out of it. He popped open the cardboard folds with a scraping sound that seemed too loud and touched the material. The old lace looked soft but it felt dry and brittle. It had mildew on it, and there was the smell of rot. He realised what it was: a wedding dress. He had a sudden image of the face in the picture, the bright eyes looking straight at him, and he let go of it with a shudder. He pushed the lid back down but it wouldn't stay shut, half opening itself again; the dress looked like an accusation.

His lungs felt full of dust. He was trapped in here with the past and the weight of time and all the lost things pressing down on him. He stepped back, reaching for the door, and found nothing but the soft pressure of clothes, no body in them. He batted against them and the brown suit slipped bonelessly to the floor, and the hanger fell on top and clattered against the wall.

Frank gulped in air, pushing open the door and spilling out. There was movement downstairs; a sudden thud. His heart was beating wildly, almost painfully, and his throat ached. He went for the door, remembering the watch chain, Mossy's frightened eyes; his brother, flailing in the mud for Sam's coppers. Then he saw the picture, the one in the silver frame, and he strode to the dresser – no use in trying to soften his footsteps now – and he grabbed it. He tried to stuff it into his pocket as he went for the door but it wouldn't fit. He ran anyway, knowing it was already too late.

CHAPTER ELEVEN

Frank kept on running, his feet banging against each tread of the stairs, as the sitting room door began to open. Its movement was slow and relentless and it didn't stop until the man's bulk came to fill it. When it did, Frank froze. Owens stood there in his dark suit, staring at him. No one said anything for a long time.

'Frank,' the man said, his voice low and a little puzzled, and that was all.

Frank started walking down the stairs. His legs felt weak. It felt as if he'd been descending for ever. The picture was in his hand and he tightened his grip on it, his fingers slippery against the cold metal, feeling the bumps and fissures of its intricate design, the smoothness of the glass that covered the woman's face.

Mr Owens took a step forward. 'Frank?' he said, and this time it was more like a question.

He was almost at the bottom of the stairs. The front door was ajar, a slot of green showing through it. He could smell the air out there, so much clearer than this. Owens didn't move, just stood there in the hallway amid all those muddy footprints. It struck Frank that there were too many to be his alone; then the thought was gone. He couldn't think about anything but the expression on Mr Owens' face. There was confusion there, and the start of disappointment. He recognised the expression at once; he had too recently seen his mother wearing it.

He knew the exact moment that Mr Owens saw the picture clutched in his hand, because when he did, he let out a roar: 'Why, you little—'

Frank ran. He yanked the door wider and surged through it, almost falling when the ground went from under him, and then he was down the steps and onto the gravel and he ran harder, hearing the spray of little stones behind him. The door behind him slammed back. Mr Owens shouted, 'Come back 'ere wi' that . . .' and then he was down the drive and at the gate, ready to grab Mossy's arm and flee before the old man could see his brother waiting there. He didn't care what happened to Sam. He'd just chuck the picture at him – he didn't want it, never wanted to see it again – and he'd hope it brained him. He thought of that woman standing behind the boy, about to reach out, to grab his shoulder maybe – *good*, he thought, *I hope you die* – and he swung around the gate, but Mossy wasn't there. Neither were Sam and Jeff.

'Shit,' he muttered. '*Shit.*' There was a hollow place in his belly. He wondered when they had run, taking his little brother with them; they surely must have made him go – Mossy wouldn't have left him like that. Maybe it was while he was in the old man's room, going through his stuff. Maybe it was the moment he'd gone inside the house, something they'd planned to do all along. Now they were gone, leaving only a place where the weeds were pressed a little flatter.

Mr Owens was coming down the drive, not running but trotting as fast as he could, his belly under the waistcoat swinging from side to side. In other circumstances, Frank might have laughed. Then he ran again, turning away from home where he hoped Mossy would be safe, and it struck him: if the dark woman was going to *get* him, it wouldn't be at home, in his own bed; it would be at the river, where the air smelled of mud and flies, and where the water kept sweeping onward, ready to cover over anything that happened there.

It was too late now. He ran alongside the wall until he reached the narrow path and swung himself into it. Behind him, Mr Owens followed.

Frank didn't slow down until he saw the bridge. It had already occurred to him that the only way back was the way he had come, but that didn't seem as pressing as his fear of the ghost. He suddenly felt sure she was real. She had been there all the time, pushing him the way she wanted him to go. No: he was only looking for someone else to blame. He was in deep trouble, beyond deep. He realised he was still holding the picture and he thought of reaching back his arm and throwing it into the mire. Somehow he couldn't do it.

The bridge was empty but he could hear a voice now, childish laughter, and his stomach dropped. *Mossy.*

He ran over the soggy ground. It actually made splashing noises under his feet. He could hear Mr Owens' panting breaths and although he knew he deserved to be caught, he still wanted to get as far away as he could. Instead of running onto the bridge he ducked low and away to the side, where the ground was soft and the grass was long. He started to sink at once. Water seeped into his boots. He crouched down as low as he could, feeling his feet press further into the ground, and he

clutched the picture in front of him. He couldn't bring himself
to look at it.

Through the grass, he saw Mr Owens reach the end of the
path. He stood for a moment, resting his hands on his knees. He
could see his cheeks puffing in and out, even from here. For a
moment, he heard him gasping for breath. He didn't like the
sound of it. A part of him wanted to step out of the grass and
walk up to the old man and give the picture back. He should
never have parted him from it. Still, somehow, he didn't move.

From somewhere beyond the bridge came another high
giggle. The old man straightened at once and headed towards it.
Frank heard the dull sound of steps on concrete and, after a few
seconds, he rustled clear of the grass. Now the path home was
clear. He could run away and try to forget any of this had
happened. But the old man would surely follow him and he'd
tell his parents everything. *A nasty little thief*, he'd say, and Frank
wouldn't be able to bear the look on his mother's face because
he'd know that it was true.

He followed the old man across the bridge, one hand skim-
ming the rail. The river was silent but Frank could smell it, a
scent that belonged to this place and here alone. It wasn't a nice
place. There was no way they should ever have come here, or
ever have gone to the house. It was odd that it was so close to his
home, his safe, warm, comfortable home, and yet he longed to
be far away from it.

Then he heard a shout; it was a child's voice, but not one he
knew. He could just see Mr Owens, picking his way ahead, and
in front of him—

He blinked. There was a child standing in front of
Mr Owens, but it wasn't anyone he had seen before. He was a

little shorter than Frank, and he looked a little like him but his clothes were different. He was wearing shorts and a shirt and a V-neck pully and his hair was lighter than Frank's, was almost glowing as the sun's low rays caught it, but Mr Owens didn't seem to have noticed the difference; he was edging towards him over the unsteady ground.

Frank went after him. He saw something else and his heart stuttered. It was the woman, standing further out, at the edge of the river, and now he could see her face. It was pale and thin, her cheeks sunken as if she hadn't eaten in a long time, her eyes shadowed. She was wearing mourning, he could see that now. It was like some dark mirror of a wedding dress. The veil was pulled back from her hair and her gown was a rich, deep shining black. She must be standing in the water, he realised. No: *on* the water. His belly contracted; his bladder nearly let go.

The child grinned as if he were playing some game and turned and ran. He was heading towards the water, quick and lithe, holding out his arms for balance as he went. Hadn't Mr Owens seen that he wasn't even carrying the picture? Frank watched as the boy pushed his way between the taller grasses and was gone.

Suddenly Frank felt afraid for Mr Owens. The man was blundering, every step clumsy. He seemed to be saying something as he went, Frank could hear the gruff tones of his voice, though he couldn't make out the words. Then he let out a wilder cry and he fell to his knees, struggling to pull his foot from the mire.

Frank stepped forward. He realised the other child was waiting after all; he had stopped just at the edge of the reeds. He had his back turned and Frank couldn't see his face. He glanced back to where the woman had been standing – no, *floating* – above the water, but now he couldn't see her at all. It did not comfort him. If she wasn't there she must be somewhere else, waiting at the foot of the path maybe, or standing right behind him. He whirled and saw nothing but more grass and beyond that, a golden, bloody sunset.

'Mr Owens,' he said. His voice was soft, but the old man heard. He pushed himself to his feet and turned.

'He hasn't got your picture, Mr Owens,' he said. He held it out. 'It's 'ere.'

He stepped towards him. He didn't even look at the picture. '*You*,' he said. '*You*. I'm going ter – you wait. You'll never 'ave 'ad—'

Mr Owens stepped towards him. Frank glanced back. The bridge was behind him now. He ran towards it and grasped hold of the rail, the rusted metal rough but welcome under his fingers, the concrete solid beneath his feet.

'It's no use runnin',' Mr Owens said. 'I'll find yer.'

And Frank knew that he would. He backed across the bridge, letting go of the rail, and he felt his foot slip off the edge. He gasped and snatched for the rail again and the picture slid from his grip. It fell and there was a dull gritting sound and the higher *chink* of splintering glass.

'You little—' Mr Owens strode towards him.

Frank turned and fled. Nettles flicked at his legs as he went, but he didn't care and he didn't stop. He wanted only to be home. It didn't matter how much trouble he was in. He wanted his dad in the front room, safe and solid, and his mum with her grumpy face and folded arms. And Mossy: he even wanted Mossy.

There was a noise behind him, a strangled, breathy sort of sound, and he turned.

Mr Owens was on the bridge. There was something wrong with him. He clutched at his throat with his hands, then shifted his grip, clawing with one hand at his collar and the other at his chest. His face had gone red, but it didn't look funny. It *wasn't* funny.

Frank blinked. The child had emerged from the reeds. He was watching Mr Owens and he had no expression on his face at all; no fear, and no pity.

Mr Owens fell to his knees, choking. He supported his weight with one outstretched hand. The picture was just in front of him and his eyes fixed on it. They looked as if they were bulging from his head. Then he fell forward with a dull smacking sound and Frank flinched. It had sounded as if something had broken, his nose maybe, or even his skull; there had been a dull crunching and something else, a wetter sound.

He stood there, frozen, until he realised that everything had fallen still. A moment longer and he couldn't even hear Mr Owens gasping for breath.

He stepped forward, his legs shaking. He walked up to Mr Owens. He was lying face down and he wasn't moving. He didn't look as if he was breathing. Shivers ran across Frank's arms. He felt cold right through. When he looked up, he realised the woman was there. Then she turned and moved away, taking the child with her, into the reeds, until he couldn't see them any more. He was alone. There was no one left to hear him and no one to help. He looked down at what had once been Mr Owens and he opened his mouth as if to speak, but he couldn't think of anything to say. This wasn't the place for words. It simply *was*.

He looked down and saw the picture, the filigree shine of broken glass. He stretched out one foot and pushed the frame closer to Mr Owens until it was touching his hand; then he saw that it was lying face-down. The old man hadn't even been able to look into his wife's face as he died.

Then he turned and ran back the way he had come, towards home, knowing that as long as he should live, he never wanted to come to the river again.

CHAPTER TWELVE

The house was no longer quiet and it was no longer dark. All of the curtains had been thrown open, letting shafts of light onto the worn carpets. They had looked better in the semi-darkness; it felt like an invasion.

There weren't many people, but because they were all wearing the same thing, it looked as if there were more: black crows pecking here and pecking there, peering into corners, tut-tutting over the worn chairs. There were ladies standing in the big room, but no one had chosen to sit in Mr Owens' seat. Frank didn't want to sit there either. He looked around for Mossy. His little brother had looked odd when they'd come here, dressed all in black too, his hair turned slick-shiny where his mother had dampened it down.

Someone had been cleaning the place. Frank sniffed. He could smell beeswax and it was a nice smell but he wished he couldn't; it didn't seem right, as if the very air had changed now that Mr Owens was gone.

Except that he wasn't gone. He was in the narrow back room. The funeral was later and now there was this; people bustling in and out doing goodness knows what. It didn't make any sense to Frank. It was as if the shadows that lay in the house had come to life and were milling about, rubbing shoulders, holding teacups or plates.

He knew most of them from church or the village. Some were from *away*, as his mum had put it, distant relatives who probably hadn't been here for years. There was an older woman with bright red lipstick that was garish against her powdered cheeks, and another of a similar age with a similar expression; they stood together, clutching tiny glasses of sherry. There was someone else he didn't know, a man who stood apart from everybody else, alternately sending dark looks around the room and examining the cornicing through his long pale eyelashes as if he was trying to work out what it cost.

The door opened and Mrs Holroyd came in, ushering Sam and Jeff ahead of her. Sam's face was pale, his lips tight; Jeff looked as if he were trying not to cry. She pushed them towards the corner where Frank stood, and he heard: 'You make sure you stay *put*.' Sam had seen him, was coming over. Frank stood his ground. He wasn't going to look as if he was afraid. There were worse things: he had seen them.

'All right,' said Sam in greeting.

'Right.' Frank didn't say anything else. He was surprised when Sam shuffled awkwardly.

'*Sorry*.' The word was barely audible.

He turned and looked the taller boy in the eye. 'He's dead.'

Sam wrinkled his nose and turned away. 'Ah know.'

'Tha shouldn't 'ave done it.'

Sam looked angry. 'It wan't me. You're t' one who went in to t' 'ouse. Does everythin' tha's told, does tha?'

Frank could feel his cheeks growing hot. 'You . . .'

'*That's* our Frank.' It was his mother's voice, raised now, loud in a room full of whispers. He looked up to see her talking to the two women he'd never met, still clutching those silly little glasses as they walked towards him. '*That's* my lad. Frank fetched 'im cake, didn't you Frank? Just the other week.' She smiled at him. The strangers nodded and smiled too, as if they didn't know what to say. Frank looked down at the floor. From the corner of his eye he could see that Sam was watching him.

'He dun't boast, our lad. But it were kind, a right kind thing to do.'

He wished, more than anything, that his mother would shut up. Sam, at his side, let out a spurt of air. It seemed the woman with the red lipstick wasn't really listening either. 'I never imagined,' she said under her breath. 'I knew the house was bad for *me*, but if I thought that Lizzie . . . so much younger than him, and yet she died so soon.'

The other woman nudged her arm. 'Look there, Antonia. It seems *someone* likes it.' She indicated the man, who was now running his hand across the walls and rubbing his fingers together.

'*Clarence.*' Antonia looked as if she'd smelled something bad. 'Well, he *would*, I suppose . . .'

Frank lost the thread as he felt a hand close on his arm. 'Why don't I watch 'im, Mrs Watts?' He turned and saw Sam's expression, his eyebrows raised, his eyes wide: all innocence. 'I can do, if you need to get on.'

She beamed at him. 'Well, that's right kind, love. I can see where our Frank gets it from. We 'ave to be getting finished up soon. Gettin' to the church.'

As they moved away, Sam's grip tightened. Frank turned and stared down at his hand and Sam let go with an exasperated sound. 'It weren't my fault. I weren't to know you was goin' to nick summat.'

Frank's eyes narrowed. 'You *teld* me ter . . .'

'Jump off a cliff, would yer?'

They were silent, staring at each other. After a moment, Sam's lip curled. 'Anyroad,' he said, 'wha's this about yer being all pally like?' He put on a falsetto voice, his head wobbling from side to side: 'Our Frank fetched 'im cake, didn't yer Frank? Just t' other week.' He leaned in close. 'Bestest friends, was yer?'

Frank pursed his lips.

'You'll 'ave seen 'im, then.'

'Eh?'

'You'll 'ave seen 'im, you bein' mates an' all.' Sam nodded towards the door that led on to the hallway. 'You know what I'm on about.'

'I don't.'

'Yes you do.' He leaned in closer so that Frank felt his breath against his ear. 'Open coffin. *I've* seen 'im.'

'You 'ave *not*.'

'You ask our Jeff.' Sam turned and gestured. His mother was standing with the vicar, nodding and talking hurriedly, and Frank noticed Jeff at her side, one hand curled at his mouth; he was sucking his thumb. Frank had known him for as far back as he could remember, but he'd never seen him suck his thumb.

'He nearly wet 'is pants. Why'd you think 'e were cryin'?'

Frank scowled. 'Tha's a git, Sam Holroyd,' he said.

'An' thee's a coward, Frank Watts.'

The accusation was so unfair that Frank's mouth fell open.

But Sam hadn't finished. 'Tha knows nowt. If you're such a big man, why dun't you go and look? You know where 'e is.' In defiance of his promise to keep an eye on Frank, he stalked off. He went to his brother and whispered in his ear, and Jeff turned and glanced at Frank and his lip twitched.

Frank turned and looked at the door. He suddenly knew he was going to go through it, though he didn't know why. It wasn't because of Sam's words; he didn't care what he thought of him any more. He was going to look because of something in himself. He had been in this room when no one else was here. He'd talked to the old man when no one had been near him in years. Now it was between him and Mr Owens, it was as simple as that. His feet were already moving, his hand reaching for the door. When he saw the old man – when he looked into his face, saw what he had *done* – he wouldn't be afraid. He was going to say that he was sorry. Mr Owens had died and Frank couldn't do anything about it. The man had been away from his house and the memory of his wife and he hadn't even been able to look at her face when he died because Frank had taken that away from him. The urge to cry was gathering in his chest and his breath hitched. He was in the hall. It was full of other people's shoes. The tiles, for once, were clean. He turned to the back room and saw that the door was ajar. There was a splash of light on the dark red wall.

He knew he was going to look. He hoped, even after everything, that the old man would somehow understand. He was with the angels now, or wherever; he'd be able to look down and see Frank and know that he hadn't meant to do the things he'd done. Everything would be all right. He had done something terrible and it would be forgotten. He wouldn't have to think of the way the old man had chased him, his face turning red, his fingers clutching at his chest. He wouldn't have to remember the sounds he'd made as he'd gasped for his last pained breaths on the old concrete bridge. He wouldn't have to see the disappointment in his eyes. It would all be gone, and everything would begin again.

Frank half expected the door wouldn't open, but it moved easily under his hand. He listened for any sound from behind him but there was only the continuous drone of voices. The room was narrow and dark and smelled slightly of damp. There was another smell too, something chemical, and layered over that the too-sweet stench of lilies. The flowers were at the back of the room, blowsy white things that were already wilting. They sent spiked shadows across the wall. They were stuck in a tall fluted vase in a nasty shade of turquoise glass. Frank realised he was staring at it because he didn't want to look at the thing that lay between him and the flowers. He could see it anyway, a dark shape like a long narrow table.

He caught his breath then winced at the sound it made. This had all made sense a minute ago, when he'd crossed the hall. Now it felt wrong. It was as if his feet weren't resting on the solid floor, as if there wasn't any air to breathe. He looked down anyway. The coffin was half-open and the part that was open revealed a face and some shoulders and a chest. The colour of the face was wrong, like putty, and he had a sudden image of a smashed egg and the broken thing inside it, of eyes that wouldn't open.

He felt his legs take a step forward. He had no idea how to stop himself as he walked to Mr Owens' side and looked down at his face. It had all gone flat somehow. The brows were lined but they weren't creased into a scowl and his lips were slack. They didn't quite seem to meet properly. All of the man's anger had gone, everything had gone, nothing left inside him. Frank let out a noise. He felt suddenly glad that no one was near, to hear him make that sound. He took a deep breath and looked down at the old man's hands, folded so neatly over his chest, and his mouth fell open.

There was that smell again, stronger than ever. He could taste it. He felt sick. He put his hand to his mouth. The suit the old man was wearing was brown, and hairy, and tweedy. It looked almost new. He knew at once who would have chosen it. His mother had been over earlier, to help out, she said, and he could picture her tut-tutting over the shiny black thing that Mr Owens wore. She would have found the second-best suit hanging in the wardrobe and held it out in front of her face. *That'll do*, she'd have said, and that would have been that, they'd have dressed him, making sure they did it all just right.

But it wasn't just right. There was another funny noise in the room and he realised it was his breath, his throat constricting, the air whistling through it. Then he heard something else, the whispered echo of a sound: *It'll be t' suit they carry me off in when I'm done, an' all.*

Except it wasn't. It *wasn't*.

Value in't just in't eye o' the beholder, tha knows. No: this 'ere's me best, an' if other folk can't see that, it's their problem.

A hand fell on his shoulder and he almost screamed. He tried to pull away and found he couldn't. He twisted, barely able to see his mother's face through the blur of his tears. For a moment it didn't even look like her and he suppressed the urge to scream a second time. Her mouth was moving and he could smell tea on

her breath but he couldn't understand a word. He had no idea
what he was going to say but anyway he couldn't speak, because
he was crying so hard.

The adults in the room gathered around him and the walls
loomed over them all, shutting everyone inside. His mother
knelt in front of him and Frank knew it was embarrassing,
seeing her there like that, but he didn't care. Behind her was
the vicar, seeming taller than ever, his face thin and without
expression.

Frank couldn't think. What was it he had been saying?
Something about Mr Owens and his wife, about how the suit
was meant for *her*, just as they both had been meant for this
place. 'It was the globe,' he blurted out, knowing already it was
the wrong thing, that he was only making it worse.

He swallowed. 'Mr Owens saw his wife's name written on the
globe.' He pointed upwards and his mother glanced at the
ceiling. He followed her gaze. There was only an old chandelier
hanging from a hook that was thickened with layers of old paint.
'Outside,' he said, 'the globe outside. And that was how he knew
he was supposed to stay and he married her and they were going
to have children, and that's why he needs his suit . . .'

The vicar frowned, shaking his head. Frank's mother leaned
in closer, blocking his view. She didn't look angry, only full of
concern, though he could feel the anger somewhere beneath it.
When she's afraid, he thought, and didn't know why: *She's most
angry when she's afraid.*

She took hold of his arm, then turned to the vicar. 'He's upset,'
she said. 'He should never ha' been in that room. He shouldn't
ha' seen what he saw.' She started to straighten and Frank pulled

away, but she wouldn't let him go. 'I'll miss t' funeral,' she said. 'I'll leave it to t' rest now. I'll take my boy 'ome.'

Frank noted in some corner of his mind that his mum must also be upset, that she had forgotten to say *have* and *home*, even though she was talking to the vicar. 'No,' he said. 'Mum, no.'

She leaned in, putting her face up close. 'Now you listen to me, Frank Watts. You've shown me up enough and you're coming 'ome wi' me, an' that's that.' Her grip tightened and Frank looked at his arm, at her fingers digging into his skin. Somewhere behind her was the blurred outline of a face: Mossy. This time his little brother didn't manage to hide his fear.

Someone put their hand on his brother's shoulder and Frank looked up and saw Sam standing behind him. 'No,' he said again, though it was no longer the old man he was thinking of: there were more important things. *It was only a suit*, he thought. *Could it really matter?* But the old man had been kind to him. He had let him into his house. He had to try. He ignored his mother's warning look. 'It wasn't the suit 'e wanted, Mum. Tha' black one – that was 'is. He said it'd be the suit they carried 'im off in.'

'Aye, well, folk dun't allus get what they want,' she said. 'Now get a move on, our Frank. It looks like you an' me's going 'ome.' And she started to drive him towards the door with little pushes, and he twisted and took another glance at her face, and he did not dare to contradict her.

It wasn't until they were halfway down the lane that he looked back at Mire House and saw the figure that was standing in one of the topmost windows. He couldn't see its face but he thought he knew who it was, and he knew that he was looking straight at him.

CHAPTER THIRTEEN

The yew tree was thick with berries. It wasn't the one nearest to Mire House and Frank was glad of that. He stood underneath it, feeling the soft sliding needles beneath his feet. This yew was near the lych-gate and it felt comfortable and close around him; the branches seemed to be hiding him. He heard the sharp *snick* of metal blades snapping shut.

When he emerged from the tree his mother was smiling and she brushed needles from his shoulders. 'You 'ave to be careful wi' yew,' she said. 'It's all poisonous. The flesh of the fruit's not but the seeds inside them are, and the wood is, and the leaves. They call 'em the death tree.' She paused, then shook her head. She held up her hands, indicating the gloves she wore. In one hand she held a dark green sprig along with her snippers.

'What's it for, Mum?'

She sighed, then shrugged. 'It's an owd custom, love. I don't rightly know where it comes from.'

'Was it that woman from t' funeral who told you?'

She gave a startled laugh. 'Antonia Hollingworth? No. Not 'er, love.'

'But you know 'er.'

'I did that. A long time ago, it was, before you was born.'

Frank frowned; it was odd to think that his mother had known people he never had. It made him think she'd had a whole other life he knew nothing about.

'Now, this yew. It's supposed to be a nice thing to do, tha's all. An' you said you wanted to do a nice thing.'

Frank nodded. He had: he'd said he would like to visit the old man. A part of him had thought that meant he'd have to go back to the house, to face the old place once more – to face whatever lay *in* the house, now – and he had been relieved when his mother suggested cutting the yew. He hadn't known what she'd meant; it wasn't something they'd ever done before.

But she hadn't finished. 'It's supposed to be summat that's right to do after the funeral,' she said. 'It's an evergreen, see – it's to do wi' eternal life. And there's something to do with spirits – or doorways, or something – it makes sure someone'll help 'im cross, that sort of thing. Help him find the other side, rest in peace or whatever. Me nan told me about it once – it's a proper old custom. Not many folk'll 'ave 'eard of it these days. Goes back years and years, long as these trees, prob'ly.' She smiled. ''Appen it means nowt at all. But it's a way of payin' your respects.'

Frank didn't really understand but he put on his own gloves and took the sprig from her fingers.

'There was druids, see,' she said. 'They said the yew tree lived in three worlds: the world above, that's the branches, and this 'un, and the one below – that's the roots. Only the yew, see, it can make doors in between.' She shrugged. 'I know it sounds daft. But still. They built the chu'ch 'ere for a reason, din't they?'

She led the way up the path, skirting the church. Frank didn't know where the old man's grave was but he wasn't surprised when they headed up the hill and towards the wall that divided the churchyard from Mire House. The other yew tree, the one on the border, was ahead of them and he could see its dark crown over his mother's shoulder. He couldn't see the bench and he couldn't see beneath the tree. He wondered who might be sitting there, and he shivered.

His mother huffed her way up the slope and then she stopped and stood aside. 'Here, love.'

The grave was close to the topmost yew, not far from the bench with its despairing words. The grass covering it looked sparse and criss-crossed with lines as if the ground had recently been chopped into pieces. The headstone looked the same as all the others except that it stood a little straighter and the letters were etched a little cleaner. Frank wondered how long it would take before it greened over with lichen and time. At least, for now, the bench was empty; the dark woman had gone. Maybe she already had whatever it was she wanted. He fingered the sprig of yew and felt those poisonous needles poking through his woollen gloves as he looked up towards the windows of Mire House and he saw the figure that was looking back at him. And he heard the whisper of words on the cold air:

This 'ere's me best, an' if other folk can't see that, it's their problem.

Frank frowned. A dull fear spread through him, making him want to shiver. He had thought he knew what those words meant – *had* known – but now it occurred to him they could mean something else too.

If other folk can't see that . . . It's their problem.

'What is it, our Frank?'

He turned and for a moment, he couldn't focus. There was only a dark shape leaning over him, one arm outstretched towards his shoulder. He took a step back and felt the raised mound of the grave under his foot. He stumbled, almost fell.

'What's up, lad? What's got into yer?'

'Nothing, Mum.'

'Summat has.'

'It's nowt.' Frank sniffed, realising he was close to tears.

'Frank?'

'I saw 'im,' he said. 'I saw 'im, Mum, the owd man. He's up the'er.' He pointed up at the window. Clouds were scudding across the sun and the glass was mottled and grey; impossible to tell if anyone was watching.

His mother was silent. Everything was still. Then she grabbed hold of his shoulder and shook him, just as she had at the funeral. 'Now, Frank. I'll not have any o' your nonsense. Not now, not ever again. Do you hear?'

'It's not nonsense. I *saw* him, after 'e'd gone, only—'

She got hold of his arm once more and Frank looked down at her fingers pressing into his coat. The last time she'd held him that way she'd left red marks on his skin. He wondered if they'd appear again in exactly the same place. She started to pull him away, back down the slope. 'Mum, no—'

He wanted to tell her that he still had the yew in his pocket, that he hadn't left it for the old man. But it was no use; it was never any use. She wouldn't listen to him. It was like before, when he'd tried to tell her about the suit. Some things were for grown-ups and some things were for children, and he should have learned to keep his mouth shut.

He followed at her heels, keeping close so that she didn't pull too hard. They rounded the corner of the church but instead of heading down towards the lych-gate and home, she led him around the path and up to the church door. She didn't pause but hauled on the heavy iron ring and the door swung open onto darkness and dust. Her shoes tapped on the stone as if she knew exactly where she was going.

Then she stopped and swung him around. 'You're a nasty little liar, Frank.'

He blinked. *Nasty little thief,* he thought, but he didn't say anything.

She jabbed a finger towards the altar. Her face had gone red. 'You should ask forgiveness.'

'But Mum, I *did* see 'im. And before that, I saw a wo—'

The slap, when it came, was hard. Frank stared at her, stunned. It took a moment for his cheek to begin to sting. He didn't put his hand to it; more shocking even than the movement or the pain or the fact that it was his mother who had inflicted it was the look upon her face. Her breathing was hard and heavy as if she'd been running. What was worse than her fury, though, was the look in her eyes before she'd struck him: it was her *fear*.

'Mum – I don't think 'e means us any harm, not really. I don't think that's—'

'Shut up. Shut *up*, Frank.' She leaned in close and he saw tears welling in her eyes. She pulled away and rubbed at them with her sleeve. Then she caught her breath. 'You'll not tell tales,' she said, 'not again, you hear? They're not good tales and I'll not hear them. Never again.' She held up her hand when he tried to answer. 'You'll make up for it. You'll ask God's forgiveness. That's wha' you'll do. An' then you'll come straight 'ome and we'll 'ave our tea and you'll say nowt to your dad and nowt to our Mossy, an' if I ever catch you talkin' o' such things ever again – *finished* things, things that are *ower*—' her eyes narrowed, 'there'll be hell to pay for it, our Frank.'

He didn't dare move and he didn't dare to look away but then she broke eye contact and walked away from him, *clip-clip-clip*, down the aisle. The door thudded behind her. He just stood there; he wasn't sure for how long. He only knew that the cold spread up from the stone floor and into his ankles and around his knees and up his back. It went deepest, though, around his arm, where his mother had gripped him so tightly. And then he started to cry.

After a while he stopped. There was no point in crying any longer. No one had come and even if someone had, he wouldn't want them to see him crying like that.

He realised he was standing by the pew he'd sat in that Sunday, so long ago. He edged into it, shuffling along the seat until he was in the place he'd sat with his mum next to him, and his dad and Mossy. He'd been in trouble then too, though it hadn't been half so bad as this. Now he felt empty. There was a depth to his mother's rage he couldn't fathom; usually her rages made sense. Usually, he could see them coming.

He kicked against the wood, sending echoes up into the shadowy rafters. The altar was a plain white table with a silver cross sitting on it. His mum liked to come and help polish it sometimes. He wondered if that would make her feel better now; probably not.

'All Things Bright and Beautiful' – they'd sung it that day. He screwed up his face and kicked harder. He'd had a bad thought then too, hadn't he? The vicar had said something about endurance and Frank had fleetingly wondered why anyone would *want* to keep faith with God if he only made bad things happen to them. Then he remembered something else and he bent and looked under the pew in front. There it was, the kneeling cushion, still soiled with mud from Matthew James' boots. He closed his eyes and imagined his mother's voice saying, *the mucky pup*. His lip twitched; he almost smiled. Then he slipped off his seat and he knelt and started to brush the dried earth from the fabric.

You'll make up fer it, his mum had said. Well, maybe he was making up for it, not for lying but for everything else he'd done; for the old man. Maybe this – doing something to help, something with his hands, was better after all. And it was what she wanted, wasn't it?

He finished cleaning up as best he could and slipped the cushion back under the seat. He actually felt better now, calmer. Ready to go home. He had a feeling his mum wouldn't say anything about this – *you'll say nowt* – but she'd let him know he was in trouble all the same, banging his plate down in front of him or giving him the burnt bits for his dinner. He'd know and so would the others, but none of them would say a thing.

He sighed. He felt older somehow, as if he'd learned some important lesson; he just wasn't sure he knew what it was. He looked up at the altar again before he left. At least he'd tried. He'd tried to make up for whatever it was he had done, even though when he looked up at the church he couldn't see God, but every time he looked up at the old house the old man was staring back at him.

He shook his head. It was probably another thought he shouldn't have had, and now he would most likely be late too.

Late for dinner, just the thing to make his mum even angrier. *Or more afraid*, he thought, but he didn't know why.

He turned to leave the church, a place where his mind only seemed to turn to darker things, to head back home where he belonged. The door banged behind him as if it was glad to see him go. He looked up and saw his mother coming down the path; she had come for him after all, maybe even forgiven him. Then he saw her expression and he knew that she had not.

'Where's Mossy?' she called out. 'I sent 'im to fetch yer for tea.'

Something cold happened inside him. It started down deep and spread up his spine. And then Frank started to run.

Frank ran so hard that his breath burned him and his lungs felt tight. The mire was ahead of him but it was Mossy he saw, his wide-open eyes, his bright grin.

Mossy. Frank opened his mouth to shout his name and somehow no sound came out and then the bridge was there, but somehow it was *more* than the bridge; it was a border. He could see each flake of rust on the handrail. He staggered to a halt and retched. If he crossed it, he would *know*. There wouldn't be any room for *perhaps he's gone up to the fields*, or *to Sam and Jeff's*. He breathed heavily, leaning on his knees and clutching those thoughts close. Then he let them go. He knew it wasn't any use hanging onto something that wasn't real.

He had a vivid image of a flash of colour amid the reeds, those endless reeds, his hand reaching out and seizing on his brother's coat, and then he couldn't help it; he was sick onto the grass in a sudden wet spatter. Inside, though, he could hear another sound; the sticky crunch of Mr Owen's face hitting the walkway.

He straightened. He knew there wasn't anything else to be done. He couldn't think where else Mossy might have gone. The woman was real and the boy who was with her and now his brother was with them. He didn't know how he knew that, but deep down, he *did*. He took a last rasping breath and then he stepped onto the bridge.

Nothing happened. He looked down and something glittered against the concrete: the shine of broken glass. *Revenge,* he thought; *the old man wanted revenge after all*, and then he shook his head – *no* – and he ran again, not stopping this time until he stood among the reeds, and the throb of his heartbeat was replaced by the rustle as he pushed them aside and he saw what it was they held.

His brother was there, but he was different now. There were his face and his hands and his short, soft hair, but his brother had gone just the same, somewhere Frank couldn't reach, and he couldn't unsee it; he knew he would never stop seeing it.

He opened his mouth to cry out but it was his own name he heard, *Frank*, and it was his mother's voice as his knees gave and he fell forward into the marsh and went into the dark, a place where there was nothing and no one at all.

PART THREE

1939 – The Last Stook

CHAPTER ONE

Aggie looked down at her arms in dismay. Her pale skin was reddened and hatched with lines where the barley had scratched her. She was coming out in a rash too; it would be a wonder if no one thought that she had the measles. The midges were biting and the sun was burning down on the top of her head and as she bent, the heat shifted to her back. The chatter-rattle of the binder filled her mind, though other sounds occasionally crept in beneath it: the low hum of bees, the snorting of the horses, the shouts of her brother Will and her dad, and the steady *thwock-thwock-thwock* of metal on stone beneath it all, coming from the big house.

She turned towards it. From here all she could see was the gentle curve of the field, each heavy ear of barley blending into a smooth stretch of near-whiteness. The line was broken only by the sharp triangle of the church spire and the merest suggestion of a chimney top beyond that, but she knew what stood there; the new house that nestled into the plot between the church and the river. *Soon*, she thought, and smiled: *soon*.

'Moocher!' The call rang out and she turned to see Will standing tall on the binder. He pointed. 'Sheaves!'

She pulled a face. The binder kept missing; a scatter of stalks lay like jackstraws. That was the reason she was here. They needed someone to trail in their wake, getting prickled by cut stems and stray thistles and the long hairs that surrounded the barley, smooth as silk along their length but barbed at the tip so that when one snagged in her cuffs, they worked all the way down her sleeves. It wasn't fair; *she* would never stop someone from doing what they wanted to do, from becoming what they needed to be. She straightened, smoothing down her shirt. For a fleeting moment she pictured the hallway in the new house, full of people wearing silks and ostrich feathers and holding glasses of champagne while a gramophone played.

Perhaps there would be young men there too. Perhaps some of them might like to dance.

'Aggie! Stop dithering about!'

She grabbed the spilled barley, pulling it into a thick bundle, the ears brushing her cheek. There was a splash of colour in it, bright red – she knew it wasn't blood, she had only been scratched, not cut – and she discarded the poppy, cut down along with the rest. She stood and went to gather the sheaves into a stook, leaning them together so that the rain would run off and the wind dry them, though not so steeply that the very next breeze would blow them down. For a second she was surrounded by a float of golden chaff that caught the sunlight and she closed her eyes against it. It was a beautiful day, a rare day. It occurred to her in that moment, standing in the warmth and the clean air, that some of the visitors to the big house might be rich.

She half-smiled, smoothing down her headscarf over her hair. Her mother had curled it so carefully the night before.

Her smile faded as she caught her ear, feeling the flare of pain where her mother had burnt the tip with the tongs she'd heated on the stove.

The binder was settling at last, the arrhythmic rattles becoming a continual chatter, the smooth dry *swish* of the blades neat and clean. The sheaves thrown down ahead of her were all neatly bound. She smiled again, moving after it to build the next stook. The last time she'd glanced across the field they had done so little, and now they were almost finished; only a narrow strip remained. She grimaced at the thought even as Will straightened, grinning, looking towards it.

'Rabbit pie tonight, Ag!'

She wrinkled her nose at him as her dad went to the lead horse's head and began the clumsy job of turning them. They were the only ones she knew who hadn't yet changed to a tractor; her dad 'didn't hold' with them. The arc was wide but Dad did it as expertly as he always had, lining up the binder square against the row. They were facing into the sun and she squinted as the remaining barley became a white blur.

'Ready,' her dad said. His voice, gruff and impossible to counter, carried easily.

Will's grin was wider than ever. From somewhere – she hadn't even seen him stash it – he'd grabbed a pitchfork. 'Shan't be long now,' he said. And the approach began, the blades spinning in a constant empty whirr, the machinery champing, and then came the sharper, dry sound of cutting. It sounded louder than ever and Aggie wanted to cover her ears. She could see the barley beginning to move along the canvas but it seemed to her that everything was still; the sense of waiting hung in the air like chaff, an unbearable lightness, and then came a dark flash in the corner of her vision as the first rabbit broke for cover. Will whooped, striding towards it, but it was too quick. It pelted across the rows until only the white flash of its tail remained, and then there was not even that. She smothered her own grin as it reached the safety of the long grass.

But it was only the first. It always went the same way: the field's small creatures retreating as the binder drew inwards until the very last of the crop was cut. They never did run until it was too late. Some were running now, but Will didn't give chase. They were small, only visible because of their movement against the brown earth: nothing but shrews and mice.

The binder moved onwards and another rabbit ran. This one headed straight towards them in its panic and Aggie winced. She could already see what would happen. It was written in the curve of her brother's back as he raised the pitchfork, in his broad shoulders and ready muscles; the concentration on his face. She didn't watch the rabbit, but she couldn't look away from her brother as his arm twitched. He struck, the movement fluid and sure. She didn't look at where the blades landed, but she heard the meaty strike of blood and bone.

She wasn't sure if the creature had cried out, but she imagined it anyway, a single high squeal that hung in the air, lingering even though the binder was even now spilling unbound sheaves from its innards and its endless rattle went on around them all.

Will pulled the pitchfork from the ground – it took two yanks to get it free – and he bent. When he straightened he swung a small limp thing from his hand, the fur stained and dampened. He turned towards the last of the barley and his face lit up. She knew there must be others, running for cover, but she couldn't bring herself to watch.

It wasn't their death – she had seen death before, many times; she had watched her mother catching chickens and wringing their necks, her hands strong and sure, and had done it herself, growing in competence each time. No, it was the fear that troubled her. It was the thought of how their terror must have grown, little by little, as their homes were taken from them. It was the thought of all the things they must feel or imagine in their frozen silence, able only to watch as their death approached.

There were stalks spilled all around her now. She would gather them up and build the sheaves and the stook and then she would be finished. She could go inside and sluice away the seeds and barbs and dust. She could release her curled hair, change her dungarees for smooth stockings and try not to think about the death-squeal of the rabbit as they all sat down for tea, her and Mum and Dad and Will, for *soon* her new life would begin and she'd never have to think about it ever again.

It occurred to her now that if the rabbits had only planned their escape, broken for cover sooner, while everyone was busy, they would have been safe. And yet that just made it worse, more pitiable: the way they had simply hidden, letting their fear grow; the way they had never known when the time had come to run.

CHAPTER TWO

Aggie lay back on her bed, letting the tiredness settle about her, the aches intensifying and fading by turns along her spine. She had washed in cold water drawn from the pump but now she felt warm again, the heat of the sun still gathered in her little room over the kitchen. Below, she could hear the clatter of pots and the rattle of pans. Soon the rich smell of her mother's stew began to rise through the gaps between the floorboards.

She closed her eyes, the hunger growing in her belly. She tried not to think of the rabbit; instead, she pictured the smooth tiled floors of the big house.

Mrs Hollingworth, the lady of the house, had come down from London for a day to oversee the proceedings. She had worn an elegant dress with a matching coat that she hadn't removed, though the day had been warm. Her hair looked freshly curled and it shone and she had a gold pencil in her hand, though she hadn't had any paper. Her expression had been a little reserved and Aggie had decided it was a sign of her superiority, her good breeding, that she hadn't smiled. She was proud at the thought of working for someone like her, someone with such self-possession. Mrs Hollingworth was dark-haired and her complexion was pale, and she had imagined her in the bustle of London, not that shell of a house which didn't yet have glass in its windows. *Solemn* was the word that came to mind, followed by *dignified*. Mrs Hollingworth's mouth had twitched, though, when she smoothed her hand down over her belly. It was as if she was already picturing the house full of children. Even with the pregnancy just visible under her coat she still looked like a lady. But then, she *was* a lady. She had a fine new house being finished around her, and beautiful clothes. What need had she of smiles? And then Aggie thought of washing those clothes, scrubbing those tiles clean, of keeping a house much finer than her mother's – and of actually being paid to do it – and she grinned even wider.

She would need new shoes, she decided. Her plain brogues had been too loud against the flooring, the dead sound echoing around the hallway and up the stairs. She would need silk stockings, not cotton lisle like her mum's. And then the rattle of the cart cut into her reverie. It meant her dad had finished his rounds with the milk and eggs and vegetables. Sure enough, she heard his voice in the room below.

She frowned. There was something wrong with his tone. He always sounded gruff, but now his voice was clipped, too, as if he had news he didn't want to impart. The door banged and Will's louder voice rang out, and he was hurriedly shushed. She knew that something had happened even before her mother started to call her name.

Later she sat with the plate in front of her, stirring the rich stew with her spoon. Around her, the others chewed. She stared down at the food. She was no longer hungry. She didn't know what she was supposed to think. No one else seemed to be thinking about it at all; they just went on eating. There were so many questions tumbling over themselves inside her mind and she didn't know if she was allowed to ask them. It didn't seem right, but all she could feel was overwhelming disappointment. She looked around at the small room. She couldn't remember a time when the kitchen wasn't full of some kind of noise, her brother's talk, her mother's washing or cooking or mending. There was always *something* to be said, but now everything was silent.

Mrs Hollingworth had gone back to London for her lying-in and the time had come and they weren't sure what had happened, other than that there would be no baby. That was all anyone seemed to know: her dad had heard it from the landlord of The Horseshoe in the village, and he had heard it from the stone-mason. No one knew when they might be coming to take up possession of the house. *Or if*, Aggie thought, and pushed the idea away.

She imagined taking cups of sugared tea to the lady as she sat alone in a grand chair. In her mind she stood at her side while she drank it, uttering soothing words. Her imagined self knew exactly what to say. She would be a helpmeet and a comfort; there would be no parties, not for a while, but she could still be there for Mrs Hollingworth. They might even develop a kind of friendship, built through adversity, even though one was a mistress and one a housemaid. Such things could happen where the need was great. She found herself smiling wistfully as her dad said, 'You'll not be going, then, Aggie.'

She turned and looked at him. Everyone fell still; no one was eating. 'Of course I'll go,' she said. 'I'm needed.'

Nothing else was said. Instead everyone returned their attention to their plates and continued to eat.

CHAPTER THREE

The harvest was almost over when Aggie heard the strike of metal on stone travelling across the hillside from the big house. She stopped at once. She had been tying a strand of wheat about a sheaf and it slipped from her fingers, but she didn't care. She stared up into the light, her eyes wide open, and a voice shouted something, but she didn't hear the words. *Now*, she thought. She's coming back *now*.

She had almost set off to run in the direction of the house when everything came back; not the stone and cool hallways that had been in her mind but the scratchy stalks and the binder's rattle and her father's glare. It didn't matter, though. The lightness was rising inside her. It was all going to happen, her whole future. It did not matter if she could not yet run to meet it.

The little lane seemed longer than it ever had when Aggie finally hurried to see what was happening at the house. The building had been done in a fine old style and it had a look about it as if it had always been there, as if it belonged to some earlier era. It certainly appeared to have been finished some time ago. The windows had been painted, the door boarded over with forbidding slats that surely would not be there forever. But the sound had meant something, and if work was beginning over again that must surely suggest that the house would be occupied at last. Perhaps some last-minute alteration was being carried out to the mistress' satisfaction.

When she reached the gates she was disappointed to see that the slats were still in place. No lights shone in the windows; no smoke rose from the chimneys. Then she saw the man standing on the lawn, one foot resting on a ladder that lay uselessly on the ground. He hadn't seen her either and his head was tilted back, as if he too was examining the building.

The silence stretched out while she looked at him, as if it were spreading from the dark building. He slowly turned his head and for a moment, he stared back at her. He started and touched a hand to his cap and bent to his ladder, only pausing when she called out a 'hallo'. He wore dark overalls, not too dissimilar to her own, save that hers were covered in chaff and his in pale dust.

'Are they coming back?' She blurted the words as she stepped towards him. 'I beg your pardon. I meant the lady of the house – Mrs Hollingworth. Has she come back?' Her gaze shifted and she saw, as if in answer to her question, the closed door.

He shook his head and gestured at the building and his mouth moved but she hardly heard the words. She looked at where he'd pointed, at the roof over the porch. She didn't know what he meant, but it hadn't been an affirmative and the disappointment was growing in her, stifling everything. She swallowed, realising with surprise that she was close to tears.

The man pointed again, down at the ground this time, and she saw a stone globe nestling in the grass. When she looked back at the house she saw others matching it set above the upper windows. She saw what he meant.

'It's not for me to ask why,' he said, 'but it dun't seem right to me.' He shrugged. 'Still, what do I know? I'm on'y t' stonemason. I does as I'm told.' He picked up the ladder, hefting it towards the porch.

Aggie went towards him, not quite knowing why, and not knowing what on earth he would think of her, a ragamuffin girl appearing from nowhere, dressed as she was, intruding on his work. She stood next to the stone globe, the last piece of a puzzle perhaps, the final touch that would make the house ready to occupy. The stone looked solid and heavy, too heavy for her to lift. Then she saw there were letters cut into the stone, wrapping around it. She twisted, reading what was written there, then she caught her breath and took an involuntary step backwards.

'Like I said, it's not what I'd 'ave on me 'ouse.' His voice was close at her ear and she jumped. She hadn't been conscious of his approach. For a moment they looked down at the globe together. She read the words again, thinking that she must have made some mistake, but there they were, carved clear and true, and still with the same meaning:

Eli Eli lama sabachthani?

Something inside her turned cold. The last piece of a puzzle? No. She shivered. She had heard the words before, in the Sunday Bible classes held in church; she knew exactly what they meant.

''Appen I'd best get on, miss,' the man said. His voice was lower. 'Missus is keeping an eye out. I'm almost done, an' all. My lad'll be back in a sec to 'elp lift. We've put 'er bench in, an' now this. I'm lookin' forrard to getting 'ome, if I'm 'onest.'

She stirred, already forming an apology for disturbing him, when something he had said sank in. 'Keeping an eye out?'

He looked surprised. 'Aye.' He cocked his head back in a sharp gesture. 'Ower in t' chu'chyard. She's mekkin' sure I've done that bench right, I'll warrant.'

She looked over his shoulder, across the lawn and through the trees towards the church. Beneath one of the bordering yews, standing under its shadow and dressed entirely in black, a lone figure looked back at her. Suddenly there didn't seem to be any air.

Then the woman raised a hand and beckoned, and Aggie didn't feel as if she was being invited into her future after all; she felt as if she'd just been trapped.

CHAPTER FOUR

The walk into the lane towards the churchyard seemed even longer than it had on the way to the house. Aggie had been there many times, to go to church services or weddings or christenings or funerals, but it was the latter she was reminded of when she glanced up and saw Mrs Hollingworth in her black gown, the veil pulled once more across her face. She was dressed all in mourning, just as if she had stepped out of some earlier time. No one heeded that formality any more, did they? But this woman did. She didn't appear to be watching Aggie. She stood facing the house, keeping perfectly still, and she didn't turn when Aggie drew close.

'Do you like it?' Her voice was smooth and cultured, just the way Aggie remembered. She had a fleeting image of the interview, the way the lady had looked upon her and hadn't smiled. The way she'd been preparing for so many things – her house, her new housemaid, her child: her life. Aggie's gaze flicked to her belly just as she turned around.

She saw only the veil and not her eyes but she felt the woman's look piercing her anyway. She was straight and unbending and she gave the merest nod towards the bench. The new stone was pale and didn't look as if it belonged in the old churchyard.

Aggie read the words – twice, just to be sure. She had known it wasn't going to be a good thing, a *nice* thing, but she still felt dismayed. The verse was written quite plainly this time, the larger surface allowing for the full translation: *My God, my God, why hast Thou forsaken me?*

Inwardly she shivered as the woman who would have been her mistress – *should* have been – slowly raised her hands and drew back her veil. Her healthful complexion had faded. Her face looked grey and her cheeks were sunken and her lips were almost blue. They had thinned to a narrow line. Only her eyes held any brightness, and Aggie found she could not look away from them.

'Do you like it?' Mrs Hollingworth asked.

Aggie nodded, but she couldn't meet her gaze.

'No. Nor did *they*.' She made a quick gesture towards the church. 'But it is Scripture, is it not? How could they argue with Scripture? And of course, they could not deny me – a woman in my circumstance. In my *condition*.' She stroked her belly, her eyes unfocused. Aggie wasn't sure what she meant by her *condition* – surely her condition was past? This woman was in no condition at all.

'And how do you like my house?'

This was safer and Aggie took in a deep breath, stepping forward so that she could see it better. The house looked solid and fine and unbearably lonely, but still she couldn't help but compare it with her own home: the low ceilings and narrow rooms that were always crowded and full of noise and where something always needed to be done. Then she realised: *my* house, the woman had called it. Hope rose and she smiled in spite of herself. 'It's beautiful, ma'am. I'm looking forward—'

'Looking *forward*.' Mrs Hollingworth drew in a long breath.

'It will be lovely,' Aggie blurted. 'It's so fine. You'll – I mean, it – will be happy again . . .' Her voice tailed away. The woman was silent, looking out on nothing, and the words hung in the air between them. 'It'll be lovely, ma'am. And you can have—'

She turned her head. 'Another?'

'I mean – I didn't mean—'

'No. Naturally, you didn't.' She sighed. 'But I do not believe I will. One cannot account for the fickleness of man, my dear, and I find I cannot account for my husband's preference at all. This – this would have saved all, but – *another* child, you say? Not from *my* belly, I doubt.' She stroked it again and Aggie tried not to focus on her pale, claw-like fingers. 'I shall not live here. I shall not set so much as a foot in the place again. Did you know, I built that house for love?' She gave a sharp laugh. 'For *love*. But love will never come to fill it.'

'Ma'am?'

'Such is my wish. There will be no laughter, no light, no *life* in that house. Do you hear me? And no children, not ever.'

Aggie had no answer. She shifted her feet, suddenly wishing she was a long way away, in their own little kitchen perhaps, squeezed in at the table as her mother's cooking bubbled on the stove, surrounded by noise and busyness and her brother's laughter. *Life*.

Mrs Hollingworth drew her lips into the semblance of a smile. 'And you, my dear. Do you think you'll have your heart's desire?'

'I beg your pardon?'

The almost-smile turned into an expression of scorn. 'Go home,' she said, 'go home and stay there. Be content.' She sighed, and when she spoke again her voice was distant. 'I fear it will not be, however. You will never be content. You shall never be happy. Never in this world.'

Aggie stared at her. She didn't think to be hurt by what the woman had said; she couldn't take it in. All she could think of was how she had been set to be a maid, at her service, to do what she might and bring comfort where she could. Now there was only the hard, too-bright stares, the strangeness of her words. She wanted to say something that would make it all right again, but she could not think of anything. She remembered the image of herself as the one bringing sugared tea and knowing exactly what to say. Now she knew that nothing was all right, that perhaps it would never be all right again. Her skin felt chilled under the woman's stare, as if it froze her where it touched. She only knew she didn't want to be here any longer, or to have this woman looking at her that way.

She took a step back and paused to give an awkward curtsey before she walked back the way she had come. She didn't look around again – she didn't dare – until she had passed under the lych-gate. She needn't have been afraid to look, however. Mrs Hollingworth was sitting on the bench again. She had turned away from her and was staring down once more towards the house.

CHAPTER FIVE

No one at church had mentioned the words carved into the bench, though it was all Aggie could think about. She wasn't sure they'd even noticed it; the mothers had gathered around the church door as usual, the men standing a little apart, talking about the weather or politics, neither of which she found of interest. She did see Will, though, standing with his friend Eddie Appleby from the next farm, and she found herself blushing when he winked at her. She didn't know whether she should laugh or be outraged, but the smile had broken out on her face before she'd really had the chance to decide. She had known him for years; he'd played sardines with them around the barn and the fold and the hayloft, before she'd grown too old to run about with the boys, to be teased and have them pull her hair. He had other brothers and a sister, but it was Eddie she knew best. He was nearest in age to Will, and the boys had always had some scheme or other to occupy them.

Now she was older, quite sixteen, and she stood a little more stiffly. She turned away from them, looking through the rows of gravestones. It was a sombre place to have so nearby, she supposed, though it had never occurred to her to think of it until today. It simply *was*. Now, with Mrs Hollingworth's bitter words carved in stone at the top of the hillside, it was more sombre still. At least her recent meeting had tempered her disappointment over her position. That future may not be hers, but surely another would soon begin, and anyway, before long there would be marriage and children and she needn't worry about going into service at all.

She frowned, unconsciously touching her hand to her belly. It wasn't something she'd considered before, although she supposed it would happen sometime. Would she have a boy or girl? How many? Would she be a good mother? If she had them, she would be kind. She would listen to all their little worries and she would understand; she would never wear a hard expression like Mrs Hollingworth. And then she remembered the woman making a similar gesture, touching her hand to her belly in just the same way, and she remembered her words: *I built this house for love.* And then: *But love will never come to fill it.*

She let her hand fall to her side and turned to look at the new house. She didn't know how she felt about it any longer. She noticed that beyond the deep green yews, the trees in the garden were beginning to turn. Was it autumn already? It didn't feel like it. Last night there had been rain; she had woken and heard it beating down, drenching the yard, but now the sun was shining, the air was clean, everything clearer after the storm.

A hand caught her arm and she jumped. She turned to see her mother, her eyebrows raised, amused at her reaction. Her dad and Will were with her and Aggie realised the gossips by the church door had dispersed. It was strangely early, and her mother's smile, when it came, was serious, as if there was no room for gossip in it. 'Come along, Dolly Daydream,' she said. 'There are things to do. And we don't want to miss the eleven o'clock.'

Aggie frowned. She couldn't think what her mum meant –
then she shrugged. They were all so serious these days, her dad
even more so than her mother. He scowled at all the broadcasts
on the wireless and she couldn't think why on earth he troubled
to listen if it upset him so. She glanced into the sky. It was blue
and peerless, dashed with scudding clouds. It didn't matter if the
trees in the garden told of the end of summer; it was clinging
still, even if there was a cooler note in the air, a breeze shivering
the hairs on her arms.

Once inside the kitchen, the others sat at the table. Her dad actually reached out and straightened the wireless before switching it
on, as if that mattered. It filled the kitchen with hissing and then
a voice started talking about how to make the best of tinned
food. Aggie looked over at her mother; she knew exactly what
she'd think of that. Aggie breathed in the smell of her mother's
roast, the air filled with the warm heady aroma. Will would be
hungry, she knew – he'd been up since dawn feeding the critters,
as her dad always put it, and he loved a Sunday roast – but when
she glanced at him, he didn't even look at her. He was watching
the wireless, his gaze serious, as if he knew something she did not.
She frowned. They were always listening to the wireless – why
should today be any different? Anyway, it was she who knew
something they did not. She could see it whenever she closed her
eyes, those words carved in stone, the woman sitting in her black
clothes, besmirching the churchyard with her despair. *Why hast
Thou forsaken me?* It felt almost blasphemous, and yet the woman
had been right: it was Scripture, after all.

She shook away the thought and her mother grasped her
shoulders, hard, as if bidding her to keep still. She wriggled in

protest as the sound changed and the prime minister began to speak, and she listened in spite of herself because somehow Chamberlain's tone was different to his other broadcasts. Now her mother seemed to have drawn in on herself, staring down at the table, which was notched with the marks from her knife and her mother's before that. Her dad sat perfectly still. Only Will met her eye and as he did, he gave a tiny shake of his head.

When she heard the words, she simply couldn't believe them. The prime minister had said he was going to stop it all and she had believed him. *Peace in our time*, he'd told them, and now there was this, something she had heard the men speak of but had never quite believed: *This country is at war with Germany*.

She had seen the gasmasks, those ridiculous bulky things that had been issued to them all, that were now stowed in the cupboard under the stairs. She had tried one on and decided it was nasty and smelly and made her feel sick, and she most certainly wasn't going to wear it. She had seen her mother hiding away the public information leaflets about blackout regulations and the best places to shelter, and she had wondered why they troubled to send them all the way out here, miles away from anybody and anything that could possibly have need of them. Now her mum stretched out her hand across the table, finding her dad's sleeve and dragging on it uselessly.

'So,' he said at last. 'That's that, then.'

Will pushed back his chair and everyone jumped as the wood scraped against the flagstones. 'They'll need everyone they can get,' he said. 'They'll be sending us to Germany.' There was an odd light in his eyes, bright and cold all at the same time, and it reminded Aggie for a moment of the woman in the churchyard.

Her dad raised a hand and slammed it down against the table. He pushed himself up from his chair and switched off the wireless, and silence came to fill the room. Then he said, 'No one's going anywhere.' He looked around as if waiting for someone to contradict him, but no one did. He glanced at Aggie and then at Will, looking long and hard into his face. 'We shall need everyone to do extra,' he said. 'We'll get that top field planted again. Might get another crop o' barley in, if t' weather keeps. You can 'elp. So can Ag.' He shifted his gaze to her but it was as if he wasn't really seeing her, and it felt as if he was really saying something else. He curled his hand into a fist and rapped at the table as if he were knocking at a door. 'They need farmers, times like this,' he said. 'They'll need all of us, you'll see – they dun't just need soldiers. They'll want all t' farmers they can get.'

He sat down again, all the tension going out of him. After a moment he waved a hand, like a teacher dismissing a class. They looked at each other. No one said anything. Aggie could hear words, though, in her mind, as close as if they were being hissed into her ear: *You will never be content. You shall never be happy.*

She shook them away as if they were physical things. She felt the coldness as it spread into her bones. It was as if it were her sitting there on that bench in the first harsh breath of autumn and thinking of the loss of everything she'd ever believed in. It was as if the woman had reached out somehow and cursed her with her words: *You shall never be happy.*

Aggie felt a pat on her arm and she turned, startled. Her mum was trying to smile but it looked as if she would burst into tears at any moment. 'Of course we'll all help, won't we, love? You can do more about the farm, can't you, Ag?'

She remembered those days in the fields, the hot sun melting on her shoulders, the scratching of barley ruining her hands, the sight of the crop spreading almost as far as she could see. And the rabbits; she remembered the rabbits, the crunch of her brother's pitchfork. She closed her eyes. If she'd gone into service already they could surely never have called her back. She would have escaped. She might not even be here, feeling the tension spreading over the room, the seriousness and the anger and the frustration – and yes, the fear.

But she shouldn't think about herself at such a time, couldn't make a fuss. She nodded at her mother without really focusing on her face. It was her brother she wanted to look at, but somehow she didn't dare; then she heard him make an odd sound in the back of his throat, as if he had something to say but didn't know how to say it. She looked at him. She saw her brother was growing into a man. He had always been taller than her, but now he stood over them all. His jaw was clenched and his hands were curled into fists. He looked older somehow; he looked *ready*. When she looked into his eyes, she saw that he too wasn't really seeing what lay before him: he was focused on something a long way away.

CHAPTER SIX

Aggie saw Mrs Hollingworth again early the next morning.

She'd been sent to collect the eggs, a task which sounded simple but which she knew would involve clambering onto the roof of the fold and into the hayloft and anywhere else the chickens may have chosen to lay. They were always coming up with new places: underneath the cart, among her mother's prickly roses, even in the back of the sty where the sow lived. They had their own nest boxes with comfortable straw inside, but they didn't seem to like them. They were shut up safe from the foxes at night but if they weren't let outside early in the morning they wouldn't lay at all. It was as if they were trying to protect them from anything that may come. This morning she had found two eggs in the boxes and had considered herself lucky until she'd seen one of them *hop-pecking* its way along the wooden ridge of the outhouse.

The outhouse had brick walls and a wooden roof, and none of it was level. A clump of leaves was caught in the guttering and she knew at once that was where the egg would be. She sighed as she fetched the ladder from the barn, knowing her hands would soon be covered in mossy slime.

The wooden ladder was heavy and the heat gathered under her bib overalls as she balanced it against the wall. She checked her pocket was empty for carrying the egg so that she wouldn't have to climb down again one-handed and then she pulled herself up. She placed both feet carefully onto each rung, cursing the chicken under her breath. When she reached the top, though, her annoyance turned to pity.

There was an egg, but it was broken. There was a shattered hole in the top and most of the insides had gone, probably stolen by a jackdaw or a magpie. She pulled a face. Then she looked up and over the roof, across the fields, and down to the church. A cool breeze lifted her hair. For a moment she thought she detected the flat taint of the river in it.

She caught her breath. Someone was sitting near the top of the churchyard. She was perfectly motionless and dressed all in black and sitting on the bench – the *cursed* bench.

No children, not ever.

She looked down at the egg. It didn't mean anything; it wasn't as if the egg had ever been going to grow into a chick. She didn't know why she'd even thought of those words. She reached out and before she could think about it she lifted the shell and dropped it to the ground, hearing it smash onto the cobbles below. She looked back towards the churchyard only once before she began her descent; the woman hadn't moved at all.

Later, Aggie helped her mother sort through their things, finding old clothes they didn't need or that were too small, blankets that had thinned in the middle, old knitting that could be unravelled. Her mother put it all in bags, adding the scraps she'd saved from her sewing for making into rag rugs or dolls. When they'd finished they loaded the bags into the cart and backed the quieter of their horses into the traces. Her dad usually did this, but he was busy in the fields; she knew he would be for ever pointing out how much more convenient it was to have horses than an engine that ran on petrol they didn't have and couldn't easily buy. The horse stamped and snorted at her. When they were ready her mother climbed up onto the seat and then she stared at Aggie, as if she was waiting.

She frowned. Then she jumped up beside her mother and took the reins. She pulled on them and the horse turned into the lane as easily as it always did for her dad. She rather liked driving. There was something about the steady hollow clop of hooves on the road and the lazy way she swayed against her mother's side, the sense of being in control, of being able to go wherever she wished.

When they passed the church she turned her head and saw Mrs Tunstall from the village, just heading inside with a bundle of rags and a tin of Mansion Polish. She liked to 'do' for the place. Her mother nodded at her, keeping both hands primly clasped over her handbag on her lap. Aggie looked towards the bench. Mrs Hollingworth was still there. She didn't look as if she had moved at all; she was still staring down at the house she had sworn never to live in.

'Well, would you look at that?' her mother said.

Aggie didn't reply.

''Appen she's come to live 'ere after all. Mebbe she'll make 'ersen useful.'

'I don't think so,' Aggie said. 'I think she's just come – to watch, or something.'

'Well, if she doesn't it's criminal, that's what it is. Building a fancy place like that, like she's some grand lady, an' leavin' it stood . . . I did 'ear 'er 'usband's staying in t' city now, though – God above knows why, wi' bombs about to fall about their ears. Wicked to keep that 'ouse empty. They're lucky it 'asn't been commandeered. They should do – they should fill it wi' folks that needs it, little mites bein' sent away from their mothers, women wi' bairns—'

It was as if she'd realised what she'd said, suddenly remembering the woman's own disappointment, and she softened her tone. 'Well, 'appen she'll sort herself out in time. Aye, 'appen she will—' and she gestured towards the road, as if Aggie had been about to wander off the track, as if the horse would have strayed into the hedgerow; as if the mare hadn't been this way a thousand times before.

The village hall was crammed. It looked like everyone Aggie had ever known was there – or at least the women. They bustled around, sorting wool and parcelling it out, cutting up old clothes, heaping scraps into a pile. The low whirr of treadles and the higher buzz of electric sewing machines came from the next room and everywhere was the press of bodies and the murmur of conversation, and an occasional whooping laugh drowning out the rest. Among them, those in Women's Voluntary Service uniforms – smart green tweed with red piping and official-looking badges – oversaw the proceedings, 'doing the national job', looking stern when the laughter pealed too loudly.

Her mother headed towards the sorting area as if she knew exactly where to go, and Aggie followed. She didn't know when she'd ever seen such a horrid crush. She barely listened to any particular words amid the general thrum, but then she caught:

'Aye, under t' yew tree.'

'It's shameful, 'avin' them words put there. Carved in stone, an' all. Shameful. An' 'er not even a local.'

'She'll tek sick, sittin' there. Anyone'll tell yer. Sittin' under a yew, it'll mek 'er sick.'

There was a lull and Aggie looked for the speaker. It was Mrs Pinchbeck, the greengrocer's wife.

'She's already sick, like as not,' her mother said in a lower voice.

'Aye, well. *Forsaken*, indeed. Someone wi' them thoughts in their 'ead – *bad* thoughts – it in't no wonder it were born dead.'

Aggie stared. It was a thin-faced woman who spoke. She lived in a cottage at the edge of the village; had been a widow for as long as Aggie could remember.

Her mother was staring too. Then she roused herself. 'We'll finish up 'ere,' she said, 'and then we'll go back t' long way. I need to call by Mrs Marsden's. Her lad joined up four months back – I want t' see 'ow she's keepin' on.' Then she spoke louder, as if she wanted everyone to hear, 'No 'arm in looking after our neighbours, is there, Aggie? No time for tittle-tattle.' She straightened and shook out the bag she carried, which was now empty.

Aggie sensed their eyes on her back as they walked away. She wasn't really thinking about the things they'd said. All she felt was relief, not only to be leaving the noisy press, but because they would be going home the long way round, by the top of the hill and down the lane. They wouldn't have to pass the house and they wouldn't pass the churchyard; they wouldn't need to see if the woman was still there, sitting all alone and perfectly still.

CHAPTER SEVEN

Aggie went into her room, ensuring the door had closed behind her. Slats of faint light from the kitchen below probed the gaps in the floorboards and she toed at her rag rug, trying to cover the worst of them. The light faded. She didn't need it, not in here. She shuffled onto her bed and pushed the window open. Cold air rushed into her face but she leaned out, resting her elbows on the broad sill.

It wasn't fully dark but the sky was already the smudged grey of a charcoal drawing. When she looked up, she couldn't see any stars. The sky looked impossibly far away and just as indifferent, and then she heard a cow lowing and the answering snuffle of a horse, and everything was familiar again, just her home once more.

She couldn't see the church spire or the house beyond it, but there was nothing strange in that. There was a blackout. Mum had even taken away her dad's matches earlier that evening so he wouldn't forget and light one of his Capstans outside. There were fines for such things; the newspaper was full of it. Besides, everybody had to do what they could.

That made her think of Eddie Appleby. Before much longer he would be gone, and no one could say when he'd be coming back. When she imagined him, he looked different; she supposed he *was* different now. He probably didn't think of her at all. He'd be standing tall in his uniform, his expression determined, and probably with that same distant look in his eyes she'd seen in her brother's. She imagined him looking a little sad too, in a way she couldn't define. She sighed. Until now she had only really thought of him as her brother's childhood friend and now he was leaving, going to the front with so many other young men. She didn't like to think of that, especially not now, looking out into the cold dark. She had wondered what a blackout would be like, but she realised that out here where there was nothing it all looked much the same as it always had. Nestled in amid the hillsides, it had always felt like they could be a thousand miles from anywhere.

She jumped as a harsh banging sounded, not on her door, but through the floorboards. Aggie caught her breath; for a moment she thought her mother knew that she'd opened the window, then she heard: 'Aggie! Downstairs – I've got summat I need you for!'

She quietly closed the window and drew the curtains across the glass, covering the pale reflection of her face. She pulled the blackout curtains right up to the edges and went to see what it was her mother wanted.

She was sitting sewing by the light of an old paraffin lamp. The electricity was off and there was only the lamp and the soft glow from the stove. Everything smelled of oil and Aggie wrinkled her nose. Did her mother think the house must be blacked out inside too? She did not dare to ask. Her mother had her *things to be doing* look on her face. She had snipped open some old socks and was stitching them together again. She was making little bags, sewing squares of paper to the front.

'It's for when they're in 'ospital,' she said, 'so the soldiers 'ave something to put their things in. They can write their names on t' front, see?'

Aggie did see, and yet she had the feeling she *didn't*. She hadn't thought of it before, young men being in hospital after being shot or gassed. She swallowed and thought of Eddie. Her throat felt dry.

'I need you to go over to that 'ouse.' Her mother didn't need to say which house; Aggie knew. 'Yer dad's 'aving a lie down and your brother's gone to see Eddie before he leaves. That woman was there on 'er tod all day. If she's in that 'ouse she might need an 'and, love. Wi' t' blackout, I mean. Just you run along and see if she's all right.'

Aggie thought of walking alone down the lane in the dark. She knew it almost as well as the farmhouse, but suddenly it was *different*.

'I'll not 'ave 'em sayin' mean things,' her mother continued. 'It's for neighbours to 'elp each other, an' that's what we'll be doing.'

What *I'll* have to do, Aggie thought, but when her mother lowered her sewing she saw how tired she looked. She couldn't possibly refuse. She nodded.

'Good girl.'

Aggie still didn't move.

'It's on'y going to get darker.'

At that Aggie grabbed her coat and waited for her mother to cover the lamp before she slipped out.

The sky looked featureless, yet it still held a certain diffuse light, as if a bright moon was hiding somewhere behind the clouds. As she crossed the yard a dark shape slipped from the shadow of the house and slid itself against her legs. Her heart leapt until she heard a brief purr. She put out a hand to stroke the cat, but it just as quickly slipped away. She peered across the yard.

Everything was silent. She remembered the sound of the air-raid siren from when they'd tested it out, rising eerily from somewhere beyond the fields, and she shivered. She pulled her collar tighter around her neck. For a moment she felt suspended between going on and going back, and then she reminded herself her mother would be furious if she didn't do what she was told. If Aggie complained of the dark, she'd only laugh and say she should eat her carrots. Anyway, she had been right: it was getting darker all the time. She went on, picking her way across the cobbles.

The surface of the lane was smoother and she walked straight down the middle. She passed the lych-gate, all thick charcoal lines against the sky, nothing visible beyond it. A part of her was glad; she didn't wish to think about what she might see there. *Only stones*, she thought. She had been there a thousand times before and she had never been afraid – only once, anyway.

The house was barely visible, just a slightly darker outline against the sky. Her mother needn't have worried. Of course Mrs Hollingworth would never have stayed there. Aggie couldn't imagine her even setting foot inside. The house had been abandoned and shrouded in darkness long before the blackout had even come to be. There was no light – *No life*, she thought – and no need to cover its windows.

She turned to leave, and then she paused. She could already hear her mother's voice in her ear: *So there were no answer at t' door then?*

Of course she would expect her to knock. If she didn't, what would she say – that she'd walked down the lane and seen that the house was dark and simply gone home again? The house was *supposed* to be dark, everywhere was. Her mother had expected her to check on its occupant. If she didn't she might even be sent out again a second time and by then the darkness would be absolute. Aggie grimaced. There was no help for it, so she walked up the drive, catching her breath at the sound of deep gravel under her feet. She thought she could see the darker rectangle of the door and she kept her eyes on it, and then her knee hit something and she pitched forward. She put out both hands to break her fall and sprawled across some object, its surface smooth and cold and hard.

She made an odd sound, then smothered it, fighting the way her breathing threatened to run out of control. She ran her hand over the thing, squinting to make out its outline. How hadn't she seen it? It was a car, nothing more – and why not? The woman must have got here somehow, and she had money; she surely wouldn't always take the train. And yet it was wildly extravagant, when there was already talk of petrol running short. She knew exactly what her mother would say: *It's wicked, that's what it is. A wicked waste.* It was the same thing she'd said about the house, standing empty when it could have sheltered so many, providing a refuge to children and women from the cities.

Aggie knew she was only delaying the thought that was in the back of her mind. She was going to have to knock after all, and the unthinkable might happen: Mrs Hollingworth might answer. She would open the door and smile that cold smile and step back and Aggie would have to go inside.

But it wasn't any use. Her mother would skin her if she went back now. She bent and rubbed her bruised knee, took in a gulp of the cold and strode up to the door and stepped under its shadow. Her first knock was tentative. She tried again. As she waited, she placed her hand flat against the door. It felt cold as stone, not something that would open, not to her. She let out the breath she had been holding. She didn't like to turn her back on the house, not now, but she would be home in hardly any time at all, quicker perhaps, since she intended to run all the way.

It was only when she reached the end of the drive that she stopped dead and looked back over her shoulder. The coldness had spread; it had come out of the night and seeped into her. It must have numbed her, stopping her from thinking, because she was stupid; stupid to think this place – that woman – had finished with her so easily.

Mrs Hollingworth wasn't home, *but the car was still here*.

She turned her head and looked into the dark. She knew exactly where she was going to be. Deep down she had always known.

Once she stepped through the lych-gate she could see the graves, indistinct slabs that faded into the dark. Beyond that it looked as if there was nothing but sky, but she could picture the hillside as clearly as if it were daylight. She knew her way to the stone seat with its bitter words and the ancient yew tree standing sentinel over it.

She wondered if Mrs Hollingworth was still staring down towards the house, her eyes unseeing, everything swallowed by the dark, and she shuddered. It occurred to her now that she could go back home and ask someone to go with her. There would be no shame in that. She could barely see and she had already done her duty; they surely wouldn't expect her to walk up here, between the graves, alone.

She started to walk anyway, but it felt like she was being drawn along, as if she didn't have any choice; as if she was supposed to *see*. Perhaps she could help after all, take the woman's arm and walk with her to the farm and show her that it was better to forgive everything and take refuge in the cheerfulness of her neighbours.

She remembered the way she'd spoken – *never be happy* – and she shook her head.

Her footsteps were silent. Somehow she didn't feel afraid of the crooked gravestones; she knew there were worse things. It was the well of darkness ahead that she dreaded. She thought the shapes were becoming more defined as she went – the yew trees, the ones her mother said had stood here for centuries, before there was even a church. It was easy to believe now – it would have been harder *not* to believe it. She could hear their whispering, like soft voices talking of things it would perhaps be better not to know. Her mother had told her once that their roots stretched down to the lips of every sleeper in their graves, finding out their secrets; perhaps, now, they were whispering the words of the dead.

Her breath was irregular and she didn't like to hear it. It was easier to tell herself that she wasn't afraid without that ragged sound in her ear. She drew a deep draught of cold air and it caught in her throat.

She must be close now. Anyone sitting there in the quiet dark must have heard her approach. They might even be looking straight at her. She forced herself to call out a soft greeting. Her voice didn't sound steady, not like the voice of someone who could help, but it was too late to take it back. Anyway, there was no reply. Was the woman sleeping? Exhaustion might have taken her, dragging her under before she could rouse herself to move. Aggie forced herself to take another step. It became darker still as she stood under the spreading branches. The seat was a paler shape against the trunk. Though the words written there were mercifully lost to sight she knew they were there, and that didn't help.

Now she could see a darker shape against the bench, but she couldn't bring herself to go nearer.

'Mrs Hollingworth?'

There was no movement, no sound except the soughing in the branches. She swallowed. There was grit in her throat. She opened her mouth to call out but no sound emerged; her voice was lost to the night air and the silence.

It'll mek 'er sick, she thought.

She took another step forward, half-believing she was caught in some awful dream. The war, the woman, all of it – none of it might be real after all. She would wake up to find herself back in the summer, her hands scratched from the harvest, and this time she wouldn't mind; she wouldn't shy away from the early rising or the hard work or the sun beaming down on her head. She would welcome it all.

She reached out towards where Mrs Hollingworth's shoulder should be. She was only half-conscious of doing it. She couldn't make out any features, hadn't heard anything at all. Her fingers met something cold and smooth. 'Ma'am?' Her voice was a whisper. There was no response; the woman didn't even move.

She stayed there a moment, her arm outstretched, just touching the silk of her dress. Then, slowly, she edged around her.

She could see the paler shape of her face under the veil. She bent closer. Now she could make out the fine black lace, the shining silk of her dress. She didn't know how she'd dared touch the fabric. She started, when she saw that the woman's eyes were open. 'I'm sorry, I—'

Mrs Hollingworth didn't move. Aggie stared down, her heart beating so fast that it almost pained her. She could hear her own breath. She could not hear the woman's.

No: she must be sleeping, that was all. She forced herself to put out a hand and touch her shoulder once more and very gently shook her. She surely wouldn't mind – she surely would be grateful to be roused and taken from such a place. She might even be afraid, waking out here on this cold night. She could come back to the farm and her mother would bustle around her, making tea or Horlicks, and everything would be all right.

The woman's hands slid forwards, her fingers so cold against Aggie's own as she tried to steady her, and all at once she *knew*. Of course she had known; as soon as she had found the house empty she should have run all the way back to the farm and light and her mother's hearth.

The woman was dead weight in her arms. If she let go, she would fall. Aggie let out a sob at the cold touch on her skin. She saw that the woman's eyes were huge and dilated, staring sightlessly into her own, and she thrust her away, not caring now if she fell, and she turned and ran.

The graveyard seemed rougher, the stones appearing suddenly in front of her so that she had to dodge from side to side, and there were mounds everywhere, all of it in tones of silver. There was no one in the world, no one to help her – then she saw the black sketch of the lych-gate and she rushed through it into the lane. Her throat felt raw. She put her head down and ran harder and that was when she hit something like a high wall where no wall should be, except that it was soft and giving and had arms that closed around her, and she screamed as she heard the answering voices calling her back.

CHAPTER EIGHT

Eventually they had to strike a match and never mind the blackout. For a moment her brother's face was lurid in the light that flickered in Eddie's hand and then his friend dropped it and she heard him blow on his fingers. 'We'd better not light another, Aggie,' he said, his voice gentle.

She shook her head, then realised they couldn't see her. She found she didn't care. Fleetingly, she wished her brother gone, and then everything flooded back. She wanted to cry. She could still feel the touch of the woman's hands on hers. She didn't trust herself to speak – and then she heard her brother, soothing her, telling her everything was all right.

Between deep breaths she told them what she had found, expecting them to comfort her, but instead her brother said something about fetching their father and she was left alone with Eddie after all. She was no longer sure it was what she wanted – she wished she had been the one to run up the lane towards her mother's kitchen. But then Eddie put a hand on her arm – she jumped when he touched her – and he said, 'Best get to the side, Aggie. If anyone comes . . .'

He was right: if a car came along in the blackout with its headlights masked, anything could happen. She was lucky it hadn't already. She had a sudden image of loose limbs flipping up and into the windscreen and the shrieking of brakes, but she pushed it away.

She stood with Eddie and he didn't speak but she could feel him there, a warm, living presence at her side. She remembered the way he'd lit a match for her, though he could have been fined ten shillings if anyone had seen. She hugged herself, then wiped her fingers against her coat. That touch was still on them: cold – *dead*. She shivered, and heard Eddie slip off his own coat and place it securely around her shoulders.

Then she heard her brother's voice, calling their names, and Eddie hailed him. 'You're to come inside,' he said. 'Mum wants Aggie indoors. She's brewing up. Dad's gone off to your house, Eddie; he wants to use your telephone.'

They sat at the table sipping cups of tea and no one looked at each other. Aggie's mum and Will had gone out to meet her father, leaving her alone with Eddie once more. She set down the cup and it rattled against the saucer.

'It'll be all right, Aggie,' he said. 'You did just the right thing. Your dad will see everything's done as best they can. I wish – I mean, you shouldn't have had to see—'

She looked up at him. He was leaving in the morning and for a time she hadn't even known it; he had told her brother first. No one had thought to tell her. He was going to be with all the rest of them, the boys with the faraway look in their eyes, but for now he was here and he was just Eddie again, the boy she'd known all her life.

He started to say something else but it turned into a tentative smile, and then he looked down at the table as if he could read something in its scars.

'What is it, Eddie?'

He half-smiled. 'I suppose it's just that sometimes you don't really *see* things,' he said, 'and then it's too late.'

She swallowed. That dry feeling was back in her throat. 'It's never—'

The door opened and she turned to see her brother standing there, his shoulders heaving as he drew in rapid breaths. 'Well,' he said, 'she's dead.'

Aggie looked away. Nobody said anything. After a while Will poured himself a cup of tea and pulled out a chair. She couldn't seem to settle her thoughts. She knew she had been about to answer Eddie, but she had no idea what she would have said. Why did Will have to come back just then?

Then her brother spoke, and when he did she saw again that he looked older, not the playful, teasing, irritating boy she had always known. 'I may as well tell you I've enlisted, Aggie.'

She whirled in her seat. 'You've done *what*?'

'I had to do *something*. I can't simply stay here, safe from everything. Someone has to stand, Aggie. Eddie's going, and I'm going too.'

'But you can't! It's impossible – Dad's going to *kill* you.'

For a while he didn't say anything at all, he just kept staring into his cup, and then he let out a hollow laugh. It wasn't really funny, but it wasn't mocking either. She thought he'd say something else, but nothing came. And then she remembered the little bags her mother had been stitching – *They can write their names on t' front, see?* – and she started again, 'Really, you can't. We need you here, Dad said so. And it's – I mean – anything could happen.' She didn't look at Eddie though she could feel his gaze; she felt as if he had touched her cheek, ever so lightly.

Will looked up at her and smiled. He gestured towards the door, the outside, the body she'd discovered in the graveyard. 'There's death everywhere, Aggie,' he said. 'It's no use waiting till it comes to find you.'

Then her mother bustled in, all questions, and what her brother had told her was pushed aside.

CHAPTER NINE

When Aggie went downstairs the next morning she could see that her mother knew what Will had done. It was there in her tight lips and her pale skin. She barely looked at Aggie. She had let her sleep late and now she saw it wasn't out of consideration so much as having her thoughts occupied with more important things. Aggie went to the stove. A cold egg lay half-congealed in a pan and she scooped it onto a plate. She sat down at the table and stared at it.

'Doctor called by, afore,' her mother said. Her voice sounded tired. Older.

Aggie scooped cold egg white into her mouth and forced herself to swallow. She didn't want to think about last night, about what had become of the woman. She didn't want to think of her as *Mrs Hollingworth*, as if the figure on the bench had been someone she *knew*. And she didn't, not really. She only knew her married name, not her own, not even her first name; she didn't have any real connection with her at all. She wished now that the woman was a long way away, that she'd never even come here, never thought of building the house.

Then she remembered the way Eddie had sat here at this very table, the way he'd looked at her and spoken to her, how he'd wrapped his coat around her, and her cheeks reddened.

'He said she likely 'ad yew poisoning.'

Aggie put down her knife and fork, her thoughts banished. 'Do you mean it's true, what they said – about her sitting under the yew? That it made her ill?' But what she was thinking of was not the yew but the bench beneath it, the letters that had been carved there. *Perhaps it was those words that poisoned her; maybe it was some kind of punishment.*

Her mother shook her head. 'No, that's rubbish – just another story about them trees, that's all. There's all sorts o' tales. But she din't take sick from sitting there. She'd etten it.'

'Etten it?'

'Aye, leaves and berries and seeds an' all, by the looks o' things. Awful business. The doctor said it would 'ave finished 'er off in no time: it made her lips turn blue and her eyes go wide-open an' her 'eart give out.'

Her eyes go wide-open. Yes, it had. Aggie shuddered at the memory. When she looked up again, her mother was staring down at the floor as if she were seeing some memory of her own; and she remembered something she'd said. As if reading her mind, her mother let out a spurt of a laugh. 'You know, those old stories,' she said, 'about the trees – some say they spread their roots 'round the graveyard to stop them who's buried there from coming back to the world. Others say that putting yew on a grave 'elps a soul find the other side. Some—' She paused, and then went on, 'Some tell as 'ow it makes gateways. There's one about 'ow people eatin' yew – they get to see the other place. The *after* place. An' then they come back.'

She turned to her sewing basket and took out some pieces of fabric, spreading them in front of her. 'So that showed them, I 'spose,' she said. ''Appen she did see the afterlife all right. But there in't no way she's coming back again.'

CHAPTER TEN

Aggie walked slowly across the field, enjoying the sensation of the breeze in her face. She turned and Jack the dog gave a little jump; he looked as if he was grinning. She smiled at him. Her limbs ached and her hands were sore, but it didn't matter. She was almost at the boundary of the farm now. She wondered how Eddie's family were coping on the next one. Another of his brothers had gone for the Air Force and she'd heard his dad had taken on Land Girls to help. She frowned. If she'd joined the Women's Land Army she'd have had fresh new breeches and a little felt hat with a fancy badge on it, and when she went into the village she'd have looked as if she was really doing something for the war. But it didn't matter. She had been doing things she never thought she'd be doing, driving the cart, managing deliveries, topping beets, cutting logs for burning. It was something different from dusting, and her father kept saying as how she'd done a 'grand job', although there was a sad look in his eyes when he said it. Still, the work was making her stronger. She even felt like she stood a little taller. Much of her spare time went on helping her mother knit blankets or sew more of those little bags, but just now she had a little reprieve, some rare time to herself, and it was nice to be up here, away from everything. She looked right across the tops of the rolling hills, dotted with trees that were losing their foliage. It seemed so short a time since the end of summer and yet so long ago, and now autumn too was beginning to fade. So much was changing and yet she was still here. It wasn't what she'd imagined. She'd thought one day she'd go far away, see whatever there was to see, leaving her brother to take over the farm. Now he was the one far away, seeing – *what?* Things, she supposed, that she never wanted to look upon.

She stood there a little longer. The lone cry of a curlew pierced the air. She half-closed her eyes. Her mother had told her once it was a bad omen, the curlew's call: sailor folk said its wailing was a warning from a drowned friend. She felt a passing relief that it wasn't the Navy Eddie had joined and then she shook the thought away – *thank goodness for Will too* – but, really, it hadn't been her brother's face she had been thinking of. She touched her cheek, remembering the way that Eddie had looked at her. What might he have said to her if Will had not come in? But it was too late to dwell on it now.

She looked down into the valley and realised she could see the chimneys of the big house from where she stood. She walked a little further so that she could see into the driveway: a car was parked on it, close by the porch. As she watched, someone stepped out. It was a man in a trilby; she couldn't see his face. She thought she could hear the metallic sound as he shut the door behind him. He tilted back his head and stared up at the windows. Even without seeing his face, she felt certain it was no one she knew. Her heart began to beat a little more quickly. She supposed she should be glad, but instead she didn't really know what she felt. She remembered her girlish excitement at the thought of being a maid in such a fine house, of working for someone, of being all grown up. It felt so distant now, as if those feelings had belonged to someone else. Now her hands were rough and she had calluses on her palms and she didn't care. It occurred to her that if she'd gone for a maid she would have been black-leading the grates and emptying the commodes and scrubbing the steps and her hands would have been ruined anyway. Now she didn't have to slave away in service; she had work, but it was all right. And at least the farm was *theirs*.

She looked back to see the man walking around the car and putting out a hand to assist someone from the passenger side. It was a tall, straight woman, her hair swept back neatly under her hat, and Aggie thought she was wearing a fox-fur stole. She let out her breath. A part of her had been expecting to see *her*, back the way she was at the beginning, big with child and full of hope; and then the two of them walked towards the house and vanished inside. They appeared to be alone. There were no children.

Nothing else happened and she looked instead towards the church. She could see the upper reaches of the graveyard and it looked quiet and empty, a place where nothing ever happened. The yew stood proud, its branches a thick crown. She narrowed her eyes. In the shadows beneath it the old twisted tree limbs were confusing to the eye; for a moment it had almost looked as if someone was sitting there, quite motionless, so that they blended with the shape of the tree.

'Bold as brass she was,' her mother said, bashing down her pastry with her rolling pin, sending flour flying from the pine table. 'Already! I know folk are quick to wed in wartime, but you'd think he'd 'ave waited a *little* longer.'

She glanced at Aggie. 'Wanted to know if we'd 'eard of any good servants. I ask you! Anyone'd think they didn't know there's a war on.'

She didn't seem to see the contradiction in what she'd said, but Aggie wasn't about to point it out. She couldn't help be curious about the newcomer. Had she really stolen Mr Hollingworth's affections before his first wife died? Thinking of the previous wife's coldness, she couldn't help but feel a twinge of sympathy.

'She was asking about eggs. I told 'er they'd need their coupons. I can't just go sneaking things on the hush-hush, not wi' them bein' new, an' all.'

Her father grunted. ''S prob'ly the on'y reason she called. They sound like snooties to me.'

'Well, snooties or not, at least she was being neighbourly.' Now her father had joined in, it was as if she wanted a reason to argue. 'An' it'll make a change to have that place full.'

'Not that full.'

'No, well, I dare say they'll rattle about in it. It's still a wicked waste o' rooms.'

'No children?' Aggie hadn't thought to say the words out loud, but now they hung in the air.

'Of course, no children.' Her mother turned on her. 'What did you think? 'E's been quick but 'e in't that quick, at least I jolly well 'ope not.' She turned the pastry and bashed it again. 'An it dun't sound like 'e's stoppin' round 'ere, anyways. Runs a fact'ry in London, so I dare say 'e won't be about much.'

Aggie thought of the new wife, alone in the big house, and shuddered.

'That woman named the place too, apparently, before she went.'

Aggie started: it was as if her mother had been thinking the same thing.

'Not a nice name, either: Mire House it is now. I dare say 'e won't change it neither, it bein' 'er last wish an' all.'

'Bad ground, that,' her dad remarked.

Aggie frowned. Had that really been the woman's last wish? She thought of the things she'd said to her: *No laughter, no light, no life in that house . . . And no children, not ever.* Somehow, she thought that naming the house had been the least of it.

'She said she'd be 'aving a soirée before long.' Her mother's nose wrinkled over the word. 'A *soirée*. Fancy that. Can you imagine?'

Aggie straightened. She opened her mouth to protest, to remind her mother that they all needed a diversion, a reason to forget about the war and the work and their worries and simply laugh, perhaps even dance, just for a while; and then she saw her expression and she closed it again.

Soirée, she thought, replaying the sound of the word as her mother talked, trying to smother the smile that was threatening to break out on her face.

CHAPTER ELEVEN

Aggie no longer liked to walk past the graveyard alone. No matter how she tried to keep her eyes fixed on the lane she couldn't help but look up through the gravestones towards the yew tree. A little part of her remained convinced that the first Mrs Hollingworth would still be sitting there, staring out at nothing, but of course she was never there. The seat was empty. She had never seen anyone sitting in that particular spot and she supposed now that it was abandoned. There was no one to look upon the words that had been written there, and she was glad of it.

And the house – *Mire House* as it was now – had people in it again. She sometimes heard voices drifting through the open windows, what she thought of as *smart* voices, *not-from-round-here* voices. She still hadn't really seen the new wife, despite her curious glances. There was no news of the 'soirée'. Perhaps even now they might be preparing for it, polishing glasses and winding the gramophone. There had been more talk in the village of them asking for servants, but everyone who might have done it had either enlisted or volunteered. Even the girls had gone for the W.V.S. or the Land Army or best of all, to the envy of the rest, the smartly dressed Wrens. They had choices aplenty now. Sometimes Aggie felt she was the only one who had been left behind, the only one whose options had actually been *reduced* by the war.

You will never be content. You shall never be happy.

She pushed the thought away. Anyway, thinking about the war meant wondering about Eddie or Will, and she didn't want to do that, not now. She certainly didn't want her mind to turn to the enemy, firing their bullets or releasing gases that choked and blinded. She pulled a face. They were supposed to carry their gasmasks everywhere and the box was hanging at her side now from its piece of string, its weight so familiar she had almost forgotten it was there.

She paused in her walk down the lane and looked at Mire House. The car parked in the driveway was a highly polished Daimler. The building looked just the same as it always had, but she thought she could see the glint of a crystal chandelier in the front room. Despite that, it still gave the impression of being abandoned, as if it had an emptiness that could never be filled.

And then she started, because she realised that someone was looking back at her. A small figure was standing on the edge of the lawn. She didn't know how she had failed to notice it before because it had bright golden curls crowning its head. She looked more closely and realised it was a boy. He wore ragged grey shorts and a shirt that had possibly once been white and a V-neck pully over the top – even from here she could see that it was full of holes. There was something pinned to the front of it, a piece of paper with lettering on it. His face was pale and streaked; it looked as if he had been crying.

He didn't look away, just kept on staring until it was past the point of rudeness. Aggie realised she was staring too. She opened her mouth to greet him, but somehow she didn't speak. She knew at once that he had come from somewhere else, a different world to the one she knew. Then a voice rang out: 'Now where *is* that other one? Come along child, it's your turn.' The voice was raised and irritated and *smart*, and before she had known she was going to move, Aggie stepped back behind the gatepost.

She peered out again in time to see the boy being pulled inside, a tall woman with light brown hair grasping his sleeve with blood-red fingertips. Aggie breathed a sigh of relief, then smiled at herself. She actually found herself thinking, *Thank goodness he is real.* What had she expected? They had taken in an evacuee, that was all. Her mother would be glad of that. Then she remembered the words, *your turn*, and she realised there must be others. So there would be children at Mire House after all.

She remembered the woman's words, as cold as the press of her hands: *No children.*

But these were somebody else's children, she argued against the voice. They would only be here for a short time, just to make sure they were safe. Surely no one would begrudge them that.

No children, not ever.

Not ever.

CHAPTER TWELVE

Aggie heard the music before the house was even in sight. She tried to remember what the tune was called as her mother tugged at her arm. She stumbled against the grass verge; the name slipped away from her and she pulled a face her mother couldn't see. It was pitch-dark and she was wearing her best clothes, the organdie dress with the little blue flowers and puffed sleeves, and her hair was perfectly curled. But it still wasn't right. She remembered staring into the mirror, trying to see that shining hair and not the mole just by her lip, and then she'd shrugged and applied the only lipstick she owned – a tiny stub of Tangee an old school friend had given her.

When she'd gone downstairs, her mother had grunted something about *good-time girls* and held out a cloth. She hadn't needed to say anything else. The colour had come off on the bleach-smelling fabric and Aggie's mouth now felt dry and cracked. She'd wanted to complain but her mother had held out her coat and they'd extinguished the lights before stepping outside.

Still, at least they were really going, and it was an actual *party*. The thought of the 'little mites' at Mire House had done much to soften her mother's feelings towards its residents. If only

Aggie had a little lipstick or some other make-up to make her look presentable; to make her look as if she might be worth dancing with.

At that thought an image of Eddie rose before her and she wondered if *this* was the place in the lane that she'd run into him, *or this, or this*. She might be standing on the very spot where he had wrapped his arms around her, but then she saw the dark outline of the house and she realised that no, she must have passed it already, without even realising. As they turned in at the gate, to bring her all the way back to reality, a fine mizzle began to drift like mist out of the dark sky.

She looked up. There were only a few stars tonight, and she couldn't make out any clouds, though she knew they must be there, blanking out the rest. The house was dark too; the new Mrs Hollingworth clearly had no need of help to manage the blackout. The windows were as blank as – *as a dead woman's eyes*, Aggie thought, and she pushed the idea away.

Another brief strain of music escaped and she recognised the simple, lilting refrain of 'Run Rabbit Run' before it was gone. It was followed by a peal of trilling laughter before that too was cut off.

Her mother pulled her arm even tighter. 'Stop dilly-dallying about,' she said. Aggie wrinkled her nose but didn't reply. Her mother had on a heavy woollen skirt and the best stockings she owned, but they were still yellowed and baggy. Her blouse was old – she had 'made it good as new', so she said, by stitching a new front onto the back of an old one. *Can't she see where they don't match?* Anyone could. They'd see and they'd laugh at them. They would probably never even have been invited if they didn't live so close by and if they didn't have a farm. When he'd heard about the invitation, her father had said, *Any farmer can find a friend in wartime*. His voice had a bitter tone when he said that. She hadn't been surprised when he'd said he wasn't coming.

They started up the drive and her mother let go of her arm and went on in front, knocking far too loudly on the big front door. After a moment it opened onto darkness. 'Come in, come in,' a woman's voice said: 'We do need to mind the blackout, you know.'

They stepped inside and the door closed behind them. Another opened and light and sound flooded out. A tripping jazz tune brought a smile to Aggie's lips and she found herself tapping her foot along to it as her mother talked. She couldn't think what had got into her, pushing out words at the hostess as if she'd never shut up: about how nice it was to be invited and what a lovely room and how her husband was indisposed, just as if they were friends, and the woman – Mrs Hollingworth – nodded and glanced over her shoulder as if she couldn't wait to get away.

Aggie looked about her. The room *was* fine. A crystal chandelier hung above it all and there was grand-looking furniture polished to a gleam, unlike their battered things at the farm. It was positioned oddly, pushed into corners or against the walls, and hope rose within her: it must be meant for dancing. Except that nobody was; people stood about in little clusters, chatting and laughing. Apparently no one worried about a scandalously hasty marriage when a party was in the offing. With dismay she realised she knew almost every single one of the other guests, and that most of them were women. She saw them all the time at the volunteer centre or in the shops or at church. She knew from Sunday mornings that they were wearing their best dresses now; some had little white gloves; one or two had fur stoles around their necks.

'Nice to 'ear about the evacuees, Mrs 'Ollingworth,' her mother was saying. 'Nice to see the place wi' a bit o' life in it.'

Mrs Hollingworth laughed, sweeping a glass of pink gin from the sideboard and passing her mother a tiny glass of sherry. Her nails clicked against it: they were long and Cutex-red and perfect, and Aggie saw with envy that her lipstick matched. She glanced around; she appeared to be the only one who had matching lips and nails.

'*Do* please call me Antonia.'

'Lovely that you're taking good care of them. Just lovely.'

'Oh goodness, you would *not* have believed. They were *filthy*. So filthy! I had to *scrub* them in carbolic, and even then, one of them insisted the dirt didn't come off. He really thought it never did! Quite tinker-class, apart from my nephew, naturally. And their *hair* . . . I never used so much insect powder in my life. Never! Well, in the end, I had to cut it off. Blond hair and blue eyes, I'd told them especially, I *do* so like blond hair and blue eyes, and now it's all gone.' She sipped at her drink, leaving a greasy red crescent on the rim. Then she looked out across the room and raised her hand as if she were greeting someone new, and with the jingling of bracelets she floated away.

Aggie frowned. She hadn't heard of one of the evacuees being a relation – but still, it was only a nephew, only temporary. She looked at her mother, who blinked and sipped at her sherry before noticing a contingent of ladies from the church flower-arranging rota and she too drifted away.

The music changed, a quick-step this time, but still no one was dancing. She glanced towards the table where the glasses stood and thought of pouring her own sherry, imagining her mother's scandalised shriek. She'd be marched home quicker than she could – *quick-step*. She pulled a face.

She could still hear Mrs Hollingworth – *Antonia* – talking, even from the other side of the room. Her voice was shrill and carried easily across the hubbub. 'Oh my, yes, isn't it an *awful* colour? Green, I ask you! *Frightfully* dull.' Aggie realised she was talking about the walls and she looked about again. The colour was calm, restful. Perhaps that was the reason Mrs Hollingworth didn't like it. Perhaps she merely wished to eradicate any trace of the woman who had chosen it.

Behind the door through which she'd entered was another table and she saw that this one was laden with slices of cake. She sauntered over there, her skirt swinging against her legs in time with the rhythm. She had so hoped for dancing and now there was only this. She could have cried with disappointment.

The Victoria sponge didn't look promising but she tried it anyway and pulled a face before she could stop herself. There was hardly any sugar and it was chewy in the middle, nothing like her mother's. She resisted the urge to spit it out. No wonder the woman needed servants if this was how she made cake. Now it was in her hand, though, she'd have to finish it or her mother would accuse her of being sinful. Food was food and cake was cake. She swallowed the heavy stuff and then she nearly *did* spit it out when the tablecloth brushed against her legs.

She stared down at it, then bent and lifted one corner. For a moment everything was grey and then she made out the white rims of a little boy's eyes. She blinked. His head was a shaven dome and it took her a moment to realise that it was the child she'd seen in the garden with his beautiful curls, awaiting his 'turn'. Now nothing about him had any colour; it was as if he had been formed from the shadows.

She realised she was just standing there, still holding the tablecloth, and she glanced over her shoulder before sinking to the floor and pulling it back into place behind her. The boy let out a stifled giggle and she was glad at once that she had done it, no matter how silly she would feel if she were caught.

'You're that lass.' His accent was broad Sheffield.

'I am that.' She smiled, though she doubted he could see it in the dim light.

'You posh?'

'Not really.' His words made her want to giggle too, as if she were a child again.

'*She's* posh.'

Aggie's eyes adjusted and she could see him more clearly; she saw the face he pulled. It didn't belong on the face of a little boy and she wondered how old he was; she had assumed he was about eight or nine, but there was a hard expression in his eyes. She wondered if that was a sign of being from the city or parted from his mother, or if it was something else.

'I don' like 'er,' he said.

'Oh. Well, that's a shame. She might grow on you.'

He didn't answer.

'At least you're safe here now, aren't you? Your mother must be very glad, knowing you're safe.'

He shrugged.

'And it *is* nice here, you know. It's colder now, but it's pretty in summer. There's fields and skylarks and hedgerows and flowers and all sorts. You'll see. Maybe she'll take you nutting, or she could bring you to see our chickens if you want. We've horses too, and pigs, and—'

'I want me mam.'

She realised from the boy's voice that he was close to tears. 'Oh – hush, it'll be all right. You'll settle in, you'll see. The school's nice. Me brother went there – you'll like it. There'll be games.'

He tilted his head and she waited for him to speak. When he did, his voice was hopeful. 'Can you play sardines?' he asked.

There were four of them: Tom, Hal, Arthur and Clarence. The one she'd found under the table was Tom. The sight of them made her uncomfortable. It wasn't so much their shorn heads as the fact that only Arthur's hair remained. He sat a little apart from the others, looking just as a little boy should, his dark fringe complementing his ruddy cheeks. In contrast, the others' eyes looked huge and their heads too big for their bodies. In the case of Hal and Tom, perhaps they *were* too big – her mother would have said they were skinny as rats in winter. They all wore shirts and grey pullies, but the quality and condition differed. Clarence, like Arthur, had clothes that looked like new, but his head too was shaved, an odd contrast with his pale eyelashes. His eyes were dull with resentment. She thought she could guess which of them all was Mrs Hollingworth's nephew.

She found herself looking at Clarence's head, all its curves and bumps and depressions, and then the sight felt too intimate and she looked away. Hal shuffled and she saw a picked-at scab half hidden in his eyebrow and a bald patch the size of a sixpence on his crown.

Never used so much insect powder in my life.

She forced herself not to grimace.

They were sitting on the stairs, near the top of the flight, and despite their number the house felt empty. The corridor faded away, each doorway forming its own dark well. It reminded her of something she couldn't quite bring to mind and then she thought of the dark slabs of stone ranked on a hillside and she pushed the thought away.

Hal stretched out one hand towards Tom, palm upwards, as if he were about to have his fortune told. The lines on his skin were too distinct, as if the recent scrubbing hadn't been quite enough to remove the dirt.

'I were s'pposed to bring cake,' Tom said. 'Well I 'aven't. Get thee own. Anyhow, we're playin' sardines now.'

Hal pulled back his lips from his teeth, making Aggie think of the skull just beneath his skin. It looked almost feral.

'I'll get us some,' Arthur said, 'afterwards.'

'Aye. She'll not shout at thee, *hairy*.'

Arthur wrinkled his nose. 'I wouldn't be too sure. But you've tried and Hal daren't, and Clarence certainly can't go.'

Clarence's expression tightened; it looked almost like hatred.

Aggie spoke quickly. 'That cake were rubbish anyway. I've tried it.'

Hal shrugged but he let his hand fall and they were silent once again. She glanced around the landing. Sardines, Tom had said, but she knew already that she couldn't enter any of those rooms. She should never have left the soirée. She certainly couldn't snoop around, peering into wardrobes or under beds, trying to find a place to hide. She didn't know why she'd even considered it.

Tom turned to her and he smiled. It made him look different again, younger and more vulnerable, and she saw that his two front teeth were broken; she imagined if Mrs Hollingworth had seen those teeth she never would have taken him in. Without the golden curls his eyes looked less bright, almost grey rather than blue, as if the colour had drained from him, or been stolen somehow. And here he was in this loveless house, out of reach of everything he had ever known.

She gave him a smile. 'We could play something else.'

His lips turned down. 'I like sardines,' he said. 'I played sardines wiv me mam.'

Aggie felt herself sinking. For a moment, it felt as if she might keep sagging deeper into the stairs until they closed over her head and the house took her. Why on earth had she said she'd play with them? And at that very moment the music drifting up the stairs grew in volume. She hadn't heard the drawing room door open but then she heard the stamp of feet on carpet, lively and rhythmic: so they'd decided to dance after all, now that she was away from everything. Still, at least dancing would keep them occupied. They wouldn't notice she was gone, not for a while yet. No one would know, and anyway, she had been in this house before they even knew it existed, hadn't she? She should have known every last part of it.

She drew a deep breath and said, 'All right, I'll be the sardine. The rest of you go down a few steps, to the corner. You can count to fifty there. You *can* count to fifty, can't you?'

'Of course,' Arthur said.

Tom sniffed. 'Mmm,' he said. 'P'raps you'd better do it all t' same. Just in case.' He glanced around at the darkened doorways. He didn't look afraid. 'I'll go first.'

She didn't want to get into a discussion about why he didn't trust the others and so she shuffled down a few steps and sat. The three boys perched below her, one with his dark hair, the others just skin and bone, and she caught the faint tang of the insect powder Mrs Hollingworth had spoken of.

Hal's hair hadn't been trimmed properly and he kept rubbing at the tufts as he turned towards the wall and closed his eyes. Clarence peered up at her through eyelashes that looked too long, almost feminine, against his angular skull.

She remembered she was supposed to be counting and she started to whisper the numbers just as the music from the drawing room gave way from 'There's a New Apple Tree' to 'Mama, I Want to Make Rhythm'. It reminded her of what this evening should have been. How odd, now, to be hiding on the stairs with these urchins.

Tom's footsteps tapped away along the corridor. It sounded as if he was heading towards the front of the house and she counted a little louder so that the others wouldn't hear. A door opened and closed, and then there was nothing but her counting: 'Forty-nine . . . fifty,' and she opened her eyes on forty-nine to make sure the others weren't peeking.

Hal was turned to the wall and Arthur's eyes were scrunched so tightly closed that creases radiated across his skin. Clarence was holding his hands across his face: had he just moved, as she looked at him? She wasn't sure.

'All right,' she said, a little too brightly. 'Time to go looking. Just one game, mind, then I'll have to go.'

Arthur looked around the landing. 'It's no good,' he said. 'Anyone could see where anyone else goes.' He looked up at her. 'Why don't you go first? One at a time. We'll count again.'

After a moment, she nodded. It would make the game longer but he was right, if someone didn't go first there would barely be a game at all. She forced a smile and pushed herself to her feet. 'Cover your eyes then,' she said.

He did, replacing his hands and bending his head into his knees. With a glare, Clarence followed suit: Hal had turned back to the wall again. Aggie hurried around the top of the landing and towards the doors at the front of the house. They all looked the same, the panelled wood pushed closed against intrusion. She didn't know which one she should take. She wondered what Mrs Hollingworth was doing now; she would surely never imagine one of her guests was up here, doing this. She pushed open the nearest door and stuck her head into the gap.

Everything was pitch-black. She willed the light to stretch from the corridor and into the room, but of course it didn't help. She pushed the door wider. She thought she could see a darker place which must be blackout curtains and the nearer hulking form of a bed. A trace of perfume hung in the air, something exotic that smelled expensive, much finer than the lily-of-the-valley her mum sometimes wore.

She couldn't imagine Tom coming in here, but she heard a breathy voice behind her counting *thirty-two, thirty-three*, and she slipped inside before she could consider it. She didn't know how the boys had reached those numbers already – they'd probably raced through them. Perhaps they couldn't count after all. She could still see little but a few blocky shapes against the wall, and then there was movement and she caught her breath, her hand rushing to her heart. 'Tom?'

She stepped forward and almost laughed. The moving shape was *her*. The thing she'd seen was a mirror. She tiptoed across the room, hoping no one could hear her in the room below. The music sounded louder than ever and yet distant too, almost ghostly. She didn't like it. She imagined her mother's horrified face if she was caught; she'd never be able to 'hold her head up'.

There was a wardrobe in the corner, an obvious hiding place. When she opened it the smell of mothballs spilled out; inside, it was full to bursting. She couldn't resist putting out a hand and running it over the velvets and silks, the fine lace, the softness of fur. There was surely no room for a child in a wardrobe such as this.

The others must have finished counting by now. She took one last look around – she was becoming a little more used to the dark – then hurried out of the room and into the next. It was smaller than the first but it too held a large bedstead and had a dark slab where the window should be. Other than that, she couldn't make out any other furnishings – perhaps it wasn't an important room. As she stepped into it she saw there was a narrow fireplace and nothing more. Perhaps Tom had been cleverer than she thought, deliberately stomping in this direction before tiptoeing away elsewhere. As she turned, though, she saw there was somewhere else to hide after all; there was another door, this one a little narrow, set into the wall near the first.

There was a scramble of feet on the landing. *Coming, ready or not.*

The door handle was cool under her fingertips and it opened onto blank darkness. She swallowed and stepped inside.

She knew at once that someone was there, but she wasn't sure how. She couldn't see a thing, even when she raised a hand in front of her face. No, there really was nothing. She held her breath and listened for the sound of someone else's breathing. It struck her how ridiculous she must look if Tom was in here crouched in the dark, and he could see her but she couldn't see him. She was no longer sure he was in here, though. She had been so sure when she'd seen the door, but now she didn't like it. It was as if she could be anywhere at all.

A faint noise came, not the giggle she was expecting – *hoping for* – but an awkward swallowing sound.

'Tom?' she whispered. 'I found you.' It sounded more like a question than a statement. She had to bite her lip to keep from shrieking as someone grasped her around her waist.

'I fought you was *'er*,' he said. 'I didn't fink it was you.'

She found his shoulder and patted it. 'Quiet, Tom. They'll hear you.'

He hushed so quickly that she wondered what on earth she'd said. Fear was pouring from him like that scent from his shorn head, which was stronger in here, chemical and unpleasant. She could feel that the space was small and she put out a hand, pawing at the air, finding what felt like a shelf.

'*You* shhh,' Tom said, and she stifled a giggle.

'It's all right,' she whispered. 'Mrs Hollingworth's still downstairs. You can hear the music, can't you?' But she realised that she couldn't hear it any more, everything was silent, as if they had been cut off from everyone.

'Not 'er,' he said. 'I thought it were that *other* 'un. The one you was with before.'

'You mean tonight? My mum?'

She felt him shake his head. 'Not tonight. The other day, when I got 'ere. When you saw us in t' garden. She were there then. She was behind you, watchin' us.'

Something inside her went cold. 'Who do you mean?'

'That 'un what wears black. An' a thing ower 'er 'ead.'

Aggie could not answer. She tried to breathe quietly through her mouth so that he wouldn't hear the way she was gulping at the air.

'I seen her after, an' all – looking ower t' wall from t' chu'ch.'

She leaned in closer. 'It's all right, Tom. No one will harm you.'

'She might.'

'No. Shush.' She straightened. Soon the others would come and they'd laugh at him, at them both; at the game they were playing.

'She dun't like me. I dun't think she likes the others, neither.'

'I'm sure that's not true.'

'My – even my mam dun't like me. She sent us away.'

'Oh, now – shh, Tom. You know that's not true. She only wanted to keep you safe.'

He paused. 'Does that other 'un want to keep us safe, an' all? She was wavin' us ower, last time I saw 'er. Arthur said she was lookin' at 'im but I dun't know. I reckon she wanted us all to go wiv 'er.'

Aggie patted his shoulder. 'I'm sure she does want to keep you safe, Tom. Quite sure. There's no need to be afraid, is there? You can – you can go to Mrs Hollingworth. Or you can always run in here and hide.' She smiled. 'You can always do that.'

Then the door opened and three shapes were standing there and she almost screamed for the second time in the last five minutes.

CHAPTER THIRTEEN

'I fell in love with the place at once, of course,' Mrs Hollingworth was saying. 'One just felt so at home. And one couldn't possibly stay in town. So much safer here, and being able to provide a refuge for some of the children – why, one has to do what one can for them. The little devils.' Her voice tailed off into shrill laughter.

Aggie shrank back against the wall as she tiptoed down the stairs. Below her, Mrs Hollingworth was emerging from the drawing room, her bejewelled arm curling around the door. She had her back turned and was talking to someone still inside. Then she stepped out and waved Mr and Mrs Ackroyd from the fishmonger's out of the room.

'Ah, wait a moment. There, I'll close the door behind you.' She did, and went towards the light switch, jingle-jangling with her arm, and she reached out and everything went dark.

Aggie moved quickly, easing behind them as Mrs Hollingworth laughed and apologised her way past her guests to let them out. She had never had cause to be grateful to the blackout before – though as she thought of it she had a brief flash of running into a warm figure in the dark – and then it was gone. She stood by the drawing room door as Mrs Hollingworth came back. She could hear her slapping her hands together as if bidding good riddance to bad rubbish and she realised she was going to switch on the light and see her standing there and that she would probably scream.

'I'll get it, Mrs Hollingworth,' she said, and snapped on the light.

The woman's mouth fell open. Her lipstick had bled into fine crimson lines about her lips. 'Why, I—'

'I *do* beg your pardon,' Aggie said in her for-the-vicar voice. 'I just stepped out to check I had my key in my coat pocket. I had an *awful* feeling I'd come out without it.'

'Why, funny girl. You gave me a shocking start.'

'My father might lock up, you know. A *terrible* nuisance.' Aggie dropped into a quick curtsey before turning and entering the drawing room. Music swelled around her, lifting her at once. It was in full swing. Mrs Smith from the bakery was red-faced and laughing, waving an empty wineglass, watching while some of the older ladies swung each other around by the arms in some semblance of dancing. She grinned; she couldn't help it. *Now* it looked like a party. A man was there – it must be the mysterious Mr Hollingworth – and he was holding out his hand to Mrs Pinchbeck, so gentlemanly; his focus shifted to Aggie and he winked and she knew she was going to dance after all, not now perhaps, but soon. The music was already in her feet, making them tap.

Then her mother bustled towards her. '*There* you are, Ag,' she said. 'Where on earth have you been?'

'I was—' Aggie sighed. 'I was talking to the children.' It wasn't an untruth; there was no need to tell her she'd been wandering into the bedrooms.

'Oh. You saw the nephews, then?' Her mother was tight-lipped.

'I saw one. Arthur, isn't it? Arthur Hollingworth, I suppose.'

'Arthur *Dean*. It's her sister's child. I don't suppose you saw t' other, then.'

'What other?'

'Clarence. I 'eard Mr Ackroyd askin' Mr Hollingworth about it, an' he said his first wife's nephew's come too, 'er sister's child – Clarence Mitchell, it is – with 'im still bein' Mr 'Ollingworth's relation, an' needin' to get out o' London an' all. An' then I saw t' look his second wife gave 'im when 'e talked about 'im. I dun't suppose that 'un's 'avin' any kind o' time of it.' She looked around, twisting her lip. The music was spinning to a close and she straightened and grasped Aggie's arm.

Aggie thought about the tight look on Clarence's face, his head shaved just like the children who were no relation at all, and she thought, *No, I don't suppose he is.* She almost missed her mother's next words. 'It's time we were going.'

'Oh – do we have to?'

'Never mind *do we 'ave to*. You've to be up early tomorrer to feed t' critters, remember? Now say thank you to Mrs Hollingworth.'

'It's quite all right,' their hostess said. She had appeared close by her mother's shoulder; Aggie wasn't sure when. 'A jolly good thing you have your keys,' she added, and Aggie's mother stared at her back as she led the way into the hall, the palms of her hands already brushing at each other as they went.

CHAPTER FOURTEEN

Aggie was in Mire House again, but she knew that she was dreaming because the new Mrs Hollingworth was standing in the hallway, talking and talking, all fur stole and ostrich feathers, but she couldn't hear a sound. The woman didn't even appear to see her as she went to the stairs and started up them. Her steps made no sound either, as if she didn't have any weight. When she put her hand on the rail, running it along the polished wood, she felt nothing under her fingers. It was as if she were made of air.

When she'd started to ascend it had been light in the house but as she climbed night was falling, quick and sudden. There was something wrong about the shadows but somehow she didn't feel afraid and that was wrong too, as if something was numbing her, stopping her from feeling. But then it occurred to her that if she *could* feel, if she could only *see*, she would not be here; she would turn and run away, as far and as fast as she could.

Now she couldn't go back. She had to find the boy. She hadn't seen him but she knew he was here and that any moment she would turn a corner and see a flash of his golden hair.

There were many doors but she knew the one she had to take and she knew before opening it the room inside would be dark.

The window was lined with black paper, as if the daylight was something that needed to be kept out. She squinted, allowing her eyes to adjust. There was a dresser that hadn't been here before. She stepped forward and saw a picture sitting on it, a pretty young woman in a lacy dress, smiling a broad smile.

She heard a soft rustling and turned to the cupboard set into the wall. In another moment she was standing in front of it and the door was open in front of her. She couldn't see what lay inside. It was darker than anything she'd known, even the expression on the woman's face when she'd grasped her hands in her cold dead fingers—

No. She stepped forward into the space and when she was inside she quickly turned and closed the door. The dark remained but now there was a sound too: the soft breathiness of a child. She waited, but he did not jump out at her. 'I found you, Tom,' she said. 'I know you're there.'

The darkness had a presence. It ate her words. She pressed her lips together. What she wanted to do was run, but she no longer felt sure there was a door behind her. If she turned and put out a hand and felt only a solid wall beneath her fingers she knew she would lose her mind. She closed her eyes and found it didn't make any difference. *Better to wait*, she thought. *Better not to know*, and she wasn't entirely sure why.

Then he spoke. 'She didn't have a baby,' he said, quite clearly, and then silence filled the space once more.

'Tom, is that you? What do you mean?' Aggie swallowed. Her throat was dry. She shuffled forward, expecting to find boxes or clothes, but there was nothing. Then she flailed and brushed past something after all; there was a bowl or a dish and it upset when she touched it, setting up a loud clatter. The smell grew stronger, chemical and nasty, and there was something cold and wet on her fingers. She snatched them back.

She took another step and felt for the boy, up high, and then lower, where he might be crouching in the dark, his head bent, not covered in golden curls but shorn and bald and with lice crawling all over it . . .

There was nothing there. Nothing there at all except the dark that was waiting, and she jerked awake and she bit her lip to smother her cry.

CHAPTER FIFTEEN

The boys looked entirely different in daylight. It wasn't their clothes – it was even more obvious now that Hal and Tom had never had a first-hand coat in their lives – but their faces. Their expressions were bright, no anxiety or trouble in them, and Tom was even smiling. It had been several days since the party and their hair was starting to grow back. Soon Arthur might not stand out so much any longer. Tom's looked like straw beginning to emerge from the ground and she reached out and rubbed it, feeling the soft prickle on her fingers. For a moment she remembered her dream and she almost expected him to disappear, but he turned to her and grinned.

'Where're we off to, then?' he said, and they all waited for her answer. She was suddenly glad she had called for them at Mire House. Inside it had been all shadows and harsh perfume and brittle manners; now they were standing in the lane, swallowing the cold air, all grins and teeth. Even Arthur looked relieved to be outside.

She carried three small wicker baskets and two of the bags she had sewn. She had taken them from the pile that was waiting to be finished; they didn't yet have the patches of paper sewn on that would bear a soldier's name. She passed them around.

'We're off nutting,' she said. She pointed towards the opening that let onto the river path, away to the side of the garden. 'There are hazels in that hedge. We're off to pick 'em.'

Hal spoke. 'I dun't know what they look like.'

'That's all right. I'll show you what's to do.'

Tom's face was threatening to crease into a frown: he evidently didn't think her plan very exciting. But then he looked back towards the house before turning to her and smiling.

She led the way towards the path and as soon as they reached it, it was as if they had escaped. They ran ahead of her, swiping at nettles with their hands, some kind of show of bravado, until Arthur yelped and gripped his palm.

'Well, don't touch them then,' Aggie said. She bent and showed him the leathery dock leaves growing beneath. 'Scrunch this up and rub it on. It'll make it better.' He pulled a face but rubbed on the sap anyway, scrubbing as if he could scrape away the bumps.

'He's an idiot,' a voice said at her ear and she looked around to see Clarence. The boy's face was screwed up with scorn.

'Now that's not nice.'

Arthur shrugged. 'It doesn't matter.'

'Yes, it does,' Aggie said. 'I'll not 'ave things o' that kind said in my 'earing, understand? 'Specially not between family.' She knew at once she'd said the wrong thing. Arthur's eyes narrowed while Clarence gawped.

'He's *not* my family,' Clarence said.

Arthur did not reply.

'But your uncle is his uncle, so—'

'He'll *never* be family. My uncle should never have got married again. If he had been nicer to my aunt instead—'

Aggie blinked. 'Whatever makes you say that?'

'They won't get away with it,' the boy said, not looking at her. He was staring over the wall.

'Clarence?'

'It's all right,' Arthur said in a low voice. 'Please can we go now? The others are getting ahead.'

She saw that he was right. 'Let's go on a bit, up towards t' river. That's where t' nuts are.'

Clarence didn't move at first, but as she started to walk she heard him trailing behind her. He was kicking at the grass. Arthur was ahead of her and she couldn't see his face, only his hair.

Then he half-turned and she heard his voice, little more than a whisper. 'Sorry. He doesn't like my aunt, that's all. She – well, she isn't very nice to him.' He paused. 'She calls him "that awful child". I don't think she especially likes children. I wanted to go to Aunt Lizzie's, but she just got married and my mother didn't think much of it – I heard her say she'd married low. She thought I'd be better off with Aunt Antonia.' He pulled a face.

Aggie frowned. It didn't seem likely that Antonia Hollingworth was particularly motherly, but all the same, she couldn't get Clarence's look out of her mind; not so much his fixed expression, but the way he had stared out over the wall and across at the slope rising away in that particular direction; as if he had been looking directly at the graveyard.

As she walked, she let her misgivings melt away. The path was still vibrantly green even though summer had passed, and the hazels were there, their generous leaves looking almost as if they were tumbling down the plant instead of growing upwards. She pushed the greenery aside and examined the nuts. She shook the tree, setting up a fine rustle, and the boys peered in, three heads close together, one a short distance away. She ignored the thought of lice and pointed. 'See, they're best when they're falling off.' She picked some up and put them in her bag. 'We'll pickle 'em. You can give some to— You can take some back to the 'ouse, when they're done.'

Tom giggled. 'I bet I can get more n' you. Bet I can get more n' anyone.' He set to work, yanking away the nuts and twigs all together and stuffing them into his bag. He separated one, peering dubiously at the green husk before putting it to his lips, then he changed his mind and dropped that into the bag, then grinned at her. She laughed. They stood in a wide-spaced line, working at the small trees. The boys were pale but the sun was in their faces and the air freshened their cheeks. They didn't appear to be thinking about being so far from home, or about Mire House or families or anything at all.

Tom was the nearest. He turned to her. 'She in't watchin us today,' he said.

'Who?'

He grasped the plant by two sturdy branches and leaned back, swinging on them. Then he straightened and looked out over the top of the wall. They could still see right across the grounds of Mire House to the slope opposite where a yew tree stood, louring and dark. She could see under its branches, well enough to know that the bench was empty. *Good*, she thought.

'She din't 'ave a baby,' he murmured.

'What did you say?'

He yanked a hazelnut from the tree as Aggie shook off the sudden chill. It must be gossip, something he'd picked up from

Clarence or Arthur, or maybe both of them. She picked a nut too, and stared at it for a moment before letting it fall into her bag, thinking of swallowing the dry, cloying thing.

'She were watchin', before.'

'What do you mean?'

He kept his eyes fixed on the tree as he plucked at the foliage with his fingers. The others had drifted away. Hal and Arthur were bunched together, their shoulders shaking; she heard stifled laughter.

'I saw 'er out o' t' window.'

'What window?' It sounded like an accusation and she tried to soften it with a smile. Time stretched out, suspended between them.

'Saw 'er a few times. Seen 'er talkin' to '*im.*' He gestured towards Clarence, who was bent close to the tree. His cheeks were pink and he looked as if he was trying to give the impression he was engaged on his task, while the others laughed. 'Dunno what she said. 'E wouldn't tell me.'

Aggie froze.

Then he said, 'She 'ad a soldier wiv 'er, last time.'

Everything stopped. Aggie's eyes widened, looking out at the yew tree's darkness. Then she grabbed the boy's shoulder and pulled him around to face her. His mouth clamped into a surly line. He met her gaze and she tried to see what was hiding in his eyes: amusement, perhaps, or cruelty, or childish glee. She couldn't make it out, and then she did: it was fear.

She took a step back and let her hands fall to her side. The bag slipped from her fingers and nuts spilled from it, rolling across the path.

'It's all right. I don't think 'e was real. I think 'e were like '*er.*'

'You *didn't* see anyone,' she said. 'You didn't see anyone because she in't real. And if you din't see 'er, you din't see no soldier either.' She leaned in close. The others had stopped what they were doing and even Clarence's eyes were fixed on her. She took a deep breath. 'There in't any lady,' she said. 'She in't there. An' there in't a soldier either, not round 'ere. They're all gone.' She immediately regretted her choice of words.

'She *is* real. I saw 'er. Ower there.' He pointed towards the graveyard. 'An she *did* 'ave someone wiv 'er. She 'ad 'er 'and on 'is shoulder, an' then she went away an' 'e did too.'

She couldn't speak. She looked away from him, forcing herself to take deep breaths. She opened her mouth to deny his words once more – *you saw nothing* – but instead she found herself asking, 'What uniform?'

'Eh?'

She was suddenly blinking away tears, furious at herself for allowing them to come, to let herself be taken in. He was a liar, a nasty little liar, and that was all. But it didn't stop her from repeating the words: 'I said, what uniform was 'e wearing?' She said it in a low voice, so that the others couldn't hear. They would only laugh at her. That was probably their whole purpose, to laugh – they must have dreamed this up between them, nothing but silly play-acting, a fine joke, and she had fallen for it like the fool she was.

She put a hand to her dress, the left side, just below her shoulder blade. 'What kind of a soldier? The uniform – were there wings on it, just here, or—?'

He shrugged.

'Or nothing? Was there—?'

'I'm off,' he said. 'I dun't like you no more.' He thrust something towards her – the bag he'd been holding, full of prickly twigs – and he pushed past, heading towards the others. When he reached them they turned and ran, all together, uncaring of the nettles thrashing against their legs.

Aggie stood alone on the path and looked down at the bag. The stitching was coming unravelled. It had never been meant for twigs and rough little hands, to be pulled around in country hedgerows. She stared at the loose threads. She knew her mother would tut over it as she unpicked the work. Then she'd steadily sew it up again before taking the thin square of paper that would bear a young man's name and stitching it to the front.

CHAPTER SIXTEEN

The water pump was coated in a thin layer of ice that disintegrated under Aggie's fingers. They were already nipped and pink with cold and her nose was running as she started to pump water into the trough. That wasn't frozen, but it would be soon; winter was almost here. She paused, letting the water's airy coughing subside. The brief low of cattle came from the fold and there was the harsher, nearer complaint of a goose. The sky was like milk, the sun not yet peering over the outbuildings, and frost coated everything.

On other days her brother would have done this, thrown down straw from the hayloft and measured out feed. Today her father had gone out early and so it was up to her. She had heard his heavy step before she'd risen, then the scrape of the door on flagstones in the kitchen below. The wood must have swollen. She wasn't sure how quickly it would turn colder – the BBC had stopped the weather forecast in case it might help an invasion – but she didn't think it would be long. Then the world would freeze, covered over in snow that smothered everything – the grass for the animals, the yard between the barn and stables, the fields. It would freeze the water on her nightstand and the insides of the windows and the cloths on the sink, if they weren't properly dried and hung. It would touch the world with silver and folk from the village would trample along the lane to the church and call it beautiful. She grimaced. It was all very well for those who didn't have a farm. Easy to enjoy winter's beauty for those whose hands weren't growing numb with cold.

She missed her brother. He was somewhere on the Belgian–French border with the British Expeditionary Force, miles and miles away, somewhere he'd probably never even imagined. She remembered Tom's words – but of course, the boy was lying. He hadn't seen what he thought he'd seen; he was nothing but a young boy dreaming of soldiers.

She knew her father thought of Will all the time and she imagined Eddie's father did the same. Her dad went about his work just as he always had, but his movements, though sure, had changed. There was something mechanical about them. He no longer smiled. The lines were etching deeper into his face as worry sank into him and his eyes, under the dullness, were full of fear.

She looked up into the sky. Sometimes planes flew over and she would stop and listen for the air-raid siren, but none ever came. They were cut off from anyone and everything that mattered in the world, and there was no helping it; without her brother, there was too much to be done. The cold clawed its way into her belly. *And if he shouldn't come back?*

She wriggled her shoulders as if she could shake off the thought.

She 'ad 'er 'and on 'is shoulder.

She started pumping water again, harder this time, no longer caring about her hands. She relished the numbness. First the trough, she reminded herself, then the chickens and the geese, then she'd see that the cows were fed and check that her father had seen to the horses, and then she'd dress for church and sing with the others, pray for the souls who were . . .

No.

She straightened and stretched out her back. Of course her brother would return, probably before too much longer. The war would soon be nothing but a memory. Anything else was unimaginable. He would come back and he would tease her the way he always had, and take the heavy loads on his shoulders so that she could go back to helping her mother, not this, being out here in the cold for always and always. And yet – she couldn't help thinking of the woman standing under the yew tree, her hand on the shoulder of a young man in uniform next to her. She just couldn't picture his face.

Eddie, she thought.

She shook her head. No, he would come back too, and perhaps he would talk to her again the way he had the night before he had left. She knew she shouldn't hope – they'd never even kissed. He was fancy-free; he hadn't said anything to her at all, not really – but she couldn't help but think she might have a life waiting for her, one other than this.

She shook her head. She had to stop thinking of it. Whenever she felt hope rising for Eddie or her brother she felt she was betraying one or the other, as if the woman in her dark veil had summoned one of them to her and it was up to Aggie to make the choice.

In church, it was impossible to think of anything other than the war. It was there in the vicar's solemn tones as he prayed for all their young men, all their brothers, and they rose to their feet to sing 'Eternal Father, Strong to Save'. It was there in Mrs Marsden's face; her son had gone for a sailor back in May. His knees had always been scabbed from cricket – he was a natural fielder, though his long limbs had made him look like a gangling calf as he ran. Now he was gone, sunk on the HMS *Rawalpindi* between the Faroes and Iceland, hopelessly outgunned by German warships. Mrs Marsden choked under the words and everyone else just kept on and on. They sang of the raging waters and the indifferent waves and Aggie couldn't help but think of the cold; huge and endless, a cold that would swallow a lost boy so easily and sink deep inside and last forever.

She glanced aside and saw Mrs Marsden was the only one still sitting, rocking herself with her hands pressed to her eyes. Mrs Pinchbeck stood next to her and she was singing, but her hand was gripping Mrs Marsden's shoulder. Aggie's mother nudged her in the ribs. She hadn't taken her own eyes from her hymn book, but Aggie knew she was aware of everything. She tried to focus on the song but she stumbled over the words. She didn't need to look around the pews to see the empty spaces: Peter Ackroyd was gone, with his freckles and red hair; Daniel, his brother, who always irritated her by kicking at his pew; Stephen Smith, who had once called Aggie 'loose' because she'd tried on Nella Tunstall's lipstick. Now Nella was here but her brother was not. Her father was gone too. There was only her mother and her gran, who rarely attended because of her health, but she was here now.

The song ended and everyone began to sit down again. The shuffling and knocking subsided and for a second all that could be heard was Mrs Marsden's dry sobbing. Aggie pressed her lips together. She glanced at her mother's hands, still holding her hymn book, so tightly her knuckles were the colour of bone. Before she could think, she had reached out and grasped them. Her mother's hands curled around her own, gripping hard. She did not let go.

Aggie closed her eyes, suddenly wanting to cry, but she knew she could not. If she did, her mother would cry too, and her mother couldn't cry here in front of everyone; she would hate it. She would believe she'd never live it down. And perhaps it would jump from one of them to the next and they would all give in, and the thing that was always threatening to swallow them would have won. She thought of the first Mrs Hollingworth, wearing her mourning dress, sitting on her bench. She had only gone a little ahead of them, after all: perhaps she had simply been the first to sense the darkness that had come.

Her mother squeezed her hand and let go at last and Aggie stared down at it. The backs were still browned from the summer. Her palms were callused, her skin dry. Then everyone was standing. It was over. As they turned to leave she leaned over and whispered, 'I'm just going for a little air,' and she hurried towards the door ahead of her mother.

She emerged into the cold. She didn't catch anyone's eye and she didn't stop, she just walked away from them all, turning the corner and striding away up the path through the graveyard. She didn't need to look where she was going and she didn't want to see ahead of her; she wasn't sure if it would be better to know if someone was waiting for her there, or if the sight of the woman would steal her resolution away. The frost was letting go of the land now, though it still crackled and hissed where the grass lay deepest. She could see the shadow of Mire

House in the corner of her eye and she realised she hadn't seen the Hollingworths in church. Too hoity-toity to be with the rest of them perhaps, to offer a neighbourly hand – someone to grip your shoulder when the unthinkable came. Well, the unthinkable would not visit *them*. Her home had always been full of noise and chatter and life and she couldn't imagine it being any different.

The grass was a vivid green against the stone, a sign of life clinging on, resisting the cold. She stomped down harder, crushing the blades. The house lay to her right, dark and silent, and the tree was ahead of her. She stopped when she reached the edge of its shadow. It moved at her feet, stretching and retreating as if trying to draw her in. She couldn't hear anything and she couldn't sense anyone but when she looked up she thought she saw a woman's straight back. For a moment, she couldn't breathe – then she saw it was only a drift of fallen needles.

After a moment she settled onto the cold stone, smoothing down her dress against her legs. She tried to imagine what Mrs Hollingworth had been thinking of as she stared down at the house. She wouldn't have guessed there was anyone inside. It wasn't full of laughter, she realised now. It hadn't been filled with life when the children came. They were hollow-eyed and confused and missing their parents, and the woman who lived there would not comfort them. The life was being sapped from them already.

She looked up into the pale blue sky. It had been different when the first Mrs Hollingworth had come here. She must have been thinking about the baby, perhaps wondering how many she would have to fill the empty rooms, wondering what her life would be like. Now there was only this, a forsaken bench in a forsaken place, and Aggie felt the sadness of it. Her anger was evaporating into the air; she only felt like crying.

Then she remembered her brother and his friend and she pushed herself up. 'You can't have them,' she said, and her words hung there, hollow and empty, smothered by the tree's heavy branches, but there was nothing and no one to hear her.

CHAPTER SEVENTEEN

Her first thought was that it didn't look like Tom at all. The morning was frost-coated and the colour had leached from the world. Everything was pale and shining and silent. Aggie couldn't even hear the cluck of a hen. She was glad to be outside. Her mum had been quiet over breakfast. Will's usual letter hadn't come and every time she looked at her Aggie had to swallow down the fear. But she didn't *know* anything, did she? A child had made up a story and that was all. As soon as Will wrote, the fear would come loose. She would be free of it. Now, just as she'd been thinking of the child, there was this: a flash of golden hair disappearing around the side of the barn.

Her first thought was, *He's playing sardines*. Her next was: *How did his hair grow back so quickly?*

But she had caught only the briefest glimpse: enough to see he had been grinning at her, as if he had decided to be friends again, and the thought warmed her. It was good to see him outside, banishing the memory of his half-lit skull as he sat on the stairs. Now he looked exactly what he was, a young boy exploring, his cheeks rosy from the cold. She had said he could come and see the animals and here he was, too shy to greet her.

She stepped carefully across the yard, the ice splintering under her boots. She put out a hand to steady herself against the rough wooden wall. The ice was thicker here, and slippery. It was odd that Tom had been able to move so quickly, but that was the way with children; they felt no fear. She looked around the corner, bracing herself for his teasing shout, but there was nothing there but a trail of footprints leading away, catching splinters of light where he'd shattered the ice under his feet. She looked towards the yard. She hadn't finished her work but it would surely wait a little longer. She walked after him, around the side of the fold. It was a little warmer against the wall and she could hear the animals shifting in the straw on the other side. When she reached the edge it was suddenly colder. She couldn't see the child at all now, but there was a sound coming from the lane: a quick high giggle.

He was playing a game. She should probably ignore him and get on with her day but she remembered the look he'd given her when they'd been nutting and instead she hurried after him. The lane was empty save for a flash of movement disappearing around the curve of the road. She thought of telling her mother where she was going – but why should she? She could take care of the animals and drive the cart and plant the fields. She wasn't a child any longer.

She pursed up her lips. Why should she follow him? He wasn't her responsibility. She wasn't sure she even liked him. Then she thought of Antonia Hollingworth crossing her arms over her thin chest, the fox fur curled around her neck, and she went on. She wasn't sure she believed the woman's words any longer about doing *what one can* and providing *a refuge*. She was beginning to suspect she hadn't volunteered to take care of the boys at all: her nephews had been foisted on her, one by a sister and one by her husband, and as for Hal and Tom – they'd probably been forced on her by the local billeting officer.

She hurried down the lane, catching herself when her feet slipped, pulling her scarf tighter. She didn't see him again until there was a flash of something golden entering the path where the hazels grew. She frowned and thought again of Mrs Hollingworth. Even if she didn't like the children being in her house she couldn't imagine her allowing him to run wild like this, away from the others, getting his clothes dirty. Whatever would she say? Aggie would have to find him and take him back – perhaps then she wouldn't be so snooty, rubbing her hands together as if brushing off something distasteful.

She moved faster when she saw a dark footprint in the ice at the foot of the path. It was muddy beneath but she didn't care about that; she was dressed for mud, not like Mrs Hollingworth, not like some fine lady. No, *she* was probably too busy, sitting in state in her fancy drawing room, having tea brought in on a silver platter. She still couldn't see him though. What on earth was he doing? She thought he'd be hiding in the hedgerow, his golden hair tangled in the twigs. There was another thin trace of a giggle, fainter now, and she wasn't quite sure she'd really heard it.

Her curiosity was hardening into anger. She didn't have time to spare to go chasing after other people's children. Instead of presenting the boy at the door of Mire House she imagined herself dragging him up the driveway by the ear.

She reached the end of the path where everything widened into a spread of frozen reeds which rustled and tapped against each other. The boy was standing on the bridge that crossed the worst of the soft ground. His hand was on the rail. He didn't grin at her and he didn't look triumphant; he just appeared to be waiting. As soon as he saw her, he whirled and was gone, the reeds quivering as he disappeared into them.

Aggie scowled and shouted, 'Tom! Come out here this minute.'

There was no movement, and silence came back, filling the space as her words faded.

'Tom?' She didn't like the way she sounded now, hesitant and weak. She shouted his name louder but there was still no reply. She couldn't leave him, not here. It wasn't safe. She'd never been allowed to play by the river when she was young.

She looked down at the splintery shine of ice on the concrete and then she went after him, her footsteps ringing out on the bridge. She paused. Had she heard Tom's footsteps when he'd run across? She didn't think she had.

Now there was laughter coming from the water's edge and she frowned again. She wasn't going to call him; she wouldn't give him the satisfaction. As she pushed aside the reeds the dry dead stems crackled. Her hands reddened and her cheeks felt pinched. The reeds were all around her and when she turned she could no longer see the clearing. She could smell the water though, a faintly metallic tang. Her next step broke the thin surface of the ice and she sank into it, brown sludge seeping around her boots. Tom only wore shoes, didn't he? He would be freezing. He would ruin them and Mrs Hollingworth would be furious and it would serve him right.

She listened, but there was still no sound. She scanned the reeds, watching for his breath rising into the air, but she couldn't see it. She was sinking deeper, so she pulled her foot free with a squelch. The boy could easily get stuck in here. She couldn't go back without him. She took another step and the water rose to her ankles. It was *cold*, even through her boots. She pulled away, grasping the reeds as she swayed, then she moved quickly, trying to take each step before the mud could suck her down. She must be almost in the water by now. Her anger was dissipating. What if he *had* got stuck? She opened her mouth to call his name, sure he would answer this time, but as she did she pushed through another thick clump of reeds and saw what lay on the other side.

She had expected that shock of golden hair, but it wasn't like that. The boy was colourless. His hair barely softened the shape of his skull and his already pale skin was whitened by the frost. Even his eyes had faded. They were wide open and staring. They did not blink. He did not stir and he did not look at her and he didn't close his eyes.

His eyes, she thought, closing her own, and then she stumbled away, gagging, clawing at the reeds so that she felt them digging into her palms, as she fought her way back towards solid ground.

The child was dead – he had been dead for some time. That was all Aggie could take in. She wasn't sure what she'd said when she'd raised the alarm but people kept arriving, the constable and the doctor among them, and eventually, Mrs Hollingworth. She wore only a thin coat and she kept clutching at it with her bony fingers. She was flanked by Mrs Appleby – Eddie's mother – and Aggie's mum, who both stood quietly and let her talk non-stop, her lipsticked mouth opening and closing, opening and closing. Her eyes were wide and incredulous and she did not blink. Aggie's discomfort grew as she looked at them. The woman must be wondering how the boy had managed to get out of the house and up here all alone. She must be blaming herself, thinking of how she should have taken care of him – she should have been with him; done *something*.

A squeal cut through the air, making Aggie think of the curlew's call and of what it meant; then she realised it wasn't a bird but a child. It was Arthur. He too had come here alone and he ran towards the marsh, his eyes fixed on what had been found there. His face was pale. Aggie put out a hand as if to stop him and then Mrs Appleby stepped forward and grabbed him around the shoulders. He fought, all the while shouting something. At first it was inarticulate, and then she heard Tom's name, and then, 'It was *me* she wanted. *Me*. I told Tom – I told him, but he wouldn't listen . . .' and he started to sob. This time when Mrs Appleby tried to lead him away, he let her. She headed for the path and Aggie saw the boy hadn't come alone after all. Clarence was there too. She saw the expression on his face and caught her breath. His hands were clenched at his sides, his eyes narrowed, and when he saw Arthur coming towards him, he whirled around and he ran.

Aggie's gaze went to Mrs Hollingworth. She saw that the woman hadn't looked at her nephew at all; she hadn't so much as glanced in his direction.

Aggie closed her eyes. She remembered standing on a slope not far from here, amid the crooked stones of the graveyard, and she remembered what she'd said: *You can't have them.* She had felt as if she was making a choice between Will and Eddie, and no matter how foolish the idea, it felt more than ever that she *had* made a choice. She had been so occupied with doing something for her brother and his friend, those whose fates she couldn't possibly affect, when instead she should have been helping the one she could. And now a child was lying dead in the cold, his last breath taken, his eyes seeing nothing in this world any longer. He was miles from his home. He never had a chance to live. He hadn't even been able to look upon his mother's face as he passed.

She remembered what he'd said to her: *That 'un what wears black . . . She dun't like me. I dun't think she likes the others, neither.*

Aggie turned to face the graveyard, but it was blocked by the sight of Mrs Hollingworth, still talking and talking. She frowned. At least *she* had sat with Tom when he spoke of his fears in the little cupboard in Mire House. She *had* comforted him, hadn't she? There was that, at least. She had done her best.

But she had told him that the woman he'd seen didn't mean him any harm. That he would be *safe*. She'd practically told him to go with her. She closed her eyes and the echoes of voices rang in her ears:

Does that other 'un want to keep us safe, an' all?
It was me *she wanted. Me. I told Tom – I told him, but he wouldn't listen . . .*
She was wavin' us ower, last time.
No children, not ever.
Not ever.

She shivered. She should have told him to *run*. She should have said, *Get as far away from her as you can*. She should have told them all: Arthur, after all, was a relative of the wife who had replaced her. He was right, he must have been the one she had wanted to take to the mire. Now Tom had gone instead.

She closed her eyes. She knew the first Mrs Hollingworth was still there. The dark woman was still reaching out to take what she wanted, to make her will felt from whatever empty place she lived now, and Aggie should have told the boys not to even look at her, not to listen if she called to them, not to let her put her cold hand on their shoulders. Now here was Tom, being carried limp and lifeless from the mire, no need to be frightened any more because it was too late for that. It was too late for anything any longer. And it was *all her fault*.

She thought she heard Mrs Hollingworth say her name and she opened her eyes and her head snapped around, anxious to think of something else, anything else, and she saw that the woman had stopped talking at last; she was standing there, her mouth hanging open as if her words had been cut off mid-flow. She just stared at Aggie, stared at her *guilt*, until Aggie was forced to look away.

CHAPTER EIGHTEEN

That woman, her mother said, afterwards. Years later Aggie would look back and realise her mother had never named Antonia Hollingworth, not ever again. Even long after Aggie had forgiven her, after she'd come to her once more looking for help and she had agreed to give it and had spent all the free time she could muster showing her how to cook and clean and run the very house that Mrs Hollingworth was coming to detest, she was always *that woman* in her mother's eyes.

'She's got a bloody cheek.'

Aggie shifted in her seat. She was sitting at the big old kitchen table, one hand curled around a cup of tea. She had watched her mother scoop three precious teaspoons full of sugar into it and stir.

'She might talk lovely, but she's got nowt good to say. Wanted to know all about it, she did. 'Ow you found 'im, 'ow you knew the boy was there, just as if . . .'

She tuned out her mother's voice and took a sip of the scalding liquid.

'As if she shouldn't 'ave known 'e were missing 'ersen. Shouldn't she!'

Aggie nodded dumbly.

'It weren't no one else's business to watch 'im, an' there she was sayin' things about other folk . . .'

Aggie let her talk. She could still see Mrs Hollingworth's face in her mind, her accusatory expression. Her mother paused and she realised she had asked her something. She blinked.

'Well, love? 'Ow did you – 'ow *did* you know where 'e was?'

Aggie paused. She did not know how to answer her mother's question in a way that would stop her from looking at her like that. She only knew that it was all her fault. She remembered her own expression when Mrs Hollingworth had turned on her, the guilt that must have been written across her face. But then it had been replaced by something else. Mrs Hollingworth's accusatory stare had faded until all there was left was recognition and then fear. And Aggie realised that Mrs Hollingworth *knew* she hadn't done anything wrong, that all Aggie had done was see something she couldn't possibly have seen, and there was only one way the woman could have realised that: because she had seen something impossible herself, or *someone*. Someone who was watching her home, and the new wife living in it, watching as she took her place. Aggie hadn't felt dislike for Mrs Hollingworth then, nor disgust nor anything like it, not any longer; she had felt pity.

The room was silent. Her mother must still be waiting for an answer, one she didn't have. There was no way she could possibly explain. Aggie looked up but found that her mother wasn't looking at her after all; she had turned to face the window. Her head was tilted to one side.

'Mum?'

She didn't turn and Aggie pushed herself up and went to her. She looked into her mother's face and saw that her eyes were staring and yet unfocused, as if she was seeing something she could not believe. She shifted her gaze and saw the telegraph boy from the village. He was standing in the yard. He had walked a few steps onto the cobbles but now he was just standing there, staring down at the envelope he held in his hands. He took a deep breath and started walking again and then he saw them standing at the window and he stopped.

Aggie's mother's hand was resting on the side of the sink. It began to shake. An odd sound filled the air and Aggie realised it was coming from her mother. That frightened her more than anything; she had never heard her make such a sound, had never heard *anyone* make a sound like that. The cold had taken hold of her. She hadn't been aware of it but now it pierced her and chilled her right to the core.

Three sharp raps rang out. Her mother started to bat at the air as if it were some physical thing that was coming: something she could ward away. Aggie couldn't move – she didn't need to; she could see it all already. The paper would open and the words would be written – *my painful duty to inform you* – and there would be nothing ever again, her brother would be gone, the rooms would be empty, there would be no noise and no life in them.

She didn't think she could move but she strode to the door and held out her hand. The boy put the telegram into it and she kept her eyes fixed on him as he touched his cap. He opened his mouth to speak and then he saw her face and instead he turned and walked away, because he could do that; he could leave this all behind.

She stepped into the yard. She knew it was cold but she couldn't feel it any longer. Her legs felt weak and she stumbled across the cobbles, stopping only when she reached the gate. She could see the church. Its bells hadn't rung since war was declared but she felt they were ringing now; there was a clangour in her ears that wouldn't stop. Her fingers opened and something fell from her hand: the paper. She could barely remember what it was. Everything had happened already; she didn't need ink on paper to tell her that. She could see it in the eyes of the woman who was walking towards the house, down the lane, her gait uncertain, as if there were no strength in her legs either. Mrs Appleby wasn't wearing a coat and her hair was escaping her scarf. Eddie's mother staggered a little as she saw Aggie waiting.

Aggie's whole body jerked. Tears were coming now, she could feel them. The day was cold and empty and that was all there was. Her brother was gone and so was Eddie. They probably had been all along. She thought how stupid she had been: what a silly little girl to think she could have changed their fate. It had been decided as soon as the woman had reached for them, her touch death, its conduit into the world, spreading from her and the house and the country and the war, come in all its forms to put its cold hand on them all.

Later, they sat at the table. Her mother put food down in front of them and Aggie knew that no one wanted to eat but they did anyway. The meat was dry but they swallowed it down and nobody spoke. The quiet spread between them, filling the empty spaces. Aggie could feel it: a solid, choking thing. At last she stood and started to gather the plates. The clatter couldn't mask the silence beneath it. Then she realised there was another sound after all, a muted gasping, and she looked around and saw it was coming from her father. His eyes were scrunched tight and his cheeks were wet; his shoulders shook, the dry, pained gasps of someone who never cried.

Aggie stood there with the dirty plates in her hands and she couldn't look away. She knew that her mother was watching too. Her mother wasn't crying; she was beyond that, she had already cried until there was nothing left inside. Aggie's hands started to shake and she set the plates back down on the table. It took a long time for her father to steady himself and then he wiped his eyes with the back of his hand and his nose with his sleeve and he blinked as if he'd just woken up.

'We shall have to bear it,' he said. His voice was small, a cracked and broken thing. 'We shall have to. An' he – he's only gone on afore,' he added. 'We'll all—' He took a deep breath and stared down at the table. 'We all go into silence in the end.'

Aggie couldn't move. She couldn't accept his words because in her mind there *wasn't* silence: she could hear it all, the shouts of men and the report of guns, shells exploding and the earth being displaced, limbs ripped apart, men's screams and women's tears and the *cry*, the cry of triumph and despair and defiance: the cry of all the forsaken. And her brother was there, she could hear him too, his lips were moving, crying out from the ground.

She felt her own scream building inside, all of the words she wanted to say, and she opened her eyes and she saw her father's face and she pressed her lips together and said nothing at all.

PART FOUR

2013 – Into Silence

CHAPTER ONE

Emma Dean opened her eyes and waited for the pain to begin. She could feel where the stairway had struck her, the place on the side of her thigh, the back of her knee, her spine – and yet everything was numb, her body and her mind. All that she could see was white, like a faded photograph. Slowly she realised that someone was standing over her and she flinched. The shape didn't move. Her vision flooded back and at first she didn't know this stranger and her eyes narrowed, and then something flickered into place and her vision righted itself. It was only Charlie, his face full of concern, leaning over her. He reached out a hand and kept it there when she didn't move.

'Are you all right?'

She raised her own hand, though not to take his; she raised it as if to fend him off.

He drew back, his expression changing to one of hurt. 'I think you must have slipped,' he said. 'Didn't you hear me? You looked as if you were sleepwalking. I told you not to get too near to the edge.'

Get out, she thought. That was what she'd heard.

'I tried to reach you but it was too late. You slipped – I tried to catch you.' He leaned in closer and concern was all she saw in his eyes. She let out a long breath. The pain still hadn't come.

'You looked as if you were watching something – were you, Emma? What did you see?' His tone had changed. She *did* remember, that was the problem. What had she seen? The ghost of an old man? She'd heard the sound of his voice.

It struck her that perhaps Charlie was right, perhaps she had been asleep. Perhaps that ghostly figure had only ever been a dream. And yet Charlie had showed her things too, hadn't he? The children's footprints in the hall – she couldn't have dreamed them. Besides, she hadn't just *seen* the ghost: she'd touched the old man's clothes, smelled his pipe. Was it possible to touch or smell things in dreams?

She braced her hands against the floor, dimly feeling the tiles against her fingers. The things she had touched in her dream had felt more vivid than this. She closed her eyes, wondering how badly she was hurt. Her head swam when she pushed herself up.

'Let me help you, Emma.'

His voice sounded deeper, more resonant, and she shook her head to clear it. Her thoughts felt cloudy. *It was better when I was lying down.*

'Careful. Come into the drawing room. You need to lie down.'

Her gaze snapped to his once more. Was he reading her thoughts? But of course that was ridiculous. It had been a natural thing to say; it was her own thinking that was disordered. Even the memory of what had happened was slipping away. When she closed her eyes she could remember the blow on each stair as she fell, and yet it felt distant, as if it had happened to someone else. And the hand in the middle of her back – had she really felt that? She was no longer sure. She thought she had, but then he said he'd been reaching for her, to try and catch her – perhaps that was all it had been.

He slipped a hand under her elbow and helped her up and she didn't pull away. She still didn't hurt but her legs felt weak and she leaned against him. He took her weight, helping her into the drawing room, but when she reached it she didn't want to lie down after all. She felt stronger. Light flooded in at the windows, the odd, lurid kind that precedes a storm. She drew away and straightened. 'It's fine, Charlie. I can stand.'

'Is it, Emma? Are you sure?'

She didn't know what to say. For a moment he hadn't sounded like the old Charlie but someone more serious. She rubbed a hand across her eyes. 'I don't know what you mean.'

'You had a nasty fall. You don't want to push yourself too far.'

'I'm all right. I'm not an invalid.'

'You should let me take care of you.'

Now she did pull away. 'I have things to do, Charlie.'

'I'm trying to—'

'I know you're only trying to help, but I'm fine. This place . . . needs me.'

'Does it?'

'I mean, I need to get on with the work.' She took a couple of steps, pausing when white spots speckled her vision. She forced herself to walk away, half expecting to feel a hand on her back, but he didn't touch her again and he didn't say anything else.

CHAPTER TWO

The hall was dark but as soon as she started to spread the fresh paint, it glowed. The air had a sickly yellow taint, as if at any moment the humidity would turn to rain. She hoped it would; a storm would clear her mind; it would wash everything clean. Her head ached and she rubbed her temple with the back of her hand. It was swollen, but the pain still hadn't set in. Everything felt numb. She didn't want to think about that hand on her back – she wasn't sure what it implied about the state of her thoughts.

She couldn't focus on anything, but as she worked she began to feel better. It was making the place feel more like hers. Soon Charlie would be gone and she would be here alone, and that was all right, now; she found she was looking forward to it.

She frowned, remembering there was a smaller room still to paint; she'd been putting it off. 'Room' was probably too grand a name for the cupboard in her bedroom. She didn't want to admit to herself that she didn't like it; that would be like giving in to some childish fear. Soon she would go in there and throw open the door and banish its ghosts. She would paint over that too, making it all new.

Time passed and the sickly light tracked its way across the tiles. Emma kept on going. She didn't feel hungry. She listened for Charlie and heard nothing at all: nothing moving in the house, no birdsong outside, nothing passing on the road. It was completely and entirely silent. Even the ghosts had quietened.

Later, the rain came down in a tumult, as if the world was raging, beating at the house, trying to tear it apart. There was thunder, but it was distant, drowned out by the pounding of the rain which assaulted brick and slate and tile. Emma walked through the house, hearing the tone of it change as she passed from room to room. It hissed against the walls and scurried through the gravel, rapping like knuckles on the windows and bleeding down the glass. She could not even hear her own footsteps.

When she entered the drawing room, the sound swelled like music and for a moment she thought she heard the strains of an old-fashioned dance tune. Then it was subsumed. She looked out of the window. Darkness had closed in, although the day wasn't over. The bare twigs of the shrubbery outside bowed and sprung back as the droplets tore down. Beyond that were black skeletal trees against a charcoal sky, their branches clawing at the world.

She had always loved storms but now she was grateful for the barrier of the glass. Everything outside moved constantly, blurring and fluid. The sky had turned to water. For a second the only motionless thing was the dark shape of the distant yew tree, so blackened it looked like a hole in the world.

When she turned, Charlie was watching her. She hadn't realised he was in the room but she did not feel startled; his eyes were soft and questioning. She gave a half-smile and he smiled back. It was his old look, open and guileless. He held out a hand and she felt a wave of disorientation; it was as if he was asking her to dance and for a moment she could hear that music again, drifting around the space. She had a sudden image of smart ladies filling the room, all wearing their finest dresses, whirling around to the music that carried them along.

'We should have something,' he said. 'We can drink wine and watch the rain.'

She nodded. She still wasn't hungry, but she was tired and a little light-headed. He was right, she should rest; she should have listened to him. He had only wanted to help. She couldn't look into his clear eyes and doubt it any longer. Now she was grateful as he took her arm, leading her where she needed to go.

CHAPTER THREE

Emma stood in the drawing room, clutching something to her. It was smooth and cool under her fingers and at first she thought of the old man's pipe; then she realised it was the telephone.

The room was dark and full of shadows and had a faintly metallic, faintly musty smell. It was cold too, making the hairs prickle along her arms.

She must have been sleepwalking. Charlie *had* been right after all. She had no recollection of getting out of bed; the only thing she could dredge from her memory was the need to speak to someone. She had wanted to ask them about Charlie. She had felt a sudden urge to know if he was really as he appeared or if he was something else after all, someone who *wanted* something else; and so she must have come down here and picked up the phone, to call – whom?

She listened for the ring tone, but there was nothing, just the dead sound of a dead line. She knew that she had no one to call, no one she could speak to. There was only Charlie and he was sleeping somewhere above her in the dark house.

She replaced the phone on its cradle and regarded it. She had brought it from her flat but she'd never even had it connected. The silence was everywhere, thick around her face, gathering until she felt she was choking in it.

CHAPTER FOUR

Emma awoke to half-light and for a moment she didn't know if it was dawn or nightfall; then she remembered the strange experience of the night before, waking in the dark room downstairs, and she frowned. Now she wasn't sure if she'd really sleepwalked or if the whole thing had been another dream.

She could hear Charlie moving around somewhere below her. It was a nice sound. It was good to know that someone was there, close by, someone she could talk to. Then she remembered the ghostly steps in the hall. For a moment, she was no longer certain that the sounds she could hear downstairs were real, but it didn't matter. She closed her eyes. The world could wait a little longer. She would burrow in deep, wrapped in the walls of Mire House, and let its boundaries close around her. It made her feel safe.

Now the footsteps were coming up the stairs and it *sounded* like Charlie. His movements were familiar to her now. There came a light knock on the door. She hadn't closed it properly and it swung inwards and there he was, his hair flattened against the side of his head so that she knew which way he had been lying as he slept.

'I brought you tea. Plenty of sugar. I thought you might need it.' He smiled.

'Thanks, Charlie.'

'I thought today, perhaps we could do with a break. I thought we might go for a walk.'

She reached out for the mug and thought at once of the river.

'We could go and see the mire,' he said, and once again she had the impression he was reading her mind. He knew her so well. 'It would do you good, I think. Both of us.'

He was right again – she'd been cooped up in here far too long. And yet she felt a twinge at the thought of leaving the house.

Ten minutes later she was standing in the hall. There were no muddy footprints on the tiles this time; the place didn't even look lived in. At least, when they came back, they could leave their own prints there.

She looked around at the work she'd done, the places where she'd tried to paint over the past. It was no use; she could still sense it, the layers upon layers soaked into the walls.

'Ready?' Charlie opened the door and it filled with the washed-out light of a pale morning. The day was beautiful. She smiled and walked into it.

The path was so close to the house she wondered why she had never followed it until now. It sloped up a gentle incline before dipping once more towards the lower ground. It was overgrown, almost closed in by long grass, and there was a hedgerow formed of dead bushes interspersed with small leaf-less trees. It didn't look like an easy path, but Charlie went ahead anyway, finding a stick in the undergrowth and swiping at the fading greenery. The foliage was wet with dew and each strike sent shining droplets flying into the air. It must have been a long time since anyone came this way. The whole place felt as empty as the house; there was not even a bird in the sky, which was clear and pale and a little cold.

When Emma glanced back, the grey stone of Mire House looked faded. Beyond it was the churchyard, everything softened by a faint haze. Only the yew tree's branches looked heavy and dense, as if they were still darkened with rain. For a brief moment she thought she saw someone standing beneath it, but no: it was an illusion born of the twisting branches. It had probably always been an illusion. For a moment she closed her eyes, imagining clawing hands reaching for her; then it was gone.

Charlie had drawn ahead and she hurried to catch up. He was blocking her view but she caught glimpses of a wider, flatter space. The path ended and there was nothing but the long grass and the susurration it made and the smell of the water.

'Watch your step,' he said, and she looked down to see that the toes of her shoes had sunk into the ground, a bright edge of water marking the line between them. She pulled them free and felt herself sinking again almost at once. 'Maybe we should go back.'

'We can go a little further. Look, there's a bridge.'

And there was, though it was nothing but a simple concrete slab with a single rusted rail. It wasn't a pretty bridge, but having seen it, she wanted to go across. That was what bridges were for.

'It's all right,' Charlie said. 'I'll go on before you.'

She followed, each footstep making a sound like a hungry mouth. She had hoped to see the water but there was nothing, only swollen-looking reeds interspersed with the grass. She could smell water, though, the iron scent of the river, and she could sense its flow, steadily leading somewhere else. The taller reeds masked it from view. They were close-pressed and stirring in the breeze, rattling against each other.

It was treacherous beyond the bridge. She took a few more steps, trying to find solid ground, but it was impossible. For a moment she couldn't see Charlie; then she realised he was standing away to the side, watching her. 'The water's high,' he called. 'It must have risen in the storm.'

He was right: the whole area was half-submerged. Emma pulled a face. There wasn't anything to see. Then she spun around to face him. How had he known that the water had risen? He had never been here before.

He saw the look on her face and smiled. 'It's all right,' he said. 'I needed you to see this. This is the edge.'

She thought at first he said *the end* and she started.

'You don't need to be afraid.'

She had a sudden image of herself falling into the water, being carried away by the tide under that endless sky, and she took a step away from him. There was only softness beneath her, the water finding its way into her shoes, lapping at her ankles, greedy for the warmth of her skin.

Charlie smiled once more and it was a broad smile, impossible not to trust, and yet she *didn't* trust it. She wanted to run, to be somewhere far away. She had that odd feeling again, like when he'd reached for her at the bottom of the stairs: as if he was Charlie but not Charlie, at once the person she thought she knew and someone else entirely.

'There is something I needed you to see.' His voice was soft, almost hypnotic, and Emma found she couldn't move. She was sinking into the ground as if she was already rooted there, a part of this place. *Becoming* part of it. He kept moving though, apparently without difficulty, until he stood in front of her. He reached out, but he did not touch her; he simply swept his hand around, indicating the reeds, the broad sky, the whole empty place. 'Look at it, Emma,' he said. 'What do you see?'

She frowned. She had seen everything already and yet she felt now that if she knew the right way to look there were depths here after all; things she had only begun to glimpse.

'Go on, Emma,' he whispered, and she did, walking away from him, moving easily after all, as if something inside her was lighter. She wanted to see the river. She wanted to catch a glimpse of where it led. The reeds opened before her to reveal something hidden behind them. For a moment she thought she saw a figure there, a small shape in the water, reaching out; and then she went dizzy and her vision speckled with white. The paleness spread. It was coming from the centre of the mire now, rising like mist from the water, hanging before her face. Everything was white, pure and clean, and she looked up at the sky to see that it had gone; everything had become that same sheer blankness. She couldn't see anything else. White: everything was white.

She tried to speak, but she was choking. What had Charlie done to her? He must have done something terrible. She batted a hand in front of her eyes as she gasped for breath. No: she was all right, she *must* be all right. It would pass. She was standing firmly on the ground. She forced herself to concentrate on that but when she shifted there was only mire beneath her feet; she couldn't even be certain of that. Then she felt his hand on her shoulder, an intimate, warm touch.

'You see now,' he said, close to her ear.

'I don't understand.' She pulled away, but he held on. His grip tightened. His hand was cold: bone-cold.

'You will. All things end, Emma. All things have new beginnings. You have hung on long enough. It is time for you to leave.'

No.

'It's time to see what's on the other side.'

She pulled away from him. Everything seemed to happen so slowly. The whiteness in front of her gave way as she turned, first to the dull colour of dead grass, and then to Charlie's smiling face. There were shadows behind it. She almost felt she could see into him, *through* him, to glimpse the truth behind his eyes. 'Who are you?' she asked.

'I came to show you the way.' He gestured towards that white light. 'You should go, now. Before it's too late.'

'I don't know what you mean.' She turned and the light was there. Fear ripped through her. She didn't know what had happened to her vision; at least he hadn't hurt her, not yet.

'I'm here to show you how to cross.'

'You're not Charlie,' she said. 'Are you? Or not *just* Charlie.'

He bowed his head, acknowledging the truth.

'So why—?'

'I needed to take a form that you would understand. A form you would not be afraid of.'

'You brought me here to— You're going to kill me.'

She watched as his eyes filled with pain. They were gentle. So *gentle*.

'No. I'm not here to hurt you. I'm here to show you the way home; to the other side, to your family.'

The thought of her father and mother cut deep. Sorrow blossomed inside her, a raw wound, and she hugged herself.

'You see it now.'

She shook her head. She didn't see anything, only blank whiteness.

'You *have* to see, Emma. This is your chance.' He pointed towards the river, towards nothing.

'I—' She looked into it. 'I don't understand. I don't know what that is.'

He gave a rueful smile. 'I can't tell you that. You have to go alone. I can't go with you.'

She turned to meet his eyes and there was a light in them she couldn't explain. She had that sense again of seeing only the surface of things, that behind them lay a deep river, something she couldn't comprehend. She knew now that the words he spoke were somehow not Charlie's. She was no longer sure he was male or female, young or old; she wasn't sure he was even human.

'There are other doorways here than those built by man.' He gestured and this time, when she turned to look, she realised that she could see the church. No: the graveyard, the yew tree at its edge standing tall and dark, looking more than ever like a hole in the world.

'There are places where the walls grow thin,' he said.

His expression was so kind that her eyes filled with tears. She blinked them away. 'What is it?' She pointed to the place where land became river and the river, land. 'What's through there?'

'Only you can find out. I can point the way, Emma, that's the reason I came. Beyond that – I don't know.' Now he looked sad. 'I've never seen it. I'm not sure I will ever know.'

She blinked. The whiteness was everywhere now, and it obscured his face. For a moment, through the blur, she thought he looked different; and then she thought she caught sight of others standing next to him, an old man in a shabby suit, a soldier, two young boys. When she rubbed her eyes, they were gone. There was a sound in her ears like a river rushing, moving onward towards a place she couldn't see.

'All you have to do is walk through.' He pointed towards the water, towards that whiteness, towards *nothing*.

Emma's eyes blurred with tears. She stepped forward and felt herself sinking deeper. It was as if the mire was trying to claim her. She shook her head. She had heard of people *going into the light*; it soothed their pain. Soon she needn't feel it any longer. She would see her father's face, and her mother's, and she would be happy again. Charlie was right. He had been right all along. She would go into that whiteness and she would simply disappear: she would be *free*.

With the next step, she sank up to her knees. The water was cold, deep cold, but she knew it wouldn't last for long. She floundered and pulled herself forwards. It was sinking inside her, the cold, touching her flesh, her bones. Death was such a simple thing, so small a barrier to cross. Now it was her time; it would all be over in moments. She felt a flood of gratitude towards Charlie. She paused only to turn, to say goodbye, and she saw the expression on his face.

She gasped and struggled to pull herself upwards. For a moment she had almost felt she could see what lay beyond the veil; for a moment, she had almost believed him. She twisted and floundered her way back across the mire towards Charlie – no: *not* Charlie. It didn't even look like him any longer. There was someone standing behind Charlie, *in* him.

The mire reached for her, trying to drag her under. For a second she thought she saw something amongst the reeds, a flash of golden hair, and then it was gone.

She turned from it and she saw Charlie's face. His expression was blank, as if he'd just woken, and there was something else, something a little like a shadow around him, as if he was surrounded by a dark halo. Then his face darkened, as if the shadows were gathering, and it suddenly sharpened, and Emma saw it was the ghostly woman she had seen in the graveyard, in front of him; no, stepping *out* of him. Her veil was drawn back. Emma could see her eyes.

The woman turned, putting her hand on Charlie's shoulder, and he slumped, his head lolling. He looked pale, exhausted. His eyes closed but he did not fall. Suddenly he shivered.

The woman looked at her.

'There's nothing there,' Emma whispered. 'Nothing but the mire.'

The woman threw back her head and laughed.

'You – you were going to trick me. I would have drowned.'

The laughter swelled. 'Oh, my dear. Oh, my dear.'

'You're *her*. The one – the one who said—'

'*My God, my God*,' she replied. 'It's so funny, don't you think? Not to despair; not to grieve; not to sorrow, but to ever believe there is a God in the first place. To believe there is someone to listen when you call.' Her face straightened. 'There is no God, Emma, not in this place. There never was.'

Emma glanced around. It was desolate, she saw that now; she didn't know why she'd ever been drawn to it.

'Because it called you to it. It called you *home*.'

Emma shook her head, as if she could deny everything: this place, the woman's presence, the death that had awaited her. She would go back and get her things, leave as soon as she could and never come back. She would *get out*. It struck her now that was exactly what Clarence Mitchell must have done. He had come here and seen the house for what it was, a place that was never a home, never meant to hold life in it. He'd seen everything and he'd fled, and when he died he had left it for her but not for love, not for the sake of family, but out of his hatred, his bitterness. *It wasn't meant for you*, he'd written to his grandson, and now here *she* was, drawn in like some foolish, trusting child. Well, she was a child no longer. She wouldn't be caught a second time.

Now his grandson had been made a part of it too, used by this woman like some puppet. He was still standing there, his eyes nothing but white slits, his cheeks deathly pale.

'It was you,' she said, 'all the time.'

'Oh, my dear, not *all* the time. Not at first. But I had to use him, you see – I couldn't speak to him the way I did his grandfather.'

'Clarence Mitchell? You knew him?'

'I knew him well. I whispered in his ear. He did not always know I was there, but we grew close, he and I. But then, we were family. He was my nephew: family, like Charles here. Perhaps that was why I could possess him so completely.'

'But why—?'

'Why you? Oh, I knew your grandfather too, my dear. He lived here for a while, along with Clarence. He was *her* blood, the woman who took my husband and this place and my life, stealing him little by little until I lost my child and everything

I had. And I almost made Arthur pay – the nearest thing *she* had to a child – but he wouldn't answer my call and I lost him in the end. But now *you* are here, his grandchild.'

'But Charlie and I – we're *related*.'

'By marriage: a tainted marriage that should never have been. But blood runs deeper still and you are *her* blood – the *last* of her blood.'

'And that's why? Because of something that happened before I was even born?' Emma gathered herself. 'Then it means you lose. I'm leaving this place. I'm not coming back. I'm done with it – I'm done with you.'

She glanced up at the sky. It was growing a deeper blue; colour was returning to the world. The woman was losing her power to drain it of life and soon Emma would return to it, leaving behind these close hillsides and the damp mire. She could leave *now*.

'There are few things more amusing than the deluded, my dear.' The woman smiled. 'This place is your home, Emma. It always has been, I knew that at once. It is impossible to deny, since you felt it yourself – the moment you looked at *my* house.'

Emma shook her head, brushing away the woman's words. She remembered the first time she had seen Mire House, its dour grey stone, its louring presence, its sense of aloneness. And yet she had seen its beauty. She had loved it at once; it was as if it called to something inside her. *No.* The woman had seen how she felt and she was twisting it, manipulating her. She didn't have to listen.

She looked at Charlie. She had doubted him, for so long, and all the time he was innocent; the woman's pawn, not a part of her plan. He might be of her blood, this dark woman's, but she couldn't leave him here like this.

'Let him go,' she said.

She had expected more, but the woman simply gave a mocking bow and stepped away from him. Charlie blinked, his eyes unfocused, and he raised his head. He frowned, as if he had no recollection of how he came to find himself at the mire.

Emma stepped forward and took his arm. He didn't react but he did listen when she said softly, 'I think that's enough of a walk, Charlie. There's nothing here. Let's go.'

He turned his head. 'I—' He paused. 'I don't—' and then he coughed, as if embarrassed. She could almost sense him trying to explain his presence here to himself.

'We've been working too hard,' Emma said. 'It's time we had a break. Get away from this place.'

He rubbed his forehead. 'You're right. I'm not sure why – I mean, yes. I should be heading home.'

She smiled. 'You should.' She could still see the woman's dark shape, outlined against the reeds at his back. She turned away from it. She took his arm and began to guide him away. There was no need for him to know what had happened. She walked towards the path, the ground beneath her feet becoming firmer with each step, and she saw the bridge ahead of her. Soon they would cross it; they would leave all of this behind. The dead need not concern her any longer, only the living.

Emma did not stop and she did not look back, but still the woman's voice followed her. She glanced at Charlie, but he showed no sign of having heard it. She paused, closing her eyes, and she felt his hand close over her arm. He said something, but she didn't listen: she could hear nothing but the woman's voice, which followed her in a whisper.

'There are few things more amusing than the deluded. There is *nothing* more amusing than someone who does not know they belong to me already.'

And then, so faintly that she wasn't sure she had really heard it: *This is your home, Emma.*

CHAPTER FIVE

Charlie seemed to wake as they went further from the mire. They crossed the bridge and reached the path and the ground was blessedly solid beneath them, and the colours intensified: the sky was deepening, and swallows were wheeling above them. Charlie pulled ahead, rubbing at the back of his neck, and she hurried to keep up. She felt lighter, freer: *alive*.

She failed, she thought. The woman had failed. She had meant for Emma to die, to drown in the mire alone and away from anyone, and she had *failed*. She relished the cool air in her lungs and Charlie, here with her and himself once again. She remembered the way she'd woken with the telephone in her hand, wanting to speak to someone, *anyone*, to find out who he was and if she could trust him, and now she knew: he wasn't evil, had never had any scheme, had never been against her. He was just Charlie, and they could get to know each other properly now, no doubts standing between them. She found herself smiling, joy tingling at the edge of her senses. She needn't be alone.

And then Charlie whirled around and she saw the expression on his face and her smile faded. His skin was pale and his eyes were wide, still unfocused. 'I have to go,' he said. 'Emma, I've stayed here too long. I'm not sure why.'

He turned his back and started to run, away down the slope towards the lane, and after a moment she ran after him. His steps were loud on the road and then he was gone, turned in at the gate. When she caught up to him he was bent double with one arm resting on his car. He let it fall and slumped onto his knees, the crunch of it loud on the gravel. She winced, but he didn't appear to feel any pain.

Slowly his head turned and he looked up at the house. The way he stared froze her. It was as if he was seeing something she couldn't see and she looked up at the windows as a shadow passed across it. She shook her head. A cloud, or a bird; it couldn't be anything else. Not now. Not here. The woman had *failed*.

Charlie bowed his head and his back jerked as if he was retching. She didn't want to touch him, but after a moment she did, resting her hand lightly on his shoulder. He didn't respond. It took him a while to raise his head. He turned to her again, and said: 'There's something wrong in there, Emma. There's something in the house.'

She shook her head, *no*, there was nothing, it was all right now; but he looked away from her, *past* her, towards the road and away. 'I have to go,' he said.

'Charlie, no. Not like this.'

'I have to *get out*.'

'Please. You could stay a while.'

He shook his head again, the movement wild, and she realised with shock that he was close to tears. 'I can't go in there,' he said. He felt at his pockets, turning even paler, and then he found his keys and clutched at his chest. 'It's all right,' he muttered. 'It's all right.'

'Charlie, come inside. You can have a drink first, rest a little—'

He pushed himself to his feet and edged around the car, supporting his weight against it once more. He reached the driver's side door and pulled it open.

'Wait. Your things . . .'

'Doesn't matter.'

'I'll get them for you.'

'No! Emma, no. You should get away from here. You should get out.' And then he paused and said, quietly, 'If you can.'

'Charlie?'

He half-fell into the car and fumbled with the keys. It started first time, ready to go, to drive away and leave her, just as they had been given this chance.

She didn't call out or grab the door as he pulled it closed. She could see it wasn't any use. He had panicked, that was all; he'd sensed something of what the woman had done to him and he wanted to get away, and she couldn't blame him. He would leave this place and he would calm down and then, soon, she would see him again. They could start over. He probably wouldn't even be able to remember why he'd wanted to go so badly. It would be all right.

He reversed onto the grass, the wheels sinking in, and then pulled forward, scattering gravel in his haste. He did not look back as he drove away; he didn't even look at her.

Emma was left standing on the drive, staring at the road, wondering how long it would be before she saw him again. *He was mine*, she thought. He was only a distant relative, but it was painfully clear now that he was the only one she had.

CHAPTER SIX

There's something in the house.

Emma closed the door behind her and she knew that Charlie had been wrong. It wasn't the house that was the problem, it never had been. It was the woman who had tainted it, cursing it with her presence.

She was grateful to be enclosed in its cool shade, its protective walls. Her fear was fading. The mire was behind her and she need never go there again. There had been no reason for Charlie to run away like that. For the first time she felt the stirrings of contempt. What on earth had he been thinking? But he too had been tainted by its ghost. He was of the woman's blood so perhaps he had simply revolted against it, wanting to cast off her spirit, to get as far away from it as he could.

And it hadn't been his fault. At least she knew now that Charlie had really been her friend. One day he too would realise that, and when he did, she would be here, waiting, when he came back.

No: she was still leaving, wasn't she? That was her plan. She had only wanted to come back here and gather her things and get out, like Charlie. She would go far away and never return. She could sell the place, get rid of it – *pass it on*. She shivered.

She realised the house was cold, even now, in the daytime. Its air had a musty taint.

Still, it was hers. *Hers.*

She had seen it in her mind, right from the beginning, a grand place with light spilling down the stairs, gleaming on the polished balustrade and the freshly painted walls, the shining floor. It was a place where she could *live*, not just exist; somewhere that made her special, that set her apart. Somewhere that made her feel as if she belonged.

She swallowed, hard, remembering her parents' house and her own small flat. They seemed impossibly far away. She didn't need to run back to them. She no longer felt so frightened. Mire House folded itself around her and calmed her and made her feel safe. She was here now, and she had nowhere else to be. She belonged here. It was *hers.*

This place is your home, Emma. It always has been.

She shook the woman's words away. She didn't have to listen to them. She had taken something that was true and right and made it twisted. Now she was here, inside, safe, she *didn't* want to leave it. She didn't want to be anywhere else; she wasn't sure she had anywhere else left to be. Mire House was the only solid thing in the world. The woman had been right: she *did* belong here – but not in the way she had meant.

Emma closed her eyes. She belonged here because the woman had *failed*. Now she was here, *alone*, but that was all right. Somehow, it always had been. Being alone needn't be frightening, not here.

She pictured her mother's face, then her father's, and they were smiling. They no longer reminded her of the hollow place inside. It had been her greatest fear, to have nothing and no one left, that she would simply disappear, but now she was *home*. She could exist in its silence and call it peace. She could breathe again.

She did just that, taking a long draught of air, but there was something wrong with it. At first she wasn't sure what it was, and then she knew: that stale taint – it hadn't been that way when she'd set out on her walk with Charlie. It had been cleaner then, refreshed by the breeze from windows left ajar, the only scent the chemical tang of paint. Now it smelled of the mire. She looked up at the stairwell. Motes of dust hung there, circling one another like long-dead dancers. She narrowed her eyes. The walls were not as she remembered. The corners were darkened with dust-coated cobwebs and the walls were festooned with dry screws of peeling paint and flecked with mould. She could smell mould now too, the scent strong and organic. She closed her eyes and pictured her own hands, working, covering the walls with fresh paint. She opened them once more and the image faded. Everything was grey. It was shadowed; it was *old*.

She stepped forward and ran her fingertips across the wall, feeling only dust beneath them. Then she went towards the back of the house and pushed open the door to the dining room, one of the last rooms she'd worked on. It was where the mould was coming from, she could tell by the sourer tang in the air. It always had been stronger here at the back of the house, the closest point to the mire.

Dark blotches had spread from the back wall, painting them anew with its clammy fingers. The carpet was uneven, rippling like swampy ground. Beneath the mould the walls were a filthy ochre: the colour of abandonment, of loss. It looked as if no one had been here in a very long time. Emma made a sound in the back of her throat. She could *see* the room as she had left it, brightened by the work of her hands, of *their* hands, hers and Charlie's. She had worked so hard to make everything new, to show that it was her own. To *make* it her own. Now its air clogged her throat; she couldn't breathe. She backed away, turning from it so that she wouldn't have to see the old house appearing once more, emerging from the past. She must have been wrong. She was only confused, that was all. It must have been one of the other rooms that she'd painted. She had made a mistake.

She stood there, just breathing, forcing herself to think. The drawing room: that was the first thing to be finished when she came here. It was the first room she'd been able to *see* in her mind, the one where her vision was clearest. She had been going to paint it green and read a book in a tall chair by the light of a lamp. Charlie had seen the colour and told her it was perfect. And it was: it *was*.

She walked unsteadily across the hall, noting that the tiles were smeared with muddy footprints. Her own? She wasn't sure and she didn't want to think about it. She reached out to push the door open and then she stopped. There were voices, low and urgent, just on the edge of hearing. They were coming from somewhere behind her. At first it sounded as if they were everywhere, echoing around the hard tiles and empty walls of the hallway, and then she heard a soft crunch as of footsteps on gravel. She breathed again. It was someone outside. She couldn't think who it might be. It occurred to her it could be the dark woman, come to reclaim the house she had built, but somehow it didn't *feel* like that. She stayed motionless. If she didn't move, they wouldn't know she was there. Soon they would go away again.

She listened for a knock but instead the murmuring came again. She couldn't make out the words but she could tell that one voice belonged to an older woman and one to a man; his voice was lower than her dry, cracked tones. With a start, she realised that she recognised it. She had heard it somewhere before, but she couldn't remember when. Then she thought:

You getting on all right, are you? Big old house, that.
It was my— a distant relative's. I inherited it.
Ah. Sorry. Or good for you, not sure which.

The voice belonged to the man from the church. What was his name? Frank, that was it. But why was he here, now? She froze and listened again. At last there was a knock at the door. She didn't move but she leaned towards it, straining to hear.

'It was never a good place.' The voice was the woman's.

'I don't suppose it was, Mum.'

'I never did like you coming 'ere that time. I never wanted you to set foot in it, not really. Not one bit—' Her voice faded.

'Aye, well. I shouldn't 'ave. I know what it led to, Mum. I still remember what 'e said, that 'e weren't scared . . .'

'I don't want to think on't, love. Not our Mossy, not 'ere.'

'No, Mum.' There was a pause. 'It were just an accident, nowt else . . .' and then, 'I was never quite easy about it, that lass coming t' live 'ere. It din't quite feel right.'

'No, well. We'll check on 'er, love.'

They fell silent. Emma stepped softly towards the door, but somehow she couldn't bring herself to open it. She didn't want visitors. She only wanted Charlie back, but if not him, she wanted to be on her own. And then the door handle turned and the catch opened with a click and she rapidly stepped back into the shadows beneath the stairs. She stared at the door and she didn't blink. If she could keep them away with her will, they wouldn't come in: they'd turn and they'd run.

The door opened.

'It's open. We'll 'ave a quick look, then you'll know she's all right. That's the best thing.' The woman's face was full of concern beneath the wrinkles. Her hair was white and pulled into a bun, stray hairs surrounding her like static electricity. She put a hand nervously to the mole just next to her lip, and then a man's hand took her arm and helped her across the threshold. It struck Emma then how colourless they looked, this old woman and the tall, thin man behind her, and yet she could almost sense the warmth they had for each other. She could see it in the gentle way he clasped her arm.

Inside the threshold, they paused and looked around. 'You was good to that old man, Frank.'

He gave a rueful smile. 'He weren't that old,' he said. 'You told me that once, though he were old enough to us. It were a shame, though. I should've gone back, after, you know. I never did say I were sorry. But then what happened happened, and it were all too late anyway and I couldn't take it back, any of it.' His smile faded as he spoke and his voice cracked and Emma realised that he was close to tears. His gaze was vague, as if he was looking at something a long way away. He still hadn't noticed her where she stood, pressed back against the wall.

She didn't quite know why she had hidden. By rights she should declare herself, demand to know what they were doing in her house, but she found she wanted to hear more.

The old woman patted his hand and leaned in towards him. 'It weren't your fault. I were punished enough when she took *them*, my brother Will, and—' She paused. 'Well, it were enough. I were a part of a future she never got to live, that was all, an' she couldn't forgive me for it. I suppose it were worse, leavin' me to carry on without 'em. 'Course, I thought it were done, after that. I thought it were ower. I never thought— I'd 'ave gone away if I'd suspected for a minute it'd tek our Mossy. Far away, where nowt'd have 'urt the pair o' you.' Her eyes filled with tears.

'Dun't go gettin' upset, Mum. P'raps you shouldn't 'ave come with me.'

'I'd not see you come 'ere alone, love. If I 'adn't—'

'Mum, don't. Our Mossy – that could 'ave been an accident, nothing more, an' anyway, we shouldn't think on't now. Not 'ere.'

'You said 'e weren't scared. He weren't, were 'e? I'd hate to think of 'im, alone and scared, in the mire, at the end.'

Emma bit her lip.

It took Frank a moment to respond. 'He – he told me he weren't scared of the old man, Mum.'

She was silent for a moment. 'But he was scared of summat else. Well, he 'ad more sense than any of us, then.' She put a hand to her face; it was shaking.

'Mum, it's all right. Step in 'ere a minute. Have a sit-down. I'm sure t' young lass wouldn't mind.' He opened the door to the drawing room and helped his mother inside.

Emma stepped forward to follow them and then she froze. They would see her; they would wonder why she hadn't spoken. Somehow she didn't want to reveal herself just yet. She felt they had more to say. She edged away from the door just as Frank came out. He paused partway, staring up at the stairs, his eyes wide open and fixed.

'Go on, love. I'll be all right. Just you 'ave a quick look, then we can go and we dun't ever 'ave to come back agin.'

'All right, Mum. You sit tight, now.' Frank stepped slowly across the hall, looking down at the black and white tiles. They were smeared with dirt and he picked his way between the footprints as if he didn't want to disturb them. He paused at the bottom of the stairs and put his hand on the rail and just stayed there, looking upwards. He roused himself and glanced around. Emma caught her breath but he didn't notice her and then he tilted back his head. 'Miss? Emma?' he called. 'Emma!'

She bit her lip. She couldn't bring herself to speak. She hadn't *asked* him to come here. She didn't *want* him here. He was an intrusive presence and soon he would leave and she would be alone once more. Then she heard a quiet murmur coming from the drawing room.

Frank tentatively made his way onto the landing, turning the corner, his footsteps moving away. He did not call out again; it didn't seem as if he really wanted to be heard. Emma glanced upwards to be sure he couldn't see her before she crossed the hall and pushed open the drawing room door.

The old woman wasn't seated. She stood with her back to Emma and she was still making that sound, although Emma realised she wasn't speaking at all; she was humming, one hand twitching at her side, as if she was trying to recall some long-forgotten tune.

'I never did get to dance,' she said.

Emma didn't breathe.

'I came here once, to a – *soirée*. It were in the war. It were then that I met the children, you know – Arthur, Clarence, Hal and Tom.' She paused. She must have heard Emma enter the room, but the way she was speaking – she did not appear to be expecting to receive a reply. She must think it was her son standing behind her, though from the sound of her words, she was a hundred miles away, lost somewhere in the past.

'After what 'appened, I came here often. I 'elped Mrs 'Ollingworth – Antonia – with the cooking and the polishing. I even helped whitewash this room, once. She had no idea what to do, bless her. She came from money and she married money, but it din't make her happy, for all that. She said she always felt like she were bein' watched. Perhaps she was.'

Emma shifted uncomfortably.

'Do you reckon that were why, love? Why she took our Mossy as well as Tom? Because I 'elped his new wife, '*er* replacement?'

For a moment Emma thought that was all; there wasn't anything else to come, but then the old woman added, 'It were all my fault, love, not yours. It were Antonia 'Ollingworth said I should start again, you see. I allus said as 'ow I'd never wed, not after what 'ad 'appened. After Tom – I said I'd never 'ave children, neither. I din't trust myself with 'em. An' I din't wed, not for a long old time, but then I met your dad, an' when 'e asked me, I remembered – I remembered what she'd said an' I dared to think I could start ower.' She let out a sob.

'I paid,' she whispered. 'I paid wi' our Mossy. Weren't never your fault, love. Don't ever think that. It were mine, it were always mine, an' I'm still paying now. I should 'ave taken you away after Mossy left us, far, far away, but I didn't 'ave the will left in me. An' I thought it were all forgot, love, but there's never anything forgotten, is there? Not in this place. This place *remembers*. I can feel it, can't you?'

Her shoulders shook and she sank into herself, burying her face in her hands. Emma took a step forward and then she remembered that the woman was expecting Frank, not her. She would only be frightened if she made herself known.

She paused to glance around the room before stepping quietly away and into the hall, sensing rather than seeing the woman whirling around to look after her. Still, she couldn't help but hear her next words: 'But it's ower, in't it, love? It's ower now.'

Emma leaned back against the wall, trying to catch her breath. Something was wrong. The walls of the drawing room had been a soft shade of green. The paint had been fresh. The room looked just the way she had imagined when she'd first seen it, and all that she could think of was that Charlie had painted it. It felt somehow as if the house had betrayed her, as if it had accepted the work of his hands and rejected her own.

She shook the thought away. Then she turned and started up the stairs after Frank.

Doors creaked as Emma trod gently on each step, as if to cover the sound of her approach. Frank didn't call out and she didn't either. She had thought she knew exactly which room he would have entered first, but he had actually begun at the opposite end of the house, towards the back. As she turned the corner of the landing she saw his thin form emerge from one doorway and enter the next. He was nearing her room. Now she felt, though she could not have said why, that he was leaving it for last.

Emma waited until he emerged again. It was as if she were in a dream, or sleepwalking, somehow aware of it without being quite awake.

There he was, a tall thin man in his colourless jumper, his hair just beginning to grey. He kept his eyes on the floor as he passed her bedroom, trying the one next to it before stepping back onto the landing, only one option remaining to him. Now, finally, he did call out, his voice breaking over the word: 'Miss?'

At the sight of his hand on the door handle of her room, anger rose; then it dissipated. After hearing his mother and the talk of their loss she was not sure why it came as a surprise to realise that he was afraid.

He turned the handle and went inside and then there was silence. Emma softly followed. She wanted to see what he would do. He hadn't closed the door behind him and she slipped through the gap he had left.

Frank was standing in the middle of the room, looking towards the door that let into the narrow cupboard. She only dimly registered that her room was a mess, her clothes strewn across the bed, her things piled all over the floor, when she realised that she too was standing in full view. At any moment he would turn and see her. He would surely be horrified to be discovered there. He turned his head; he looked straight towards her and then he turned back to the narrow door, just as if he hadn't seen her at all.

Emma's throat was suddenly dry. She watched as he stepped forward, his movements stilted, and reached out one shaking hand towards the door. She put out her own hand to stop him. She opened her mouth to speak. She forgot about needing to be silent and wanting to be alone and everything else. She only wanted to stop him from opening the door. She didn't want to see, didn't want *him* to see. She didn't want to know anything else about this place; she only wanted for him to go and for her to lie down and sleep for a very long time.

She was cold, right through. It felt as if something were waiting for her on the other side of the door. She was suddenly certain it would be the old man who had stood at the foot of her bed in the middle of the night; the old man's *ghost*. He would be searching for his suit. He would know that she had been the one to throw it away. He would be angry with her. She could sense his anger, could almost *smell* it. It was sour and ripe and stuck in her throat. At the same time she wanted only to run, as hard and as fast as she could, even as far as the mire, to that empty place.

And she realised that Frank hadn't opened the door after all. He had turned the handle but he hadn't opened it and relief flooded her. Then she looked at him, really looked at him, and she followed his gaze. He was staring at the floor. He was looking at the things that had been stacked against the wall; at the things that had fallen in front of the door, preventing it from being opened.

He bent and started to push them away. A clothes rail had slipped behind a pile of boxes. She watched as he moved them, methodically, one by one. She couldn't see his face. He hadn't turned and he hadn't looked at her again. She couldn't move and she couldn't breathe; it felt as if time had stopped and it would only start again when he opened the door and she wanted, more than anything, that he would not do that. That he'd put back her things and turn around and walk away, take his mother by the arm, and that they would both go. But instead he finished clearing the things from in front of the door, the one place left that he hadn't looked, and she moved behind him as he turned the handle once more and pulled and this time the door swung open.

She caught only the merest glimpse of what lay inside before Frank whirled around. His face was white. He pressed his hand to his mouth as he staggered away and started gagging, as if he was going to be sick. A moment later she caught the stench that was flooding into the room.

Frank didn't say anything, didn't even look at her as he fell to his knees, retching, then he pushed himself up, batting at the air in front of his face, as if he could expel the thing he had seen, as if he could rid himself of that *smell*. Emma didn't turn as he stumbled past her. She heard him, though, as he left the room, the door slamming, the irregular sound of footsteps moving away down the corridor.

For a long time, she didn't hear anything at all. She only looked.

She saw the dark and the thing that was slumped against the wall, the thing that had once been her. Her body looked small, shrunken somehow, and her hands were bent into claws, as if she was scratching her way out through the walls. Her face was greyed and blotched and mercifully in shadow. There was an overturned bowl at her side, the faint tang of bleach doing nothing to stifle the stench of rot, and an old man's pipe, splintered and broken at the stem, clutched tightly between her fingers. The holes it had made in her skin were no longer bleeding; the dark pool it had left at her feet had long since dried.

CHAPTER SEVEN

At first she thought the smell of her own decay would choke her, but after a while she found it did not, and later she did not notice it any longer. On returning to the house she had been alone and had not wanted it to be any different, but now she did not merely *know* that to be true: she *felt* it in her bones. There would be no one to take her by the hand and lead her away, and so she stayed. There was no one to comfort her, and so she would not be comforted. She simply stood there and she did not look away.

She had been in there all the time. All the time she had thought she was working on the house, building a life for herself, and she had been in this room, in a trap of her own making. She closed her eyes and remembered the woman's words:

There are few things more amusing than the deluded. There is nothing more amusing than someone who does not know they belong to me already.

She remembered being trapped in this room, the way that Charlie had come back and saved her, or she *thought* he had. She could still remember stepping out of it, into freedom, the light that, for a moment, had dazzled her eyes. All of it was false; none of it was real. No: it *had* been real – the only thing that hadn't been real was *her*. And Charlie, of course: he had been in the thrall of the woman's ghost. She remembered what he'd said, his confusion when she'd asked him why he'd returned to Mire House: *I'm not sure what made me come back*. The woman wouldn't have permitted him to see the truth.

She looked back at the corpse in the narrow room. She closed her eyes, opened them again and looked down at her own hands. They appeared to be solid, but she couldn't feel them any longer.

After a time, she allowed the tears to fall. They were cold against her cold cheeks.

CHAPTER EIGHT

There is nothing more amusing than someone who does not know they belong to me already.

Emma couldn't get those words out of her mind as she walked through the house, seeing the mouldering carpets, the grey walls, the paper hanging off in shreds, the cracked paint, the wood that had split, revealing the blackness inside it. The smell of the mire was stronger than ever. The woman had wanted her to walk into it and now it was here, swallowing the house, subsuming her. She was lost in the house and she knew now that it wasn't hers, had never been hers. She had allowed it to charm her, had listened to its call – no, the *woman's* call. And she didn't even know her name.

Now the house was empty and there was no voice to speak, not even her own.

She went through a door and entered a room and stopped. She hadn't consciously chosen this place but she realised she had come back to where, for her, it had ended: she was standing in front of the narrow door that led to the narrow room in which she had died. She did not want to look into it again; she had seen it already. Instead she covered her face with her hands. She didn't move for a long time; she didn't know if she slept or if she dreamed.

We all go into silence in the end, she thought, and she did not know why.

CHAPTER NINE

The shadows lay dark in Mire House, making corners soft and vision uncertain. Dampness spread across the ceiling, its fingers reaching from the earth outside, the mire beyond. The humidity in the air constantly formed new shadows, new shapes. The house had been built to be a home, for *life*, but life had no part in it, Emma knew that now. It had always been empty and always would be. The corridors were still, and any small sound – the rustle of leaves against glass, the lonely cry of a curlew – resonated long and empty.

When her body had been removed, she had thought that she would leave somehow, melt away from this place or find a new door set into some corridor; it would open for her and she would walk through it. Maybe – she dared to hope – someone she loved would come to her and take her by the hand. Or perhaps she would see another bright light.

Her discomfort grew at the thought of it. She had thought the woman was trying to trick her into stepping into that whiteness, lure her into drowning in the mire, but now another fear had taken root. When she had been faced by that brilliant light, had that been her chance after all? The ghostly woman might have tricked her, not by having her step into the marsh but by its opposite. What if the light had been real – a doorway opening into the world, leading somewhere else – somewhere better? Perhaps the woman had known that Emma would turn away. Perhaps that had been her true revenge.

There must be somewhere she was supposed to be – but if there was, she didn't know where to find it. The men who took away her remains had closed up the house behind them, and whatever light they had let in had withdrawn. Now it felt as if the walls would never let go of her. There was only silence left. Sometimes she thought she heard the strains of some long-forgotten music coming from another room, but as soon as she entered there would be nothing and no one there.

She wasn't sure how much time had passed when the day came that she wandered into the hall and found the front door standing open.

She could sense the fresh air beyond it. Without looking, she knew that it was the brightest part of a clear day, and she walked towards the door, dazzled after so long in the dark. When she reached the threshold she simply stood there, breathing it in. Then she stepped outside, half expecting herself to disappear as she crossed the boundary, and then she was outside and she turned and saw the one who was waiting for her.

She was beautiful: she could see that now, the straight-backed woman with the dark hair and the black dress. Her complexion was clear, her cheeks softly rounded, her lips full. Her veil had been thrown back and her expression was soft; it took a moment for Emma to realise that her eyes remained cold.

She opened her mouth to speak, but the woman stopped her with a look. Then she smiled. Emma didn't trust that smile.

'I thought it would end,' the woman said. 'Perhaps it has, now. There is no one else left.'

Emma did not answer.

'You are the last.' The woman looked her up and down. 'I hated you all for so long. Now . . .' She did not finish the sentence.

Emma frowned.

'It is time for me to go.' She gave that smile again. 'But you will stay, will you not? You will stay here, in my house.'

Emma shook her head. 'But you said – at the river – you said it was my time, my chance to leave—'

The woman tilted back her head and sent a trill of laughter into the clear air. 'Indulge the ways of an old woman, dear. I lost all hope before I left the world behind me. I had lost my husband, my child – my family that should have been. But I rather enjoyed the taste of *your* hope. When you actually thought that you would simply be able to leave – that you would *live* . . .' She smiled, and it was a real smile this time. Her eyes shone. 'It tasted so sweet,' she said.

'And now you're going to leave me here? In the house – for what?'

There was no answer. The woman took in a deep breath, as if she was savouring the air, and then she turned to Emma. 'Enjoy her, my dear,' she said.

Enjoy her. Those had been the words in the letter, hadn't they? Clarence Mitchell's letter. Emma had a sudden image of the woman whispering in the old man's ear, him hearing nothing but nodding anyway, clutching his bed sheets tighter as the life faded from him and he formed his plans. She blinked the image away.

The woman drew herself up. 'The house was built for love,' she said, 'but love never came to fill it. Now you must do your best.'

She stepped out of the door and the sunlight gleamed on the black silk of her dress. She pulled the veil down over her face as she walked away. Her footsteps made no sound and she did not look back. Emma watched as she reached the lane and turned not towards the mire but towards the church, where the yew trees stood, ancient and dark. There was no sound, none at all.

Emma watched until the woman passed out of sight and then she turned and went back into the house that was waiting for her.

CHAPTER TEN

As time passed, the woman's last words drifted around Emma's mind again and again: *Love never came to fill it . . . you must do your best.* She wasn't sure what she had meant, not really, but she did know that she had been wrong: Mire House was not empty.

At first it was only the echoes of things she had seen before: the strains of music coming from the drawing room, a child's high giggle, the gruffer tones of an older man, but later, they came to her. The children were first, one with shaved hair that made his skull appear too big for his body, his eyes mistrustful, the other a quiet boy who edged around a doorway with his thumb in his mouth. She felt dread gathering inside her at the sight of them, revulsion at these *things*, and then she saw the fear in their eyes and she forced herself to swallow it down. Instead she gave a wavering smile and held out her hands. They came to her and she held them, and she thought: *It doesn't have to be the way* she *wanted it.*

The house didn't have to remain as it had been created, full of fear and emptiness and loss. There didn't have to be silence. There could be laughter and joy and *love*, because she could bring them here, those things which had mattered to her in life;

she could hold on to them. She could make sure that they were the things which would last.

Do your best, she thought. Yes, she would; and she gathered the children in close and she told them stories. And as she did they smiled up at her and she thought she understood: there was no happy ending, not really. Things just went on. In stories, princesses got married and heroes prevailed over their enemies, but what next? They would grow old and die. Their strength would fail. The longer they lived the nearer they would come to losing everything, because that was where loss belonged, wasn't it? In *life*, because in the end time would carry everything away, the good and the bad alike. Happy endings were only ever a beginning. Real endings had loss, death, sorrow. But for her, it hadn't been the end. Now she had Mossy and she had Tom. Not all stories had to end in loss; some of them only began that way.

She heard a high giggle behind her. She recognised it as Tom's, but she knew that Mossy would be with him. They were rarely apart – and anyway, Tom wouldn't laugh if he was alone. He didn't like to be alone. A shadow crossed her face and she brushed the thought away. Now that she was here, he didn't have to be alone. He didn't have to be afraid. She smiled. She knew that things were better now because Tom's hair was growing back; it was golden.

The pair of them would be playing a game. Soon she would find them and squeeze into whatever small space they had found in which to hide. She thought she knew where that would be, and that was all right; whatever dark things had once happened there had passed.

Another faint giggle circled the room and she smiled. Tom had been lost once; they all had. Now it was time to go and find them.

CHAPTER ELEVEN

Emma stood in the small blue bedroom and looked out of the window. She could see into the lane and the pathway next to it. She had thought of simply walking away from the house as the woman had done, several times, but she had never tried. Partly this was because the door was never open, but it was also because she knew that the woman had been right; it was not her time. And the others needed her.

She heard a dull sound through the glass and she touched the pane with her fingers. She knew it must be cold but she didn't really feel it. There was a car passing in the lane outside. A small blue car with a man driving and a young boy pressed up against the passenger window. For a moment he looked up at her before he turned away, straightening in his seat. She wasn't sure if he had seen her. Out there, time was passing; in here, it stood still. Time didn't steal the things she loved. In Mire House, things lingered: it had been built to last.

The old man was standing behind her, by the wall, smoking his pipe. She had begun to see him more and more often and she was no longer afraid of him. *Get out*, he had said to her once, and she had thought of it as hostility. Now she was no longer sure; perhaps he had only been trying to warn her, after all. She had been frightened of him when she had thought of him as someone else's ghost, unconnected with her; now he was her own.

Still, he hadn't explained and wasn't welcoming. Sometimes, his expression even reflected those words back at her: *Get out*. But whenever Emma considered the possibility of leaving, she reminded herself of the day she had stood in front of the mire and seen the white light in front of her, the glimpse of the death she had thought was waiting for her there, and the way she had turned away from it; the longing for more *time*. Now she had all the time she wanted. She was here: she was *alive*. Perhaps it was as good a place as any.

When she looked outside again, there was someone she knew standing in the garden. He was looking up at her and for a moment he seemed to be staring directly into her eyes, but no, he glanced around and she knew he had seen only a reflection of the sky shining back at him. He turned to the woman at his side and took her hand. He was holding something in the other – it looked like a sprig of yew.

It was Frank and his mother. Emma frowned. Why had they come? It felt like a reminder of some other time, another place, one that made a vague longing rise within her again, something a little like pain. Her frown deepened, becoming a scowl. It wasn't fair; it wasn't *right*. They shouldn't have come here where they didn't belong. They shouldn't have come here knowing they could simply walk away again.

She turned from the window and walked down the stairs, slowly and steadily, running her hand along the rail. She remembered thinking once that it would be a little like this, that she'd walk down these stairs wearing some silken gown, like a *lady*. Like a lady of the house.

She could hear Frank and his mother outside, talking to each other just as if they knew everything about the place. She could hear it in their tone, the casualness, the *presumption*. Then she heard them say her name and with a *frisson* she realised they thought they knew everything about *her*: who she was, what she would have wanted. She heard that phrase now: *What she would have wanted*, the woman saying it to her son, just as if they had ever even met – and there was a soft rustle of something being set down on the step.

Emma reached out a hand towards the door. She hadn't tried it before and she didn't like to touch it now. She closed her eyes, trying to listen, and when she opened them again she was right in front of their faces. She was standing on the top step, just outside the door. The man and the woman in front of her did not react. They showed no sign of having seen her.

Frank was wearing his grey jumper again, and he wore an expression to match. He glanced up once more, nervously, as if he thought he could see in at the windows from where he stood. His mother was holding his arm. She was a little more stooped than when Emma had last seen her, and she shifted now as if she was catching something of her son's disquiet.

'We wish her well,' Frank intoned, as if murmuring some ritual.

'We wish her well,' his mother repeated.

He tucked her arm a little tighter under his own and for a moment they just stood there, staring at the house, their eyes focused on the door. Emma glanced down. They had placed the sprig of yew on the step below the one on which she stood. It had been freshly cut; she could smell it, a sharp, not altogether natural smell. She could sense its poison.

The woman looked down at it too. 'It'll 'opefully 'elp 'er cross,' she said. 'It'll 'elp her get wherever she's going.'

Emma scowled. Help her cross *where*? She wasn't leaving. She wasn't going anywhere. This place was hers. *Hers.*

Frank nodded. His eyes were pale and weak, his hands whitened where they curled over his mother's, as if he was gripping a little too tightly. Emma stretched out a hand towards them, without quite touching their skin. She could feel their warmth and somehow that was worse than anything else: their warmth, their touch, and longing rose within her. Tears pricked at her eyes. She withdrew her hand and touched her cheek. It was cold. *Cold.*

She shook her head. Why had they come here? She had been happier before. She hadn't thought about other places in so long, other possibilities, of the touch of a hand upon hers.

'I'm sorry,' the old woman said.

Emma started. She had thought she was speaking to her, but no: she had pulled away from her son and turned to face him.

'I was angry,' she said, 'when you said you saw something in this place. I'm sorry. It weren't that I din't believe you. It were just that I were afraid. I din't want it t' be true.'

'Mum, it's in the past.'

'But if I 'adn't—' She paused. 'I thought it were all ower by then, you see. This place – it 'as a way of 'olding onto things. It dun't let 'em pass.'

Emma stared down at the yew at her feet.

'Now 'er last relative's gone – the last of Antonia 'Ollingworth's, I mean. The woman who she thought 'ad took everything from 'er: that's 'er line finished, I reckon. So it must be ower now, in't it? She's 'ad 'er revenge.'

Frank opened his mouth to speak, but she cut in once more. 'So she'd not be thinkin' of me any more, would she? Of us, the way I 'elped Mrs 'Ollingworth. The fact that – that I went *on* an' she didn't. For – for being part of a future she never 'ad. For – '*oping*.'

'Of course not, Mum. Don't get upset. It's in the past.'

This place, thought Emma. *It has a way of holding onto things. It doesn't let them pass.*

'But there's more, Frank. I'd tried not to think on't, but – it were *me*, you see. When Antonia sold up and left, it were *me*. She'd talked me into starting agin, an' – well, in a way, I did the same. She thought she should stay 'ere, and it were me as said – I told 'er she 'ad a choice. I said if she 'ated the place so much, she should leave. Some of us never 'ad much of a choice of what we did, but she 'ad one and it were me as said she should use it. And that's why she left when she did, why she got away – *escaped* from this place. Do you think it remembers, Frank? Do you think it remembers that?'

'Mum, please—'

'We should've done something, Frank. We should have teld that girl, soon as we knew – told 'er to get out an' all. Soon as you said she'd come to live 'ere, we should've done something. We shouldn't 'ave let it be.'

Emma listened and she knew that it was true: they *should* have done something. They should have helped her, warned her somehow. They could have saved her from all of it. She clenched her fists at her side and found herself stepping forward, across the sprig of yew lying useless and dead at her feet. Anger took her, and something else: a wild, insane jealousy. They were *warm*. They had *life*.

'But Mum, we didn't *know*.' Frank's voice faded to a whisper. 'When I saw 'er, in't church – she weren't *real*. They said she were already—'

'They could've been wrong, Frank.'

'Aye. Mebbe.'

'It'll 'elp her cross.'

'Mebbe.'

'We should've done summat anyroad. This place – it in't right. It'll never be right. We should've found a way. We *knew*.'

Emma drank in those words. She was greedy for them. She was greedy for their warmth. They *should* have helped her.

This time when she stretched out towards them, her hand trembled. She was barely conscious of her actions; she only watched as her fingers curled into a clawed, grasping shape as she reached for the old woman's shoulder.

The touch, when it came, was a shock of ice. The woman's whole body convulsed. The breath hissed from her and she pulled away and staggered. If it wasn't for her son, she would have fallen. He caught her, grasping her arm tightly once more, calling her back. The old woman's eyes were bulging from her head.

'What is it, Mum? Mum?'

She shook her head. She looked almost funny now, her face blanched, her mouth opening and closing, opening and closing. Emma watched as she gasped at the air, drawing in a deep whistling breath, and then she leaned in towards her and stared directly into her eyes.

For a moment, nothing happened. Then she grasped at her chest, her thin fingers scrabbling against her coat. It seemed a long time before she began to breathe regularly again, in-out, in-out, and she patted at Frank's hand until he eased his grip.

'Mum?'

'It's nothing, Frank. I'm fine. It was nothing – it *must* have been nothing.'

Emma smiled. The touch on the woman's shoulder had stayed with her, a splinter of ice she cradled, sensing the *promise* it held. Now she turned to Frank. He was still fussing over the old woman, just as if he could help her, just as if she wouldn't soon be gone from him; as if she wouldn't be called to where she really belonged.

Emma tilted her head. The woman belonged at this house; they both did. She could see that now. It was as if some pattern had become clear, its lines stretching down through the years and ending here. They needed one last piece to be put in place before it was complete. And she was the one who was supposed to do it. Frank and his mother were bound up with the house and it with them: they were a part of it. And it meant she didn't have to be alone, not ever. It didn't need to end with her. There could be others; the house could have life after all.

The house was built for love, but love never came to fill it.

After a moment she reached out and she grasped Frank's shoulder.

Now you must do your best.

And she would. She *would*. She would do her best for the house. She would try to fill its empty rooms and echoing corridors and that other space, the one inside her, the one that was empty too: abandoned. *Forsaken.* And at last she knew why the house had called to her, why she'd entered its cold rooms, seen the dust hanging in the air, the doors that swung open onto darkness, and yet she had loved it at once, had felt connected to it even though she had never seen it before.

She looked into Frank's eyes. He met her gaze and his was full of pain. It was full of fear. He shook his head and she smiled as he pulled away. He turned from her and the house as if he could banish them from his mind – from his *future* – and he helped his mother down the steps, hurrying her down the driveway as if he thought they could leave it behind them.

Soon, Emma thought. *Soon.*

She turned to go back inside, kicking the sprig of yew away as she went. She already felt a little warmer than she had before, a little lighter. The rooms in front of her already felt a little less empty.

CHAPTER TWELVE

Emma awoke, or thought she did. She had heard something, a sound that was louder and closer than the usual creaking of the house, the footsteps of its ghosts. It came again, the slamming of a car door, the grinding of feet on gravel.

She went to the window. A car was parked on the driveway. It was small and rather battered, and someone was standing beside it. She recognised him at once. The sun was rising and it caught his hair, which was untidy and a little too long. It was Charlie. He was alone. As she watched, he went to the boot and pulled out an overstuffed rucksack.

For a moment she wondered if it was *really* him, but then he looked up at the house and she saw that it was. His eyes were clear and guileless and a little sad. He put his hand into his pocket and withdrew it holding a key; then she lost sight of him, but she heard the rattle of metal in the lock.

When she went downstairs she found him standing in the hall, looking around at the dark corners with a blank expression. She stood near the bottom of the stairs, but she didn't need to be cautious; he didn't see her or hear her or even sense she was there. He didn't appear to be afraid any longer. He put down his bag and went towards the drawing room, pausing on the threshold, looking inside. She wondered what it was that he saw.

After a while he shook his head and turned to go up the stairs. She followed him as he went, slowly stepping onto each tread. When he reached the top he surprised her by entering not the master bedroom, but hers.

He went inside and just stood there, looking at the narrow door. He stayed there for a long time. Emma stood behind him; she no longer wished to see the expression on his face.

He whispered something, so brief and quiet she couldn't make it out, but she felt a rush of warmth for him. She had doubted him and suspected him, and all the time he had simply been caught in the tide, being manipulated by the dark woman who had started it all. Now he was free: he was a young man who had done nothing – no, not nothing; he had come to visit Emma just because they were connected somehow, just because of something in their distant past. He had worked with her and talked with her and laughed with her. He had held her once, putting his arms around her and soothing her fears. She found herself smiling at him, though a part of her was a little sad too: she found herself wishing there could have been more.

She remembered the kiss they'd shared, warm and good. She would have liked to know him better – the real Charlie, not the way he had been when she thought he'd come back to her and found only *her* beneath his face, the woman clothing herself in his bones and skin and flesh.

He pulled something from his pocket, a crumpled sheet of paper, and he straightened it out. It was a letter, densely typed with an official-looking crest across the top, signed with a flourish of ink. She stood close by his shoulder, without touching him, examining it. She stared. She should have known as soon as she saw him standing in the driveway, as soon as he produced the key.

Charlie had inherited Mire House after all. He had come home.

For a moment she didn't know how she felt. She froze, staring down at the letter, and then she stepped back into the corner of the room. She saw that the old man who had stood at the end of her bed was there again. She could see him only dimly, the white curl of smoke from his pipe rising against the walls, and he looked at her without smiling and he shook his head.

She turned away from him to find that Charlie was gone. She could hear his footsteps, though, moving down the corridor. She went out and saw him coming out of a doorway and entering the next room, and the next. She followed. He didn't stay long in any of them but she saw his expression; he was looking at the walls with an appraising look, a considering look. It was as if he was already wondering what colour to paint them, as if he was making plans.

It was her house. Hers.

It was as if she was seeing two versions of Charlie as she followed him around the corridors of Mire House: someone who was almost her friend, almost something more – and *her* Charlie, the dark woman's relative, not by marriage but by blood, the last of her line. Now he had inherited and it was *his* house. He would live here and be happy, just as *she* had no doubt intended. The house that had passed from her grasp had been returned to her and her own, for always. Emma could almost sense her triumph. And then it struck her: Charlie's kiss. Had that really been *him*? She could remember the touch of his lips on hers, their warmth, the way it had recalled all the feelings she'd suppressed: the sense of *life*. And she remembered his touch on her shoulder. It had been cold. *Cold.*

When he kissed her – that had been after she had become trapped in the narrow room. After Charlie had come back – *but it hadn't been Charlie*. Would he have kissed her at all if he hadn't been influenced by the dark woman? Did he ever even have feelings for her? The kiss – it might have been nothing but mockery. And she had clung to it, her moment of connection, and it hadn't even been real. How the dark woman must have laughed. Emma clenched her fists.

Charlie reached the stairs once more and began to go down them, placing his feet so very carefully on every step. She reached out towards him, her hand wavering, almost, but not quite, touching his back.

He reached the hall and looked around once more, just as if he hadn't seen it already, as if it wasn't *his*. The grandson of Clarence Mitchell, who had gifted her this place, not out of love or family connection but out of revenge for something that happened before she had even been born. He'd intended her for this place, chosen her for its own before he'd even met her or known her.

Slowly she smiled. She had been *meant* to be trapped here, for always, in an empty existence, watching as the last of the woman's line moved in and was happy and *lived*. It was her last revenge, willed down through the years, passed on through her cold touch until there was no one left to receive it.

But Emma *was* here. Her story wasn't finished. She didn't have to despair; she didn't have to fade.

She pictured herself reaching out and seizing Charlie's shoulder, imagining the expression on his face as he felt the ice of it, the promise it held.

She remembered the way she had worked with him, side by side, Charlie whistling or humming some tune under his breath. She had liked him then. She remembered the way she had run to him when she'd been afraid, the way his arms had wrapped around her body. It had been good. She hadn't felt alone any longer. Now she didn't need to be afraid; perhaps it was time for other people to be afraid of *her*.

She began to smile. Downstairs, Mossy and Tom had come out from wherever they'd been hiding. She could hear them running about the hallway, playing some new game. One of them – Mossy – had started to sing.

Emma felt like singing too. She was smiling now; she felt that smile would never end. It never *needed* to end. Charlie was here and he would stay; how could he not? The house was beautiful. It was forbidding and proud and alone, but it was beautiful. He would live here and he would love this place, and she would live here too, at his side. She would stay close to him. And Mire House would hold him within its walls, keeping him safe, keeping him near. Making him one with the rest of them; saving him from ever being alone. Making him *belong*.

THE END

ACKNOWLEDGEMENTS

First of all, massive thanks to Jo Fletcher for the wonderful editing and for helping to make this a better book. Thanks too to the teams at Jo Fletcher Books UK and USA and to my agent, Oli Munson.

To Roy Gray, who insists I don't need to keep thanking him – I wouldn't be writing this if you hadn't encouraged me to submit *A Cold Season* – so thank you! Thanks too to Wayne McManus for looking after my website, despite my best efforts to break it.

Thanks to all of the editors producing magazines and short story anthologies in the independent presses who've continued to support me. You are awesome people. Special shouts go to Stephen Jones, Scott Harrison, Jonathan Oliver, Ian Whates, Paula Guran, Jan Edwards, Gary Fry, Ellen Datlow, John Joseph Adams, Allen Ashley, and Pete, Nicky and Mike of PS Publishing.

I also want to thank the friends who have been there with cheers, calming words, the benefit of their wisdom, or indeed wine, particularly the Fantasycon crowd, and my dear friends Gary, Heather, Lauren, Craig, and Karen – whose amazing book-themed cakes deserve a mention all of their own.

To Ann and Trevor Littlewood, for always being there, love and thanks. Fergus, you've supported me for twenty years, shared the successes and carried me through the tough times. I owe you more than I can say.

Last but never least, I would like to thank the readers who've taken their time to share my journeys into these imaginary worlds.

Alison Littlewood
West Yorkshire
December 2013